THE TROOPER'S WIFE

THE TROOPER'S WIFE

Sara Fraser

Severn House Large Print
London & New York

This first large print edition published in Great Britain 2005 by
SEVERN HOUSE LARGE PRINT BOOKS LTD of
9-15 High Street, Sutton, Surrey, SM1 1DF.
First world regular print edition published 2004 by
Severn House Publishers, London and New York.
This first large print edition published in the USA 2006 by
SEVERN HOUSE PUBLISHERS INC., of
595 Madison Avenue, New York, NY 10022.

British Library Cataloguing in Publication Data

Fraser, Sara
   The trooper's wife - Large print ed.
   1.   Crimean War, 1853 – 1856 - Fiction
   2.   Army spouses - History - 19th century - Fiction
   3.   Historical fiction
   4.   Large type books
   I.   Title
   823.9'14 [F]

   ISBN-10: 0-7278-7477-2

Printed and bound in Great Britain by
MPG Books Ltd, Bodmin, Cornwall.

One

It was late afternoon beneath dark louring skies when the angry crowd of men and women came up the narrow lane towards the small cottage. As they neared the isolated building, several of them began to shout threateningly.

'We'em come for you, you old witch!'

'You'm going to pay for what you bin doing!'

Within the cottage, Hester Pearson reacted instantly, grabbing her granddaughter's arm and pushing her through the rear door, urging frantically.

'Run, Rosie! Run and hide! Run, sweet-heart, run!'

Whimpering with fear and distress, the small girl ran stumbling across the newly ploughed field. A high-pitched scream carried on the icy gusting wind echoed in her ears, deepening her terror. On she went across the deep furrows, muddy earth clodding on her bare feet. She climbed over a barred gate and took shelter behind a hedgerow, gasping for breath, heart thumping wildly, the wind cutting through her thin clothing, chilling her sweating body.

Inside the cottage, Hester Pearson was on her knees, blood dripping from her nose and mouth as she stubbornly refused to answer the bawled questions.

'Where's that devil's spawn whelp o' yours, you evil old bastard?'

'I aren't going to ask you again, witch, where's your devil's spawn got to?' A hobnailed boot thudded into her ribs and once again she screamed in agony as her frail bones cracked.

The echoing scream brought Rosie to her feet, conflicting emotions battling for mastery, the terrible fear for her grandmother against the desperate desire to flee further away.

A heated argument arose inside the thatched-roofed hovel.

'Let's do what we come to do. We can deal with the girl later.'

'No! We needs to catch both of 'um now.'

'Tom Steven's right. That devil's spawn might be as well able to cast bad spells as this old bugger.'

'But her could have took any shape.'

'O' course her could. And until we gets this old bastard under the water then the little 'un can keep herself so that we can't see her proper. So I says let's deal with the one we got and then the other won't be able to escape us.'

6

'That's right, that is! The little'un'll have to take a proper human form then.'

More voices shouted in agreement, and brutal hands dragged Hester Pearson to her feet and dragged her bodily from the cottage, while other hands hastened to lift burning scraps of wood from the tiny hearth fire and hold the flames to the thick thatch of the roof.

Shivering in her hiding place, Rosie caught her breath and her heart pounded afresh as she saw her grandmother being dragged out of the cottage, the men and women surrounding her shouting abuse and jostling to rain blows on their helpless captive. Rosie's love for her grandmother overcame all else and she stepped from her hiding place and began to run back towards the cottage.

'Look there!' a woman shouted, pointing at the small figure stumbling across the furrowed earth. 'It's the little 'un!'

'Come on, lads,' a man bawled. 'Let's get her.'

Baying like hunting dogs, half a dozen men ran to intercept Rosie. She was near enough now to see her grandmother's bleeding face and she became possessed by a madness of fury which drove out all her fear. The men reached her, their hands seeking to grab and hold, and she fought them like a small wildcat until a fist clubbed her senseless.

One of the men slung her limp body across his shoulder, chuckling in wry admiration. 'Bloody hell, her's a fighter, aren't her? You got to give the little bitch credit for that.'

Talking and gesticulating excitedly, the crowd retraced their steps along the narrow lane, taking their captives with them, while smoke and flame began to billow from the cottage.

Eugenia Pacemore was sitting at her bedroom window, gazing out across the winter landscape. The bleakness of the bare fields and lifeless trees beneath the dark grey sky began to depress her, and in an effort to shake off the burgeoning sombreness of her mood, she rose from her chair and went to stand in front of the fire burning in the small grate. Above the mantleshelf the wall mirror reflected her thin pale face, her black hair severely drawn back and tied in a tight bun.

She stared at her image and muttered disparagingly. 'What a plain, dull object you are.'

Her gaze moved to the miniature painting on the mantleshelf. It was a portrait of an exceptionally handsome youth dressed in military uniform.

A rueful smile curved her lips.

'What stranger would ever believe that we're related, Charlie? Why did you have to take all the good looks in this family for yourself?'

Charles Bronton was her first cousin on her mother's side, and as children they had been very close. Now she saw him only rarely, but still cared for him as if he were a brother.

The small carriage clock on the mantleshelf began to chime the hour and Eugenia experienced a familiar sense of relief mingled with despondency. Another empty, boring, seemingly pointless day was nearly over; another empty, boring, seemingly pointless evening stretched before her, and at this moment it seemed to her that it had been this way for her entire twenty-two years of life.

Footsteps sounded on the planking of the corridor, a loud knock came on the bedroom door, and an elderly maidservant bustled into the room.

'Your mam wants to know if you'm a-coming downstairs for your tea, Miss Eugenia,' she demanded aggressively. 'Or am you a-going to be messing about up here for much longer? I don't want to have to keep on coming up here every five minutes. I'm getting too old for gallivanting up and down all these stairs all the time.'

'I'm coming directly, Martha.' Eugenia smiled, amused. She was very fond of this irascible old crone who had been her childhood nurse.

The sounds of furiously barking dogs came from outside, and Old Martha began ranting aggrievedly. 'Just hark at them savage beasts. They oughtn't to be let run loose, they oughtn't. I don't know what your feyther was thinking on, to have brung 'um here in the first place. I don't know, I'm sure.'

'He brought them here as watchdogs, Martha, as you well know. And they're not

9

savage at all. In fact they're perfectly harmless. All bark and no bite.'

'That's what you says now. But you'll talk different when they tears the throat out of you,' the old crone riposted over her shoulder as she went down the broad staircase.

The dogs were still barking and, curious to see what was disturbing them, Eugenia went to the window and looked down, but couldn't see either animal. Her gaze lifted and she sighted the clouds of black smoke rising from the far side of a tree-lined ridge where she knew a cottage stood.

'Oh my God!' she exclaimed, and rushed out of the room, down the stairs and into the drawing room where a lady, dressed in a green satin gown, wearing an ornate, snowy-white lace cap on her grey hair, was sitting by the fireside in a large armchair.

The lady lifted a gold-handled lorgnette to her eyes and tutted with surprise. 'What on earth is the matter? Why are you rushing so, Eugenia?'

'I think the cottage beyond the ridge is on fire. Ring for Joseph while I find my bonnet and shawl.'

Mrs Pacemore shook her head in puzzlement. 'But why should that concern you?'

'There's a woman and a child living there, Mamma. They could be in need of help. I must go and see,' Eugenia snapped curtly as she tied her bonnet strings.

Martha had come into the room and heard the exchange between mother and daughter, and she intervened vexatiously. 'You'll do no such thing, Miss Eugenia. You keep well away from that cottage.'

'Why?' Eugenia was baffled.

'Because that woman who lives there is a black witch. Her's the one who's been casting the evil eye all over the countryside.'

'Don't be so ridiculous, there are no such creatures as witches,' Eugenia snapped.

'Oh, aren't there now? Then how did Billy Johnson's two cows come to sicken and die like they did? And what killed Mrs Gilmore's geese, all five of 'um? And how did the Izzards' boy come to drown in the river, and him able to swim like a fish? And why has it all happened in the past twelve months?' Old Martha demanded, and immediately answered her own questions. 'Because it was that witch-woman who put the evil eye on 'um. That's well known, that is. All this badness started when that witch come to that cottage twelve months past. All the folk hereabouts knows it.'

'Not another word from you, Martha,' Eugenia ordered firmly. 'Now go and find Joseph and tell him to follow me on to the cottage.'

The old crone glared for a brief moment, but recognizing that her young mistress's fiery temper was becoming roused, turned and went away muttering indignantly to herself.

Eugenia wrapped a shawl around her shoulders and hurried from the house, taking the footpath which led up to and over the half-mile-distant ridge.

By the time she reached her goal, the cottage had become an inferno, and Eugenia could only stare helplessly at the roaring flames before making a hurried search of the surroundings, calling in case anyone might be nearby.

Meeting no reply she stood for some moments pondering as to what best she could do, and decided to go to the village, a mile away along the turnpike road.

As Rosie's captors passed along the main road of the straggling village, their tumultuous number was increased by excited men, women and children coming hurrying to join them. Hester Pearson was being dragged along by a rope tied around her neck. Rosie was on foot now, tightly clutching her grandmother's skirt, her swelling jaw agonizingly painful, her head and body aching, a nauseous fear gripping her.

The village green was a muddy square surrounded by buildings, and the crowd came to a halt on the banks of the wide pond that comprised a third of the square.

Frightened sobs tore from Rosie's throat as she was forcibly separated from her grandmother, and again she fought desperately against her captors until they flung her to the ground and tied her hands and feet with thick ropes.

'Rosie! Rosie! Don't cry, sweetheart. Don't

12

cry. We'll be alright, Rosie. Really we will. Don't be feared, darling,' Hester Pearson shouted in a desperate attempt to soothe her grandchild, and she begged her captors, 'Please, let the child go. Do whatever you want to me, but don't harm the child. Please, please don't harm her.'

'Shut your rattle, you old bitch.' A man silenced her pleas with a vicious backhander across her mouth, sending her staggering backwards.

'Let's get on with what we got to do,' the man named Tom Steven directed the others. 'Strip the bugger.'

It was the women who hastened to obey him, tearing at Hester Pearson's clothing, ripping the gown and petticoat and long drawers from her body. The old woman wept in shame as her tormentors pulled her shielding hands from her private parts and stood her upright, spreadeagled, jeering obscenely at her wrinkled skin and shrivelled flesh.

Then her arms were roped behind her, her legs tied together, and she was hurled into the scum-topped pond. Rosie screamed in terrified anguish as her grandmother's frail body splashed into the water and disappeared. The next instant her view was blocked by the clamorous crowd as they jostled for vantage points on the bank.

Eugenia could hear shouting and jeering as she came walking rapidly into the village. She entered the square just as Hester Pearson was being dragged from the water by the rope

13

around her neck.

'Out her comes!'

The crowd howled with savage delight.

'And back her goes!'

Eugenia came to an abrupt halt, staring horrified at the spectacle she faced. Then her anger flared. Lifting her long skirts with both hands, she ran forwards, shouting at the top of her voice.

'Stop this! Stop this!'

Faces turned towards her.

'It's Pacemore's daughter,' people muttered. 'It's Colonel Pacemore's girl.'

The recognition spread like lightning through the crowd and bodies moved to give her passage.

She reached the man who was standing with the end of the long rope in his hands, and furiously confronted him. 'What are you doing, Tom Steven? Get that poor woman out of the water this instant! My father will have something to say about this.'

His broad red face twisted with fear. 'Her's a witch, Miss Pacemore. We'em only doing what has to be done.'

'Get her out,' Eugenia screamed at him and, grabbing the rope herself, pulled frantically on it.

Others came to her aid and within seconds Hester Pearson was dragged up on to the bank and laid face down.

'If she's dead, you'll hang for it,' Eugenia shouted at Tom Steven. She went down on to her knees and with both hands pumped

14

on the old woman's cold white flesh. Water belched from Hester Pearson's gaping mouth.

While Eugenia worked to revive the old woman, the crowd scattered, anxious to distance themselves from what had happened.

A horseman rode into the square and Eugenia shouted to him. 'Doctor! Doctor Whitmore! Come quick! Come quick!'

The middle-aged horseman dismounted and hurried to Eugenia's side. He knelt facing her across Hester Pearson's body, bleary-eyed and florid-faced, wafting out the fumes of gin and peppermint with every wheezy exhalation of his breath. He pressed his fingers into the old woman's throat, searching for the pulse of the carotid artery, but, frowning, shook his head.

'She's gone, Miss Pacemore.'

'Nanna? Nanna?'

Eugenia heard the frantic calls and rose to her feet, again stunned into horrified shock when she saw the small figure lying bound upon the muddy earth.

'Oh my God!' she cried and ran to where Rosie lay.

She quickly freed Rosie from her bonds and hugged the small figure to her breast. Stroking the girl's long hair, she said, 'It's over now, child. You're safe now. No one shall harm you now.'

'My nanna! What's happened to my nanna?' Rosie begged piteously.

'You must try to be brave, my dear,'

15

Eugenia told her. 'Your nanna is dead.'

Rosie threw back her head and screamed her anguish to the skies.

Rosie was still sobbing, heartbroken, when Eugenia brought her back to the house to be met in the hallway by her mother and Old Martha. Eugenia quickly related what had happened in the village.

'But why have you brought the girl back here? What are you going to do with her?' Mrs Pacemore questioned.

'Care for her, of course, until we can find out if she has any other relatives,' Eugenia said firmly.

'But what will your father say?' The older woman looked anxious.

Eugenia shrugged. 'He will say whatever he wishes to say, as he always does.' She turned and told Old Martha, 'Make her up a bed in my room.'

'But her's filthy dirty!' the crone protested.

'Then we shall have to bathe her, won't we, so tell Susan to begin warming some water.'

When the old crone made no move, Eugenia snapped curtly, 'Just do as I say, will you, Martha.'

There ensued a brief, silent battle of wills before Martha surrendered and hurried away, muttering angrily to herself.

Mrs Pacemore's soft pale face creased in dismay. 'Oh dear! Why must you upset Martha so? And I hardly dare to think of how your father will react when he returns. You've

16

no right to bring beggars into this house.'

Eugenia frowned in exasperation. 'Don't you understand what has happened, Mother? This poor child has just lost her grandmother in the most awful circumstances.' She brushed past her mother and led the sobbing girl into the large drawing room, seating her on the armchair by the fireside.

Drowning in her own grief, Rosie was hardly aware of what was happening around her; she could only weep for her grandmother.

Eugenia stood looking down at the girl, her expressive features full of pity. She waited patiently for many minutes until the heart-rending sobbing gradually eased and died away, and then lifted Rosie's tear-stained, woebegone face with gentle hands.

'What's your name, child? And how old are you?'

'Please, miss, I'm ten years old. My proper name is Rosalind Stannard. But everyone always calls me Rosie.'

'Then that is what I shall call you.' Eugenia smiled. 'Do you have family other than your grandmother, Rosie?'

'Please, miss, my mother's dead, and I don't know where my father is.'

'You don't know?'

'No, miss. My nanna took me with her, and we ran away from him when my mother died.' Tears again began to fall from Rosie's eyes as she haltingly muttered, 'My nanna was afraid of him, miss. That's why we kept moving from

17

place to place.'

'Why was she afraid?' Eugenia frowned with concern.

'Because whenever he got drunk he used to beat her, and beat my mother as well. When she died, the Spirits told my nanna to take me and run away and hide from him. So that's what she did.'

'The Spirits?' Eugenia was momentarily confused. 'What Spirits?'

'The Spirits that came to tell my nanna things. She used to make a magic spell to bring them to her. I couldn't see them, but my nanna could. She said she could see them as clear as she could see me.'

'There now! What did I tell you?' Old Martha had entered the room unheard by Eugenia and had been listening to the girl's story. 'That woman was a black witch who used to summon demons from hell...'

'Hold your tongue, Martha!' Eugenia rounded on her furiously. 'This poor child is suffering too much already. How can you be so cruel?'

'I'm not cruel,' the old crone protested. 'And you knows very well I'm not.' She glanced uneasily at Rosie's wan tear-wet face. 'I'm only saying what everybody hereabouts is saying.'

'And I'll hear no more of such rubbish from you, or anyone else.' Eugenia's thin face was flushed with anger. 'Now go away! I can't bear the sight of you at this moment.'

As the old crone retreated, Rosie defended

18

her grandmother. 'My nanna wasn't a witch, miss. She wasn't. She only used to talk to the Spirits. She was good, miss. Truly she was.'

'I'm sure she was good, child.' Eugenia stroked Rosie's head comfortingly. 'You mustn't mind what Martha says. She's only a very foolish old woman.'

Mrs Pacemore had sat silently listening and observing through her gold-handled lorgnette, and now she rose from her chair and went to the sideboard where a decanter of wine and glasses stood. She poured wine into a glass and added some fluid from a small dark phial. She put the glass into Rosie's hand.

'Drink this down, girl. It will do you good.'

Rosie obediently gulped the sweet-tasting wine.

Mrs Pacemore took the glass back from her and told her daughter, 'I think she should be put to bed now, before the laudanum takes effect. She can be bathed in the morning. Though I dread to think what your father will say about us giving her shelter.'

Grateful that her mother was now supporting her, Eugenia agreed with her suggestion, and took Rosie by the hand to lead her along the corridor, up the stairs and into the bedroom.

Rosie was overawed by the opulence of the house. The gleaming polished floors, the pictures on the walls, the glinting of silver and brasswork, the leaping flames in the great glistening black grates. In her innocence she thought it must be as splendid as the Queen's palaces that her grandmother had told her stories about.

By the time they reached the bedroom the dose of laudanum, coupled with the exhaustion of her ordeal, was already taking effect, and dizzying waves of sleepiness were engulfing Rosie. Noting this, Eugenia didn't make the girl undress, but only led her to the made-up bed and tucked her within the lavender-scented sheets. Then she sat on its edge and stroked Rosie's long hair until the child drifted into a deep sleep.

Eugenia went back to her mother and announced, 'I'm going into the village.'

'Whatever for?'

'I'm going to find the constable and demand that he arrests Tom Steven.' Eugenia lifted her hand to forestall her mother's protests. 'No! Don't try to stop me. I'm going, and that's final.'

The long, low-beamed, stone-flagged taproom of the Red Lion tavern was thronged with men and a noisy hubbub of talk and laughter filled its smoke-thick air.

Eugenia entered the tavern and halted just inside the doorway, peering around the dimly lamp-lit taproom for a glimpse of the man she sought. When the crowd became aware of her presence the talk and laughter died away into silence and a score of suspicious stares were directed at the newcomer.

'What's her want here?' a hoarse voice

questioned.

As the crowd stared at Eugenia an almost tangible atmosphere of hostility emanated from them, which struck home to her, causing her to feel nervous.

She drew a long breath and, quelling her nervous tremor, asked, 'Is the constable, Master Simpson, here? I need to speak with him urgently.'

'Oh, the constable's here alright, Miss Pacemore.' The stocky, white-aproned innkeeper chuckled grimly.

Hobnailed boots scraped against the stone flags and a passage was cleared to allow Eugenia a view of a man slumped, head on arms, upon a table, snoring in a drunken slumber.

'He's here alright. But he aren't going to be of much use to you, is he, missy? Perhaps there might be summat as I can do for you instead?' A man leered suggestively and winked at her.

She heard the sniggers and saw the grinning faces ranged around her and her fiery temper sparked. But she forced her voice to remain even.

'And Tom Steven, where is he?'

'God only knows where Tom Steven is. Because for sure, he aren't here.' The innkeeper appeared to be ill at ease. 'Listen, Miss Pacemore, this aren't the best place for you to be at this time. Feelings are running high in the village, and while I got the greatest respect for you and your family, I don't think

21

that you ought to be interfering in matters which are none of your concern.'

Growling hostility reverberated through the room.

Eugenia stood silent for several seconds. Then, her previous nervousness now replaced by her anger at these men's attitude, she heatedly stated, 'Tom Steven murdered a poor old woman today. I don't doubt that most of you, if not all, were present when he did so. He must be taken into custody until the magistrates can deal with him. I need help to arrest him. Will some of you please come and help me?'

She was answered with sullen, unresponsive stares.

Desperation started to goad Eugenia. 'I'll pay anyone who'll help. I'll pay them well!'

The man nearest her noisily hawked and spat on the floor by her feet, then slowly and deliberately turned his back on her. Within moments every man in the room followed suit.

She stared around her in angry impotence, but, realizing the futility of making any further attempts to persuade them, she could only walk out of the room. As she stepped out into the muddy road, an uproar of jeering cheers and laughter saluted her retreat.

'God, I wish I were a man!' she thought bitterly. 'I'd make you all laugh on the other side of your faces.' She sighed in frustration and trudged wearily homewards through the darkness and the cold dank wind.

Two

Worcester City

The middle-aged man toasting a piece of cheese at the lodging-house kitchen fire was shabbily dressed and wore his shapeless hat pulled down low on a shock of long, matted hair. Although ravaged by drink and weather there could be discerned in his features traces of the handsome youth he had once been, and beneath his shabby clothing there was still a taut, muscular body.

There were other men sitting on the rough benches ranged around the smoke-blackened walls of the odorous room, some talking, some dozing, all poorly dressed and down-at-heel.

A ragged tramper appeared through the low doorway and came to crouch by the fireside. He held his hands close to the glowing coals. 'It's bloody freezing out there, and I've been on the cadge all bloody day and aren't been give a penny piece by the miserable bastards,' he complained.

He stared longingly at the piece of cheese on the end of the long toasting fork, then glanced sideways and exclaimed in recognition.

'I knows you. I seen you at Aston Fair. You couldn't spare me a taste o' that cheese, could you? I'm bloody well starving with the hunger.'

Peter Stannard kept his gaze upon the cheese and shrugged dismissively. 'What's that to me?'

'I'll pay you back for it tomorrow. I got a mate following me here who's got plenty of the readies with him.'

'Then you'll be having a feast tomorrow, won't you?' Stannard sneered. 'So you don't want to risk spoiling your appetite now.'

He stood and went to sit on a bench, blowing on the cheese to cool it.

'Ah well!' The tramper took the rebuff philosophically, then announced to the room at large: 'I been trying me luck down around Appleby Village but there's all sorts o' shit flying about there at the minute, and any poor moocher is likely to be blamed for what he didn't do.'

'What sort of shit?' another man enquired casually.

'The bloody locals got hold of an old woman and drownded her in the village pond. They reckoned she was a witch.'

'How does you know that?' someone asked.

'Because I was there when it happened, two days since. I saw it all. The buggers had got hold of a little maid as well, and I reckon that they'd have drownded her next, but then this young gentlewoman come charging up and stopped them...'

The mention of an old woman and child had caught Peter Stannard's attention, and he was listening intently as the tramper went on.

'She didn't half lay into the bloke who had hold of the rope, I'll tell you. She told him that she'd see him hung, and he looked scared to death when she told him that. Oh, it was a hell of a game, it was. I never seen anybody drownded like that before, you know. To tell you the truth it give me a bit of a turn. I was glad to bugger off quick, before the bloody beaks and constables come sniffing around.' He paused for several seconds and then asked hopefully, 'Has anybody got a bit o' scran to spare? I'm bloody well starving with the hunger.'

His audience quickly averted their eyes and ignored him. But Peter Stannard left the bench and came to crouch by the man's side and spoke in a low voice.

'I want you to tell me everything you can remember about what you saw and heard at Appleby.' He broke off a morsel of cheese and handed it to the other man. 'And when I've heard sufficient, you can have the rest of this cheese. But tell me quietly.'

The man nodded eagerly and in hoarse whispers related all he knew.

'And the name of this old woman? What was her name?' Stannard questioned.

The tramper shrugged. 'I dunno.'

'Think, man,' Stannard pressed. 'Think

hard. Somebody must have said what name she bore.'

The tramper's grime-thick brows furrowed in concentration, and he said slowly, 'Now I comes to think on it, the old woman shouted to the little maid. I reckon she called the maid Rosie, or something similar.'

'And how old was the girl?'

'Bloody hell, matey!' the tramper swore impatiently. 'How the hell should I know how old the kid was? Perhaps nine or ten. I warn't paying that much heed to her, was I?'

'Alright.' Deep in thought, Peter Stannard rose upright and started to turn away. The tramper grabbed his sleeve.

'What about that bit o' scran then? You promised to give me that bit o' scran.'

Stannard's face twisted in sudden fury and he snarled menacingly, 'Get your filthy hands off me or I'll break your back.'

Frightened by Stannard's murderous glare, the tramper hastily released his grip, and stuttered, 'No, no. I meant no harm, master! Don't take against me. I meant no harm.'

Keeping his murderous glare fixed on the tramper, Stannard crammed the cheese into his own mouth, and slowly chewed and swallowed. Then, sneering contemptuously, he turned and left the kitchen.

'Did you hear that? Did you hear him threatening me? Telling me that he'd break me back?' the tramper blustered. 'It's lucky for him that I'm in a good mood, or I'd have give him a hammering, else.'

26

'It's lucky for you that he can't hear you saying that,' an elderly man informed him. 'I've seen him fight. He's a vicious bastard. A real nasty piece of work. He'd eat three like you for breakfast. Aren't that right, lads?'

There was a rumbling of agreement. Deciding that discretion was the better part of valour, the tramper said no more.

Three

Six days had passed since the death of Hester Pearson and Rosie had been transformed from the muddied, wan-faced urchin that Eugenia had brought home into a fresh-complexioned, remarkably pretty girl, with long, shiny auburn hair and lucent dark eyes. Though still mourning for her grandmother, the natural resilience of youth had served to blunt the sharp edges of her pain, and she now sat at the breakfast table with Eugenia and Mrs Pacemore, eating a boiled egg and toast with considerable relish.

Old Martha bustled into the room with a bundle of clothing in her arms, complaining irritably. 'I'se had such trouble altering these. Me eyes are burning in me head. I shouldn't be forced to do it, neither. I'm getting too old to do fine needlework.'

Eugenia sighed resignedly. 'If you recall,

Martha, it was you who insisted upon altering them all by yourself. No one forced you to do it.'

The old crone ignored her, and instead snapped at Rosie. 'Will you be quick and finish stuffing your face. I needs you to try these on so I can see the fit.'

'Let the poor girl finish her breakfast in peace,' Mrs Pacemore intervened. 'There'll be time enough for trying on clothes afterwards.'

Eugenia smiled inwardly. During the brief time Rosie had been staying with them, she had become something of a pet of both the older women, and they constantly vied with each other to spoil her in little ways. Eugenia's own fondness for the girl was also increasing every day. She had found Rosie to be pleasant-natured, highly intelligent and eager to reciprocate any kindness being shown to her. Despite the dark cloud of the tragedy that hung over them, there was a quiet sense of happiness pervading the house. Eugenia could even envisage Rosie eventually becoming accepted as a member of her family. But this would depend upon Eugenia's father's reaction to the girl being there. Herbert Pacemore was an old soldier, kindly enough at heart, but during the past few years his health had greatly deteriorated and he was in constant bodily pain, which made him sour-mooded and irascible at times. Presently he was in the city of Bath, enduring a variety of water cures in an effort to alleviate his bodily sufferings, and his date of return was still uncertain.

During long conversations with Rosie, Eugenia had garnered a great deal about the child's antecedents.

Rosie's maternal grandfather, Henry Pearson, had been the proprietor of a small gunsmith's workshop in Birmingham. Her father, Peter Stannard, had married the Pearsons' only daughter, Gabrielle, and when Henry Pearson died, the couple moved into the family home to live with Hester Pearson. From Rosie's account it seemed that Peter Stannard was a drunken, violent bully who terrorized the small family, and she had been a witness to many of the beatings her mother had endured. Three years past, Rosie's mother had died suddenly, and her grandmother had then become the main target of Peter Stannard's violent outbursts. After one particularly brutal assault, Hester Pearson had taken the child and run away from her son-in-law. For a short while the pair had moved from place to place, and then a year ago they had settled in the small cottage in Appleby.

Although Eugenia had spent a comparatively privileged, sheltered life, the child's stories of domestic violence did not shock her unduly. In this modern, rapidly industrializing, supposedly enlightened nation, men still had the legal right to beat their dependants. Violence inflicted upon women and children in their own homes was as commonplace in the rural areas as in the teeming cities, and was not confined to any particular social class. Eugenia knew several women of her own social standing whom it was rumoured had more than once felt the weight of their husband's or father's fists.

'But how were you able to buy food and shelter, my dear?' Eugenia had asked the child.

'My nanna had a store of money,' Rosie told her solemnly. 'On the day we ran away, my father wasn't at home, and a man with a horse and cart came to see my nanna. He gave Nanna money and took away a great many things from our house. Then after he was gone my nanna said we must run away very quickly, because my father would go mad when he came back and found out what she'd done.'

Eugenia was forced to hide a wry smile when she heard this, and felt pleased that Hester Pearson had at least managed to strike back in this small way at her brutal son-in-law.

'Did your grandmother still have some of that money left, my dear?'

'I don't think so.' The child shook her head. 'Because she used to cry sometimes and worry that we might have to go into the workhouse very soon.'

'Well, you may rest easy on that score, Rosie.' Eugenia smiled. 'I won't let you go into any workhouse.'

With that she let the topic rest.

Breakfast was over and while Susan, the cook, cleared the table, Old Martha and Mrs Pacemore supervised Rosie while she tried on the various altered dresses. The two women squabbled heatedly over the fittings, and Eugenia sat watching them with amusement. None of them was aware of the horseman dismounting in the front forecourt of the house until the doorbell jangled.

Eugenia went to answer to the summons.

Doctor Whitmore's florid face was glistening with sweat, despite the chill air, and he was breathing wheezily as he raised his top hat in polite salutation.

'Forgive my calling on you without appointment, Miss Pacemore. I won't step inside, for I'm in great haste and have other pressing calls to make.'

'How can I help you, Doctor?' Eugenia invited.

His plump cheeks puffed out and he exploded in gin-fuelled indignation. 'While I was at breakfast this morning, the coroner saw fit to inform me that he is to hold his inquest this very day. At the village tavern. Really, the fellow is no gentleman! He should have given me due warning about this, instead of sending his lackey to me while I was still breakfasting. I shall take him to task about it, believe me! I shall give him a piece of my mind!'

Eugenia waited patiently.

'And then, to top it all, the damned lackey swore that he had gone lame, and so was

31

unable to journey up here to inform your good self that you are required to attend the inquest as a material witness, and the girl Rosalind Stannard as well. So I'm reduced to the status of a mere messenger.'

Dismay burgeoned in Eugenia's mind as she listened. She feared that when Rosie was forced to give her evidence before a crowd of onlookers, all the trauma of that dreadful day would return to her, and set back the progress she had made in coming to terms with her grief.

'Is it really necessary that Rosie should give her evidence in public? I'm fearful that the proceedings will cause her much distress,' she explained. 'Cannot she tell the coroner quietly, in private, what was done to her and her grandmother?'

Whitmore shook his head. 'No, Miss Pacemore. I've been a witness at inquests, and all must be done openly and in public. The girl will be alright, I'm sure. You will be close by her as she testifies. Now I must get on. The coroner requests that all we witnesses are present in the tavern at two o'clock sharp. Good day to you until then, Miss Pacemore.'

He bustled away, leaving her with an uneasy sense of foreboding, which, try as she might to dispel it, inexorably strengthened its hold upon her mind.

The taproom of the Red Lion tavern was close-packed with men and women, its air polluted with the reek of foul breath, unwashed bodies, work-soiled clothing and rank tobacco smoke. Another avidly curious, noisy crowd of men, women and children clustered outside on the street, pushing and squabbling for their turn to peer through the leaded windowpanes at the scene of the corner's inquest taking place inside.

At one end of the taproom, two trestle tables had been set up. Behind one of these tables sat the coroner, a well-dressed, self-important gentleman, flanked by a quill-wielding clerk who had an open ledger, an inkpot and cellar of blotting powder on the table before him.

On the second table lay Hester Pearson in her open coffin, arms crossed upon her withered breasts, her mouth bulging with the peeled onion that had been inserted in a vain attempt to delay the onset of the stench of death's decay.

Near to the tables were a row of high stools on two of which sat Doctor Whitmore and the pasty-faced young curate of the parish church, the Reverend Phineas Cutwell. In front of them the jurymen were seated on a long bench.

When Eugenia came into the taproom leading Rosie by the hand, all heads turned toward them and excited murmurings ran through the crowd.

'It's Miss Pacemore and the Stannard girl, sir,' Whitmore informed the coroner, who nodded and banged his gavel hard upon the table top.

'Order! Order! Be silent!' He frowned at Eugenia. 'You are late, ma'am. Be so kind as to seat yourself there.' He pointed his gavel at the row of stools.

Rosie's heart was thudding rapidly and she felt tremulous as Eugenia led her towards the far end of the long room. When she saw her grandmother's waxen face so grotesquely distorted by the onion crammed into the gaping mouth, she cried out in distress and, jerking free from Eugenia's restraining hand, ran to the side of the coffin.

Eugenia came behind her and embraced her. 'Come, my dear. Come and sit with me.' She turned her head and beseeched the coroner, 'Cannot you excuse the child from this hearing, sir? You can see how distressed she is.'

The coroner shook his head and told her sympathetically, 'I regret, ma'am, that she cannot be excused. She is a material witness. However, I am prepared to allow you to stand with her while she gives her evidence, and I will hear her first so that what must be an ordeal for her may be over and done with more quickly.'

'Thank you, sir.' Eugenia drew Rosie away from the coffin and stood with a supporting arm around her as she was gently questioned by the coroner about the events of the terrible day her grandmother was killed.

'And did you see who actually forced your grandmother into the pool?' was his final question.

'No, sir. There were too many people. They blocked my sight.'

'Very well. You may sit.' He dismissed her and invited Eugenia to begin giving evidence.

Perched on the high stool, Rosie could see into the coffin, and she stared continuously at Hester Pearson's pallid, waxen face, her grief gnawing at her like a physical pain.

Eugenia was followed by Doctor Whitmore, and when he had finished there was a buzz of talk from the crowd.

The coroner rapped his gavel on the table top. 'Order! Order!'

An expectant silence fell on the room.

The coroner scowled irritably. 'I find it almost impossible to comprehend how in this modern age the superstitious belief in malignant witches can still survive. Such deluded ignorance is deplorable. I am satisfied that the deceased, Hester Pearson, was assaulted by a number of people in this village during the afternoon of the eighteenth of January of this year. Yet despite the extensive enquiries made by the constables, only these three witnesses now present have come forward. It would seem that the rest of the people of this parish were all mysteriously struck blind, deaf and dumb during the afternoon of the eighteenth of January.

'To bring in a verdict of murder requires the proof that murder was intended. I have not heard sufficient evidence to prove that it was the intention of Hester Pearson's assailants to kill her. But I am completely satisfied that the

35

unfortunate woman died as a direct result of the assault made upon her. However, it is the jury who must decide upon the verdict. Therefore, gentlemen of the jury, I would request that you retire and consider your verdict.'

The jurymen, who consisted of local farmers and tradesmen, whispered together for several moments, and then their foreman rose to his feet and addressed the coroner.

'If it please you, sir, we don't need to retire. We're all of the same mind and in full agreement. Our verdict is that it was an accidental death.'

There was a ripple of applause from the spectators, and the coroner banged his gavel hard and shouted furiously. 'Be silent! Be silent!'

He scowled in disgust at the jurymen. 'It is not the verdict that I would have arrived at myself. However, so be it. Let it be entered in the record.'

The clerk's pen diligently scratched, and the coroner went on.

'Furthermore, I order that the corpse of Hester Pearson be now released from the custody of my office. Is there anyone present who will take responsibility for the expenses of interment?'

'I will, sir,' Eugenia said and could not help but glare angrily at the jurymen for their blatant disregard for justice.

The coroner nodded acknowledgement, and glanced with sympathetic eyes at Rosie's forlorn expression. 'I trust that the Parish Vestry will decide in due course what is to be done with Rosalind Stannard in accordance with the laws appertaining to pauper orphans.'

'There is no need for the Parish Vestry to decide anything, sir,' Eugenia spoke out firmly. 'I will take the girl into my own home and care for her.'

'Well, I might have something to say about that!' a voice shouted from the rear of the crowd. Rosie's eyes widened and she gasped in shock. Peter Stannard pushed through the crowd and came to stand in front of the table where his dead mother-in-law lay.

'I'm Peter Stannard, and Hester Pearson's daughter was my wife, sir.' Then he pointed at Rosie's shock-whitened face. 'And I'm this girl's father, so I shall be taking care of her.'

'Is this true, girl?' the coroner asked Rosie, who could only nod and stammer nervously.

'Y–yes, sir. He's my f–father.'

The dramatic intervention sparked an explosion of uproarious excitement, and the cacophony was increased by those outside shouting through the windows.

'Order! Order!' The coroner hammered his gavel upon the table, shouting at the top of his voice. 'Order! Order! Order!'

Eugenia went to Rosie and hugged the girl protectively to her breasts. Rosie clung to her and begged in frightened whispers, 'Don't let my father take me! Please don't let him take me away from you!'

'I won't, my dear, I won't,' Eugenia assured her, but even as the words left her lips, she knew with a sickening certainty that she was legally powerless to prevent Peter Stannard from doing whatsoever he wished with his own daughter.

Four

In the small, bare room at the rear of the tavern, Eugenia Pacemore and Peter Stannard stood facing each other across an upturned barrel on which a single smoky-flamed candle cast its small wavering pool of light. Rosie was standing behind her father, her hands tightly clenched together, her face betraying her fearful anxiety.

Through the intervening walls the noise from the taproom was muffled, individual voices rendered unintelligible.

'Well, miss? You asked to speak with me in private. So say your piece,' Peter Stannard invited.

Eugenia did not reply immediately. From the first moment she had seen this man, she had instinctively distrusted and disliked him. So now she considered her words carefully.

'During the short time we've known Rosie, Mr Stannard, my mother and myself have become very fond of her, and we feel that we would like to offer her a home with us.'

He bared his strong, tobacco-stained teeth in a sneering grin. 'You want to offer her a home, do you? What as? A bloody unpaid skivvy?'

'Certainly not!' Eugenia denied indignantly. 'Our intention is that she shall be treated as one of our family.'

'And be encouraged to forget and disown her own family?' he accused.

Eugenia was finding it hard to quell her fiery temper, and could not keep a hard edge from intruding into her tone. 'That is the last thing we want, Mr Stannard. You would, of course, be free to visit her whenever you wished to do so.'

'Well, that's very kind of you. Allowing me the freedom to visit my own daughter!' he exclaimed sarcastically. 'However, I shan't be troubling you with any visits. She's coming with me.'

Rosie could not repress a moan of distress. Seeing the girl's stricken face, Eugenia's own dismay impelled her to challenge forcefully. 'Taking her from here at this time surely cannot be in her best interests, Mr Stannard. You must recognize the advantages she will gain by remaining here with my family.'

'I've had enough of this!' he hissed impatiently and, grasping Rosie's arm, pulled her with him as he strode to the door and flung it open. 'If you're so eager to have a kid, then birth one of your own. You're not getting this one, that's for sure.'

The suddenness of his move took Eugenia completely by surprise, and for a couple of moments she stood motionless. Then she hastened after him along the dark passageway, back into the taproom.

Peter Stannard dragged Rosie up to the bar counter and called for a glass of gin. Hester Pearson's coffin had been removed and the coroner was stood at the street door having a final word with Doctor Whitmore.

Eugenia appealed to the two men. 'Will you please help me, gentlemen. That man mustn't be allowed to take the girl.'

They both looked at her as if she were a madwoman, and the coroner raised his eyebrows expressively. 'She is his daughter, ma'am. He can do whatsoever he chooses with her, just so long as it is legal.'

'I'm sure she will be perfectly safe with her own father, Miss Pacemore.' Doctor Whitmore offered his wheezy reassurance. 'And that is the proper place for her to be. With her own flesh and blood.'

'You don't understand, gentlemen,' Eugenia tried desperately to persuade them.' The man is a brute who used to abuse his wife and mother-in-law. The girl is terrified of him, and with good reason. He'll treat her badly. I know he will.'

'I don't doubt that you mean well, ma'am.' The coroner smiled patronizingly. 'But have you not considered that the girl might have told you untruths about her father? After all, in your home she has tasted what to her must seem luxury, and so of course she is not happy to revert to her own lowly station in life.'

This exchange took place in a hush of silence as everyone in the taproom listened curiously. At the bar Peter Stannard drained the glass of gin and ordered another one, while by his side Rosie stood in tearful misery, enduring the pain of her father's cruelly hard grip upon the back of her neck.

'Will you stop him taking the girl, gentlemen?' Eugenia demanded, pointing at Rosie's face. 'Just look at her. See how unhappy the poor child is.'

The coroner's eyes were uneasy as he glanced briefly at the girl. But he only shrugged his shoulders. 'Even if what you claim about Mr Stannard's treatment of his wife were true, there is nothing in law to prevent him taking his daughter with him. You must accept that fact. I bid you goodnight, ma'am, Doctor.' He bowed curtly and went outside to his carriage.

Doctor Whitmore's florid features also showed a degree of unease, but he only said, 'There's nothing to be done, Miss Pacemore.' Then he bowed and left her.

In desperation, Eugenia decided to try another tack. She walked up to Peter Stannard and said bluntly, 'I'll pay you to leave Rosie with me. I'll pay you well.'

Stannard swung to confront her, a savage snarl on his thick-stubbled features. 'If you don't bugger off and let me be, I'll break your

41

face for you, you bitch!' He turned his head from side to side, appealing to the onlookers. 'Have you ever seen the likes of this? A woman trying to buy a daughter from her own father? How brass-necked can you get?' He clenched his fist and raised it threateningly before Eugenia's face. 'Get away from me and my daughter, or you'll get a taste o' this. Now bugger off!'

The innkeeper hurried to interpose himself bodily between the couple. 'You must leave it be, Miss Pacemore. You're in the wrong here. You must leave it be.' Then he said to Stannard, 'And you go straight now from this village, and take your girl with you. We don't want any more trouble here.'

'Oh, I'll go alright,' Stannard growled. 'But you'll sell me a bottle o' gin first.'

Eugenia was struggling to regain her composure. Stannard's threat of violence had shaken her, because never before in her life had she been threatened with physical assault.

Stannard brandished the dark-green bottle triumphantly aloft as he swaggered from the inn, dragging the weeping Rosie with him.

'No!' Eugenia cried out in protest and tried to go after him, but the innkeeper blocked her way, physically restraining her.

'No, Miss Pacemore. Leave them go! You must leave them go!'

'Let me pass! Let me pass, will you!' Eugenia fought to break free of his grip, but was powerless against his bulk and strength.

42

Tears of distress and frustration stung her eyes. 'If you don't let me go this instant, I'll have the law on you.'

The big man grimly shook his head. 'If I was to let you go, then I'd have your dad after my blood. Because God only knows what will happen if you catches up to that pair, the state you're in. You'm going nowhere, Miss Pacemore. Not until they've gone clear away from here. So it's no use you struggling, because I'm not going to let you go after them.'

Slowly and reluctantly she was forced to accept defeat, and she ceased to struggle.

'Now, you sit yourself down. You're going to stay here until you've come to your senses, and then I'm going to escort you back to your house.'

He gently but firmly pushed her down on to a bench and released his grip, but remained standing directly in front of her, watching her closely.

Eugenia buried her face in her hands, tortured by the mental image of Rosie's pitiful tears, and her own uncontrollable grief burst from her.

'I've failed you, child. I've so miserably failed you.'

The night was wild and windy. Fierce, brief showers of sleety rain had soaked Rosie to her skin, her whole body ached and she was near to exhaustion when after what seemed interminable hours, Peter Stannard finally slowed

43

his pace and halted. He lifted the gin bottle to his lips, tilting it high, then shouted in fury and hurled the empty bottle on to the ground, shattering it to pieces.

'It's all gone! All gone! And where am I to get more?' Clouds rifted and a shaft of moonlight fleetingly illuminated Peter Stannard's contorted features as he bent low, bellowing like a drunken madman into Rosie's face. 'Tell me! Bloody well tell me!'

She cried out in pain as his fingers dug deep into her tender flesh.

Stannard suddenly staggered and fell, dragging her down with him. He rolled on to his back and began to rave incoherently. Rosie scrambled to her feet and stood staring with wide frightened eyes at her father. The clouds closed, blotting out the moonlight, plunging the countryside once again into inky darkness. Stannard began to kick out with both feet, screaming at the top of his voice at some phantasm conjured by his drink-fevered brain.

'Get away from me! I'll kill you! Get off me!'

Panic overwhelmed Rosie and she turned and ran stumbling and tripping over the deep ruts of the trackway. She passed through a coppice of trees and saw a light glimmering in the distance on her right-hand side. She left the trackway and headed across the bracken-studded heath towards the flickering glow. As she drew nearer she could see a large round tent, a cart and a tethered horse, and four

44

soldiers in red coats sitting around a camp-fire. Heads turned as she came into the firelight, and a grizzled-haired sergeant exclaimed: 'Where the hell has she sprung from?'

Gasping for breath, she pleaded frantically, 'Please help me! My dad is back down the road there. There's something wrong with him.'

'What's the matter with him? Is he hurt?' the sergeant asked.

'He drank a whole bottle of gin and then he fell down and he's lying on the ground shouting and kicking at somebody, but there's no one there.'

Her questioner chuckled. 'Sounds like the DTs to me.'

'Can you help me? Please can you help me?' she begged.

His shrewd eyes examined her intently for some seconds. 'How far away is he?'

'He's on the road beyond the trees. I can take you there.'

'There's no need. My lads will find him easy enough. You stay here with me. You looks knackered.'

He issued rapid commands, the other three soldiers went to harness the horse into the shafts of the cart, and within scant minutes the cart trundled away.

'Now then, what's your name?' The sergeant smiled kindly at her.

She bobbed a polite curtsey to him. 'My name's Rosalind Stannard, sir. But everybody

45

calls me Rosie.'

'Well, you don't have to call me sir, I'm a sergeant not an officer. Sergeant William Thomas of the Twenty-ninth of Foot, at your service, Rosie. Now sit you down and rest.'

Feeling weak with exhaustion, Rosie sank down beside the leaping flames. From an iron cooking pot suspended above the fire, Thomas ladled stew into a mess tin and handed it to her together with a spoon.

'You get that across your chest, Rosie, and have a drink o' this cider.' He placed a small flagon by her side.

The savoury smell of the stew made Rosie realize just how very hungry she was, and she ate and drank with a will, scraping every last remnant of the food from the mess tin.

'Have you had enough?' He smiled.

'Yes. Thank you very much, sir.'

He lifted his finger in remonstrance. 'Not *sir*, Rosie. Sergeant Thomas, or just Sergeant will do.'

'Thank you very much, Sergeant Thomas.' She smiled.

He filled a short clay pipe with tobacco and lit it with an ember from the fire. 'Tell me all about yourself, Rosie. And what brings you out on such a dark night?'

She felt instinctively she could trust this weather-beaten, grizzled-haired man, and readily related all that had befallen her during these latter days.

Puffing out occasional clouds of rank-smelling smoke, he listened in motionless silence, his brown eyes warmly sympathetic. When she had finished her recital he shook his head thoughtfully 'And you've no idea where your dad is taking you?'

'No, Sergeant Thomas.'

He seemed about to say something more, but then the sound of a horse and cart brought him to his feet.

'You stay here,' he told her, and went to meet the returning party.

Peter Stannard was lying on the floor of the vehice, unconscious, and trussed up with rope.

'He was off his head when we got to him, Sarge. He wouldn't come quiet, so I had to tap him one.'

'Bit more than a tap by the look of it.' Thomas grinned. 'Wrap a blanket round him and put him under the cart, but leave him tied. I don't want him waking up and causing ructions.'

He went back to Rosie. 'Your dad's alright, Rosie. He's sleeping now. He'll be as right as rain. You can sleep in the tent with us, and in the morning we'll see what's what.'

Thankful relief flooded through her that the ordeal of the journey had ended, for this night at least.

'Right then, let's get our heads down,' Sergeant Thomas instructed. 'You take the first watch, Billy. Second watch, Mack. Third watch, you, Pat. I'll take the last watch.'

'I see you're taking the easiest for yourself again, Sarge,' Pat jibed cheekily, and Thomas chuckled. 'That's one of the privileges of command, my bucko.' He beckoned to the girl. 'Come on, Rosie, let's find you some bedding and get you settled down.' As an afterthought, he asked, 'Do you want to have a look at your dad, so you can see he's alright?'

She shook her head in emphatic refusal.

'No, I shouldn't want to look at the bugger myself if I was in your shoes, you poor little devil,' Thomas thought pityingly, but said nothing, only smiled and nodded acceptance.

She went with him to the tent, and he handed her two rough blankets. 'Wrap these tight around you, my duck, and you'll be as snug as a bug in a rug. You can sleep there at the back, then you won't be disturbed by us coming and going.'

The men followed her into the tent, quickly settled themselves and very soon were all asleep.

Exhausted though she was, sleep did not come quickly to Rosie. Her brain was seething too vividly with all the memories of the last few traumatic days. She lay wrapped in the coarse blankets with the snores of the sleeping men sounding in her ears. After a while she snuggled up close to Sergeant Thomas, drawing comfort from his warm bulk, and finally drifted into sleep.

'I wish that my dad was like you, Sergeant Thomas,' she thought. 'I really do wish that you could be my dad.'

Five

The winds in the night had cleared the skies of clouds and the dawn was clear and chilly-fresh. The soldiers left Rosie asleep in the tent while they prepared for their day's march.

Sergeant Thomas grasped Peter Stannard's booted feet and hauled him bodily from under the cart.

'What's happened? Why am I tied up like this?' Stannard snarled aggressively. 'What am I doing here with you bloody redcoats?' His tirade was cut short by the sergeant's boot thudding hard into his stomach.

'Shut your mouth, you drunken scum!' Thomas snapped. 'Or I'll kick your bloody head in.'

Peter Stannard could see from the other man's expression that this was no idle threat, and subsided into scowling silence.

'Now I'm going to set you free,' Thomas told him. 'So behave yourself.' He loosened the ropes and stepped back a pace.

Stannard struggled to his feet, groaning from the pain of a pounding headache and stiff muscles. His bloodshot eyes took in his surroundings, and his well-honed cunning quickly reasserted its dominance.

'I'm very sorry for what I just said, Sergeant.' He hastened to try and mollify the grim-faced soldier. 'It was just the shock of finding myself in such a strait. What's happened to me? And where's my daughter? Is she alright?'

'She's sleeping back in the tent there, and she's in much better shape than you are, judging by the looks of you,' Thomas said evenly. 'She come running to us last night for help. You were raving like a loony, mad with the drink. So we tied you up and kept you here with us.'

Stannard projected a remorse that he was very far from feeling. 'Oh my God! I feel so ashamed! It's true, I took a few drinks. But there must have been something poisonous in the gin to send me off my head like that. It's never happened to me before, I swear on my child's life.'

Thomas's expression was deliberately ambiguous. 'She told me about what's been happening to her lately. About her grandmother being killed and suchlike. But she didn't seem to know where you're taking her to now.'

'Why, back to her rightful home, of course. Back to my house in Birmingham.' Stannard shook his head sorrowfully. 'The poor child has suffered a great deal, and now I'm going to make sure that she's well loved and cared for.'

'Well, you make sure that you do that.' The sergeant's wide experience of men and life made him strongly doubt that the girl would ever be well loved and cared for by this shabby, debauched, bleary-eyed man before him. 'She's a very likeable kid.'

'Oh yes, yes, I intend to make sure of it, Sergeant. I swear to it.'

'You'd both best have a bite to eat with us before we part company,' Thomas invited, wanting to at least ensure that Rosie was fed before she left their camp.

'Come on, kiddo. It's reveille.' Thomas gently roused the sleeping girl, and was struck by a poignant memory of his own dead children buried far away in India. 'My daughters would have been about your age by now.' He smiled sadly at her pretty face.

Rosie reluctantly awoke. She had been dreaming that she was walking through woods and fields with her grandmother, and with wakefulness came the renewed desolation of her loss.

'Here, take this.' Thomas gave her a strip of towelling and a sliver of soap. 'There's a stream at the rear of the tent. You go and wash yourself, and then come and have some breakfast.'

The stream was clear and fast-running, and the cold water caused Rosie to gasp as she splashed it over her arms and face and neck. She broke twigs from a hazel bush and, crushing their ends between stones, used them to scrub her white teeth.

Her waking sense of desolation ebbed and was replaced by an escalating trepidation about what might lay ahead of her. Yet mingled with that trepidation there was also the burgeoning excitement of a new adventure.

She joined the men at the campfire, where the appetizing scent of bacon frying in the iron skillet filled the air. When Thomas handed her a thick wedge of bread and crisp bacon she ate it with gusto.

'By Christ, she's boltin' that grub down like she's a bleedin' grenadier!' one of the men chortled.

Rosie blushed with embarrassment, and Sergeant Thomas chuckled.

'You get it down you, kiddo. I was a grenadier meself, and you're doing me proud, so you are.'

Immersed in his own thoughts, Peter Stannard sat chewing his own ration of food, paying no attention to his companions. It was not any degree of love or concern for his child that had impelled Stannard to bring Rosie with him. It was pure selfishness that motivated him. To him, she was merely a possession. His property, and a potential source of income. Many children as young as only five or six years of age were put to work to earn wages. At ten years old, Rosie was more than capable of working and earning money, and Stannard was pondering how best she could do just that.

He saw how pretty she was, and how these hardbitten men were treating her with an asexual, fatherly kindness. But Stannard

52

knew of other types of men. He knew of men who did not look upon pretty children with kindly eyes. Instead, these men's eyes were predatory, their sexual appetites perverse and degenerate. Such men were willing to pay, and pay well, for the satisfaction of those appetites.

'Annie will know how best to handle that business. She'll know how to get the best price,' Stannard told himself. 'So I'll leave it all to her. There's no need to rush at it like a bull at a gate, is there?'

He looked at his daughter, and mentally blessed the good fortune that had brought her back within his power.

The tent was packed on the cart, the soldiers shouldered their muskets, and Sergeant Thomas smiled down at Rosie.

'We have to part company now, Rosie.'

She bobbed a curtsey. 'Thank you ever so much for helping me, Sergeant Thomas.'

'It's been my pleasure.' He took her hand and pressed a small object into her palm. 'If ever you're in need of a friend, then this will help you to find me. Goodbye now.'

Rosie felt a lump rise in her throat as she stood watching the group of redcoats march away down the track, the horse and cart trundling behind them.

She looked at the object in her hand. It was a brass button tied on to a length of ribbon, with the number twenty-nine inscribed upon its shiny surface.

Tears stung her eyes as she murmured

53

aloud: 'Sergeant William Thomas of the Twenty-ninth of Foot, at your service, Rosie.'

'What did you say?' Peter Stannard came up behind her.

She quickly secreted the button in her pocket. 'Nothing, Dad. I said nothing.'

'Come on.' He jerked his head. 'We've still a long way to go.'

She took one last look at the now distant redcoats, drew a deep breath and followed her father, surreptitiously tying the ribbon around her neck so that the brass button lay next to her heart.

Six

The second day's journey was physically easier for Rosie. There was little wind, the sky was clear and the wintry sun tempered the chill of the air. There was sparse traffic on this country road, just an occasional farm cart or trudging labourers, whom they passed without greeting. Her father, suffering the after-effects of his previous night's debauch, walked slowly, frequently halting to take brief rests. He spoke little, but when he did so his tone was pleasant enough. Rosie's earlier sense of trepidation gradually dispelled and she began to feel more optimistic about what might lie ahead for her.

As the sun sank low to the horizon her father said, 'The place we're going to is about a mile further on.'

Rosie, very hungry and increasingly footsore, was relieved to hear that she was almost at journey's end.

The house stood well back from the road, surrounded by a stone wall with an arched gateway. From a distance the building appeared to be a substantial residence, but close up it presented a sorry sight of decay. There were rags stuffed into broken windowpanes, peeling paint and rotting woodwork, broken tiles in the sagging roof, crumbling brickwork surrounded by a rank overgrowth of weeds and shrubs.

'Where the bloody hell have you been, and what's you got there?' Annie Sparks stood beneath the stone archway, her arms akimbo.

'You know that I've been searching for my daughter.' Peter Stannard pushed Rosie forward. 'Well, I finally found her down by Worcester.'

Rosie stared apprehensively at the fat, rouge-plastered face frowning down at her.

'She looks like she's been dragged through a bloody midden.'

'Then she won't look out of place in this shithouse, will she?' Stannard rejoined.

'And what makes you think that I'm going to take you back in, Peter Stannard? After the way you've played me up.' The fat face was petulant.

'Now Annie, darling, you know you won't

be happy without me.' Stannard chuckled confidently and moved to take the blowsy woman in his arms and kiss her noisily on her scarlet-painted lips. 'And I've got plans to earn money. Good money.'

'And pigs'll bloody fly, won't they?' She sniffed scornfully, but made no attempt to break free of his encircling arms.

Rosie's earlier sense of rising optimism about her future ebbed rapidly as she stood looking at the house, her father and the fat woman.

Stannard was now smiling cajolingly and whispering into the woman's ear, his hands roaming over her body. Her petulant frown faltered and then she cackled with raucous laughter and surrendered to his blandishments.

'Alright, you rotten bastard. I'll forgive you. But this is the last time you gets around me. Next time you plays me up, it'll be the finish.'

'There'll be no next time, darling,' he assured her fervently. 'From now on, it'll be just you and me, I swear on my child's life!'

Annie Sparks pursed her lips thoughtfully as she stared intently at Rosie. She pushed Stannard's arms away and came to the child.

'Let's have a look at your teeth, my duck.' Her fingers tapped on Rosie's lips. 'Open wide now.'

Rosie dutifully obeyed, and Annie Sparks nodded her satisfaction. 'Yes, they'm nice and white and even, aren't they?' She turned to Stannard. 'You've got a real pretty kid here,

Pete. I know just where to place her.'

He chuckled and nodded. 'I was sure of that, darling, that's why I brought her straight here.' Then he hesitated before adding in a more serious manner, 'But I want my fair share, mind.'

'You'll get it,' she agreed readily. 'But I'll deduct what you owes me from your share.'

He scowled, but said nothing.

Annie Sparks' pudgy hand stroked Rosie's cheek. 'Won't you come inside, my duck, and have a bite to eat with me? I've got a nice bit of meat all ready for cooking. Does that sound nice to you?'

Rosie's empty stomach rumbled painfully and, bobbing a curtsey, she agreed readily. 'If you please, ma'am, it sounds very nice indeed. Thank you, ma'am.'

The garishly painted mouth gaped wide and the hanging jowls shook with a cackling of raucous laughter. 'Her's quite the little lady, aren't her? I'll bet it's her mam who she takes after.'

'Oh, yes,' Peter Stannard sneered. 'My wife always had a bob on herself. She was full of airs and graces.'

The fat woman smiled at Rosie. 'I think that you and me shall become real good friends, my duck.' She took her by the hand and led her into the house.

It's gloomy, shadowed interior was as ruinously decayed as the exterior. The finely crafted ceiling plaster was falling away from the slats, the walls streaked with greasy damp, the bare wooden floors covered with filth and rubbish. The air was musty and dank.

Annie Sparks saw Rosie's dismayed expression and cackled with laughter. 'Don't you fret yourself, my duck. I don't live in this part. This is where I lives, down here.'

She led the way along a dark, stone-flagged passageway and thrust open the door at its end. Rosie blinked as lamp light struck her eyes and warm, pleasantly scented air enveloped her.

'Come in, come in, my duck,' Annie Sparks invited, and Peter Stannard followed them in.

The room was long and wide, dominated by a great inglenook at one end, where a log fire was crackling and spitting. The opposite end of the room contained a huge, curtained four-poster bed. Iron-bound chests and sets of drawers lined the white-limed walls and a great table flanked with rush-bottomed chairs filled the room's centre, while ranged in a semi-circle before the inglenook were several large upholstered armchairs. Hanging from the ceiling beams, at least six oil lamps were casting their light.

Perched on one of the armchairs, leaning forwards upon the silver-topped cane he held in his gnarled hands, was a cadaverous elderly man. He was clean-shaven, parchment-complexioned, with long white hair tied back in a ponytail.

'Now, my duck, you must meet my father, "The Reverend".' The fat woman once again cackled with laughter as she ushered Rosie to stand before the old man. 'This is Pete's daughter, Father.'

The old man's watery blue eyes squinted at Rosie. 'What's your name, girl?'

Rosie bobbed a curtsey. 'If you please, sir, my name is Rosalind Stannard. But everyone calls me Rosie.'

He sucked audibly on his toothless gums while his squinted eyes examined her face and form.

Rosie, made uncomfortable by this silent, ever-lengthening scrutiny, tried to stand absolutely motionless and kept her own eyes politely downcast.

Annie Sparks smiled at Rosie. 'You can come and help me in the kitchen, my duck. I might be able to find a piece of ginger-snap for you to eat as well.'

The kitchen was another surprise for Rosie. Adjoining the long room, and equally well-lit, it was a mass of polished black cooking ranges and burnished, gleaming copper and brass pots and pans. There was a great stone sink equipped with its own small hand pump, and a huge dresser that almost covered one wall, its shelves lined with blue and white patterned plates and dishes and other crockeries of all descriptions.

The shrewd, puffy eyes of the woman dwelt on the girl's expressive face, and she cackled with laughter.

'I can see that you weren't expecting to find such a grand kitchen as this, were you, my duck?'

Rosie shook her head. 'No, ma'am. It's bigger than Miss Pacemore's kitchen, even.'

Annie Sparks smiled with self-satisfaction. 'Yes, I haven't done so badly for myself, when all's said and done.' She touched Rosie's cheek. 'And you can do as well for yourself, my duck. That's if you're a good, obedient girl, and you do as I tell you to do.'

'Am I to stay here then, ma'am? To live with you?'

'Would you like to live here with me?' The woman returned question for question.

Rosie pondered a moment before answering gravely. 'I don't know, ma'am. I suppose I would like it well enough if we are suited to each other.'

The fat jowls shook with raucous laughter. 'What a funny little article you are, duck. Do you know, it's hard to believe that you'm Peter Stannard's daughter. You don't seem to have anything of him in you.'

From a cupboard, Annie Sparks took out some beefsteaks and onions, and from another cupboard a round loaf and butter.

'Now you watch close, my duck, and then you'll know how to cook your meat.'

'If you please, ma'am, I know already. My nanna taught me how to cook all sorts of things.'

'Did she now! And what else did your nanna teach you?'

'How to read, and write, and do my numberings.'

'So you're a scholar then, are you?'

'Well, my nanna said I had the makings of becoming a scholar, ma'am.'

As the savoury aromas of the frying meat and onions rose from the big cast-iron pan on the cooking range, Annie Sparks asked seemingly innocuous, disconnected questions to cunningly garner a great deal of information concerning Rosie's antecedents.

The girl's artless answers painted a much different story to Peter Stannard's accounts of his previous life, but this came as no surprise to Annie Sparks. She was widely experienced in the ways of the world, and already knew only too well that he was a habitual liar. She stored the information about Eugenia Pacemore in her capacious memory, as she did any information that might serve as a future source of potential financial or material gain.

For her part, Rosie was feeling increasingly comfortable in Annie Sparks' company, and as she enjoyed the sweet piece of ginger-snap that the fat woman had given her, she was starting to hope that all her troubles had passed.

After the meal was eaten, the four of them sat in the armchairs before the inglenook fire. The three adults drank gin and smoked short clay pipes. Her full stomach, the warmth of the room and the comfort of the armchair quickly lulled Rosie into a sound sleep.

The atmosphere between the two men was a little less hostile now, both their moods mellowed by good food, gin and tobacco. For some considerable time there was no conversation in the room, and the copious amounts of gin the trio of adults were drinking took its inevitable toll, rendering them all half-drunk.

Sucking his gums, The Reverend squinted contemplatively at the sleeping girl.

'What are you thinking, Father?' Annie Sparks asked.

'I'm thinking she'd do very well for the "ship-wrecked missionary's orphan" dodge. I could work the Welsh border with her. Nobody knows me in those parts.'

'But that'd only be small pickings,' Peter Stannard objected. 'There's quicker ways of making good money out of her. I know some who'd pay very well for a pretty kid like she is.'

'What sort of a wicked unnatural parent are you?' the old man challenged with apparent disgust. 'To be ready to sell your own daughter as a whore.'

'Exactly the same sort of parent that you was, you old hypocrite!' Annie Sparks snapped, but without any real rancour in her voice. 'You was willing enough to sell me for a whore, as I recall it.'

'Now, Annie, it was a case of "needs must, when the devil drives", as you knows very well. We'd have starved to death otherwise. And I took care that none of the marks was ever let to knock you about, didn't I?'

'So where do you get off, you old bastard?' It was Peter Stannard's turn to challenge the old man. 'Calling me wicked and unnatural?

When you've done exactly the same as what I'm proposing to do?'

'Don't start, you two!' Annie Sparks ordered sharply. 'This is a business discussion, not a prize fight.'

'Exactly so, darling,' Peter Stannard was quick to agree.

'And I'm the head of this business!' she stated forcefully. 'And it'll be me who decides what's to be done with the kid. Not neither of you. Is that understood?' She glared at both of them until they signified their acquiescence.

'Right, that's it then.' She rose ponderously to her feet. 'Leave the kid here for tonight. I'll make her a bed up tomorrow. You get to your own bed, Father. Now!'

'Alright, alright.' He shuffled to the kitchen door and went through it, grumbling under his breath.

'Come on you.' She grabbed Peter Stannard's coat collar and, hauling him bodily from his chair, pulled him towards the four-poster bed. 'You'd better be able to do the needful tonight, you bastard, or else I'll be finding meself a man who can.'

Snuggled peacefully in the capacious armchair, Rosie smiled as in her dreams she walked with her grandmother through sunlit green meadows.

Seven

Three weeks had passed since Rosie's arrival at Annie Sparks' house and, although she still mourned for her grandmother, the initial raw pain of her bereavement had greatly eased. Annie Sparks had treated her with constant kindness, and Rosie reciprocated with an ever-increasing trust and liking for her new friend, so that when Annie Sparks suggested that she should call her Auntie, the girl was only too happy to comply.

The Reverend and Peter Stannard had gone away together early that morning while Rosie was still asleep, and when she asked Annie Sparks where and why they had gone, the fat woman said, 'They've gone up Nottingham way, my duck. My dad's doing the Lord's work, and your dad's helping him.'

'What is the Lord's work, Auntie?'

'It's helping people to ease their consciences by relieving them of some of their sinful gains, my duck, and passing the money on to the poor.'

'Which poor are those?' Rosie asked curiously, and Annie Sparks' raucous laughter cackled.

'They're us, my duck. Me and you, and my

64

dad and your dad.'

Rosie thought about this information for some time. 'Are we very poor then, Auntie?'

'Oh yes.' The fat woman nodded emphatically, then smiled. 'But that's nothing for you to worry your head about, my duck. I shall take good care of you, no matter how poor we might be.'

There came a thunderous hammering on the kitchen's rear door, and Annie Sparks scowled. 'Run and see who that is, my duck, before the bloody door gets knocked off its hinges.'

Rosie ran to open the door and was greeted by a swarthy-featured man in a voluminous multi-caped coat, a small round hat perched on his long black ringlets.

'Hello, pretty 'un.' He grinned. 'Tell the missus it's Solly Solomons come bearing gifts again.'

Solomons was a hawker, who travelled the district with a horse and cart laden with foodstuffs and domestic articles, trinkets and geegaws.

Annie Sparks came out from the inner room.

'Did you deliver that note I gave you?' she asked the hawker.

'I did, missus. And here's the reply to it.' With a flourish he produced a sealed envelope, which Annie Sparks snatched from his hand. She opened it and quickly scanned the note, then smiled with satisfaction.

'Right, now I wants oil, bacon, eggs, soap,

flour...' She rattled off a list as she and Rosie accompanied him to the horse and cart standing on the roadway outside the arched gate.

When Rosie took some of the goods back into the house, Solly Solomons winked meaningfully at Annie Sparks.

'That's a real pretty little niece you got there, missus. How long has she been in the family then?'

'Since she was birthed, of course, you fool. How could she be my niece else?' The fat woman scowled.

'Oh I know that, missus.' He grinned teasingly. 'It just seems that you're a family that's been blessed with an uncommon amount of little nieces. Only none of them never seems to stay here with you for very long, do they?'

Annie Sparks made no reply, and the hawker pressed on. 'That last one who was here, the gingery-haired 'un. Where's she gone to?'

Annie Sparks' pudgy fingers suddenly clamped on to his large fleshy nose, squeezed and twisted hard, forcing a cry of pain from the man. 'Ask no questions, and you'll hear no lies,' she hissed. 'And if you don't keep your long conk out of my business, then I've got friends who'll tear it off your face.'

As Rosie came running back from the house, Annie Sparks released her grip.

Solly Solomons, his eyes watering, gingerly fingered his nose. 'I was only taking a friendly interest, missus. There was no need to damage me.'

The fat woman's raucous laughter cackled loud and long. Rosie stared curiously at the couple. 'You take the rest of this stuff inside, my duck. I'll follow you in directly. I just wants a last word with this gentleman.'

When Rosie had left them with her arms piled high, Annie Sparks asked, 'Are you going back to Brummagem tonight?'

Solomons nodded.

'Then you call on the gentleman who sent me this note, and tell him that tomorrow night will be most satisfactory. Have you got that?'

Still fingering his sore nose, he nodded sourly.

'Here.' She rummaged in her gown pocket and produced some coins. Solly Solomons' eyes gleamed.

'You just remember to keep your nose out of my business, and you'll keep on doing well out of me.' She put the money into his cupped palm, and her yellowed teeth showed in a feral snarl. 'But if you ever cross me, you won't have a nose left.'

'Don't you worry, missus. From now on I'm like the three wise monkeys. I can't see, hear or speak,' he fervidly assured her.

Eight

'Hester Person. Died January 23rd, 1844. Safe with God.' Eugenia Pacemore softly repeated the words inscribed on the small plain gravestone, and sighed despondently. 'I hope you're safe and well, Rosie.'

In the weeks since she had parted from Rosie Stannard, not a day had passed without her thinking, with deep concern, about what might be happening to the young girl she had befriended.

'Genia?' a voice called.

She turned and exclaimed in delighted surprise. 'What are you doing here?'

Gathering her skirts with both hands she ran through the rows of graves to meet her cousin, Charles Bronton.

He laughed and embraced her with such fervour that her feet left the ground and her poke bonnet was knocked askew.

'Oh, Charlie, it's been so long since I last saw you. Why didn't you write and tell me that you were coming?' she demanded reproachfully, and he chuckled.

'I wanted to surprise you, Cousin.'

'Well, let me look at you.'

She stood back, her dark eyes filled with

loving tenderness. 'You look wonderful,' she told him. 'Absolutely wonderful.'

He did indeed present a fine figure. Tall, handsome and sun-bronzed, his top hat at a rakish angle on his thick, brown hair, he was a relative to be proud of. They kissed and hugged again, and then it was his turn to break off their embrace.

'Are you perfectly well? You look so pale and tired.'

'Of course I'm perfectly well. I had a restless night, that's all.' She linked her arm with his. 'Come, let's talk, and you shall tell me all about your new regiment.'

'Not before you tell me why you're refusing Colin Bateman's offer. When Uncle wrote to me about it, he seemed to be very angry.' A hint of scolding entered his voice. 'Why must you always go out of your way to provoke him so, Genia?'

'Oh, you know what Pa's like.' She smiled dismissively. 'He must always have something to growl about.'

Her cousin's answering smile was rueful. 'Don't I know it. But don't avoid the subject! Why won't you marry Colin Bateman? I thought that you were very fond of him.'

'I am fond of him,' Eugenia agreed readily. 'He's truly good and kind. But he bores me. His sole interest in life is fox-hunting. I can't marry a man who devotes a lifetime to chasing after foxes.'

'Then what sort of man do you want to marry, Genia? Good men are hard to find, and Bateman, as you admit yourself, is a good man. You're not getting any younger, are you? Do you want to end your days as an old maid?'

She answered with a hint of asperity, 'Please, Charlie, spare me. I endure enough of this nagging from Pa and Ma.'

'I don't mean to nag, Genia. It's only that I'm concerned for your future. I want to see you happily married, and with your own children to love you.'

'And I want to see you married and with children of your own,' she riposted.

He chuckled and accepted defeat. 'I'm not the marrying sort, Cousin, and I shall say no more at present on the subject of marriage.'

'Good!' She hugged his arm. 'Now tell me about your new regiment ... How did they receive you?'

'Well enough. I'm not the first to transfer from the heavy to the light cavalry, you know, Genia. Fellows switch regiments all the time. Most of the mess are good sorts. But a few of them are awful muffs. All they want to do is hunt all day, every day. I confess that there are times when their company bores me to tears.'

The couple strolled slowly away from the graveyard and along the narrow green lanes, totally and happily immersed in each other's company.

As she listened to her cousin relating his stories of army life, Eugenia couldn't help but feel strong pangs of envy. Her own life seemed so dull and restricted and boring in comparison, and although she had no wish to have been born a man, yet she wished with all her heart that she could enjoy the same worldly freedoms that men enjoyed.

When Charles had exhausted his stock of fresh stories, Eugenia told him in full detail about the brutal killing of Hester Pearson and of her concern for the fate of Rosalind Stannard.

'She was such a sweet, intelligent girl, Charlie, and her father appeared to be a complete brute. I hate to think of what might be happening to her. I can't help but feel that I could have done much more to help her.'

'You did everything that you could for her, Genia. You've nothing to blame yourself for,' Charles consoled, and leaned to kiss her cheek. 'You're a kind, good soul, and you make me proud to be your cousin.'

'Will you do me one favour, Charlie?' she asked. 'Will you come with me to Birmingham tomorrow? Rosie told me the address where she used to live. I want to make sure that her father has taken her back there.'

'We'll go first thing tomorrow morning,' he promised.

They turned their footsteps towards home and walked on in companionable silence.

Nine

Birmingham

The small side street of semi-detached houses close to the city centre presented a visual testimony to the respectability of its inhabitants. Polished windows sparkled in the sunlight, doorsteps were scrubbed to whiteness, the minute front gardens were free of rubbish and foul-smelling waste.

Eugenia Pacemore experienced a sense of relief. 'Well, this looks a pleasant enough place, Charlie.'

Her cousin nodded, and stopped a man who had just come out from a nearby doorway. 'Tell me, sir, do you know which house belongs to the Stannard family?'

The man thought briefly, then shook his head. 'I don't know anyone of that name who lives hereabouts, sir.'

'Pearson?' Eugenia intervened. 'Is there a family of that name?'

The man shook his head again. 'Not to my knowledge. But I've only moved here meself a few months since. If you knock on that door,' he pointed to a neighbouring house,

72

and grinned, 'there's a woman lives there who's been here for years. She pokes her nose into everybody's business. She'll most likely be able to tell you something.'

'Many thanks, sir.' Eugenia smiled.

The woman who answered the door stared with avid curiosity at her callers, and when asked if she knew of anyone named Stannard or Pearson, reacted with an immediate, aggressive challenge.

'Why should you ask me that? Who are you, anyway?'

Eugenia introduced herself, and explained that she was anxious to trace a young girl, Rosalind Stannard, and her father, Peter Stannard.

The woman frowned supiciously, and Charles smiled. 'We have come with the best of intentions towards these people, ma'am. And I'm willing to pay well for any help in finding them.'

The woman poked her head forwards and peered quickly in each direction. Then, satisfied no one was watching, jerked her head as a signal for them to step into the house. She closed the door behind them and spoke rapidly.

'There's a lot I can tell you, but you must swear that you'll never tell who you heard it from, because I'm putting meself in mortal danger by telling you anything at all.'

'You've nothing to fear on that score, ma'am,' Charles solemnly promised. 'Our lips shall be sealed.'

'God help that poor little mite if her dad's got hold of her, that's all I can say. Peter Stannard is an evil man, and the woman he's been carrying on with for years is as bad and wicked as he is. It was a happy day for this street when Stannard cleared off, and I pray to God that he never steps foot in these parts again. Good riddance to bad rubbish!' She pursed her lips tightly and shook her head rapidly from side to side, her hands clasped in front of her narrow chest.

Alarm shocked through Eugenia, causing her heartbeat to quicken. 'Please, ma'am, will you tell us all that you know about Peter Stannard?'

The woman coughed, and muttered, 'This gentleman mentioned payment.'

Charles hastily took a gold sovereign from his pocket, and held it in front of the woman's ferret-like eyes.

She stayed silent until he added a second sovereign, and said, 'This is all I intend to pay.'

She snatched the coins from him, bit on them, then slipped them into the top of her bodice.

'Right, sir, you just listen to me then...'

She spoke for some considerable time, and Eugenia listened with escalating horror.

When they left the house, Eugenia walked with her head bent, her brows furrowed with deep anxiety. Charles took her arm and passed it through his own, and she looked up at him with tear-filled eyes.

'Oh, Charlie, what am I going to do?'

He shrugged helplessly. 'I don't believe that there's anything more you *can* do. But try not to worry yourself so. The girl may be perfectly well and happy.'

'But you heard what that woman told us.' She flared with sudden anger. 'Peter Stannard is an evil man, and his mistress is a prostitute. God only knows what they might force Rosie to become. We have to find the child, and save her from them.'

They were now traversing the bustling, teeming streets of the city centre, and Charles grimaced. 'And where do you propose to look for her, Cousin? It will be like looking for a needle in a haystack. That's even supposing that she is still in this city. She could be anywhere in the country by now, or even abroad.'

'We shall go to the police and ask them to help us find her.'

Charles sighed in resignation as he looked at his cousin's determined face. He knew from experience that in her present mood nothing he could say or do would persuade her otherwise.

They made their way to the principal station and headquarters of the First Division of the Birmingham City Police Force in Moseley Street, where their status as gentry quickly gained them access to the office of a genial-mannered, rotund inspector. He listened intently to Eugenia's story, then called a constable into the office and issued instructions. The man returned in scant

75

minutes.

'Sergeant Hall says to tell you that Peter Stannard and the woman, Annie Sparks, are not known to us, sir. We've no records of them.'

The inspector smiled regretfully at his visitors. 'Well, this being the case, I'm afraid that there's nothing more I can do, ma'am, sir.'

'But surely you could put men out to search for them?' Eugenia protested.

'For what reason? Neither of them have been reported to us as having committed any crime.'

'But that poor girl will come to great harm if she is not found!' Eugenia pressed. 'You must institute a search for her.'

The policeman's genial manner hardened. 'There are estimated to be nearly a quarter of a million people in this city, ma'am, and among them the dangerous classes number many thousands. It's all the Force can do to maintain order on our streets. I can't spare men to go searching for some girl who is in the lawful care of her own father.'

'But I'm convinced that he will compel her to prostitute herself, and she's only a child!' Eugenia argued stubbornly. 'Surely that constitutes a crime, doesn't it? To force a child into prostitution?'

The inspector frowned and, shaking his head dismissively, told her, 'All I can suggest, ma'am, is that if and when you discover that this man, Peter Stannard, is forcing his daughter to prostitute herself, then you can inform this office of his whereabouts. I shall then order whatever action I think necessary to be taken on that information. But until that day dawns, then there is nothing I can do against a man who, as far as I know, has broken no law. Now, I've many other urgent matters to attend to, ma'am. So I'll bid you a good day.'

Seething with anger, Eugenia wanted to stand her ground, but Charles took her arm and firmly led her from the room.

On the street she would have rounded on him furiously, but he laid his finger across her lip. 'No! Not one word, Genia! We're going home!'

She pushed his finger from her lips and retorted, 'You go home if you wish. Be selfish and leave me on my own, if that pleases you. But I'm going to stay here and search for Rosie.'

He gazed at her for long moments, then a wry smile appeared on his lips and, shrugging his shoulders, he gave in. 'Very well. I shall stay and help you search for Rosie. Now, where shall we begin? Perhaps the bullring?'

Eugenia realized that she was behaving badly towards her beloved cousin, and with that realization came the cooling of her fiery temper. A wave of reluctant acceptance swept over her.

'I'm being foolish, aren't I? We've more chance of finding a needle in a haystack than we have of finding Rosie. As you said, she could be anywhere in this country, or even abroad.' She sighed in sad resignation. 'Come, my dear, let's go home.'

Ten

It was a Sunday afternoon when Annie Sparks lit the fire beneath the copper boiler in the scullery and then brought a large tin hip bath from the outside shed to place before the kitchen cooking range.

'It'll be nice and warm in here for you to have a bath, my duck,' she told Rosie.

The last hot bath Rosie had enjoyed had been at the Pacemores' house. Since her arrival here, her ablutions had been shiveringly performed at the cold-water pump with a rag flannel and hard yellow soap.

'Why am I to have a hot bath?' she asked.

'Because we've got a fine rich gentleman coming to make a social call, and we don't want him to think that we're dirty scruffs, do we now?' Annie Sparks smiled.

'A fine gentleman? Coming to visit us?' Rosie was intrigued. While she had been here, the only visitor had been Solly Solomons, and her experience of life was sufficient to cause her to wonder why a fine rich gentleman would want to make a social call on poor people like themselves who lived in a house which was, in part, a derelict ruin.

'That's right, and he's a very nice and kind gentleman as well. So I want you to look pretty, and be on your best behaviour when he comes.'

'I'll try to, Auntie,' Rosie promised, feeling stirrings of excitement about this mysterious visitor.

When the hip bath was filled with warm water, Annie Sparks produced a cake of scented soap. 'When you've used this, you'll smell like a rose, my duck.' She cackled with laughter. 'Come on, get undressed.'

Rosie obeyed, her natural shyness about her own nudity making her feel self-conscious. She laid aside her dress, petticoats, long drawers, stockings and shoes and went to step into the bath, but the fat woman stopped her.

'Come and stand here in front of me, my duck. I needs to take a closer look at you.'

Rosie obeyed, modestly shielding her genitals with both hands.

Annie Sparks clucked her tongue impatiently. 'Put your hands by your sides, girl, so I can see you properly.'

Rosie blushed, and reluctantly moved her hands.

'Now turn around, slowly.'

As the girl turned, Annie Sparks smiled with approval.

'You're a real little beauty, my duck,' the fat woman said. 'Into the tub now, and let's get you smelling like roses.'

While Rosie luxuriated in the scented warm

water, Annie Sparks went into the other room, opened one of the iron-bound chests and sorted through the clothing it contained, finally selecting a flimsy white shift.

She came to help Rosie wash her long hair, and then waited while she dried herself in front of the range fire. When the girl went to dress in her discarded clothing, Annie Sparks stopped her. 'Leave them lay, my duck, and put this on.'

Rosie pulled the white shift over her head, and again went to pick up her other clothing.

'I told you to leave them lay, didn't I?'

Rosie looked up in consternation, not understanding why Annie Sparks' normally kindly tone had suddenly become so sharp.

The raucous laughter cackled. 'There's no call to look at me like that, my duck.' It was the kindly, jovial Annie Sparks again. 'Them clothes of yours needs washing, don't they? You'll do well enough in that nice gown I've give you until these are all washed and clean again.'

She grunted with the strain of bending to gather up the small pile of clothing. 'You go and sit by the inglenook now, and dry your hair properly. I'll give it a good brushing after.'

Later, Annie Sparks brushed Rosie's hair for long minutes until it shone like burnished bronze in the firelight, before tying it loosely back with a golden silk ribbon. Cocking her head to one side, she regarded her handiwork, smiling with satisfaction.

'You looks as pretty as a picture, my duck. You shall have a little treat now.' She bustled into the kitchen to return with a large piece of ginger-snap. 'Here, my duck, you get that down you. All we got to do now is wait for our fine rich gentleman to come. He'll soon be here.'

A faint apprehension impelled Rosie to ask, 'But shouldn't I put some more clothes on before he comes, Auntie? This gown is very thin, isn't it? Shouldn't I have my drawers on at least?'

'There's no need.' The pudgy hands waved in airy dismissal. 'That covers you well enough.'

'But...' Rosie tried to argue.

'I said, there's no need!' The fat face scowled and the hard-edged tone re-entered her voice. 'God love me! What's got into you, girl? Why are you trying to upset me so?'

'I'm not!' The accusation filled Rosie with dismay. 'I'm not trying to upset you, Auntie. It's just that...'

Annie Sparks gave her no chance to explain. 'I don't want to hear another word! I'm really hurt that you should be so ungrateful, after all I've done for you. Haven't I looked after you like you was my own daughter? Haven't I been good and kind to you ever since you come here? And this is the thanks I get! This is how you repays me! If I wasn't so hurt, I'd be vexed, I really would!' She pulled a piece of rag from out of her sleeve and began to dab her eyes with it. 'But I'm too hurt to be

81

vexed. I'm hurt in my heart, and that's the truth!'

Rosie was totally confused. She shook her head helplessly. 'I'm sorry, Auntie. What have I done wrong? I didn't mean to hurt you. Honestly I didn't.'

'Come here to me.' The pudgy hands beckoned, and when Rosie obeyed, Annie Sparks held her at arms' length, staring intently into her face. 'Now, are you going to be a good girl, and not hurt me any more?'

'Yes, Auntie.' Rosie nodded solemnly.

Annie Sparks hugged her affectionately. 'That's it then. I forgive you, my duck. We shall say no more about what's happened. It's all forgot!'

Rosie's rush of relief that her friend had forgiven her overlay the fact that she still couldn't comprehend what she had done to necessitate any such forgiveness.

Still cuddling her close, the fat woman spoke urgently. 'You must trust me, my duck. I only want to do what's best for you. I want you to have lots of nice things, and lots of money, and a fine house of your very own. And you'll have all that someday, if you only trust me, and do as I want you to do.'

'I will, Auntie. I will,' Rosie promised.

It was dark and the lamps were lit when the visitor arrived and rapped on the rear door of the house.

'You stand there, my duck, under that lamp,' Annie Sparks directed Rosie, and

bustled to answer the summons. She returned to the room accompanied by a tall man
wearing a top hat, his figure shrouded in a
knee-length caped cloak.

'Here she is, sir,' Annie Sparks announced
with a lilt of pride in her voice. 'Didn't I tell
you that she was a rare little beauty? Come
and greet the gentleman, Rosalind.'

Shy and nervous, Rosie advanced a couple
of steps and bobbed a curtsey. 'How do you
do, sir.'

'I do very well, thank you, Miss Rosalind.'
His voice was low and husky. He leaned forwards and, with the tip of his forefinger,
raised her downcast face to the lamplight,
and exclaimed appreciatively. 'By God, Mrs
Sparks, for the first time during our acquaintance, I'm forced to admit that you've not
over-gilded the lily.'

'Will you sit down and take a little refreshment, sir?' Annie Sparks invited.

He nodded and, unhooking his cloak,
passed it together with his top hat into Annie
Sparks' hands, revealing the dark frock coat
he wore beneath.

Rosie peeped shyly at his plump pleasant
face, longish black hair and side whiskers,
and he smiled at her in a friendly manner.

'Will you do me the honour of taking some
refreshment in my company, Miss Rosalind?'

'Yes, if it pleases you, sir.' She bobbed
another curtsey.

'It will please me greatly.' He chuckled and,
seating himself in front of the inglenook fire,

gestured with a be-ringed hand to a chair facing his own. 'Sit there so that I can see you without having to turn my head all the time.' He made a mock grimace and held his hand to his high white collar and cravat. 'Modern fashion impels me to half strangle myself with these hangman's nooses around my neck.'

The man sat with folded arms, staring at the girl, the tip of his tongue protruding between his fleshy lips, his eyes moist with lust.

Rosie was aware that the strange gentleman was staring fixedly at her, but having been taught from infancy that it was impolite to stare back, and not to speak unless first spoken to, she resisted the urge to fidget and remained as motionless as she could.

Annie Sparks reappeared, carrying a bottle of wine and three glasses. Her puffball eyes shrewdly assessed her visitor's expression as he continued to keep his attention focussed solely on Rosie. 'The bastard's already hooked! If I play this right I'll make a bloody fortune out of him,' she thought.

She instantly decided to alter her planned agenda and, leaving the bottle and glasses on the table, went back into the kitchen. From a concealed recess she extracted a small phial containing laudanum and, secreting it in her hand, returned to the main room.

'Here you are, sir, it's the very finest madeira.' Annie Sparks handed the man a glass of wine, and then said to Rosie, 'And as a special treat, you shall have a glass of wine as well, my duck. Come now, you must be a good girl and drink it all up.'

Rosie enjoyed the rich, sweet taste of the madeira and needed no second urging. Annie Sparks sipped from her own glass, and waited patiently for the soporific drug to take its effect.

Rosie began to feel waves of sleepiness threatening to engulf her, and desperately tried to fight them back. Worried that if she surrendered to this overpowering urge to sleep, Annie Sparks would be angry at her for being so ill-mannered as to fall asleep in front of their visitor. But fight it though she might, the drug exercised its irresistible effect, and soon she lost all consciousness and fell slowly back into the capacious chair.

The man rose and moved to bend low over the girl, satisfying himself that she was completely unconscious.

'I'll use the bed there. You can wait in the kitchen until I'm finished,' he said. He lifted Rosie's limp body in his arms and carried her to the four-poster bed. He laid the child on the top of the coverlet and started to take off his coat.

'You can keep your coat on, sir.' Annie Sparks intervened her fat body between man and bed. 'You're not having this kid tonight.'

He gaped at her in disbelief for an instant. 'What's got into you, woman?'

'We haven't talked prices yet, have we, sir? Just you look close at her.' She smiled pleasantly, and deftly stripped the flimsy shift from

Rosie and arranged her on her back in a blatantly sexual position. 'This is prime goods, sir. The prettiest little thing I've ever come across. And virgin in every way. Never even been fingered by a man. I guarantee you that.'

'Oh, I see. You want to up the usual price. Very well. If I'm satisfied after I've had her that she is indeed a virgin, then I'll give you a little extra.'

Annie Sparks slowly shook her head. 'No, sir. You won't be giving me a little bit extra. You'll be paying me a whole lot extra, and paying before you so much as lays a hand on her.'

His fleshy lips pouted petulantly. 'And how much extra are we talking about?'

'Two hundred sovs, at the least.'

'What?' he ejaculated incredulously. 'Two hundred? I could have a hundred little whores for that!'

'Of course you could, sir,' Annie Sparks agreed readily. 'In fact, for two hundred sovs you could probably have their mothers as well. But Rosie here aren't no little whore. She's an innocent child, sir. A pure virgin. Just look close at her, and then try and tell me if she's not. There's no bag of blood pushed up inside her.'

He did look, and his lust rampaged, and Annie Sparks began whispering sibilantly in his ear.

'You're not the only gentleman that I do business with, sir. In fact there's several other gentlemen who've arranged to come and see her in the next few days. She'll be going to the highest bidder, sir. My offer to you of two hundred sovs was made because you've always been a good customer of mine. But I'm certain sure that I can get more for her than that. But I'd have preferred you to have her because, like I said, you've always been such a good customer, and I knows that you won't be over-rough with her. She's very tender-fleshed, you see, sir. She could be easy torn if a man was over-rough with her. But I know how you likes to take it slow and gentle-like with a young 'un.'

He was breathing heavily, his plump face sheened with sweat. 'How long would I get with her?'

'Why, you can have the whole night. Have her as many times as you like. If she starts to wake up, I'll dose her for you again.'

He nodded jerkily. 'Alright. I'll pay what you ask.'

'When? When do I get the money?' Annie Sparks pressed.

'Goddam it, woman! I don't carry such an amount on me.' He rounded on her irritably. 'You know me well enough to trust me to pay you, don't you? Have I ever broken my word to you before?'

She shrugged her shoulders. 'No, you haven't. But I want your written and signed agreement to pay me two hundred sovs. If you can't give me that, then you'd best leave now, sir.'

'Wait a moment.' He was struggling to make a decision. Then his eyes moved to the sleeping girl once more, and he drew a long hiss of breath. 'Very well. Bring me pen and paper.'

She hastened to comply, and he sat at the table and wrote out a promissory note, which he dated and signed. 'You may present this at my office whenever you please, and my clerk will pay you the full amount.'

She inclined her head in gracious agreement. 'That's satisfactory to me, sir. I'll leave you now. I shall be in the kitchen if you need me for anything at all. I'll say goodnight to you, sir.'

Even before she reached the door he had shucked off his frock coat and was tearing at his cravat.

Eleven

'There now, my duck, what a nice long sleep you've had.'

Rosie blinked her eyes and slowly the fuzzy outline of Annie Sparks' smiling face became clear.

Rosie's head was pounding, her stomach nauseous, her mouth dry. She pushed herself upright and hissed aloud as the movement caused a sharp pain to lance through her genitals.

'It's nearly noontime, and you've missed your breakfast. Never mind, here's a nice drink of milk for you, my duck.' Annie Sparks pressed the rim of the mug against Rosie's lips, tilting it so that she was forced to gulp the liquid. 'Don't worry if you're a bit sore, down you-know-where. It'll soon pass.'

'What's happened to me?' Rosie lifted the bottom of her flimsy shift and was frightened when she saw the bloodstains on the soft inner flesh of her thighs. 'Why am I hurting so, and why is there blood on me like this?'

'It's nothing to worry about,' Annie Sparks was quick to reassure her. 'You've become a woman, that's all. Don't fret yourself, my duck.'

'What's happened to me, Auntie?' she pleaded pitifully. 'Has something bad happened to me?'

'Of course not, you silly girl!' Annie Sparks snapped impatiently. 'Now, stop asking me such daft questions and go to the pump and wash that blood off you.'

In pain, distressed and confused, Rosie did as she was told.

Annie Sparks stood in the doorway watching while the girl washed and dried her body. 'You'll grow to like it in time, my duck. Every girl grows to like it.'

'To like what, Auntie?'

'To like the feel of a man inside you.' Annie Sparks cackled. 'There's times it feels so good

89

it's like you're in heaven. And you're a very lucky girl, because the gentleman was nice and gentle with you. I've made sure of that. You're hardly ripped at all.'

The words impacted like physical blows on Rosie. She felt nauseous and faint, and her hands grabbed and held the stone sink as her senses reeled.

Annie Sparks observed Rosie closely. 'Come on, my duck.' She loosened Rosie's tight-clenched hands from their grip on the sink. 'You come and sit by the fire.'

Rosie felt dazed and strangely disembodied. She allowed herself to be led over to the inglenook fire, and she sat hunched on the edge of the chair, staring fixedly into the leaping flames.

Annie Sparks sat on the arm of the chair and stroked Rosie's head, speaking to her in a tone of warm sympathy. 'It's all come as a bit of a shock to you, hasn't it, my duck? I knows that, and I'm truly sorry for it. But believe me, you'll soon be feeling yourself again. That nice kind gentleman left me some money to give you, and you shall have every penny of it spent on nice things for your very own self. I'm going to take you with me to Birmingham soon and buy you lots of nice things. You shall have a new dress and a pretty bonnet and lots of silk ribbons, and even some silk slippers if you wants them. You're a very lucky girl.'

A sharp image of the man's face came into Rosie's mind, and fear shuddered through her. 'Is he coming back to hurt me again?' she asked anxiously.

'I don't know if he'll come back.' Annie Sparks shrugged. 'But there'll be other kind gentlemen will come to visit you, and to give you lots of money to buy things with.'

'Oh no!' Rosie moaned in distress. 'Why are you going to let them hurt me? Why?'

'Now stop being such a crybabby! They won't hurt you, because I shan't let them. And I've already told you that every girl grows to like having men to do such things to her. And how else are you going to earn money to live on? Money don't grow on bloody trees, girl! You have to earn it.'

'I could work!' Rosie protested desperately. 'Other girls smaller than me go to work to earn money, don't they?'

'I've heard enough of this nonsense,' Annie Sparks warned. 'You'll do as I tell you, and be nice to the kind gentlemen. And that's that.'

Young though she was, Rosie possessed a courageous spirit, and now rebellion fired in her. 'I won't do as you say! You're not my mother, and you can't tell me what to do. And I'll tell my dad about what's happened when he comes back.'

The woman's fat face purpled with rage and, grabbing Rosie's long hair with both hands, she dragged the girl from the chair and forced her to the floor. 'You'll tell your dad, will you, you little bitch? Well, it's him as brought you here to do whatever I tell you to do. I've tried to be kind to you, but you're nothing but an ungrateful little bleeder. So now I'll show you the other side of the coin.'

Grunting with effort, she dragged Rosie screaming and struggling across the floor and into the kitchen, lifted a big trapdoor set in the stone-flagged floor, and kicked Rosie into the black hole beneath. She slammed the trapdoor down and slotted its bolt into position, then stood with hands on hips, panting heavily. 'You can stay down there until you've learned your manners. You can stay there until your dad gets back, and then you'll see what's what!' She swung on her heels and went back into the other room.

Rosie lay on her back in chill, damp blackness, racked by bodily pain and mental anguish. Images of her mother and grandmother filled her mind, and bitter sobs tore from her throat. Never in her life had she experienced such absolute loneliness and despair, such total emotional desolation.

Twelve

It was many hours since Rosie had been kicked into her prison and she had lost track of time. The hole was too cramped for her to either stand upright or stretch fully out upon the floor. She sat shivering, hugging her knees close to her chest in a fruitless effort to find warmth. Deep in the recesses of her being, the atavistic instinct for self-survival was stirring. This instinct, coupled with her own courageous spirit and intelligence, was slowly fuelling Rosie's determination to fight back against her captor and escape from her predicament.

She was cold, thirsty and hungry, but despite these discomforts, sheer bodily weariness periodically overcame her and she fell into brief snatches of uneasy sleep. She awoke from one such brief sleep with the urgent need to relieve herself. Naturally fastidious though she was, she was forced to comply with the dictates of her body, crouching in the corner of the hole. She felt ashamed and degraded, and gave way to tears.

More than forty-eight hours had passed when the trapdoor was lifted and Annie Sparks loomed, colossus-like above the hole.

'Come on out of there,' she ordered.

Her cramped muscles stiff and painful, her eyes blinking against the daylight, Rosie slowly clambered out and stood stiffly upright before the fat woman.

'Are you going to be a good girl now?' Annie Sparks frowned sternly.

For a split second, Rosie's urge was to shout her defiance, but instinct kept her silent and, after a moment or two, she nodded her head, keeping her gaze directed at the floor.

'Are you going to do what I tells you to?'

Once more Rosie nodded in submissive acquiescence.

Annie Sparks' yellowed teeth bared in a

triumphant snarl. 'Now you're being a clever girl, my duck. And clever girls gets rewarded. Are you hungry?'

Rosie nodded.

'Then you shall have something nice to eat. But first we'll get you all cleaned up, because you stinks.'

Rosie needed no urging to strip off the shift and cleanse herself at the pump. Afterwards, dressed in fresh clothing and feeling ravenously hungry, she made short work of the platter of bacon and eggs that Annie Sparks cooked for her.

Annie Sparks watched the girl eating. 'She's got a lot of the gutter devil in her. I think it might be better if I sell her on, sooner than have the trouble of keeping her here.'

Later that night, lying warm and comfortable in the four-poster bed next to Annie Sparks' snoring bulk, Rosie realized for herself that she did indeed possess a plentiful quantity of what Annie Sparks called 'gutter devil', the rebellious spirit that could impel the physically weak to strike back against much stronger tormentors, even though that striking back would inevitably bring down harsh punishment upon them.

'I'll escape from all this,' Rosie promised herself. 'I'll escape some day. Just see if I don't!'

Thirteen

It was almost two weeks after Rosie's ordeal in the hole that Solly Solomons came to the house in the dark hour before dawn.

Annie Sparks and Rosie were already up and dressed. The fat woman was in a jovial mood and invited the hawker to take a glass of gin. He accepted with alacrity, and while he noisily slurped the spirit into his loose-lipped mouth, his dark eyes flickered back and forth between the two females.

Annie Sparks was not powdered or rouged today, and her black clothing resembled a widow's weeds, while Rosie was dressed neatly in shabby but clean and well-pressed dress and jacket. The wings of her bonnet framed her pretty face and shining hair.

Solomons winked slyly at the woman. 'What's it to be today then, Mrs S.? The poor forlorn widow woman?'

She cackled with raucous laughter. 'Never you mind, you nosy bleeder! I'm paying you to take me there and back, and that's all you needs to know.'

'Where am I taking you exactly?'

'You'll find out when we gets there.'

He grinned knowingly, and nodded his

95

head towards the girl. 'I'll bet it's another customer for you-knows-who.'

'Shut your mouth!' Annie Sparks snapped and, knowing that he was risking an eruption of her violent temper, Solly Solomons contented himself with another sly wink and said no more.

Rosie was sitting with her head demurely downcast, her hands clasped upon her lap, taking no apparent interest in what the adults were saying, but secretly listening intently.

Since her spell in the hole she had behaved with a docile submissiveness, and her relationship with Annie Sparks had been amicable. So long as she did what Annie Sparks instructed her to do, then the fat woman treated her with kindness. With a maturity beyond her years, Rosie realized that to simply run away from the woman could merely worsen her predicament. In this perilous world a child tramping the roads alone, particularly a girl, faced innumerable dangers.

Realizing that no further glasses of gin were to be forthcoming, Solly Solomons sighed regretfully. 'Shall we get going, then?'

The cart was empty, and the three of them clambered under its hooped tarpaulin roof and settled themselves for the journey.

'I take it we're going to Brum?' Solomons asked, and when Annie Sparks nodded, he cracked the long whip over the horse's rump and the cart lurched into motion.

'When we gets there go straight through

into the Bull Ring,' Annie Sparks added.

Surrounding the open space of the Bull Ring marketplace, the narrow streets were smoke-palled, stench-filled, and thick with filth. Waggons and carts struggled to make progress through the swarming crowds, and from the innumerable factories and workshops came the hammering dins of industry.

Annie Sparks halted the cart outside one factory premises in a street close to the Bull Ring, and disappeared through the office door, only to reappear shortly afterwards with a broad smile on her face.

Solly Solomons winked slyly at Rosie and whispered hoarsely, 'I see the cat's swallowed the cream again, kiddo.'

'I heard that, Solomons.' Annie Sparks scowled at him threateningly.

But he only chuckled. 'Where to now then, Your Majesty?'

'Go up New Street first. I want to buy some fine clothes for Rosie.' She smiled warmly at the girl. 'You see, my duck, I keep my promises, don't I? Because you've been a good girl, you shall have all the nice things I promised I would buy for you.'

Rosie experienced a rush of excited anticipation. Like the vast majority of young girls, she enjoyed being bedecked in fine dresses.

The next two hours were spent in a variety of shops, and ended with Rosie dressed in brand new dress, bonnet and bootees. She couldn't help but peep delightedly at her image in every reflective surface that she passed.

The shopping completed, Annie Sparks took Rosie into a genteel eating establishment where they feasted on cream cakes and drank sweet madeira wine. Ever since they had left the house, Annie Sparks had been treating Rosie so lovingly that she now found herself wondering if in fact she had not misjudged the fat woman. Perhaps she really was a good, kind-hearted creature after all, and it was only poverty that had forced her to let that gentleman do what he had done.

When they emerged back out on to the busy street to find that Solly Solomons had disappeared from view, Rosie asked where he'd gone.

'He's doing a little errand for me, my duck. Now I want to take you to meet a very nice lady I know.'

She hailed a cab, and they left the bustling city centre and entered a quiet leafy suburb where large opulent houses stood in extensive grounds surrounded by tall hedges and walls.

Dismissing the cab, Annie Sparks led Rosie to the ornate ironwork gate of the nearest house, and tugged on the bell.

Rosie stared curiously at the shiny brass plaque fixed high on the brick pillar and read its scrolled lettering aloud. 'Redemption Orphan Asylum.'

Beneath this in smaller letters was another inscription: 'Suffer the little children to come unto me, and they shall be saved.'

A dour-featured woman wearing a black gown and mob cap, with a big bunch of keys hanging from her waist-belt, appeared from around the side of the house and came to the gate.

'Will you tell your mistress that Mrs Sparks wishes to see her,' Annie Sparks asked.

The woman unlocked the gate and stood aside for them to enter, then locked the gate again before leading them into the house. The spacious hallway smelled of fresh beeswax polish and was richly decorated.

'Mrs Sparks, what an unexpected pleasure.' An elegantly coiffed and gowned woman came from a side door to greet them, and dismissed the maid. 'You may leave us, Bridget. Do come in and take some refreshment with me, my dear Mrs Sparks.' The lady led them into the opulently furnished room.

'Thank you, Mrs Wentworth, ma'am, but we've just had something to eat and drink,' Annie Sparks said politely.

'Let's all sit down and be comfortable, shall we.' The woman gestured towards ornately brocaded chairs and, when they were seated, turned her attention for the first time towards Rosie.

'So, I take it that this is the Rosalind Stannard you mentioned in your note, Mrs Sparks.' Her eyes met Rosie's, and she smiled. 'She truly is as pretty as a picture.'

'She is indeed, ma'am.'

'Stand up, my dear, and come here to me.' The woman gestured with her long, ring-laden fingers. Rosie obeyed. 'Come a little closer, my dear. Open your mouth. Wider, my dear, open it wider.'

The woman leaned forward and peered closely into Rosie's mouth. 'Excellent. She has very good teeth.'

She turned to Annie Sparks. 'That is so important, Mrs Sparks, as you well know. There is nothing more off-putting to a fastidious client than a mouthful of rotting teeth.'

'You are quite right, ma'am,' Annie Sparks agreed solemnly.

The woman turned back to Rosie. 'Now my dear, I want you to undress.'

'What?' Rosie was shocked.

The woman laughed. 'Bless the girl! There's no need for you to be embarrassed, my dear. You are among well-wishers here. Now, please take off your clothes.'

'But I don't want to,' Rosie protested.

'Do as the lady says, and don't be so silly!' Annie Sparks' voice was harsh. 'You know what will happen if you don't behave and do as you're told. Now take them off, or I'll do it for you.'

Blushing self-consciously, Rosie slowly removed her clothing and stood naked.

The woman smiled encouragingly. 'Now, let me see you walk, my dear. Come now, walk to the door and back.'

Rosie did as she was bid, and had walked the several paces to the door and back many times before the woman said, 'Thank you, my dear. Now you may get dressed.'

'Well, ma'am. What's your opinion?' Annie Sparks enquired eagerly.

The woman nodded. 'I'm prepared to take this young lady under my wing, for our customary terms.'

Annie Sparks frowned slightly. 'No, that won't do, ma'am. I'm looking for better terms for this one. She's an exceptional fine and fresh piece of goods. She's not a slum rat. She's been raised respectable.'

The woman's attitude hardened instantly. 'I can see that she's no slum rat, Mrs Sparks. But don't try taking me for a fool, by claiming that she's still a virgin. I know you too well to believe that.'

Annie Sparks didn't react indignantly, but only chuckled. 'We both know each other too well for me to try and gammon you, ma'am. Of course she's not a virgin. I had an offer that was too good to resist. But I swear on my dear mother's grave that she's been used by only one gentleman, and for one night only. And I'd dosed her well, so there was little damage done. You won't have to start shoving pigeon's blood up her for a while yet.'

Rosie was listening to this exchange with escalating fear and dread. Although she could not entirely comprehend the full connotations of what the women were talking about, she sensed all too clearly that it boded badly for herself.

The elegant Mrs Wentworth frowned. 'There is no need for such coarseness of expression, Mrs Sparks.'

Annie Sparks grinned confidently. 'So then, ma'am, we're agreed on different terms for this one?'

Mrs Wentworth smiled and nodded in acceptance, then lifted a small silver handbell from the floor at the side of her chair and rang it forcefully. Within a few seconds the dour-featured woman entered.

'Go and tell Mister Julian to come to me,' Mrs Wentworth ordered, then frowned at Rosie. 'Listen very carefully to what I'm going to tell you, girl. If you don't behave yourself, then I shall deal with you very severely. If, on the other hand, you are obedient and dutiful, then you will lead a comfortable life here in my establishment, and, what is more, when the time comes for you to leave here, you will be very well rewarded.'

'Did you send for me, madam?' A lisping, high-pitched voice sounded and Rosie's eyes widened in shock as she saw the gigantic figure of a frock-coated black man, his shaven scalp almost touching the door lintel, his massive bulk filling the doorway.

'Yes, Julian. This young lady's name is Rosalind. She is joining our establishment. Introduce her to my other young ladies and gentlemen, if you please.'

'Certainly, madam. It shall be my pleasure.' He moved towards Rosie with an effeminately mincing gait, holding out his huge be-ringed hands towards her. 'Come along, my dear. Come with Julian, there's a good girl.

I'm not going to harm you.'

Rosie gulped fearfully as he loomed above her, but when he took hold of her shoulders his grip was gentle and his white teeth flashed in a friendly smile. 'You've no need to be afraid of me, Rosalind.' He bent down to bring his face close to hers. 'Just so long as you do what my madam and myself tells you to do.'

She blinked unbelievingly at his rouged cheeks and scarlet-painted lips, and her nostrils were filled with the heady sweetness of his perfume.

Julian took Rosie down a flight of steps and along a dark passageway. She caught her breath apprehensively, and sensing her fear, Julian hastened to reassure her.

'You don't have nothing to be afraid of, Rosalind. Nothing's going to harm you. That's what my job is, you know. To look after you and the other kids and take care that nothing harms any of you.'

He unlocked the iron-barred door at the end of the passage and ushered her into the large room that lay beyond.

Rosie had only time enough to glimpse two rows of neatly made single beds lining, the white-limed walls before she was suddenly surrounded by a clamorous questioning group of children.

'Where you from?'

'What's your name?'

'Got any money?'

'Get away from her!' Julian shouted. 'Now,

shut your noise and get stood by your beds!'

One girl was slow to obey and, moving with a speed that belied his outsized body, Julian sprang at her and knocked her to the floor with a back-handed cuff across the side of her head. She scrambled away on hands and knees and levered herself to a standing position by one of the beds.

Rosie could only gaze about her in bewilderment. There were three girls, one of whom was dark-skinned, and a boy, all dressed alike in knee-length brown smocks, their legs and feet bare. The room's furnishings consisted of six single beds, three on each side, and in the centre space between the rows was a plain deal table and backless wooden benches. The sole window was high on the far wall and covered with a heavy iron grille, while two oil lamps hung from the rafters overhead.

Noting Rosie's expression, Julian chuckled. 'It's a very plain and simple room, isn't it, Rosalind, but that makes it so much easier to keep it clean. My madam is a stickler for cleanliness. That will be your bed at the end there. The sheets have been freshly changed, so there aren't any bugs waiting to feast on your exquisite flesh. Now take those clothes off and put on the smock that is on top of your pillow there.' When she hesitated, his smile instantly metamorphosed into a snarling grimace.

'You'd best do what he says, matey,' one

girl whispered. 'Or he'll have your guts for garters.'

Rosie moved to the side of her allotted bed and began to undress. To her own surprise she found that this time she felt less embarrassment about her nudity. She was becoming inured to having her intimate body revealed before others.

The huge negro was jovial and kindly spoken again when she pulled the brown smock over her nakedness and handed him her fine new clothes.

'Now, don't fret yourself about these clothes of yours, Rosalind. They shall all be kept in safe storage for you.'

He went from the room, locking the door behind him. Her new companions instantly clustered around Rosie, hurling eager questions at her.

There was no hostility or suspicion in the interrogation, merely a friendly curiosity, and Rosie warmed to them immediately. When she spoke of Annie Sparks, one of the children – a diminutive, freckle-faced, red-haired girl – spat out venomously.

'That old cow! It was her who put me on the game. She give me a hard time of it as well. It was her who held me down while her old bastard of a dad had his way with me! It didn't half hurt as well.'

When Rosie told them how she had been drugged and violated, another girl, slightly older and taller with blonde hair and impish, snub-nosed features, said, 'That's what happened to me the first few times I was sold. Me mam told me that some of the Bloods likes it better when you'm lying there like a stiff 'un. And she reckoned it was the best way for me to be broke in for the game. She said she was doing me a kindness.'

The next few hours proved to be a horrific revelation to Rosie as, one after another, the girls related their own individual stories of abuse, something that they appeared to accept as their natural lot in life.

'But why haven't you run away from here? It must be horrible having to let men do all those dirty things to you. How can you bear it? Don't you hate that woman upstairs, and that black man for keeping you locked up like this, and making you do all those things?'

To her amazement, they answered with a vociferous defence of their captors.

'It's alright here.'

'It's a sight better than where I was before.'

'The madam and Julian aren't so bad at all.'

'We eats and drinks like lords and ladies. And we lives warm and comfortable.' Bridie, the blonde-haired girl, grinned impishly. 'And we don't get knocked about, so long as we does what we're told. And they don't let the Bloods serve us bad, neither. One bloke started to try and choke me one night, and Julian near on killed the bastard. It warn't like that when I was flogging meself on the streets, I'll tell you. I used to get nigh on murdered sometimes by the Bloods who picked me up then.'

'And the madam gives us smokes and pongo regular, and she's saving most of our earnings for us to have when we gets too old to stay and work here,' the gentle-featured, softly spoken youth chimed in. 'The rotten bastard who pimped me before took every penny I earned, and beat me up regular as well.'

Rosie stared at him in silent puzzlement, and Tembi, the half-caste girl, laughed. 'Look at her stare! She don't know what you does, Angel.'

Then she explained. 'There's some blokes that likes boys, Rosie. We calls them sort the Turks. They're the ones that Angel services. Only he's getting too old for his Bloods now. They likes littler kids.'

Rosie gasped with horror, her stomach churning and nauseous fear invading her.

'Stop trying to frighten her, Tembi!' Bridie reproved sharply, and patted Rosie's shoulder soothingly. 'You needn't worry about it, kid. The madam don't force any of us girls to get Turked if we don't want to be. And anyway, she'll be selling you as a virgin for ages yet.' She paused and grinned salaciously.

'If they're so good, why are we all locked in here?' Rosie argued.

'It's to stop us going out on the razzle and catching the clap.' Seeing Rosie's utter lack of comprehension, they hastened to explain to her what the clap was.

'What do they do to you if they find out that you've got a disease like that?'

Theresa, the red-haired girl, mimed the making of a hangman's noose and, dropping her head to one side, opened her eyes wide and made choking noises.

Rosie burst into tears of fear and anguish.

The youth, Angel, came to cuddle and try to soothe her. 'Take no notice of Theresa. She's just a stupid cow! It's alright in here, Rosie. You'll soon get used to everything. It's alright when you get used to it. You should see some of the places where I was before, and the bad way I got treated. This is good in here.' She clung to him in desperate need of comfort.

On the other side of the door, Julian had been bending down with his ear pressed to the keyhole, listening intently to all that was said within the room. He decided he had heard enough and returned to Mrs Wentworth.

Annie Sparks had gone and Mrs Wentworth was smoking a small cigar, breathing the smoke deep into her lungs and then allowing it to dribble slowly from her lips. She smiled at the big negro.

'Well, Julian? What do you think?'

'She's crying her eyes out at the minute, madam. I think we'll have to allow her a bit of extra time to settle in. She's not a slum rat, is she?'

'Yes, I agree.' Mrs Wentworth drew deeply of the fragrant smoke and allowed it to dribble from her lips. 'What do you think might be the best way to introduce her to our

Bloods, when she's ready for it?'

'I think we should stage a pose plastique, the "Sleeping Beauty" one, madam, and use her as the centrepiece. Then auction her. She'll fetch a very high price for being such a pretty little virgin.'

'There might be a small problem with that.' Mrs Wentworth frowned. 'She's already lost her cherry. Sparks claims it was just the one Blood, for a single night only, but that woman is such a liar I can't be sure of it. The girl could have been had by a dozen for all I know. I don't want any of my regular Bloods ranting and raving that he's been palmed off with second-hand goods.'

Julian's large white teeth shone as he chuckled. 'Have I ever failed to produce a cherry for you, madam? Just leave everything to me.'

Fourteen

For several weeks following her arrival at the big house, Rosie was progressively initiated into the bizarre way of life of her new community. She found that her companions had told the truth about living in warmth and comfort. The food was good and plentiful. The children's basement living quarters were warm, dry and well furnished. Adjoining the dormitory were a kitchen and pantry, a wash house and a large furnished living room. At the rear was a narrow sunken yard completely enclosed by a high brick wall topped with vicious iron spikes. Every window was also barred by iron-spiked grilles.

The basement complex had only two entrances: the passage door and the door set into the yard wall. Both were kept locked at all times. It was, in effect, a self-contained secure prison, and Rosie was told repeatedly that any attempt to escape from its confines would bring a terrible reckoning down upon her head.

Yet she did not find this confinement unduly oppressive. In fact she found that she quite enjoyed this new experience of living within a familial group of children. There was no sense of solitary loneliness here. Fleeting troubles and joys could be shared. There were toys and board games and packs of cards with which they could amuse themselves, and almost daily Julian brought in clay pipes, tobacco and bottles of gin for them to share.

Initially, Rosie was shocked to see the children smoking and drinking like seasoned topers. But when they pressed Rosie to join them in their revelry, she readily did so. The first tentative sip of the raw spirit caused her to cough and splutter, and her eyes to water. But the second sip went down easier, and the third and fourth sips induced a warm glow and a burgeoning sensation of dizzy exhilaration. She puffed on a proffered clay pipe, and again was racked by a fit of coughing as the rank-smelling tobacco smoke assaulted her throat. But, like the gin, each succeeding puff had a less traumatic effect. Within an hour she was reeling drunk, laughing hysterically, crazed with excitement.

Most evenings, after supper, Julian took one or more of the children out with him, and they would not return until the following morning.

Driven by avid curiosity, Rosie would ask them what had happened to them during the night, and listened with bated breath to their stories.

She learned that Mrs Wentworth used another house near to the centre of the city as the actual brothel. Rosie listened wide-eyed as her new friends laughingly described in graphic detail some of the grotesque antics that the customers indulged in.

'There's some of them who don't even touch us,' Bridie told her. 'We just has to dance about naked in front of them, while they play with themselves.'

'And if you're sharp with it, you can get some of them so worked up that it's over before they get near you.' Theresa giggled.

As day followed day and night followed night, her companions' complete lack of modesty or inhibitions, their acceptance of how they lived as a perfectly fortunate and pleasurable existence, quickly began to exert an insidious effect upon Rosie. What previously would have shocked and distressed her

111

now ceased to do so. As time passed she found herself listening enviously to the accounts of her companions' adventures of the night, when they boasted of the fine wines and sweetmeats they had shared with their Bloods, or showed her some flashy trinket that a Blood had given them. She laughed with them when they related how they had coaxed a Blood to profess to be romantically in love with them.

'You can't credit what stupid old sods some of the Bloods am. You can tell 'um anything, and they'll swallow it,' Theresa crowed delightedly.

It was Angel who awakened Rosie's own sexuality. After one session of drinking and smoking, when the others were asleep, he came to her bedside in the darkness of the night and began to kiss her on the lips, and gently caress her body. She found herself enjoying it, and lay passively while his fingers explored her, stroking, fondling, causing her to gasp at the thrills of pleasure that shuddered through her. He took her hand and guided it on to his erect member, and she in turn squeezed and stroked its firm length.

After that first encounter, Angel would come to her bed whenever there was opportunity, and they would lie together for hours, kissing, cuddling, fondling each other. Then, one night Angel moved on top of her and, pressing her thighs apart, entered her. She experienced a slight pain, which was quickly overtaken by sensations of acute pleasure, and she clutched his frail body close as he thrust rapidly into her for a few brief moments before groaning and collapsing upon her, panting for breath.

A full ten weeks had passed since Rosie's arrival at the house, and one morning Julian called her to him and took her upstairs to the drawing room.

Rosie had not set eyes on Mrs Wentworth since the day she had entered the house, and now she felt a trace of shyness as she stood before the seated, elegantly dressed woman.

'How are you, Rosalind?' Mrs Wentworth smiled kindly.

'I'm very well, thank you, ma'am.' Rosie bobbed a polite curtsey.

'And are you happy living here with the other children?'

'Yes, ma'am.'

'Good! It's very pleasing to me that you are happy living here with our little family group. Because that is what we are, you know: a family, and I would hope that you now consider yourself to be a part of it. One of us. A member of our family.' She paused.

Uncertain as to what reaction was expected of her, Rosie could only bob another curtsey and reply, 'Yes, ma'am. Thank you, ma'am.'

Mrs Wentworth nodded her elaborately coiffed head in gracious acknowledgement.

'Well now, Rosalind, as a family member it is your duty to help maintain the family. So tonight you shall commence work. Do it well, and you shall be rewarded for it.' She waved

113

her hand in languid dismissal and Julian took Rosie by the shoulder and led her out of the room and back downstairs to the dormitory.

'Gather round, kids,' he ordered, and when they had clustered about him, he said, 'We'll be doing the "Sleeping Beauty" pose plastique tonight. And Rosie will be the beauty.'

'That aren't fair!' Tembi protested petulantly. 'It should be my turn to do the beauty.'

Julian sighed. 'How many times do I have to tell you, Tembi, that you're not suitable for that role.'

'Why not? I'm as pretty as the others,' she argued.

'You can't do it because everybody knows that the beauty is white,' Theresa chimed in. 'Besides, she's a princess, aren't she? And you'm only a bloody slave.'

The next instant she shouted in pain as Julian's great hand clamped around her upper arm, and his fingers tightened and crushed into her flesh. His white teeth glinted in a feral snarl as he hissed savagely, 'One more word from you, and I'll break your neck, you bog-Irish sow!'

She howled in agony, and he hurled her across the room to crash down and lie in a crumpled, sobbing heap on the floor.

Rosie felt a rush of fear when the huge man turned to her, but he only smiled. 'Don't worry about tonight, Rosie. I shall be there to look after you.'

Then he told the others, 'I'll be taking Bridie and Tembi with me as well. You and

114

Theresa have got the night off, Angel. See you all later.'

Now that she knew she was finally to be introduced to the Bloods, Rosie began to feel increasingly nervous. Later, when the room had quietened once more, she asked Bridie, 'What will I have to do tonight?'

'Just go to sleep, o' course.' The snub-nosed girl chortled. 'It aren't nothing to bother about, matey. I've been the beauty at least a dozen times. The madam gets a few of her rich Bloods together in the big room at the other house and we does a few poses in front of 'um, to get 'um all hot like. You'll be laying out on the cushions, and me and Tembi 'ull be doing the hard work, dancing around with nothing on, looking like a pair o' prats because neither of us can dance proper. Then, when the Bloods are all excited, the madam 'ull sell you to the highest bidder as a virgin. It's what they calls a cherry auction. But you won't know anything about what's going on, because you'll have had a dose o' laudanum, and you'll be sound asleep. That's why it's called the "Sleeping Beauty".'

'Why can't I just pretend to be asleep?' Rosie asked curiously.

The other girl shrugged her narrow shoulders. 'Who knows, matey! That's just the way it is. We takes the dose, and sleeps proper.'

'But I'm not a virgin now. How can the madam sell me as such?'

Now Bridie gurgled with laughter. 'Bloody hell! You'm still as raw as they come, aren't

115

you? It's easy done. Julian pushes a little skin bag full of fresh pigeon blood up you. It's like I said to you before, the Bloods are all easy to fool. They'll swallow anything that they'm told.'

A little later, Rosie was sitting on her bed alone in the dormitory, thinking about the night ahead, apprehension for the unknown still gnawing at her. Angel came to sit at her side, and put his arm comfortingly around her shoulders.

'Don't be fretting about tonight, Rosie. Julian knows how to dose you proper. You'll most likely sleep right through till tomorrow and be back here with me before you even wakes up.'

She snuggled closer against him, drawing comfort from his warmth and kindness. 'I can't help feeling scared, Angel. What if somebody does something really bad to me tonight while I'm asleep?'

He shook his head. 'Julian will be watching over you. There's hidden spy holes to every room, and Julian keeps a close eye on everything what goes on. He won't let anybody damage you.' His voice hardened, his youthful features suddenly metamorphosed into an aged, bitter mask. 'He keeps us all safe because we're saleable goods, and he will do until we're a bit too old to attract the Bloods. Then we'll be kicked out on to the streets, and then there won't be anybody to keep us safe. The streets are awful cold and cruel, Rosie. Awful cold and cruel.'

Fifteen

There were half a dozen men, young and old, sitting around the walls of the large, dimly lit room, all intently watching the two young naked girls dancing to the strains of Julian's fiddle. Against one wall there was a four-poster bed with its curtains drawn shut. The air was wreathed with the smoke of cheroots and smelled of wine and brandy fumes, expensive pomades and Macassar oils. Mrs Wentworth stood next to the door, her hard eyes closely studying the faces of the men.

The tune came to an end and the two girls sank gracefully to the floor, kneeling in attitudes of submission, while the audience applauded loudly.

Mrs Wentworth moved to the centre of the room, standing over the girls. 'Well, gentlemen, are you ready to see my new offering? My new little "Sleeping Beauty"?'

There was vociferous assent, and Mrs Wentworth's smile broadened. 'Very well, gentlemen.' She nodded to Julian, who laid aside his fiddle and took Bridie and Tembi out of the room.

Mrs Wentworth went to the side of the bed and beckoned the men to follow her. They eagerly clustered around the bed as Mrs Wentworth pulled the velvet cord and the curtains swished fully open.

Rosie was comatose, lying on her back, covered with a red silk sheet so that only her face was visible, her long hair spreading across the pillow.

Mrs Wentworth took the top edge of the sheet and, with a tantalizing slowness, drew it down to reveal Rosie's naked body, which was greeted with a collective intake of breaths and appreciative murmurs.

'There now, gentlemen.' Mrs Wentworth's voice rang with proprietorial pride. 'Is she not a truly exceptional little beauty? And you have my solemn guarantee that she is absolutely pure. She is not some street urchin, but comes from good family. Untouched virgin flesh, gentlemen.'

She fell silent, her gaze moving from one to another of the faces around the bed. She saw the lust in their eyes, the slackening lips, the heightened tension of their bodies, the quickening breaths, and inwardly smiled with contempt.

'What am I bid for this untouched virgin flesh, gentlemen? Who'll start the bidding?'

'Forty pounds,' an elderly man quavered.

Mrs Wentworth chuckled mockingly. 'You are insulting me, sir. I won't sell for a hundred even. Come now, gentlemen, this is a quite exceptional opportunity to enjoy a true virgin beauty. A once-in-a-lifetime chance for a night to remember.'

'I'll go a hundred and ten,' another man offered.

'Make that a hundred and fifteen.'

'A hundred and sixteen.'

The bids came ever quicker, ever higher, and Mrs Wentworth glowed with satisfaction, knowing that tonight would prove to be a very profitable night indeed.

Sixteen

Rosie was auctioned and re-auctioned as a virgin several times more during the following weeks and months, taken to different towns and cities by Mrs Wentworth and Julian until their extensive client list had been fully covered. Then, her novelty exhausted and selling price consequently lowered in value, she lost her starring status and simply serviced the clients at the house in Birmingham. She quickly developed a hardened, outer facade. Yet buried deep within her essential being there still survived the core of her innate goodness and decency. She would never be able to reconcile herself to the degradation of what she had been forced to become.

As time passed, her relationship with Julian subtly altered. A peculiar sense of fellowship gradually evolved between them, and although he remained the ruthless enforcer of Mrs Wentworth's will, and the physical embodiment of her power, Rosie came to realize that in his way he was as helplessly entrapped as herself.

Over time Theresa became ill, and died. Then Bridie disappeared one night without warning. They were quickly replaced by younger girls. In their turn these younger girls disappeared to be replaced by others, who in their turn were also replaced. Angel disappeared, to be followed by a succession of younger boys. Rosie wept for his loss in those secret hours when no one could see and mock her tears.

When she asked Julian what had happened to Angel and Bridie, he sympathetically patted her shoulder. 'The Bloods got tired of them, honey. So the madam give them the money she's been saving for them, and sent them away. They'll be living rich and comfortable now, and so will you when it's your time to leave here with your pockets full of gold.'

'I wish the Bloods had got tired of me,' she said with heartfelt longing. 'Because I'm sick to death of this life.'

He shook his head. 'You still look too young and pretty for her to send you away, Rosie.'

'Then being pretty is a bitter curse for me,' she retorted in sudden anger.

Tembi, however, had not left with pockets full of gold. She stole money from a client, and her theft was discovered. Julian locked the other children into the living room and they could hear Tembi's piercing screams through the dormitory door as he beat her mercilessly. They never saw her again, and when Rosie questioned Julian as to Tembi's whereabouts, the huge man snarled fiercely at her.

'The thievin' little cow has been taught a lesson that she'll never forget, and she's been kicked out of here with nothing. Just you make sure that the same thing don't happen to you.'

Rosie knew better than to press, and never mentioned Tembi's name again.

Rosie had learned to stoically endure her existence as a prostitute, but she desperately longed for the day when, with pockets full of gold, she would be set free from her bondage.

'I'll go far away from here, to somewhere nobody knows me. I'll build a new life for myself. A decent, respectable life,' she promised herself.

Seventeen

Worcestershire, April, 1849

Eugenia Pacemore sat in her favourite seat, staring out of the open bedroom window at the expansive countryside. Another spring had come, another quickening of verdant life, new lambs playing in the fields, birds fluttering among trees and bushes budding with fresh green growth. The sun warmed the air, and the breeze was gentle.

The wall clock whirred and chimed the hour and Eugenia sighed and rose from her seat. Another long, seemingly pointless morning had passed, and another long, seemingly pointless afternoon and evening stretched before her.

She went to stand and gaze at herself in the mirror above the mantlepiece. The passing years had been physically kind to her. Her thin pale face was still clear-skinned and unlined, her eyes still lucent, her dark hair still thick and glossy.

She heard the sounds of horses' hooves crunching on the gravelled forecourt beneath her window, and went to see who had arrived.

It was a solitary horseman, top-hatted, booted and cloaked: her family's solicitor of many years' standing.

Eugenia opened the casement and called to him. 'Good evening, Mr Burston, I'll come down directly.'

She reached the bottom of the staircase as the maidservant opened the door to the visitor, and went forward to greet him with outstretched hands.

His pale, heavily lined features were grave as their hands met. 'These are sad days for you, ma'am. You have my sincerest condolences.'

'Thank you, sir. I take comfort from the fact that my parents died instantaneously at the moment of collision. The railway engineers have assured me of that. They say that with the train travelling at such a speed, my parents would have known nothing after the initial moment of impact.'

Burston shook his head, clicking his tongue. 'This modern passion for speed, ma'am, it's a madness that's afflicting the world.'

She led him into the drawing room, and when they were seated said to the maid, 'Will you bring some tea, Lizzie, and some food ... I'm sure you must be in sore need of refreshment, sir. You have ridden a long distance.'

He lifted his hand. 'No food, I thank you, ma'am, but tea will be very welcome.'

He had carried in a small leather case, which he now opened upon his knees and took out a sheaf of papers. His expression was troubled, and a sense of foreboding invaded Eugenia.

'If you have bad news for me, sir, then please tell me without hestitation.'

He nodded abruptly. 'Very well, ma'am. The fact is that your family's financial position has worsened greatly during these past ten years. Some of your father's investments were unwisely made, to say the least, and he lost a great deal of money as a result. There are also considerable debts, and the creditors are pressing hard for settlement. They are threatening to take legal action if they do not receive payment in full.'

Eugenia frowned with concern. 'Is there money enough to settle those debts?' Burston shook his head. 'Then what do you advise, sir?'

'Your cousin, Lieutenant Bronton, is he in a position to help you financially?'

'No. Charlie has very little money. He's been a lieutenant for a long time because he cannot afford to purchase any promotion in rank.' Her face saddened. 'There are only we two surviving in our family.'

'And where is he now?'

'He's presently in Ireland with his regiment.'

Burston nodded gravely. 'Then, regretfully there is no other course open to you but to sell this house and land. I've already approached some interested parties concerning this action, and I'm confident that the sale of the estate will bring enough capital for you to settle all debts in full, and leave sufficient to purchase an annuity for yourself. It should provide sufficient income to live on, albeit very simply and without extravagance. Naturally I shall be only too happy to aid in any way that I can in arranging the annuity for you.' He fell silent, waiting for her reaction to this disturbing information.

Eugenia sat with her head bowed, assimilating what she had heard. Inwardly she smiled at the irony of this unexpected turn in her fortunes. The dullness of her life, with which she had been so dissatisfied, had abruptly altered. Now she was faced with radical change. Excitement suddenly burgeoned.

The solicitor was surprised when she smiled broadly at him. 'Do you know, sir, I do believe that this will turn out to be exactly what I've been needing. Please arrange for the sale of this estate to be completed as soon as possible.'

'What will you do now?' Burston seemed genuinely concerned.

She smiled happily. 'I shall do something that I've long had a hankering for, but have never had courage enough to do. I shall take up useful employment.'

Burston looked doubtful. 'I'm not sure what type of employment you might find, ma'am. There are very few gainful employments that are fitting for a lady of your gentle birth.'

'This employment won't be for any financial gain to me, sir. I intend to enter the

Institute of Protestant Deaconesses at Kaiserswerth.'

'The what?' he asked, bemused.

'It's in the south of Germany,' she explained. 'It was founded in 1833 by a Protestant
pastor named Theodore Fliedner. Now the
Institute includes a hospital, an orphan
asylum, an infant school, a training school for
female teachers, and also a penitentiary.
When I went with my father to Carlsbad Spa,
I met with some of the deaconesses, and later
visited them at the Institute.'

'But what will you do there?' Burston
asked, blinking several times in surprise.

'I shall train as a sick nurse, and hopefully
also help to care for the orphans.'

'But you're a gentlewoman! It wouldn't be
fitting for you to work in such a menial
capacity,' he protested.

'I think that to become a deaconess at
Kaiserswerth is more than befitting for any
gentlewoman, sir. In fact, if I succeed in joining them, then I shall count it as an honour,'
she told him firmly.

After Burston had left, Eugenia sat for some
time thinking of the new life ahead of her.
Excitement throbbed through her senses,
making her restless. She took her bonnet and
shawl and left the house, walking towards the
village, her goal the ancient churchyard in
which her parents lay, along with her beloved
old nurse, Martha.

Since her parents' deaths, she had come
several times each week to spend time sitting

on the gravestone adjoining their expensive, ornately carved and lettered tomb, an ostentatious edifice that social convention insisted upon, but which did not appeal to her own taste. Her grief for her parents did not need to be proclaimed to the world by extravagant ornaments of stone and gold gilt; she carried it in her heart.

There was no one else in the tree-shaded churchyard, and she took her customary seat. She had fallen into the habit of talking to her parents' grave as though they were present with her in spirit, could hear her, and now she quietly related what had happened, and the decision she had taken.

'So you see, I shall not be able to visit with you as often as I do now. But I'll come back whenever possible, and anyway, you'll always be with me in my thoughts wherever I shall be.'

She rose from her seat and started to walk quickly towards the lychgate, only to slow her steps and come to a halt opposite the simple headstone she had had placed to mark Hester Pearson's grave. The vivid memories of the pretty child she had tried unsuccessfully to keep with her all those years ago invaded her thoughts.

'What has happened to you, Rosie? Are you well and happy?'

Eighteen

It was Sunday night and Rosie had been drinking gin for some hours when Julian led a tiny, dirty-faced ragged girl child into the dormitory.

'Who's this?' she asked.

'This is Mary, and madam wants you to clean her up. She's been brought in especially for a new Blood, so make sure that you get rid of any lice, and that she's nice and pink. And make sure to brush her hair well and clean her teeth. From what madam tells me, this new Blood is a very important man who likes everything to be just so. It won't do to upset him.'

Rosie felt a horrified disgust, which impelled her to protest forcefully. 'But she's only a baby! You can't let a Blood use her! Look how tiny she is!'

The huge negro frowned. 'What's got into you?'

'Look how tiny she is!' Rosie repeated. 'She'll be torn to bits inside. You can't let a

128

Blood have her. You can't!'

'Madam can do whatever she wants,' Julian stated reasonably. 'She pays the piper, and so she calls the tune.'

'But this is wrong!' Rosie's voice rose sharply, became strident. 'She's just a baby, and it's wrong!'

The man shrugged his broad shoulders. 'Right, wrong, what's the bloody difference to us?'

'It might not make any difference to us, Julian. But this is an evil thing to do to her, and you know it is. It could be the death of her,' Rosie argued doggedly.

Julian's thick lips parted as he exhaled a sigh of impatience. 'Look, Rosie, you should know very well by now that what madam says, goes. She's the organ grinder here, and we're just the monkeys.'

Just then, something snapped in Rosie's brain, and she struggled to control herself. Shaking her head, she shouted furiously, 'I don't care if I am only a monkey, I'm not going to let the bloody organ grinder do such badness to this baby.'

Before he could move to stop her, she had darted past him and through the unlocked door. She hurled herself down the dark passage and up the flights of stairs that ran through the house, along the landings, slamming the doors open in search of Mrs Wentworth.

'What in hell's name...' Mrs Wentworth gasped in surprise and rose from her chair as

Rosie burst into the room.

'I'm not going to let you do it to that baby!' Rosie shouted furiously. 'Can you hear me? I'm not going to let you do such badness to her!'

Mrs Wentworth glowered down at the girl. 'Get out of here.'

'I'm leaving this house!' Rosie shouted. 'And I'm taking that poor little mite with me. And if you try and stop me, I'll bloody kill you, you evil old cow!'

Mrs Wentworth's face became a writhing, savage mask. Without warning, she grabbed a bronze statuette from the mantleshelf and smashed it into the side of Rosie's head, lacerating skin and flesh, spraying bright-red blood everywhere.

Rosie staggered sideways, colliding with the small table on which an oil lamp burned. The table crashed over and the lamp hit the floor. Its glass reservoir shattered and oil spilled across the thick-pile carpet.

Screaming in maniacal fury, Mrs Wentworth attacked again. Rosie ducked under the wildly flailing statuette and grappled with the taller, heavier woman, trying desperately to tear the statuette from her hand.

Then the spilled oil caught fire and the flames spread rapidly, voraciously feeding on the tinder-dry carpet, licking at the furniture, filling the air with glare and smoke.

The struggling women tripped and fell, with Rosie uppermost, and the impact of her weight momentarily loosened Mrs Wentworth's grip on the statuette, enabling Rosie to tear it from her. Mrs Wentworth's long fingernails instantly raked at Rosie's eyes as the scorching smoke and flames engulfed them, and with a strength born of terror, Rosie broke free and scrabbled on hands and knees towards the door.

She dragged it open and stumbled on to the landing. Coughing and retching, eyes streaming, half blinded, she fumbled her way down the stairs. Terrible shrieks of agony came from above her, and the thumping of boots and Julian's shouting from below.

Instinct gripped her, overwhelming all conscious thought, dominating every fibre of her being. Somehow she knew she must escape.

Not knowing how she got there, she suddenly found herself outside the house, and she began to run through the darkness of the night without thought, without direction, a mindless creature, fuelled by blind terror.

Nineteen

Dawn was seeping over the eastern horizon and Tommy Heston was moving cautiously through the dark-shadowed wood, using a stick to search the ground in front of him for any newly hidden man-traps and tripwires laid by the gamekeepers. Despite the darkness, he knew the wood well enough to be able to head directly towards his target: a shallow, bowl-like hollow of gorse bushes and grasses.

He reached his destination and crouched low, listening intently, his eyes searching the broad hollow and its surrounding trees for any sign of a gamekeeper waiting in ambush, or a rival poacher at work.

Satisfied he was alone, he moved quickly down through the bushes, checking the dozen snares he had set up the previous night. Three of them held rabbits. Two of the animals were dead, strangled by the nooses. The third was still living, and he expertly put an end to its suffering with a chopping blow to the base of its skull. He placed the three animals in the haversack slung on his back and then recovered all the snares. He would not target this particular warren again for some time and wanted to leave no telltale traces behind him.

He left the hollow and took a different route through the wood that would bring him out on to the public roadway and a wide stretch of heathland. Tommy Heston knew from experience that once he was on the heath he was safe from any of the local gamekeepers because he could sight them at a distance and outrun them.

The road was a chalky paleness, and Tommy made a careful survey of its length and the heath beyond before breaking from his cover. He went some fifty yards into the heath before turning and walking parallel to the road. Then, in the far distance, he saw a small, dark figure approaching along the road. His caution was instantly aroused. The road was little used during the daytime hours, and hardly ever at night. He ran to hide behind a clump of gorse where he could keep the oncoming figure in view.

Making slow progress, the dark shape drew nearer, moving erratically, jerkily zigzagging, halting for long periods, then coming on ever more slowly, until finally it halted and collapsed on to the road to stay motionless.

'Well it don't look like any animal I've ever met with. So it's got to be humankind,' Tommy Heston concluded. 'Might it be a keeper tryin' to gull me, I wonder. Trying to draw me out into the open?' He stayed hidden in his vantage point.

An hour passed and then it was full day, and the huddled figure was still lying motionless where it had fallen.

Tommy Heston's curiosity overcame his caution and, stowing the dead rabbits in the thickest part of the gorse, he broke cover and moved warily towards the road.

He gasped in astonishment when he realized that the fallen figure was a woman, and hurried towards her, only to come to an abrupt standstill when he saw her blood-caked wounded features.

'What's happened to your face, girl?'
He stepped to her side and bent over to

examine her closely, noting that her clothing and skin were covered with smoke smut, and her hair badly singed.

'It looks like you've been in a fire.' He touched her brow, which felt hot. 'And you feels feverish.'

Rosie's body was collapsed in utter exhaustion, her senses swirling giddily in a black void, and she had no awareness of anything around her.

'I'd better see what you're carrying, girl.'

Tommy Heston's deft fingers quickly searched her clothing, and her flesh, finding the ribbon around her neck and tracing it down between her breasts to pull out a small round metal object.

'Is this gold or silver?' He held it close to his eyes, and cursed in disgust when he recognized what it was. 'Oh, bollocks! It's just a bleedin' sodger's brass button!'

He leaned back on his haunches, staring speculatively at Rosie's face.

'What am I going to do wi' you? I could just walk away and leave you to it. You got nothing! Not even a bloody cheap trinket on you! You could be a real bad lot, for all I know. I mean to say, why should I trouble meself about you? What's in it for me?' He grimaced resentfully. 'Nothing! That's what'll be in it for me. Nothing! I'll bet a hundred sovs on that. But you're somebody's daughter. And I got daughters of me own ... Oh, bollocks to it!'

Twenty

Rosie slowly returned to consciousness and could hear voices, but could not make out what they were saying. She became aware of throbbing pain in her face and in her body. Pain which, as her senses returned, sharply intensified, causing her to emit a drawn-out groan.

'Come quick, Tommy! Her's waking up properly,' a woman's voice shouted.

Rosie opened her eyes, blinking repeatedly to clear her blurred sight. Her dry mouth tasted foul, and her stomach was heaving with nausea.

'Hand me that jug o' water,' a man's voice ordered.

As Rosie's sight cleared she saw his weather-beaten face looking down at her. She tried to speak, but only an unintelligible croaking issued from her lips.

'Don't try to talk yet, girl. Have a drink o' this first.' Tommy Heston gently raised her to a sitting position and held the jug of water to her mouth.

Rosie eagerly gulped the icy-cold liquid, spilling some of it down herself. As her thirst was assuaged, full recollection of what had happened in Birmingham rushed back to her. She stared in confusion around her, unable to understand how she had come to be here, on a rough wooden pallet inside what seemed to be a crude plank and canvas shelter. Her fingers went to her face, tentatively tracing the sore, swollen wounds.

'Is my face badly torn?' she asked fearfully.

'Well, it's a mess alright,' Tommy Heston told her bluntly. 'But it'll heal, and then it won't look so bad.'

Again she looked about her. Standing behind the man were two grimy-featured, wild-haired women, one middle-aged, the other younger, staring doubtfully at her as though she were some exotic animal they had never seen before. All three of them were roughly dressed, their clothing ragged and earth-stained.

'Where am I? How did I come to be here?' Rosie was totally mystified. Her last memory was of the pale chalk road stretching endlessly before her.

'What's your name, girl? Where's your family? Who done this to you?' Tommy Heston began to fire questions at her.

'My name's Rosalind Stannard. I've got no family. I'm alone in the world.'

The man's lined features displayed acute disappointment at hearing this.

'You got nobody at all who'll pay any reward for any news of you, then? No friends or suchlike?'

'No. There's no one,' she reiterated.

'Well, you must have been living some-wheres,' Heston snapped irritably. 'Where was it? And what was you doing to get your bed and board?'

'For pity's sake, leave her be, Tommy!' the older woman said sharply. 'Gerrout and get a bit o' work done, and leave her be. Don't be so bloody hard-hearted. You can see she's suffering.'

'Me? Hard-hearted?' he protested indignantly. 'I saved her bloody life, woman. If it warn't for me, she'd still be lying on the road. I'm too *soft*-hearted for me own good, I am.'

'Oh, just piss off and do some work!' She pushed him aside and came to Rosie. 'There now, my duck, don't you fret none. I'll see that you're alright, don't worry.' She stroked Rosie's bowed head with her black-nailed, work-hardened hand. 'You lay back and rest yourself now, and later on we'll have summat to eat. And then after that you can tell us whatever you wants to, or not tell us, as the case may be. Is that alright, my duck?'

Rosie nodded gratefully. 'Yes, thank you, ma'am. Thank you very much.'

The woman threw back her head and laughed delightedly. 'Did you hear that? She's just called me ma'am. Nobody's ever called me that before in me life. *Ma'am*.' She savoured the title. *'Ma'am*. She called me ma'am, as if I was a gentlewoman, no less.'

'I could call you something a bit different, and it wouldn't be ma'am,' Tommy Heston said as a parting shot over his shoulder as he left the shelter.

'Piss off!' she said with contempt. 'You'd best go and give him a hand, Abi, or he'll only be moaning and groaning all day.'

As soon as they were alone in the shelter, the woman smiled kindly at Rosie. 'First of all, let me tell you where you be, my duck. You'm in our camp in the middle of the Lickey Woods, about half a dozen miles from Brummagem. Me husband found you a-laying on the old quarry road nigh on a week past, and he fetched me and we carried you here. You've had a bad fever, my duck. But it's well broke now, and you just needs to rest while you gets your strength back.'

'But who are you?' Rosie asked.

'Me name is Abi Heston, and that was me daughter, Abi. They calls me Old Abi, and they calls her Young Abi. And that bloke is me husband, Tommy Heston. We'em charcoal burners. That's why we camps here in the woods.'

Rosie was jolted by a spasm of giddy weakness, and she slumped back against the coarse linen of the lumpy pillow beneath her head.

'That's it, my duck.' Old Abi smiled pityingly. 'You lay and rest, and don't be fretted about anything. You'll be safe here with us.'

'Please, ma'am, have you a looking-glass? I want to see my face for myself,' Rosie pleaded.

Old Abi pursed her lips with doubt.

'Please, ma'am. I shan't be able to rest until

I've seen for myself.'

'Alright then,' the woman conceded reluctantly. 'But remember that it looks a lot worse now than it really is. The swellings 'ull soon go down, and the scars will fade as you gets older.'

She rummaged in one of the battered wooden chests that were dotted about the shelter, and took out a jagged piece of broken mirror to give to Rosie.

'Here, my duck, use this. I busted it the day before I married my husband and it's brought me bad luck ever since. Now I got to go and help the others, but I'll be back tonight and then we'll all have some grub and a talk.'

Rosie was thankful to be left alone to marshal the maelstrom of her thoughts. Her heart beating with trepidation, she lifted the piece of mirror and studied her reflection.

The left side of her face was a swollen purple-red surrounding a long livid gash, and around both eyes were the deep scratches left by Mrs Wentworth's fingernails. Rosie studied her reflection for long, long minutes, mental anguish pulsing through her.

'What's going to become of me now?' she sobbed.

Twenty-One

August, 1849

The heat of the noontime shimmered in the air as Rosie carried the wicker basket into the extensive clearing where the Hestons were toiling to build a cone-shaped pile of timber that would eventually metamorphose into charcoal. The pile was six feet high and thirty feet in diameter and, with skill born of long practice, Tommy Heston had fashioned the central cylinder and the long flues through the consecutive circles of timber to ensure that the whole mass burned evenly. The final pieces of wood were being set in place as she joined them, and Tommy Heston grinned in welcome.

'Thank Christ you've come wi' the grub. Me stomach was starting to think that me throat had been cut.'

Rosie took a linen sheet from the basket and spread it out on the grass, then emptied the contents of the basket on to it. There was a loaf of bread, a large lump of cheese, a crock dish filled with pieces of cooked rabbit, and a big jug of cider.

The Hestons sat down around the sheet and began their meal.

'Is there something I can get on with, Tommy?' asked Rosie, who had already eaten.

'You can make a start on cutting the turfs and covering the pile, my duck. Remember now, its grass-side laid next to the wood, and make sure that they'm deep-cut blocks.'

'Rosie knows that very well already, Dad. Stop speaking to her as though she's a halfwit like you,' his daughter gibed, and Rosie laughed as she loaded the turf cutter on to the wooden wheelbarrow and trundled away to a wide swathe of greensward. There she started to cut out rectangular blocks of turf and load them on to the barrow. She hummed contentedly to herself as she worked, enjoying the fluid play of her muscles, the warm, scented air and the songs of birds floating through the trees.

Despite the heavy burden of her memories, Rosie was happy here in this wooded isolation sharing in the hard, wearisome, poverty-stricken life of the Heston family. She was happy to toil for long arduous day after long arduous day. To work until every muscle in her body ached. To labour like a beast of burden.

The Hestons had cared for her throughout her fever and convalescence, and their rough kindliness had deeply moved Rosie, eroding the hard defensive shell of cynicism that had formed during her years in the brothel. Now, with her physical strength fully recovered, she was trying to repay them by helping in every way she could with their grinding labours.

Naturally enough, the Hestons had asked her many questions concerning the past, and Rosie, afraid that they would turn from her in disgust if they knew the full truth, had instead related an edited version, which had at least some grounding in fact.

She told the Hestons that when Tommy found her she had been running away from her violently cruel father and stepmother following a particularly brutal beating during which her stepmother had inflicted the gash on her face. She had no other family, and so was now completely alone in the world. She had begged the Hestons to say nothing about her to anyone else, because she was terrified that her father might discover her where-abouts and come after her again.

The warm sympathy with which the Hestons had reacted to her story caused Rosie to feel guilty about her deceit. But she was genuinely living in fear of discovery. The memories of Mrs Wentworth's shrieks of agony still reverberated in her mind, and Rosie feared that the woman may have been burned to death in the fire. If that was indeed the case, then she, Rosie, would be blamed for the woman's death, perhaps even accused of deliberately murdering her. Rosie's ex-perience of the world had given her little reason to trust in any form of legal justice, and she naturally had no wish to be hung as a murderer.

A fierce hatred – for her father, for Annie Sparks, for Mrs Wentworth, for all the men who had abused her – burned constantly within her. Yet, paradoxically, the shame of guilt also nagged in her mind. She blamed herself for having passively submitted to all those long years of degradation. The passing of time did not lessen her sense of shame and guilt; if anything it became more of a torment to her.

When the Hestons had eaten, they came to join Rosie at her task, Tommy Heston cutting the turf and the three women carrying the blocks to the pile. When the turf covering was completed, leaving only the hole above the central cylinder, they heaped dry earth all around the base of the pile, ramming it hard to create an airtight layer. It took many hours to complete the work, and darkness had fallen when Tommy Heston finally called a halt.

'That'll do for now. I'll start the firing first thing tomorrow.'

They made their way back to the camp to find a man sitting on a large wooden box by the side of the cooking fire, his face half-concealed by a wide-brimmed hat pulled down low over his eyes.

Isolated deep in the woods as they were, this was the first time that Rosie had seen anyone other than the Hestons since her arrival, and at the first glimpse of him a frisson of fear that it might be Julian shivered through her. Then she realized that he was white-skinned and she chided herself for reacting so irrationally.

'It's our Jack!' Old Abi cried out in joyful surprise. At the sound of her voice the man stood up, cast aside his hat and hurried towards them. He was in his mid-twenties, tall, rangy, pleasant-featured, with short curly brown hair.

'Auntie, Uncle, Cousin Abi!' He embraced them one by one, and they simultaneously hurled questions at him, forcing him to hold up his hands. 'One at a time, one at a time.'

Rosie stared at him curiously. Old Abi had spoken several times of her dead sister who had married a soldier, and died giving birth to a son: Jack Collier.

'What are you doing here? I thought you was in Ireland,' Old Abi said. 'How did you know where to find us?'

'And so I was, but the regiment come back last month. I've been granted a six-week furlough, so I thought I'd come and spend it with you. I went to your lodgings in Digbeth, and they told me that you was charcoaling here in the Lickeys. I've been tramping around these bloody woods all day trying to find you.'

'But where's your fine uniform?' Young Abi sounded disappointed.

'Back in Coventry barracks, Cousin Abi. I'm a full corporal now, and our adjutant give me permission to wear plain clothes while I'm on furlough ... And who's this pretty

144

creature?'

He smiled at Rosie and instinctively she turned her head to hide the long scar on the left side of her face.

'This is our friend, Rosie. She's been helping us this summer,' his aunt told him.

'Well, I'm very pleased to meet you, Miss Rosie.' After a momentary hesitation, Rosie shook his proffered hand, then steeled herself to turn her face squarely towards him.

His smile faltered for a brief instant, and dismay enveloped her.

He pressed her fingers and said, 'Well, you're one of the prettiest girls I've seen for manys the long day. I'll bet you've got all the lads hereabouts chasing after you. I'm of a mind to join them, as well.'

Rosie felt herself beginning to blush, and Old Abi scolded him good-naturedly. 'Will you let the poor girl have her hand back, our Jack? If you keeps hold of it any longer she'll start to think she's lost it for good.'

Jack chuckled and released Rosie's fingers, then opened his arms wide in an expansive gesture of invitation.

'Come and see what I've brought you.'

He returned to the box he had been sitting on and, opening its lid, took out some silk shawls that shimmered in the firelight. He gave one each to his aunt and cousin, and demanded a kiss on his cheek from them both in payment. Then he turned to Rosie.

'Will you do me the honour of accepting this shawl, Miss Rosie? And don't worry, I shan't expect you to kiss me in payment.'

Deeply touched by his kindness, she found herself blushing yet again, and she bobbed a curtsey. 'Thank you very much, Mr Collier.'

As he held the shawl towards her, suddenly the memories came flooding back of all those men giving her gifts of trinkets, and she was overcome with a terrible sense of shame, a shame so cruelly all-encompassing that she could only turn and run, tears of anguish flooding from her eyes.

Jack Collier gaped in perplexed astonishment. 'What did I do? Why did I upset her so? What did I do wrong?'

'Nothing, Jack. You did nothing wrong,' Old Abi hastened to assure him.

'But why is she so upset?'

'The poor girl's had a hard time of it, Jack,' Tommy Heston put in.

'Yes, she has. She's been cruelly used.' Old Abi shook her head sadly.

'How so?' her nephew demanded.

His aunt continued to shake her head. 'That's for her to tell you if ever she wishes.'

'Alright, but shouldn't we go after her?'

'No. Let her alone. She'll come back by and by.'

'Alright, Auntie.' He went back to his box and took from it several dark bottles. 'Now, let's get stuck into this gin, shall we, and enjoy ourselves.'

In the darkness of the woods, Rosie was slumped down on her knees, her face buried in her hands, struggling with the bitter realization that, try though she might to leave her past behind her, she would never be able to escape it. The maturity, the stoicism, the mental toughness engendered by her years of enslaved prostitution were being tested to the limit as the need to unburden herself, to shed the crushing load of secrecy, became over-powering. She was beginning to realize that confession was the only way she might finally achieve full peace of mind.

It was the early hours of morning when Rosie returned, cold and weary, to the camp and crouched by the smouldering embers of the fire. She could hear snoring coming from the shelter, and felt relieved that she would not have to face her friends for hours yet. She went to fetch fresh wood to replenish the fire, then stood holding her hands to the heat of the leaping flames.

She thought of Jack Collier. 'How will he look at me if he finds out what I was? He smiled at me as if I were a good, clean-living girl, but he'll never smile at me in that way again,' she thought sadly.

She heard movement inside the shelter and looked up to see the subject of her thoughts emerging. His teeth gleamed white as he smiled.

'I'm glad to see you back safe and sound, my pretty.' He came to stand on the other side of the fire. 'What made you run off like that, Miss Rosie? Did I do something to offend you? Because, believe me, that's the last thing I want to do.'

'No!' She was dismayed by his question. 'No, Mr Collier, you did nothing to offend. It was just me being stupid.'

He chuckled. 'That's alright then.'

'Did I wake you, Mr Collier, when I was chucking wood on the fire?'

He shook his head. 'I was already awake. And I wish that you'd call me Jack. I'm hoping that you and me will become good friends, and friends don't have to be so formal, do they?'

He radiated good humour, and Rosie experienced a feeling of warmth towards him, along with sudden curiosity.

'What sort of soldier are you, Mr – sorry – Jack?'

'A bloody good one, I trust.' He laughed.

She was embarrassed by the clumsiness of her question, but noting her expression, he went on quickly. 'I'm a cavalryman, Rosie. A Light Dragoon.'

On impulse, she pulled the brass button out from her bodice and showed it to him. 'A soldier gave me this years ago. His name was Sergeant William Thomas, and he was in the Twenty-ninth Foot. He was very kind to me.'

'Good, I'm glad to hear it. And so should everybody be kind to you, Rosie, especially us soldier-men.'

A fleeting frown troubled her face. Jack Collier noted this, and he asked with a deliberate casualness, 'You haven't been ill-treated by any soldiers, have you?'

She shook her head.

'How old are you, Rosie? Are your parents still living? Do you have family?'

She became instantly wary, afraid of the direction that the conversation was heading in and hesitated for several seconds. 'I turned sixteen two months past. My mother and grandparents died years since. But I don't know whether my father is still alive or not.'

'That's a sad thing.' He smiled sympathetically. 'So how long have you been with my aunt and uncle?'

'A few months.'

'Where were you before then?' His voice was insistent. 'Who was looking after you?'

She was torn with indecision. She didn't enjoy lying repeatedly.

Taking her extended silence for a rebuff, Jack Collier apologized. 'I'm sorry. I'm being terrible nosy. I shouldn't be pestering you with all these questions.'

A struggle began to rage within Rosie's mind. The impulse to unburden herself fought against her fear of the consequences.

He broke the silence again. 'You ought to go inside and rest, Rosie. You must be needing some sleep.'

Gratefully she seized this opportunity to escape. 'Yes, I'm very tired. I'll go and lay down for a while.'

She went into the shelter and lay down upon her straw-filled mattress, hugging the blankets close around her. She closed her eyes, longing for sleep to come and release her from the burden of her thoughts. But her emotions were too disturbed to allow her to rest, and when day broke she was still lying awake.

Around her the Hestons were rising from their own mattresses, yawning, stretching, grunting, and the acrid stench of their unwashed bodies and clothes filled her nostrils. The smell did not offend Rosie, although she herself bathed daily in a clear pool in the woods and washed her clothing as often as she could. Unwashed flesh and stale clothes were the norm among the labouring classes, and Rosie had been accustomed to tolerate this fact since birth.

They gathered around the camp fire to find that Jack Collier had already cooked a pot of onion porridge for their breakfast. After greeting them, the young soldier said no more, and the only sounds to break the silence were those of eating and drinking, but his blue eyes continually flickered towards Rosie's downcast face.

'Right then, let's get to it.' Tommy Heston led the small group towards the work site. Rosie was bringing up the rear and Jack Collier fell back to walk beside her.

'Did you get some sleep, Rosie? Only you look tired. You're not feeling unwell, I hope.' There was concern in his voice.

'No, I'm fine, thank you.' She felt shy and awkward.

He dropped his tone to a whisper so that the others could not overhear him. 'Listen,

I'm sorry for pestering you with all those questions last night. I won't do it again, I promise. Can we be friends?'

She peeped at him from beneath her long lashes and nodded in pleased assent.

He laughed with satisfaction, and Rosie was suddenly overwhelmed with a strange sensation of recognition.

'I've known this man before! Somehow, somewhere, sometime, I've known this man before. This has happened before! But where, and when, and how?' Her mind was full of unanswered questions.

The sensation left her as suddenly as it had arrived, leaving only a residual trace of instinctive feeling that this young man was destined to play an important and relevant role in her future, and that their meeting in the woods had been fated to happen.

Twenty-Two

September, 1849

Summer had passed and the damp gusty winds of autumn had begun to strip the early dying leaves from their branches.

The work on the final pile of wood had been completed and it was now to be fired.

Tommy Heston climbed up to the opening on top of the central cylinder and the others formed a human chain down its slope to the small bonfire at the base.

'Right then.' Tommy's few stubs of teeth grinned happily. 'Let's be having it.'

Old Abi lifted flaming sticks and chips of wood from the bonfire and passed them upwards along the chain to Tommy, who dropped them into the depths of the cylinder funnel. This process was repeated for several hours until the kindling of the pile of wood was fully complete, the fire spreading evenly throughout the mass.

Then, at Tommy's command, there ensued a frantic scramble to close the top centre hole with turf and earth, and to drive small round air holes through the base layer of hard-packed clay. White smoke streamed from the pile, and Rosie stood watching it with the others by her side.

Nothing further would be done to this particular pile until about fourteen days' time when the smoke would change to a thin blueish transparency. As soon as this occurred, all the air holes around the base would be blocked, and more earth spread over the pile and tramped down hard and airtight so that the fire could no longer obtain oxygen, and extinguish itself. Then the pile would be left for several weeks to allow it to cool throughout. Once cooled, it would be opened up and the charcoal extracted and bagged up to be sold.

'That'll do very well, so I reckon that's our lot for this year,' Tommy Heston announced. 'I'll take a walk into Rednal and get some bacca.'

'I'll come with you,' his wife said.

'And me,' Young Abi added eagerly. 'Are you coming as well, Rosie?'

Subconsciously, Rosie's hand went to her scarred cheek as she shook her head. 'No, I think I'd sooner stay here. I need to bathe and wash my clothes.'

'So do I.' Jack Collier looked ruefully down at his work-soiled trousers and boots, and fingered his thick stubble. 'It'll take me hours to shave this lot off and scrape the dirt off me.'

Tommy Heston grinned. 'You two 'ull never be true charcoal burners until you stops worrying about being dirty and stinking. That's the badge of our trade.'

Jack Collier chuckled. 'Well, spit and polish is the badge of my trade, Uncle, not dirt and stink. And I'd best get into practice with it again, because I have to get back to the regiment tomorrow.'

The Hestons walked away through the trees, and Rosie and Jack Collier left the clearing and went back to the camp.

'Shall I use the pool first, Jack, or will you?' Rosie smiled at the soldier. During his extended stay she had come to like him a lot, and was saddened to think that soon they would part, perhaps forever.

'You go first, Rosie, and I'll stay here. Wait

a second though.' He went into the shelter and, opening his box, took out a cake of scented soap, which he handed to her. 'Here's a present for you. I bought it from a pedlar down in Rednal a couple of weeks ago. He said it comes from France.'

She sniffed its sweet fragrance. 'It smells lovely. But you shouldn't waste your money on me.'

'I'd spend every penny I've got on you, Rosie, and think it money well spent.'

'Oh, what a sweet-talker you are.' She smiled, then took up a strip of rough towelling, the cake of soap and a change of clean clothing, and hurried towards the thick clump of undergrowth beyond which lay a clear pool of water fed from a nearby spring.

The young man stared hungrily at her retreating figure. On impulse he started after her, but she had disappeared beyond the undergrowth. He slowed his pace, but was unable to resist the urge to follow further, to reach the screen of bushes and peer through the thick tangle of leaves and branches. What he saw caused him to draw his breath sharply, and his heart to pound.

Rosie had loosened her long hair to fall freely about her shoulders, and was unlacing her rough-sacking working dress, slipping it down from her shoulders and over her hips and stepping free of its enveloping folds.

Rosie slid into the water and Jack, fearing that he might be caught acting the peeping tom, forced himself to sneak away.

'I've got to have you, Rosie. I've never met a woman that I wanted as much as I do you. I've a mind to marry you,' he said to himself.

Jack Collier was a man ruled by impulse and physicality. Now that the idea of marriage was in his mind, the more advantages he could see in having a dutiful and obedient wife. Born in barracks, raised in barracks, army life was all that Jack Collier had ever known. His sexual needs had always been catered for by the prostitutes who swarmed around the barracks and camps. But the vast majority of them were diseased, unclean drabs, and Jack Collier was tired of risking his health every time he slaked his sexual appetites. If Rosie was his wife, he need no longer take such risks. Plus, there were the added benefits of having her as his own personal servant to cater to any of his other needs.

Rosie was very thoughtful as she bathed her body and washed her dirty clothing. Now that the current charcoal-burning season had finished, the Hestons would be returning to their permanent lodgings in the centre of Birmingham for the winter months. They had invited her to go with them, but Rosie dared not return to live in Birmingham. Here in this isolated camp deep in the woods she had felt safe, but the city and its environs held too much menace for her. So she had told them that she needed to move further away from the city in case her father managed to track her down.

Rosie knew that she would sorely miss the Hestons, of whom she had become very fond, but sadly accepted that she would once more be alone and friendless. She must take to the roads again and head further away from Birmingham, find work and shelter in a place where no one knew anything about her.

When Rosie returned to the camp, Jack went to the pool and bathed, scrubbing his skin hard until it glowed. Before dressing in his clean clothes, he washed his discarded clothing and spread it out alongside Rosie's on the tops of the bushes so that it would dry in the sunlight. Lastly he shaved carefully, and found himself momentarily wishing that he had some cologne water to rub into his throat and cheeks. Then he chided himself. 'Soldiers have got no business to be smelling like a clerk in a counting house. We have to smell like real men.'

He began to walk back to the camp, his mind full of images of Rosie's shapely body. 'If she was mine, every bloke in the regiment would envy me, having a good-looking wife like her. I'm going to do it. I'm going to ask her to marry me.'

But he was suddenly racked by doubt. 'She won't accept a common soldier like me, will she? Not when she could have her pick of civilians. She won't want to be a soldier's wife.'

In his world the respectable, God-fearing elements of society shunned soldiers and whores alike as being two sides of the same

156

coin. Any woman who dared to marry a soldier was considered to have ruined herself and was little better than a prostitute in their eyes.

Rosie was standing outside the shelter brushing her hair, its long auburn mass shining richly in the sunlight. A lump of tension came into Jack's throat when he saw her. The long-faded scar on the left side of her face did not detract from her desirability in his eyes. Her many other physical attributes more than compensated for this flaw.

'Now then, boy,' he ordered himself. 'Don't hang back any longer. Go for it straight away.'

He walked up to her and cleared his throat. Seeing his tense expression, she asked in surprise, 'Why do you look at me like that? What's the matter?'

He cleared his throat once more. 'I want you to marry me,' he blurted.

Her brushing hand stilled, her full moist lips parted in shock. 'Marry you?' She murmured the words disbelievingly. 'You want me to marry you?'

'Just so. I want you to be my wife.'

Her hand went to her mouth and she shook her head in an involuntary reaction. His expression filled with dismay.

'Are you saying no to me, Rosie?'

Her thoughts were in turmoil, and she could form no words to answer him. A note of desperate urgency entered his voice. 'I know that I've sprung this on you. But I shan't be just a corporal forever, Rosie. I'll be a sergeant-major before I'm done, and then you'll live like a lady. You'll want for nothing, I swear to that.'

'Now then, what are you saying to Rosie, our Jack? She looks all moithered,' Old Abi said as she walked up to them.

'I thought you was going into Rednal,' Jack said.

'I changed me mind. Now what's you been saying to Rosie to make her look so moithered?'

'I've just asked her to marry me.'

Old Abi grinned knowingly. 'I had a notion that you was going to do that, our Jack. I could see that you're sweet on her.'

'Say yes, Rosie,' he urged. 'I'll be a good husband to you. Say yes!'

Abi also urged her. 'You should marry him, Rosie. He's not a bad lad, for all that he's too fond of the drink. You should marry him. He'll keep you safe from your father. Nobody will be able to treat you bad again. Our Jack will keep you safe.'

'Safe!' The word reverberated in Rosie's mind.

She didn't love Jack Collier, but she had long since abandoned any girlish day-dreams of marrying for love. She liked him, and found him physically attractive. Faced as she was with the daunting prospect of having to go alone and friendless into the world once more, for a brief moment she was sorely tempted to accept his proposal.

'Safe! I'd be safe with him. For the first time

in my life, I'd be safe. And I'd be a respectable married woman. I'd have put the past behind me. Buried it forever. I'd be safe with him,' she thought over and over.

Words of acceptance trembled on her lips, but then another voice sounded in her mind. A powerful, demanding voice. The voice of her conscience.

'And how will you be able to rest easy, if you're living a lie? Having to always guard your tongue in case you let something slip about your past. And think of all the men who've had you through the years. There's always the chance that someday one of them might see you, and then the truth will come out. Jack Collier might be the answer to your problems, but you can't hide your past from him. You have to tell him the truth about yourself. You have to.'

Rosie drew a long, deep breath, summoning all her courage and resolution. She forced herself to look into his eyes, her mouth dry with apprehension.

'I think that I must tell you the truth about myself.'

He nodded encouragingly. 'I want to hear everything about you. Every last detail.'

Her resolve quailed momentarily, but then she swallowed hard and began to relate her story, wavering at times, but forcing herself on, leaving nothing out, making no excuses, speaking only the harsh, bitter truth.

He visibly flinched on first hearing that she had been a prostitute, but then his expression hardened to a grim mask. Old Abi expelled her breath in a sharp hiss, and pressed her knuckles against her mouth.

Finally, Rosie finished her story, and with the sting of tears in her eyes, waited apprehensively for the others' reaction.

Jack stood silently for what seemed like endless hours, then finally shook his head, turned and walked away into the trees.

Old Abi exploded with rage. 'We took you in and give you shelter, and all the time you was lying to us! Making fools of us. And now you've made a fool of our poor Jack.'

'No!' Rosie protested desperately. 'No, it wasn't like that, Abi. I just didn't dare to tell you, that's all.'

'No! I should think you bloody well didn't dare tell us. Because we might be poor, but we've always lived decent. No woman in my family's ever turned whore. And to think that you've been sleeping under our roof all these months. God knows what foul diseases you're carrying.'

Rosie said nothing, realizing that Old Abi was too consumed with rage to listen to any explanation. The woman went into the shack but soon hurried out again, brandishing her fist in the air. Rosie flinched as Old Abi grabbed her hand and slammed her clenched fist down upon Rosie's open palm.

'You've taken us for fools, you bloody little whore. But bad as you are, I won't cheat you out of what you've earned.' She opened her clenched fist to release a few coins into

Rosie's hand. 'Take this and bugger off, before I fetch you a smack in your chops. Take your sack and get out of my sight. And don't you dare come back near me or mine ever again. Now bugger off!'

Rosie managed to hold back the tears until she was many yards from the camp, then broke down and, sobbing bitterly, hurried away towards the road.

Deep in the woods Jack Collier came to a fallen tree and sat down on its trunk, mulling over Rosie's story.

He had not expected her to be a virgin. A truly chaste sixteen-year-old girl was a rarity in his level of society. The workhouses were full of unmarried young pregnant women. But her confession that she had been a child prostitute had come as a stunning shock to him.

The hours passed and gradually he began to come to terms with this unpleasant discovery.

'I can't really blame her for what she was. The blame is on the bastards who forced her into it. And she's been honest, telling me everything about her past. That took guts, that did.' He smiled sardonically. 'And there was me worrying about her thinking she'd be lowering herself in the world by marrying a soldier, when all the time we've been on the same level.'

He stood up and began to walk quickly back towards the camp. 'I'll still marry her.

And if she don't behave as I want, then I'll just have to knock her into line until she does.'

The possibility that there might come a time when Rosie's past would be discovered by his comrades didn't cause him any concern. It was the veteran soldier's cynical precept that reformed whores made the best wives, since they knew best how to serve and satisfy their men, and Jack was a hard-bitten veteran.

It was dusk when he reached the camp and he found the Hestons sitting around the fire sharing a bottle of gin.

'Where's Rosie?' he asked.

'I've buggered her off. The lying cow's made fools out of us.' Old Abi was still furious.

'Where's she gone to?' he demanded.

'I don't know, nor care! It's good riddance to bad rubbish!' Tommy Heston grunted.

'How long's she been gone?'

'Hours since. She's probably back flogging her mutton in Brummagem, by now.' Old Abi stared at Jack's dismayed expression, and with sympathy added, 'Don't take it to heart, son. You're well rid of her.'

'I'll be the judge of that,' he snapped, and ran back into the trees, shouting Rosie's name. But only the echoes of his own voice sounded in reply.

Twenty-Three

Kaiserswerth, Southern Germany,
April, 1850

At five o'clock in the morning the rising bells rang throughout the complex of buildings that constituted the Institute of Protestant Deaconesses.

Eugenia Pacemore rose from the pallet in her small cell-like room on the top floor of the hospital and readied herself to face another day of hard, rigorous work. She washed her hands and face in the basin of cold water, then mixed a small amount of paste, using powdered chalk, pulverized gum myrrh and camphor. She cleaned her teeth with the mixture, and completed her morning toilette by brushing her hair and binding it into a tight knot on the nape of her neck.

Dressed in the uniform of a trainee nurse, a grey serge gown, stout boots and thick black stockings, her hair covered by a black head cloth, she went to join her fellow workers in the entrance hall.

The double line of buxom, fresh-faced country girls stood in silence, with only an occasional cough sounding from their ranks.

The matron, Head Deaconess Ursula von Meissner, entered the hall followed by two large women dressed in the black gowns and white headdresses of trained nurses. The trio stood facing the front of the group. The matron's pallid, patrician features were severe.

'Good morning, students. God's mercy be upon you.'

'Good morning, Sister Matron. God's mercy be upon you.'

There was one girl who did not add her voice to the chorused reply. She was standing next to Eugenia, her lip twitching nervously, apprehension in her eyes.

The matron called the roll: 'Schultz, Knaubel, Zimann, Rechtenburg, Pacemore, Maroslavitz...'

And the swift answers came back. 'I am present, Sister Matron.' Over and over again.

'There is only one student remaining. She knows why I have kept her until last,' the matron stated. 'Her name is Rauter.'

When this final name was called, Eugenia heard her neighbour's sharp intake of breath.

'Rauter?' The matron's hard blue eyes fixed on the girl, who swallowed hard.

'I am present, Sister Matron.'

The matron's voice was clipped and cold. 'You are present for the last time, Rauter. I've grown tired of reprimanding you. You are expelled from this Institute, as of this moment. Sister Hochheim, Sister Winkle-

164

horn, you will escort Rauter to the gatehouse and hand her into the custody of the head porter. He will carry out the necessary procedures.'

Her two companions came to take hold of the girl's arms.

'But I didn't mean to do wrong. I didn't mean to sin. It's just my way of speaking, that's all. Just my way of speaking,' Rauter wailed in distress.

The matron gestured in dismissal, and the girl was propelled swiftly away.

A rustle of excited reaction came from the onlookers, which was immediately stilled by the matron's warning frown.

'Let this be a lesson to you all,' the matron told them. 'That wretched creature was guilty of the sin of blasphemy. Take heed, all of you, that the name of the Lord God is only to be spoken with the utmost reverence and humility. Now, let us humbly worship our Lord.'

She prayed long and fervently until the distant chiming of a bell sounded. Then she dismissed them and marched out of the hall.

Trays of salted, buttered black bread and jugs of coffee were brought in, and the students were allowed ten minutes to consume this austere breakfast. No talking was permitted, and the silence was strictly enforced by senior deaconesses.

Eugenia ate and drank her entire portion, knowing that she would need every ounce of energy and sustenance that the unappetising fare contained. The working hours would extend until night fell, and there would only be another three ten-minute breaks allowed for taking food and drink during that time.

After breakfast the students were ordered to their work. As Eugenia walked through the long corridors towards her allotted ward, she heard her name whispered urgently. She stopped and smiled at the mischievous blonde-haired Dutch girl who joined her.

'What about poor Rauter?' Bertha Makkink whispered in English. 'The poor cow only used to say "Sweet Jesus!" or "Great God" when something surprised her. Fancy expelling her for that!'

The next instant, Bertha glanced over Eugenia's shoulder, clasped her hands before her face, closed her eyes tight shut, and began to pray loudly.

'Oh Lord, please help this wretched sinner to carry out her duties this day, in a manner which is pleasing to your sight, Lord. Dear Lord, I beg you to endow me with courage and determination and the spirit of humble obedience to those whom you have set above me...'

Struggling to keep the amused smile from her lips, Eugenia also assumed a posture of rapt devotion. The matron and a spade-bearded, frock-coated surgeon swept past them, the matron nodding approvingly at Bertha.

Once they were gone, Bertha giggled. 'Sweet Jesus! Great God! Sweet Jesus! Great

God! I do enjoy finishing my prayers with a little blasphemy.'

Eugenia couldn't help but giggle at her friend's impish irreverence.

The driving force of the Institute was an almost fanatical religious ardour. Several evenings in the week were devoted to Bible studies, where deaconesses and students gathered en masse in the Great Hall. They were taught and expected to pray aloud extempore and call on God for aid if any incident should occur during the day, such as a patient or an orphan misbehaving. Eugenia had initially found this practice of public individual prayer an embarrassment, but time had accustomed her to it, just as she was growing used to her spartan existence of hard, rigorous work, simple diet and few comforts.

She was training and working mainly in the hospital and had already witnessed several surgical operations, steeling herself to endure the screams of the patients under the knife, the blood and body wastes. She was fast becoming inured to the awful sights and stenches of diseased flesh, and had learned how to bring comfort to the sick and to ease the last hours of the dying.

Eugenia gave little or no thought to her future; she was totally and happily absorbed in the present. Instead of her pointless existence in genteel boredom, she now felt that she was living life to the full. Eugenia Pacemore had found in the Institute what she had been hungering for since she was a young girl: involvement. Physical and mental involvement in the multi-faceted dramas of humanity.

Twenty-Four

Environs of Windsor, April, 1850

The dancing booth was a large wooden hall with a planked floor, a raised platform for the band at one end, and a drinks bar stretching along one side wall. The thumping of polka-dancing feet, the tunes of fiddles, trumpet and drum, the singing, shouting, and laughing of the dense throng created a cacophony of sound. It was Saturday night, and the clerks, mechanics, factory girls, servants, soldiers, thieves and whores took refuge from the grinding hardships of their lives in the enjoyment of these few brief hours of revelry.

Behind the long bar, white-aproned barmen and barmaids struggled to keep pace with the demands of the drinkers, serving ales and ciders, wines and spirits, cheroots and short clay pipes ready-filled with rank-smelling tobacco.

'Give us three bottled beers, my love.'

'Give me a double gin.'

Loud voices constantly bombarded Rosie. Her face was hot and flushed, and she could feel sweat trickling down her body as she filled tankard after tankard, glass after glasss, taking money from hands that tried to clutch her fingers. She in turn handed the coins to the hatchet-faced harridan who sat on the raised podium as keeper of the cash desk.

The long hours passed. The hot, humid air stank of acrid sweat, cheap scent, spilled liquor and tobacco smoke. Rosie's body was weary, her head ached from the ceaseless thumping noise, and she had lost all sense of time. The ever-changing, shifting faces before her became a blurred kaleidoscope, the voices lost all individuality and became merely a series of orders, which she mechanically obeyed.

'Time, please, ladies and gentlemen! Time! Time! Time to go home!'

The last tune ended and the bellowing of the bouncers brought the gathering to its close and emptied the booth. The weary bar staff collected in and washed the empty tankards and glasses in tubs of greasy water, then removed their aprons and put on their coats, shawls, hats and bonnets before forming a group in front of the cash desk.

'Mr Gee, will you come here please? I'm ready to make the pay-out,' the hatchet-featured cashier called.

'I'm here, Mrs Smith.'

Angus Gee, squat-statured, barrel-bellied, puce-complexioned, came to stand beside the cashier, his eyes flitting along the queue, his hands fingering the heavy gold chain that dangled across his blue satin waistcoat.

'Albert Tomkins?' Mrs Smith shouted, and an elderly man shuffled forwards.

'One shilling and fourpence owing, less sixpence for breakages, leaves tenpence. Sign here.' Her black grimed fingernail pointed to the ledger line, and with his tongue protruding, the old man laboriously made his scrawling signature.

'And don't bother coming back to work for me again,' Angus Gee growled.

Tomkins reacted with obvious alarm. 'Why not, gaffer? What's wrong?'

'You're too slow, that's what's wrong. I've pissed more ale tonight than you've served. Now get out o' my sight.'

The old man stood his ground. 'But that ain't fair, gaffer.'

Angus Gee lifted his hand and immediately two of the bouncers came to grab the old man and dragged him to the entrance, ejecting him with savage kicks.

Gee's threatening gaze moved across the now apprehensive faces of the remaining bar staff before he turned and tapped the cashier's shoulder. 'Get on wi' paying these lazy useless buggers.'

Rosie was at the rear of the group, deliberately keeping her eyes down, but well aware that Angus Gee was staring hard at her. When it was Rosie's turn to be paid, Angus Gee said to the cashier, 'I'll deal with this one.'

With a jerk of his head, he signalled Rosie to follow him to the far end of the booth where they could not be easily overheard.

Walking behind his waddling bulk, hearing his heavy rasping breathing, Rosie was already resigning herself to some sort of proposition. Gee halted and faced her.

'You're a mystery, aren't you, Rosie? Nobody seems to know anything about you, apart from the fact that you've took lodgings with Old Millie Errol down by the riverside.'

Rosie shrugged her shoulders. 'Why should anyone want to know anything about me, Mr Gee?'

He chuckled wheezily. 'I always makes it my business to have enquiries made about anybody who comes to work for me. And I takes an especial interest in the pretty ones, like you.' He stepped closer so that his barrel-belly pressed against her, his hands feeling for her slender waist, and she instantly pushed free and stepped back.

'Don't maul me about!'

He held up both hands palms outwards. 'No need to get your dander up, Rosie. I'm just being friendly, that's all. There's no harm in that, is there?'

'No. There's no harm in being friendly, Mr Gee,' she conceded. 'So if you'll just pay me my wages, I'll say a friendly goodnight to you.'

He pushed his hand into his trouser pocket and jingled the coins it held. 'How much are you owed, Rosie?'

171

'I've worked four nights at a shilling and fourpence, so you owe me five shillings and fourpence.'

'How many breakages have I got to stop out of your wages?' He leered at her. 'You surely must have had breakages and spillings?'

'There's been none by me!' She shook her head, irritably aware that at the other end of the booth the bouncers and cashier were watching and smirking.

He pulled his hand from his pocket and opened his palm to disclose some gleaming gold sovereigns. 'There now, Rosie. Ain't they a pretty sight? Just think how you could enjoy yourself spending these.'

She didn't answer, and he went on in a low, cajoling tone. 'I've seen the way you handle the men. You ain't spent your life in a bloody convent, Rosie, that's for sure! I reckon that you've handled more than a few men in your time.'

Rosie's temper was rising fast. Hot words teetered on the edge of her tongue, but she bit them back, knowing from bitter experience that men like Angus Gee did not hesitate to use physical violence against women who provoked them. She injected a hint of pleading into her tone. 'Look, Mr Gee, I'm not well. Can I please just have my wages? I need to get to my lodgings and take some physic.'

'You don't look sickly to me.' He grinned. 'In fact you look as rosy and sweet and juicy as a ripe peach.'

He chinked the sovereigns in his palm and lifted them closer to her eyes. 'Just look at them, Rosie. If you play your cards right, these could all be in your pocket instead of mine. All you have to do to earn these is to be nice and willing.' He winked again. 'I'm sure you get my meaning, Rosie.' He stepped aside and leered. 'You go and get your rest. We'll talk again when you come back tomorrow.'

'What do you mean, come back?' She was taken by surprise. 'The booth's not open tomorrow.'

'No it ain't,' he agreed equably. 'But I'm having a private gathering here, and I need you to barmaid it. So come at two o'clock.'

'But I want what I'm owed now, tonight.' Even as she said this, she was invaded by the sickening realization of her helplessness.

'But if I pay you tonight, then I can't be sure that you'll turn up for work tomorrow, can I? You might go on the lush and forget to come.'

Rosie forced herself to plead humbly. 'Please, Mr Gee, I need money tonight. I've the rent to pay.'

'And physic to buy as well, don't forget,' he mocked, and at the far end of the tent the bouncers laughed.

His tongue snaked out across his fleshy lips, and he winked salaciously at her. 'Don't worry, Rosie. I guarantee that you'll get all your money tomorrow. And a big bonus as well, if you plays your cards right. Be here

173

sharp at two o'clock.' With that he waddled away, and was followed from the booth by the cashier and two of the bouncers.

The remaining bouncer moved around the booth, extinguishing all but one of the lamps. Rosie stood motionless.

'Are you going home, girl? Or do you want to stay here with me tonight and help me keep watch?' The man grinned at her.

She glared at him, and spat back, 'All I wanted tonight was to do my work and be paid my wages, not to be mucked around and insulted by that rotten fat bastard!'

The bouncer grimaced sympathetically. 'I know how you feel, Rosie. Just between you, me and the gatepost, I think Angus Gee is a rotten fat bastard as well. But he's a *rich* rotten fat bastard, and I'm only a poor penniless bastard. So there ain't nothing for it but for me to hold me tongue and do whatever he tells me to do. We're in the same boat, you and me, girl. God help us!'

The bouncer grinned and, muttering angrily beneath her breath, Rosie stamped out of the booth.

The night air was fresh and cool, and she breathed it gratefully, drawing it deep into her lungs as she lifted her face to the full, clear moon above.

She began to trudge wearily across the wide stretch of meadowland that surrounded the booth, heading for the distant huddle of buildings and the great tower and ramparts of the castle looming over them.

She skirted the outer walls of the castle and came to the mean terrace of hovels flanking the river side. The weak glow of a candle shone through the dirty cracked window-panes and Rosie sighed despondently.

'The old witch is waiting up for me.'

She lifted the latch of the door and reluctantly went in to be enveloped by damp, musty air, thick with the reek of burning tallow candles.

'Where's me rent money?' Millie Errol was sitting on a three-legged stool, crouched over the dead ashes in the rusted fire grate.

Rosie forced herself to smile at the hunchbacked smelly old crone. 'I don't get paid until tomorrow, Mrs Errol.'

The crone's toothless jaws worked frantically as she noisily sucked her gums. 'That's bullshit, that is. I knows for a fact that Angus Gee always pays out on Saturday nights.'

'Well, he wants me to go in to work tomorrow, and he'll pay me then,' Rosie explained.

'That's bullshit, that is. I knows for a fact that there's no dancing and gallivanting allowed on a Sunday.'

'He's having a private party, Mrs Errol. There won't be any dancing.' Despite her resentment at being accused of lying, Rosie tried to keep her tone neutral. 'You'll get your rent the moment I come back from work tomorrow, I promise you.'

'I'd better, or else I'll be fetching me sons to deal with you, and they won't be as soft with you as I am.'

175

Rosie was bone-weary, and wanted only to end this exchange. 'I'll say goodnight to you, Mrs Errol.'

She climbed up the ladder that connected the main room to the single tiny bedroom above. Her bed was a rug on the bare floorboards and a single threadbare blanket. For a pillow she used the sack bag that held her spare dress, underclothes, stockings and her pathetically few toilette articles.

She unlaced her bootees and slipped them from her sore feet, then lay back on the makeshift bed. Sufficient moonlight penetrated the broken windowpane to show the greasy, damp-stained walls and the dust-thick cobwebs festooning the rafters.

'Jesus Christ!' Rosie thought in disgust. 'The Hestons' shanty was a palace compared to this pigsty.'

Her stomach rumbled, reminding her that she had not eaten that day. In fact, she had not eaten since the previous afternoon, and then it had been only a small loaf bought with her last few pence.

Depression momentarily welled over her, but Rosie refused to allow it to take hold. Instead she forced herself to think about what she would do with her wages.

'I'll pay the old witch what I owe, and then I'll go and find something nice to eat. A broiled beefsteak, new bread and fresh butter, and for afters, a fruit tart ... Or should I have a dish of lamb chops, with peas and roasted parsnips, and a jam duff and custard for afters ... Or maybe ham and eggs, and apple pie...'

She fell asleep planning her feast.

Twenty-Five

Rosie woke at daybreak and, taking her soap and towel, descended as quietly as she could down the ladder so as not to disturb Millie Errol, who was snoring on the mattress in front of the fire grate. Rosie pulled her shawl close around her head and shoulders and went outside.

The sky was dark and a chill breeze skimmed across the wide, grey River Thames. Rosie walked upstream along the footpath, past the bridge that connected Windsor to its satellite village of Eton. She was heading for her bathing place, a secluded spot beyond the town where a small streamlet fed its clean, fresh waters into the polluted river.

Normally Rosie enjoyed the walk, but this morning she was troubled by what might await her later that day when she went to the dancing booth. She was certain that Angus Gee was going to try to take advantage of her, and she knew that she would need all her cunning and hard-won experience to get the money she was owed without surrendering to him. Head bent, deeply engrossed in her thoughts, she was unaware of the distant troop of cavalry approaching the opposite bank of the broad river.

'Form line to front! March!' Sergeant-Major Henry Peebles' stentorian orders rang out above the muffled thudding of hooves and jingling of harnesses. 'Prepare to halt! Halt! Prepare to dismount! Dismount! Make much of your horses!'

As the men patted and stroked their mounts, Peebles dismounted and gave his own horse into the keeping of the nearest soldier, then walked along the long single rank of the troop.

In his early thirties, powerfully built, his florid features adorned with black mutton-chop whiskers, Henry Peebles possessed brutal good looks that greatly appealed to certain types of women. He frowned disgruntedly as he took in the dusty, travel-grimed appearance of horses and men, in sharp contrast to his own glittering resplendence and glossy-groomed horse.

'All NCOs to me on the double!' he roared.

'Here, Bernie, take me horse.' Jack Collier handed the reins to the man next to him and ran in answer to the summons.

Henry Peebles scowled at the small group gathered in front of him.

'Stand to attention! I don't know how the hell any of you lot ever got your stripes. This troop's in shit order. I've seen cleaner dustmen. You call yourselves soldiers? This morning's been my first sight of you lot, and

I hope to God it's going to be my last.'

The sergeant and two corporals exchanged resentful glances, and Peebles instantly challenged them. 'If any of you has got anything to say, then let's be hearing it. Speak up, Sergeant.'

The grey-haired Sergeant Doolan said nothing, and Peebles ordered sharply, 'Speak up, Sergeant. Give me your thoughts. That's an order.'

Doolan cleared his throat and in a lilting Irish brogue stammered nervously, 'Sure now, Sergeant-Major, we been on the march for four days and nights and only stopping to snatch a couple or three hours' kip of a night. We've had no chance to do any cleaning or grooming.'

Peebles turned to the corporals. 'And what about you two? Have you got any bollocks excuses to give me?' He deliberately allowed the silence to lengthen interminably. The NCOs stood motionless, eyes fixed to the front, their faces expressionless.

Peebles sneered. 'No, you'll wait till me back's turned, won't you? And then you'll be shooting your mouths off. That's the coward's way, aren't it?'

Jack Collier was stung into giving an angry reply. 'We're not cowards, Sergeant-Major! And for your information, I don't think that what Sergeant Doolan told you is bollocks. It's no wonder we're in shit order after marching like we've been. You'd be looking like us if you'd been with us on the march.'

Peebles assumed an expression of dismay. 'Oh my God! It speaks!' He stepped close to Jack Collier so that their faces were only inches apart. 'What's your name,' he hissed.

'Collier, Sergeant-Major. Corporal Jack Collier.'

'Well, for your information, Corporal Jack Collier, I'm only delivering you lot to Hounslow Barracks, then I'm posted elsewhere. And that's a bloody good job for you, my buck, because I don't like your attitude.'

He stepped back. 'You've got half an hour to get this shower of shit looking something like soldiers. Get on with it.'

Jack went back to his horse, seething with anger.

'I knew that Peebles 'ud had a go at you, Jack. I knows the bastard of old. I've come across him a lot of times,' Bernie said sympathetically.

'But where has he sprung from?' Jack was mystified. 'I've been in this regiment man and boy, and never clapped eyes on him until this morning.'

'Nor probably won't ever again, because he's a proper will-o'-the-wisp.' Bernie grinned wryly. 'He was with the Seventeenth Lancers for a bit while I was serving with them. Only a trumpeter then, he was. Next time I saw him, he was full sergeant in the Eleventh Hussars. And now here he is popping up again as a bloody troop sergeant-major in our mob! I reckon he's some high-up officer's bastard, because he keeps on getting promoted but he serves his time playing drill instructor to the bloody yeomanry regiments.' Bernie chuckled enviously. 'Nice work if you can get it. He's a jammy bugger, right enough.'

Jack scowled. 'I just hope that I'm equal in rank if ever I meet up with him again, because then he won't be able to hide behind his stripes and crown.'

Returning along the river bank, Rosie noticed the soldiers across the broad flow of grey water. She stared curiously, wondering what type of cavalrymen they were, the vivid image of Jack Collier springing up in her mind. Rosie recalled him talking to her of Heavies and Lights, Hussars, Lancers and Dragoons.

Her shawl slipped down to her shoulders, and she walked on with her head uncovered, her long, luxuriant auburn hair flowing free down her back.

'Stand to your horses! Prepare to mount! Mount!' Henry Peebles bellowed, and the long line of men sprang into their saddles with a practised ease.

'Threes right! March! Leading threes left wheel! Forward! Trot!'

The troop column, with Henry Peebles at their head, moved parallel with and ahead of Rosie on the opposite side of the river.

She was some twenty yards from the bridge as the leading horsemen stepped on to it on the Eton side, and she halted to watch them pass. Her appearance invoked lewd smirks and whispered comments from the cavalry-men.

'Be silent, damn you!' Henry Peebles roared. 'I'll have the next man who makes a sound on a charge!'

But one man was too shocked to do anything but stare in silent disbelief, twisting his head to keep her in sight for as long as he could.

'It can't be her!' Jack Collier doubted his own eyesight. 'I can't be seeing right. It can't be Rosie! It can't be...'

Twenty-Six

'A toast, Gennulmen! I give you a toast!' Angus Gee clambered to his feet and stood swaying drunkenly, spilling wine from his glass as he raised it high.

The half-dozen men around the long table were all in stages of advanced inebriation, from glassy-eyed owlish stares to comatose collapse. Only one of them managed to rise to his feet, and the next instant he crumpled to the ground in slow motion.

'To our prosperous future, all the drink we'll swallow, and all the women we'll have,' Angus Gee slurred, then sat heavily down on his chair, dropping his glass. 'Rosie, bring me a drink,' he shouted.

Behind the long bar, Rosie sighed wearily and filled a fresh glass with wine, then brought it to the man. He leared blearily at her.

'Can I please have my wages, Mr Gee? It's long past midnight, and I'm very tired. I want to go to my lodging.'

'I need you here,' he mumbled. 'To serve my friends.'

Rosie shook her head. 'They don't need any more serving, Mr Gee. They're all too drunk to be able to drink any more.'

'Come here and give me a kiss.' He threw the fresh glass aside and grabbed at Rosie, but she had been expecting this and easily evaded his hands.

'Just give me my wages, will you please?'

'You'll get your wages after you've given me what I want.' He became surly.

'And what's that, Mr Gee?' she asked, already knowing what the answer would be.

'I want you!'

'You're getting nothing from me,' she told him angrily. 'Now please give me what you owe me, and let me leave.'

He belched, then patted his pocket, chinking the coins it held. 'Here's your wages. Come and take them.'

Drunk though he was, Angus Gee was still an exceptionally strong man, and Rosie knew that he totally outmatched her physically. If he managed to grab her, she would stand little or no chance against him.

'Put them on the table there.' She pointed

to a spot beyond his reach. 'Just toss my money there.'

'Alright, if that's what you want.'

To her surprise he readily agreed, and to her even greater surprise, he said, 'And I'm giving you the bonus I promised as well.'

Pulling two golden sovereigns out of his pocket he held them under the lamplight, moving them so that they glimmered temptingly.

'Here, Rosie, you take them.' He rolled the coins along the table, and they swerved and fell off the edge.

Rosie instinctively tried to catch them, and in that fleeting instant when she was off-guard, Angus Gee made his move, suddenly propelling himself from the chair. His hands grabbed her long billowing skirt, jerking hard, bringing her stumbling towards him. Their bodies collided and his arms locked around her, crushing the breath from her lungs, trapping both her arms.

'I gotcha now!' His stinking breath gusted into her face and his slobbering wet lips clamped upon her mouth.

Rosie felt as if she were choking, but she fought desperately to twist free, trying to kick his shins.

His right hand moved downwards to tug her skirt upwards and this released her left arm. She clenched her small fist and hammered it on the side of his head, but the blows had no effect. She felt his fingernails clawing at the flesh of her inner thighs, tearing the

184

soft skin, and in sheer desperation she stiffened her thumb and rammed it into his right eyeball. Gee bellowed in pain, his grip slackened and she broke free.

'You bitch! I'll kill you!' he bawled, and came at her with swinging fists, his face murderous.

Panicking, Rosie turned and ran for the door, wrenched it open and escaped into the night. Gee gave chase, but after only a few dozen yards he came to a standstill and doubled over, retching and gasping for breath.

Once her initial panic subsided, Rosie realized that she was no longer being chased and, panting heavily, slowed to a walk. As her jangled nerves calmed a wave of despair washed over her instead.

'Dear Christ! What do I do now?'

Her sweating body and face chilled rapidly in the cold night breezes. She untied the white serving apron from her waist and wrapped it around her upper body.

'The bastard's even got the best of this swop, hasn't he? I've got his rotten cotton apron, and he's got my wool shawl.'

A splattering of raindrops flurried on the breeze, and the prospect of being drenched to her skin added to Rosie's misery.

'I'll have to get into shelter. The last thing I need now is to catch my death of cold. I just hope the old witch is asleep.'

Light-headed with hunger, her body aching with weariness, Rosie trudged slowly back to

Old Millie Errol's hovel.

Her heart sank even lower when she reached the warped front door and saw the glimmer of candlelight through the window. For a moment or two she stood undecided, wondering whether it might be best for her to try and find shelter elsewhere, but then the rain turned into a downpour, and, reluctantly choosing the lesser of two evils, Rosie steeled herself, lifted the latch and stepped inside.

A blue-uniformed soldier with a round forage cap perched rakishly on his head was sitting on the stool before the fireless grate, a gin bottle on the floor beside him.

'Hello Rosie,' he said quietly.

Rosie's jaw dropped in stupefied shock. Jack Collier rose and came to her, taking her hands in his, drawing her away from the open door, and pushing it shut with his foot.

'Now I don't want you running away from me again. Not before I've had a chance to talk to you.'

'How did you find me?' she managed to blurt out.

'It took me bloody hours. I must have knocked on nearly every door in Windsor.'

'But how did you know I was in Windsor?'

'This morning, when we were crossing the bridge. I saw you this morning. I couldn't believe me own eyes at first.' He grinned happily.

'Where's Millie Errol?' Rosie asked, bemused.

He let go her hands and pointed upwards.

'She's up there sleeping off the best part of a pint of gin. Don't worry, I've paid her your rent.'

'You shouldn't have. I've no money to pay you back with,' she protested.

He waved her protest aside and, putting his hands on her shoulders, gently pressed her down to sit on the stool.

'Just sit quiet and hear me out. I've missed you, Rosie. I've missed you real bad. It was like some sort of miracle when I saw you this morning.' His manner became deadly serious. 'I still want to marry you, and I don't give a bugger what you were in the past, and I don't blame you for it neither. I blame the evil bastards who forced you into it. So marry me, and forget all about what's past.'

It seemed unbelievable. This man wanted to marry her? He knew all about her past, and yet still he wanted to marry her?

Weary, hungry, cold and penniless, her flesh bruised and raw from Angus Gee's brutal assault, this offer of marriage seemed like a God-sent miracle to Rosie. Emotion welled up in her, and she broke down, sobbing helplessly.

'Bloody hell, Rosie! I'm asking you to marry me, not sentencing you to be hung,' he complained ruefully.

Blinded by her tears, she reached out for him, and he lifted her from the stool and cuddled her against him.

'I'll take it that you're saying yes, then, shall I?' He chuckled.

Rosie, her body shuddering with sobs, her eyes streaming, could only nod her head in wordless agreement.

Twenty-Seven

Hounslow Cavalry Barracks, October, 1853

Wearing civilian clothes, Lieutenant Charles Bronton left the barracks mid-morning. The breeze was exhilarating and the weak sunlight cheered the bleak aspect of the surrounding countryside. He cantered across the great swathe of Hounslow Heath where the blue-coated soldiers of his regiment were hard at work practising mounted sword drill and the hoarse commands of the troop sergeants carried clearly through the crisp air. Burnished blades glinted as the men drilled mechanically in perfect concert. There was not a single officer to be seen.

Charles Bronton frowned. During the years he had been serving in the cavalry, he had become thoroughly disenchanted with certain aspects of his profession. He had come to despise many of his fellow officers for their stupidity, their ignorance, their languid affectations. They had little interest in the practicalities of their profession, and even less in the welfare of the men they commanded. A good half of their number were absent on leave from the regiment at any one time, and the majority of those present spent their days fox-hunting and their nights gambling and drinking, living in luxury while their men festered in squalor.

The day-to-day administration and training of the regiment was left almost entirely in the hands of the senior NCOs and the training consisted of endless, mind-deadening ceremonial drill. Any teaching of fieldcraft, reconnaissance, outpost and skirmishing skills was virtually non-existent.

Charles's frown deepened. 'This system only serves to produce mindless automatons, brutalized by abuse, and disciplined by the lash. If I ever rise to command a regiment, I'll change things.'

But within scant seconds came the despondent realization that he would never rise to command any regiment. The system of purchase ensured that only wealthy officers could afford to pay the price for high rank. Men like himself, of straitened means, had no hope of promotion above his present rank. He would remain a lieutenant until the end of his service.

'Unless I marry into money. But where will I find a rich woman who'll take a penniless soldier for her husband?' he pondered.

Today was to be a rare holiday outing for him. He was going to meet his cousin, Eugenia, at Windsor station and spend the day with her. He touched spurs to his mount's flanks and set it to the gallop.

Periodic showers of red-hot smuts from the funnel of the engine spattered against the windows of the first-class carriage, and Eugenia Pacemore felt considerable sympathy for the less fortunate third-class passengers in their open carriages.

She peered out of the dirty glass pane at the green fields, huge market gardens and small clusters of buildings that the train was travelling past at what she considered to be breakneck speed.

The elegantly dressed, mustachioed man sitting opposite to her leaned forwards. 'That's Hounslow over there, Miss Pacemore. The cavalry barracks lies beyond, on the edge of the heath. But you'll not be able to see them from here.'

She smiled and nodded. 'I must ask my cousin to take me there, Captain Nolan, if his duties permit him, of course.'

His lustrous eyes twinkled. 'Well, if he can't then I will, Miss Pacemore, whether or no my duties permit me.'

Her smile broadened. 'But I won't permit you to neglect your duties on my account, Captain Nolan.'

Captain Louis Edward Nolan had travelled with Eugenia all the way from Carlsbad, after having been formally introduced by a mutual acquaintance following her departure from the Kaiserswerth Institute. During the journey back to England, Louis Nolan had proved to be a very pleasant companion and, despite the brevity of their acquaintance, a mutual fondness had blossomed.

The long train snaked around a curve and Nolan pointed through the window. 'Look, there's Windsor Castle. At this speed we'll be arriving soon.'

Eugenia stared at the distant ramparts with keen anticipation. 'I'm so looking forward to seeing my cousin again. It's been three years since I was last in England.'

Nolan smiled warmly at her. 'I expect that you'll be visiting your old friends as well.'

She shook her head. 'Truth to tell, I've many old acquaintances in this country, but no one that could be termed an old friend. Because of my father's ill health we lived a very solitary life. I shan't be doing any social visiting.'

A gleam of sympathy showed in the Irishman's lustrous dark eyes. 'Well, be assured of one fact, Miss Pacemore. You have a new friend, who admires you greatly, and who hopes to visit you as often as you will allow.'

His words caused her to feel a little shy and flustered. Sensing her reaction, he hastened to apologize. 'Do forgive me if I've presumed too much, and by doing so have offended you, Miss Pacemore. I've always been far to ready to rush in where others might fear to enter.'

'Oh no!' she was quick to reassure him. 'I'm not at all offended. I should greatly like to see you again in the future.'

'That's settled then.' He beamed happily. 'You shall introduce me to your cousin when we arrive at Windsor, and before we part we shall make arrangements for our next meeting. That will be very soon, I hope. In fact, I want to invite you both to dine with me at the Castle Hotel this very evening. Please say that you'll accept.'

Eugenia hesitated. 'But my cousin may already have made plans for this evening.'

'I'm sure that I can persuade him to alter any plans, if I'm given the opportunity to do so.'

'Very well.' She surrendered without any great reluctance. 'You shall have the opportunity, Captain Nolan.'

'Excellent!' Radiating satisfaction, he settled contentedly back into his seat.

Eugenia felt both pleased and flattered that this man should be so keen to further their relationship, and for a few seconds she fancifully wondered where it might lead. Then she forced herself to face the unpalatable fact that an old maid with little money and fast-fading looks could never hope for anything other than a platonic friendship with a man as physically attractive and personable as Louis Nolan.

'Never mind,' she thought philosophically. 'Enjoy his friendship for its own sake, and don't indulge in foolish fancies.'

The cousins hugged each other in the midst

of the noise and bustle of the station platform, and Louis Nolan stood back, watching them closely. He had been drawn towards Eugenia Pacemore from the very first time they met. To the fleeting glance, her thin features and figure were unremarkable, her beauty not immediately apparent, but the longer he had spent in her company, the stronger his initial feelings had become.

'The old saying is true, isn't it?' he told himself now. 'Beauty is in the eye of the beholder. And in my eyes she is beautiful, and her company delights me.' His gaze rested on Charles Bronton's remarkably handsome face and fine figure. 'I'm going to have to get into your good books very quickly, I think, because your cousin thinks the world of you, doesn't she?'

Eugenia led Charles up to Nolan and introduced the two men. Upon hearing the other man's name, Charles reacted with obvious excitement.

'Are you Captain Nolan, the author, sir? Captain Nolan of the Fifteenth Hussars?' he asked.

Louis Nolan grinned. 'The very same, sir.'

Charles was greatly impressed. 'It's an honour to meet you, sir. I've studied all your works. Would it be possible for us to meet at some time and talk together? There are many things I want to ask you about.'

Nolan chuckled and winked at Eugenia. 'There now, Miss Pacemore, did I not say that given the opportunity I might well be able to persuade your cousin and yourself to dine with me this evening at the Castle Hotel?'

'Indeed, we will happily dine with you, sir,' Charles said enthusiastically. 'By coincidence I've taken rooms at that same hotel for my cousin and myself, so will you do us both the honour of being our guest this evening?'

'Only on condition that you, in return, will do me the honour of being my guest tomorrow?' The Irishman bowed to Eugenia. 'Will you agree to those terms, Miss Pacemore?'

She felt a glow of happiness. 'Indeed I will, sir.'

'That's settled then. And now I'll have our baggage taken up to the hotel. I'm sure that you have much to say to each other, so I'll leave you in peace until this evening.' He beamed at them, then gestured excitedly at a passing porter. 'You there! Come with me, I've a job for you.'

Eugenia and Charles turned and hugged once more, then linked arms and walked from the station. They spent the hours until dinner talking, and Eugenia told him all about her life at Kaiserswerth.

Charles listened silently and when she finished, he kissed her cheek.

'I'm so proud of you, Genia. But I have to confess that it worries me to see how thin and pale you've become. You've been over-taxing your strength. I know of a cottage that you can rent not far from the barracks. I want you to stay there to rest and recuperate, and live as befits your station in life.'

'But I'm in perfect health, Charlie,' she argued. 'And I've no intention of reverting to my old useless way of living. I enjoy working as a sick-nurse.'

'But you surely can't intend to continue doing such work here in England,' he said incredulously. 'The hospital nurses are the dregs of humanity – dirty, drunken, thieving harridans.'

'I've no wish to quarrel with you, Charlie, but I will not be dictated to by you or anyone else,' she said with quiet determination. 'I shall be working as a sick-nurse here in England.' She lifted her hand to ward off his protest. 'I totally agree with what you say about the nurses in the general hospitals. But I've applied for a nursing post in London, in the Institution for the Care of Sick Gentlewomen. The superintendent there is a lady of good family, a Miss Florence Nightingale, who was trained at Kaiserswerth like me. I met her there shortly before she returned to England. You've no cause for concern about the standards she expects of her staff. Miss Nightingale does not tolerate dirty, drunken, thieving harridans, I assure you. She is a highly moral Christian lady, and, I might add, has many friends in high places.'

'Yes, but...'

'No buts, Charlie!' She did not give him any chance to renew the argument. 'I shall be going to London to work in that institution, and nothing that you can do or say will change my mind about it.'

Knowing how stubborn she could be, Charles reluctantly accepted defeat.

In the dining room that evening, Louis Nolan was waiting for them in company with another man, whom he introduced as Major William Beaston, an old friend of his.

Beaston – tall, heavily built, sun-bronzed and balding – was an Indian veteran like Nolan, and had recently won great distinction fighting as a mercenary with the Turkish army against the Russians.

The conversation over dinner was a revelation to Charles, who was glad that he was not alone in his misgivings about the British Army. Listening to the forthright strictures of the two men, he began to hope that things could be changed for the better if only there were sufficient men like them prepared to challenge the incompetence of the aristocratic high command.

'The army is fit only for the parade ground. It has been turned into a tailor's dummy, all gold braid and finery. I wonder that we don't form a Corps of Milliners.'

'Wellington has proven to be the ruination of today's army. He's been dead for two years and still he rules, because all the senior commanders can think of is the successes he gained fifty years ago. Any new ideas are stifled. But what was successful fifty years ago will not be successful in this modern day.'

'We need to rid ourselves of the control of

the aristocracy. Promotion must be gained on merit, not on wealth and family connections. We should get rid of the entire command staff and replace them with younger men who have seen active service in India and elsewhere.'

'The French have learned much from their Algerian campaigns, and have adapted their tactics and modernized. They will prove immeasurably superior to us when on campaign.'

'The British cavalry is the most disciplined, best-mounted cavalry in the world, and it's led by the most stupid, useless muffs the world has ever seen. Its training is no preparation for modern warfare.'

Charles could not help but feel a sense of vindication as he heard many of his own opinions confirmed by these hardened veterans.

'Where do you go next, sir?' he asked Major Beaston.

'I'm returning to Constantinople within the week. I am to command a corps of Bashi-Bazouks. They're the irregular cavalry of the Turks. A prize bunch of thieves, cut-throats and jailbirds, but they put the wind up the Russians.'

'Can they match the Cossacks?' Charles asked.

'No.' Beaston shook his head. 'Because the Cossacks are tribal, and fight for the honour of their clans. The Bashi-Bazouks are a mixture drawn from a dozen races. Mongrels with no pedigree.' He smiled. 'But it is great fun to lead them.'

'I wish I had experience of war,' Charles said wistfully.

'And you will experience it before too long,' Beaston declared positively. 'My friends in the government have assured me that we are going to fight the Russians, because we can't allow them to take Constantinople, and so gain control of the Dardanelles Straits. If they gain that control they will be able to challenge us for dominance of the Mediterranean. So the next time that we all meet again, it might well be on the battlefield.'

'Let's drink to that,' Nolan said excitedly and raised his glass. 'To the battlefield that we'll meet on!'

'To the battlefield that we'll meet on!' Charles echoed, and fervently hoped that it would soon become reality.

Eugenia's enjoyment was suddenly overshadowed by the fear that her beloved cousin might have to go to war, and she felt her heart chill at the prospect.

'God, please don't let it happen,' she prayed silently. 'Please don't let there be a war between us and the Russians.'

Twenty-Eight

Hounslow Cavalry Barracks, November, 1853

As the first bleak grey light of dawn entered the fetid gloom of the barrack room, the strident trumpet call of reveille echoed over the vast parade ground and the long, two-storeyed, red-brick blocks that surrounded it. The bottom storey of each block served as stables, with the men's living quarters above.

Rosie Collier opened her eyes and for a few brief moments stared up at the stained plaster of the ceiling. Beside her in the narrow cot her husband snorted into wakefulness. Rosie slipped from beneath the sheets, pulled her gown down over her head and thrust aside the hanging blanket that shielded this corner of the room. She stood for a moment accustoming her eyes to the gloom.

The long, narrow, low-ceilinged room stank of stale cooking and unwashed flesh, along with the sour pungency of the wooden barrel which served as a night urinal, and the acrid reek rising from the stables below. Two rows of close-set wooden cots for the men lined the walls, and each of the room's corners was occupied by the married families, their only privacy afforded by hanging blankets from ropes. The walls were lined with spaced shelves on which the men's equipments were neatly stacked. Swords and shakoes hung from wooden wall pegs.

B Troop were awaking now, yawning, stretching, groaning and scratching. Dressing themselves in white canvas jackets and tunics, pulling leather wellington boots on to their feet, they belched, farted, and fouled the air with myriad body odours. Behind the blanketed corners, babies squalled and children squabbled.

A sense of depression overwhelmed Rosie. For four years now she had lived in squalid quarters like these, cooking, cleaning, laundering for the men in her barrack room, in return for which she received half-rations and, if she was lucky, a few pence as wages from the men.

Behind her, her husband groaned. 'My bleedin' head's splitting. What are you standing there for? Get the coffee ready, will you?'

Rosie made no reply. Very soon after their marriage, her husband had begun to display the major flaw in his character. He was a heavy drinker, and when drunk, or hungover as he was this morning, he could become violently angry towards anyone who crossed or provoked him in any way. Rosie had quickly learned when it was wisest to stay silent.

A greasy-haired middle-aged woman was

bending over the fireplace, which was set midway along the wall. Rosie fought off her momentary depression and went to join her.

'Morning, Dorcas.'

'Morning, Rosie. The coffee's boiled.' Dorcas Murphy stirred the brown liquid that was bubbling in a large iron pot suspended from a chain above the fire. 'Any news?'

'Yes. I came on during the night.'

'Another false alarm then.'

'Yes, it was,' Rosie agreed sadly. 'But better to have a false alarm than know I'm carrying and then lose it like I did the others.'

She had already suffered two miscarriages since her marriage, and above all else she was hungering for a child of her own to love and cherish. She also hoped that having a child of their own might make Jack control his drinking.

Two more women appeared from their own corners and busied themselves in setting up trestle tables and benches between the rows of cots.

'Morning, Annie. Morning, Nell,' said Rosie.

From the tall cupboard standing to one side of the fireplace, Rosie lifted a pile of tin basins and spaced them along the tabletops.

Some of the men seated themselves on the benches, and Dorcas Murphy carried the iron pot and set it down on the table. She ladled coffee into the basins while Rosie distributed chunks of grey-looking stale bread.

Her husband glowered at her as she handed

him his portion, so she kept her eyes downcast, knowing that in his present mood he would lash out at her on the slightest provocation.

There was little conversation, only a few muttered exchanges, and the general mood was surly. The men had been paid the previous day, and the majority of them had spent their meagre wages on drink that same night. Now they were sullenly contemplating another penniless week.

Colum Murphy, the male image of his wife, tasted the gritty, unsweetened coffee, and angrily accused Dorcas. 'You've not scoured the pot out this morning, have you, you dirty cow? I can taste piss in this coffee. You're useless!'

Her decayed teeth bared in a grotesque parody of a seductive smile as she ran her hands down over her huge, flaccid breasts.

'You wasn't calling me useless last night, was you, Murphy? It's no wonder I hadn't got the strength left to scour the pot, after the seeing-to you give me last night.'

Then she said to the other women, 'I don't think! He couldn't get it up again. He aren't been able to get it up for years.'

Murphy's temper exploded. He cursed and hurled the tin basin at her head, sending its contents splashing over the men nearest him, who ducked and angrily cursed in their turn.

The basin hit Dorcas on her forehead and her eyes blazed in rage. Moving with a cat-like agility that belied her bulk, she snatched a long sabre from its peg-hung scabbard and came for her husband, jabbing the sharp point at his throat.

Jack Collier reacted instantaneously, grabbing Dorcas's sabre-wielding arm and twisting it brutally until she cried out in pain and dropped the weapon.

'That's enough from both of you,' Collier roared. 'You get on down to the stables, Murphy, and you put the blade back where you got it from, Dorcas. Or I'll have you both on a charge.'

Still mouthing threats at each other, they obeyed him nonetheless. Jack Collier tasted from his own basin, and swore in disgust.

'It does taste of piss.' He turned furiously on his companions. 'If I catch the dirty bastard who's pissing in the cook pot, I'll have his guts for garters.'

A leathery-featured veteran picked up his basin and gulped the contents down his whiskered throat, then belched and said contemptuously, 'I've drunk water with shit floating in it many's the time when I was out in the Sikh wars. We was real soldiers back then, though. Not a set o' soft bloody nancy boys like you lot are today.'

Jack Collier glared at the man. 'If I hear another word from you about your time in India, Conky, I swear I'll break your head for you.'

Before Conky White could reply, a trumpet pealed from the parade ground.

'All of you get downstairs. Can't you hear

Stables being sounded?'

As the men clattered out of the door, along the outside verandah and down the steps, Jack Collier said to Rosie, 'Make sure everything is properly done before you comes to Windsor. I don't want to give that bastard Peebles any excuse to put me on a charge.'

He hurried out to join his comrades, and Rosie sighed. Henry Peebles had rejoined the regiment the previous week as sergeant-major of B Troop, and for some reason unknown to Rosie there had been instant enmity between him and Jack.

'Come on you kids. Come and get your breakfasts,' Dorcas bellowed, and a swarm of half-naked, tousle-haired urchins came hurrying to receive their bread and coffee from Rosie's hands.

Both Nell Harrison and Annie Bartleet, whose frail, emaciated body was periodically racked by fits of tubercular coughing, fetched out swaddled babies and proceeded to breast-feed them.

'How are we going to split it today, Rosie?' Dorcas asked.

Although she was the youngest in the room, Rosie was the accepted leader of the women, a fact which owed as much to her intelligence and strong mentality as to her husband being the ranking NCO.

'Me, you and Annie will do the laundering, and Nell can clean the room and keep the kids quiet. As soon as we're done with the work, we'll go to Windsor.'

Nell, a small, wizened woman, who looked far older than her twenty-five years, complained. 'That aren't fair, leaving me to clean up by meself, and watch all these bloody kids.'

'Oh, give over, will you,' Dorcas snapped irritably. 'You're always whingeing about summat or other. That's all we ever hears from you, except when you're causing trouble for others.'

Rosie quickly intervened before the quarrel worsened. 'Leave it now, both of you. Just do what you can manage, Nell, and when I get back, I'll help you.'

'Well, it just aren't fair to leave me by meself,' the woman snarled, and went back to her corner bed.

Nell Harrison was an unpleasant woman, who continually carped and moaned about her lot in life, and frequently caused trouble in the room.

'And how am I going to carry me babby all the way to Windsor? I aren't feeling very well today. It's alright for you lot, you'm all a sight stronger than me,' Nell's voice whined from behind the blanket curtain.

Rosie fought down her irritation. 'You won't have to carry him. I've got a ride fixed up for us with the ration carts.'

'Oh yeah. You've been making eyes at the commissary again, have you, girl? What else have you been doing to him, that's what I'd like to know,' Dorcas gibed, then pushed her finger into her mouth and made lewd sucking sounds.

'Get stuffed, will you,' Rosie retorted good-naturedly.

There was a thump and jingle of spurred boots on the wooden-planked verandah and the door was pushed open. The women turned their heads and, in unison, aggressively challenged the entrance of a corporal.

'What's you want, Smailes?'

The man chuckled. 'And a fine good morning to you also, ladies. I've brung you a new guest to share your palace.'

Nell Harrison immediately came back to join the others and stared with avid interest at the young man who followed the corporal into the room. He was tall and slender, with a sweep of long blond hair on which a velvet cap was slanted at a dashing angle. His clothing, although bearing the scuffs and dirt of hard usage, was elegantly tailored. His grimy, greasy features were almost effeminately good-looking.

'This Johnny Raw is to billet with your troop for a couple of days,' Smailes informed them. To the newcomer he said, 'Report to the stores after dinner to collect your slops. You'll be given further instructions then.' He saluted the women mockingly. 'I shall now leave this fine gentleman to your tender mercies, ladies. And God help the poor bastard!' He exited under a volley of jeers.

'Come and sit here, my 'andsome,' Dorcas Murphy beckoned. After a moment's hesitation, the young man came to sit on the end of the bench.

The urchins around the tables were silent, staring with wide-eyed curiosity at the new recruit, the 'Johnny Raw'.

Dorcas proffered a chunk of bread. 'Have summat to eat.'

'No, thank you, ma'am,' he said politely. 'I'm not hungry.'

She grinned with a lascivious wink. 'Well, maybe you've the hunger for summat else, my 'andsome. And I might be sweet-talked into giving you a bit o' that, if you plays your cards right.'

Her companions laughed raucously. 'Steady on, Dorcas, you'll have him thinking that he's come among a load o' trollops who'm after his money.'

'I wasn't thinking o' charging him for it. He can 'ave it for nothing!'

There was another outburst of shrieking laughter, and the young man appeared ill at ease.

'Leave him alone now,' Rosie chided. 'Pay no attention to them,' she said to him. 'Here, drink this.' She handed him a pannikin of coffee. 'What's your name?'

'Arthur Sinclair, ma'am.' His voice was soft, his diction that of a gentleman.

'Oh, he talks just like the officers does, don't he?' Annie exclaimed admiringly.

'Where d'you come from? You looks like you've had a hard time of it. Why have you 'listed?' Dorcas volleyed questions at him.

Rosie could see the purple shadows beneath

his hazel-coloured eyes, the drawn weariness of near exhaustion in his face, and interjected sympathetically. 'You look very tired. When did you last get some sleep?'

He kneaded his face with his long, slender fingers. 'The night before last, ma'am. I must confess, I'm feeling very tired at the moment.'

'Then you'd better get some rest. Use that bed there at the end, next to the corner space, if you want to,' Rosie said.

'But that's Billy Jones's pit,' Nell objected.

'And Billy Jones won't come out of the cells until next week, will he?' Rosie quelled the objection. 'Go on, Arthur Sinclair, use the bed. I'll wake you when dinner's ready.'

Sinclair's head was spinning with tiredness. 'Thank you for your kindness, ma'am. If you'll excuse me now, ladies, I really do need to rest for a little while.'

He stood up, bowed his head politely and went to the cot. Removing only his cap, he lay down on the straw-filled canvas palliasse and within moments collapsed into exhausted sleep.

Rosie went to her corner and brought out a brown blanket. As she covered him, he moved restlessly, and muttered as if he was afflicted by bad dreams.

Vaguely troubled, Rosie stood looking down at his effeminately handsome face, unwelcome memories welling up in her mind.

'Angel! You remind me of Angel!' she suddenly realized. 'Well, I hope for your own sake that you're not soft and gentle like he was. Because your life won't be worth living if you are. There's no place for the soft and gentle in this army.'

Twenty-Nine

In Windsor Great Park the glittering squadrons of cavalry wheeled and advanced and retired in obedience to the calls of the battle bugles, and the crowds of spectators applauded each succeeding evolution, men cheering, women waving their handkerchiefs like a forest of small banners fluttering above their bonnets.

Eugenia Pacemore and Louis Nolan were standing in the dense crowd some little distance from the raised platform on which Archduke Johannes of Guter-Waldgrave was sitting in company with resplendently uniformed senior officers and a bevy of courtiers.

It was almost a month since Eugenia had arrived in Windsor, and during that period she and Louis Nolan had spent many hours together, meeting virtually every day or evening. In fact, she had seen more of Nolan than of her cousin, whose duties had claimed much of his time. Her feelings for Louis Nolan had deepened with each passing day, and though she tried to fight against it hope burgeoned in her heart that this excitable Irishman might well return her affection for him, that there might be a chance of marriage in the future.

'Well, Eugenia, what do you think of them?' he asked her now.

'I think they are very fine, Louis.' Admiration throbbed in her voice. 'They look superb.'

'Indeed they do.' Nolan chuckled drily. 'But a couple of weeks' campaigning would reduce them to pitiful scarecrows.'

Gloved fingers tapped him hard on his shoulder and he turned to be confronted by the angry scowl of an exquisitely dressed and lavishly mustachioed young man.

'Did I hear you cowwectly, sir?' the young man demanded, his brandy-laden breath gusting against Nolan's face. 'Did you wefer to my wegiment as pitiful scarecwows?'

The young man's trio of companions, equally exquisitely tailored and lavishly mustachioed, crowded in upon their friend's shoulders.

'What's the cad saying, Rufus?'

'Is he being insulting?'

Nolan's face glowed with quick anger. He instantly recognized these young men as being cavalry officers of the type he despised, commonly known as Plungers and Heavy Swells: rich men's sons and cadets of aristocratic families, who had joined the cavalry merely because it was the fashionable thing to do, and whose military service was spent in self-indulgence and pleasure-seeking. Plungers and Heavy Swells deliberately affected speech impediments, drawling their words and clipping sentences short. They always assumed an air of languid boredom, except when they were looking for trouble and excitement, as these four undoubtedly were.

Nolan glared at the young soldier. 'You are intruding upon a private conversation, young man. Be kind enough to go about your business.'

'Don't take that tone with me,' Lieutenant, the Honourable Rufus Tytherleigh Bart snarled threateningly. 'I shall have to teach you to show respect, else.'

Charles Bronton, wearing the blue and silver dress uniform and high-plumed shako of the 20th Light Dragoons, interposed himself between the two men, and pushed the young man back.

'I think you should apologize for your rudeness towards this gentleman, Mr Tytherleigh, and then leave us alone,' he stated firmly.

Tytherleigh took a further step backwards, a defiant sneer twisting his lips. 'And what do we have here, gentlemen? Our own adjutant springing to the defence of a cad who, by the look of him, is a distressed commissary.'

His friends erupted with loud guffaws and bawled plaudits.

'Distwessed Commissawy! That's pwiceless, Wufus. Oh, I do like that one, weally I do!

Pwiceless! Pwiceless!'

'What's amiss here, gentlemen?' A tall officer, also in the blue and silver full dress uniform, came pushing through the crowd.

The four young men stiffened and Tytherleigh blustered. 'This civilian was insulting the regiment, sir.'

The newcomer's light-blue eyes were hard beneath the polished black peak of his white-plumed shako.

'Indeed I was not, sir,' Louis Nolan protested angrily. 'It is I who has been insulted here.'

'Might I enquire your name, sir?' the newcomer asked.

'My name, sir, is Nolan. Captain Louis Nolan of the Fifteenth Hussars. And you, sir, who might you be?'

The officer's light-blue eyes sparked in recognition as he heard the name, and his manner was suddenly tinged with respect. He touched his hand to his shako brim in salute.

'Major Philip Fothergill, Twentieth Light Dragoons. I have heard much about you, Captain Nolan.' He gestured at the four young exquisites. 'Pray accept my most sincere apologies for whatever offence these gentlemen have caused you, sir. Be assured that I shall have harsh words with them.'

'I accept that apology, sir.' Nolan bowed slightly.

Fothergill scowled at the offenders, who made a hurried retreat, and then smiled pleasantly at Nolan. 'I hope that we may meet again, sir, and further our acquaintance. Regretfully, my duties require me to leave you now.' With a final salute, he departed.

Charles watched the flowing white plume of Fothergill's tall black shako bobbing among the heads of the crowd, then turned and grinned ruefully.

'Well, so much for my comrades-in-arms. Charming fellows, aren't they?'

Nolan's expression was sour. 'Stupid clowns! But there will be some good men also in your mess, I'm sure. What is Major Fothergill like?'

'A rigid martinet. Very keen on ceremonial drills, but takes little interest in anything else. Personally, I find him to be an arrogant, pompous snob.'

Nolan chuckled as his good temper re-asserted itself. 'I've known a couple of Fothergills in the past. They were also arrogant, pompous snobs, as I recall. It must come with the name.'

Eugenia uneasily recalled how Major Philip Fothergill had totally ignored her cousin. 'Have you quarrelled with him, Charlie? Only he didn't even give you the courtesy of a greeting.'

Charles smiled wryly. 'It's as I said, Genia. Fothergill is an arrogant snob who sucks up to the rich and powerful. Since I'm sadly lacking in either personal wealth or social standing, however, he does his best to ignore my very existence.'

'How stupid the man must be!' Eugenia

snapped, angry that her beloved cousin could be slighted in this way.

'Oh, I doubt that he's stupid, Eugenia,' Louis Nolan observed shrewdly. 'Men like him are rarely stupid in the way they pursue their own selfish ends. On the contrary, they're normally ruthlessly cunning, and will tread anyone down into the mud to gain their goals. I'd advise you to be wary of him, Charlie.'

A cold premonition suddenly shivered through Eugenia, and instinctively she silently begged, 'Dear God, don't let that man Fothergill do anything to harm my Charlie. Please, don't let him.'

A sprawl of tents, stalls, sideshows and fairground rides had been erected beyond the outermost edges of the crowd, and hucksters, pedlars and showmen of all descriptions were patiently waiting for the Grand Review to come to an end.

A pair of two-horsed ration carts skirted the fairground and headed towards the area where the regimental tent and horse lines were laid out in rigid rows.

Sergeant-Major Henry Peebles rode alongside the cart on which Rosie was perched among the bulging sacks and small wooden kegs behind the driver. He grinned at her.

'My Christ, but you're looking very toothsome, Rosie Collier. If you was put between two pieces of bread, I'd eat you and love every single mouthful.'

'You'll need stronger teeth than you've got now to be able to chew me, Sergeant-Major. I'm a lot tougher than I look,' she bantered light-heartedly.

'I reckon you ought to have a drink with me while we're here, Rosie. Just for friendship. What do you say?'

She shook her head in refusal. 'I'm a married woman.'

At Rosie's side, Nell Harrison's baby began to wail. 'This bloody babby is wearing me to a shadow. He wants more feeding than the bloody regiment.' She unbuttoned her bodice and pulled out her flaccid, drooping breast.

Henry Peebles' florid face scowled. 'Cover yourself up, woman. There's gentry who can see what you're doing and be offended by it.'

'I'm only doing what's natural,' she retorted defiantly. 'And if anybody's offended by a babby being fed, then bollocks to 'em!'

'Don't you be giving me any of your lip,' Peebles warned. 'Or you'll be saying hello to trouble.'

'Trouble?' Nell scoffed angrily. 'Trouble? That's the only thing I've ever known since I come to this bloody regiment.'

'And you're going the right way to knowing it even better,' he warned. 'I'll be having a word with the adjutant about you. We'll see how much you like being kicked out from the regiment, shall we?'

Rosie saw the anger glinting in Peebles' bloodshot eyes and realized that he was not merely blustering empty threats. She had

215

witnessed the fate of other soldiers' wives who had been expelled from the barracks for numerous reasons and misdemeanours. Even if their husbands gave them all the wages they earned, it would still only be a beggarly pittance. Not nearly enough to buy food, clothes or shelter of even the meanest sort. All too many of these expelled women were forced into prostitution to keep their children and themselves from starving. It was either that or enter the workhouse, where they would be forcibly separated from their children and would lead an existence of bleak hopelessness.

Although Rosie disliked Nell Harrison, she did not wish such a fate upon her children. She quickly slipped the shawl from her shoulders and draped it around the other woman, so that its folds shielded the feeding baby. Then she tried to deflect the irate man's attention from Nell.

'Now she's all covered up, and can't offend anybody, can she?' Rosie smiled coquettishly. 'And about that drink you invited me to have. I wouldn't say no to a drop of gin later on, just for the sake of friendship.'

Her ploy succeeded, and he instantly lost interest in Nell Harrison. 'You shall have a bottle of it, if you want, Rosie, my sweet.' He preened. 'When you're a friend of Henry Peebles, you can live on the fat of the land.'

She demurely dropped her gaze. 'A drop of gin will be quite enough for me. Only the one, though, and I'll have to tell my husband about it.'

'Alright then. Once the duty's finished, we'll have that drink.' Grinning with satisfaction, he cantered on ahead of the carts.

Rosie immediately regretted the impulse that had made her intervene in the dispute. Nell frowned disparagingly. 'I shouldn't think that your Jack 'ull take kindly to hearing that his missus is so friendly with Henry Peebles. A corporal's woman going on the razzle with a sergeant-major? That's acting like a whore, that is!'

For a brief second, Rosie couldn't believe what she was hearing. Then resentment flared at this injustice, and she retorted angrily, 'I don't want to drink with Peebles! I only agreed to it to save your neck, you ungrateful cow!'

'Don't you call me a cow!' Nell spat out venomously. 'Who do you think you are? Acting like Lady Muck all the time, giving out your orders. One of these days I'll finish the job some other bugger started to do on your face, you stuck-up bitch!'

Rosie was very close to hitting the other woman, and only the presence of the baby stopped her. 'You'd do well to shut your mouth, you miserable cow, before I do it for you,' she shouted.

The cart lurched to a halt, and the driver turned his head and jeered. 'That's it, girls. Start tearing each other's eyes out, why don't you? The adjutant's standing over there, and I reckon he'll enjoy seeing a good fight.'

217

Both women stared to where, some distance away, Charles Bronton was standing in company with a man and woman. Knowing that any public disorder among the regimental women was strictly forbidden, they instantly abandoned their quarrel. The driver grinned and set the cart into motion once more.

The cavalry squadrons were now trotting from the review ground to be replaced by marching companies of scarlet-coated infantry. Henry Peebles rode back to the carts. 'Pull up over there in front of our tents,' he ordered.

When they stopped, Rosie helped the driver to unload the sacks of bread and hard cheeses, and to set up the kegs of beer ready for broaching. By the time this was done, her husband's troop had dismounted and were tethering their horses to the long rope lines, adjusting harnesses, brushing dirt and grasses from sweating hides.

Peter Moston, one of B Troop's sergeants, rode up to the carts and dismounted to talk with Henry Peebles. After an exchange of words, both men laughed and turned to stare in Rosie's direction.

Nell Harrison was at the horse lines, whispering excitedly into her husband's ear, and after a few moments he also began to stare in Rosie's direction. Unaware of this concerted attention, Rosie worked on.

The excited children were shrieking and running about as Philip Fothergill cantered up to the carts.

'Get the men fed and watered as quick as you can, Sarn't-Major. And keep these damned brats in order.'

'Yes, sir!' Peebles broke off his exchange with the sergeant, and roared at the men. 'You men get fell in in front of the carts, and you women get a hold of your whelps.'

The women and children gathered into a group to wait until the men had been issued with their food and drink. Only then would they be able to draw rations for themselves.

Philip Fothergill trotted up to the women, scowling. 'Keep your brats under control. Don't get drunk. If any of you misbehave in any way or bring the name of this regiment into disrepute, it will go hard against you. This is not a threat, it is a guaranteed certainty.'

They stared mutely up at him, and even the most rebellious among them did their best to keep their expressions submissive, knowing from past experience Philip Fothergill's reputation as a harsh disciplinarian.

He wheeled his horse and cantered away, and only when he was out of earshot did the boldest spirits dare to snarl their defiance after him.

'I'll get as drunk as I bloody well wants to!'
'Bollocks to you, Fothergill!'
'I 'opes your horse tumbles and you breaks your bleedin' neck!'

As soon as the last men had drawn rations, the women and children formed a queue at the carts and were issued with their food and drink: half a man's ration for a woman, a quarter for a child.

They went to mingle with their menfolk, and Rosie joined her husband who was sitting on the ground tearing voraciously at his food. He ignored her as she sat down opposite him, and Rosie accepted with resignation that he was still in a foul mood.

She had little appetite for her bread and cheese. 'Do you want this, Jack? I don't feel hungry.'

Now he looked directly at her, his eyes glinting angrily. 'Have you got something that you ought to tell me about?'

Momentarily puzzled, she asked, 'Is there something that I should be telling you about?'

'Oh yes.' He nodded, and his teeth bared in a rictus-like grin. 'I reckon my own missus ought to tell me about her arranging to go drinking with another man.'

'I've not arranged to go drinking with another man,' she hastily tried to explain. 'Henry Peebles asked me to have a drink with him when the duty's done, and I said I would. I only agreed to it because Nell Harrison was getting him all riled up. She was in danger of getting kicked out of barracks.'

Jack Collier's grin became a threatening snarl. 'What sort of a game do you think you're playing at? What's that going to make me look like? My missus drinking with another man? The whole of the bloody troop knows about it and are laughing behind their hands, and only me not knowing of it.'

'Don't be angry. I was going to tell you all about it now,' she appealed. 'I only intended to have the one drink, that's all, and then to come and find you.'

'You won't need to come and find me, because you aren't going to be drinking with that bastard in the first place. I'm not having my missus acting like a whore!' he shouted furiously.

All around them people were watching the confrontation, some merely curious, some showing concern, and others sniggering with enjoyment. Although uncomfortably aware of the onlookers, Rosie could not help but feel resentment at her husband's reaction, and she protested spiritedly. 'I don't know why you're making such a fuss about this, Jack. You've never minded me having a drink with anybody before. Having one single drink with Henry Peebles isn't acting like a whore.'

'Well, you'd know all about what acting like a whore is, wouldn't you? Seeing as that's all you've ever been!' he growled savagely.

The words struck her like physical blows. Then, beyond her husband's shoulder, she sighted Nell Harrison's wizened face grinning with spiteful delight, and her anger fired.

'Ask Nell Harrison why I agreed to have a drink with Peebles, Jack.' She pointed at the woman. 'She can tell you that I did it to save her neck. Go on, ask her.'

Collier got to his feet and swung round as Nell Harrison shook her head in emphatic denial. 'It's nothing to do wi' me,' she

221

declared aggrievedly. 'Don't try blaming me for what your missus gets up to. It's nothing to do wi' me. She's been making eyes at Peebles since he come to this troop. She makes eyes at any bloke who'll look at her.'

'You bloody rotten bitch!' Rosie's anger exploded into a red-hazed fury, and she jumped up and started towards the other woman. 'I'll tear your lying tongue out!'

Jack Collier's hand clamped on Rosie's upper arm and she struggled to drag herself free, clawing at his fingers and thumb, tearing his skin with her nails.

'Goddam you!' he roared, and clubbed her to the ground with his clenched fist. 'You make one move and I'll kick your bloody lights out.'

She remained slumped on the ground, her head ringing from the force of the blow, too dazed to attempt to rise.

The trumpet brayed, and Sergeant Moston came bellowing through the circle of on-lookers. 'Come on now! Let's be having you! Get fell in! Get fell in!'

A knowing smile lurked at the corners of his mouth as he took in the sight of Jack Collier and Rosie.

'Having a little bit of upset wi' your woman, are you, Corporal Collier? Well they all needs to be shown who's the boss, sooner or later, don't they? Now get fell in, man, or I'll have to be showing *you* who's your boss, won't I?'

Several women came to cluster around Rosie, loudly expressing their sympathy, calling curses down on the heads of all men, bewailing the hard lot of all women. Rosie remained slumped on the ground, shame, grief, anger and despair all exerting their mastery over her in a rapid, repetitive sequence.

Across the wide expanse of the park, Louis Nolan voiced his dismay. 'But surely you don't have to go to London tomorrow, Eugenia? Can't you stay here for another day or two?'

'No.' Eugenia Pacemore shook her head with genuine regret. 'I have to report to the Institution by tomorrow afternoon at the very latest, and commence my duties there.'

'Then I shall come there every day to visit you,' he declared.

'No, that's not possible, I'm afraid.' Again, she regretfully shook her head. 'The staff are strictly forbidden to receive gentlemen callers.'

He pondered for a few moments, then his eyes sparkled and he grinned like a mischievous urchin. 'The *staff* may be forbidden to have gentlemen callers, but I'll wager that the patients are not. I shall visit one of the Sick Gentlewomen. While I'm doing so, there is nothing that forbids me to have a chat with her nurse, is there?'

She couldn't repress a giggle of amusement at his audacity. 'But you don't know any patient there, do you?'

He chuckled merrily. 'I'm a cavalryman,

Eugenia. The cavalry's task is to carry out reconnaissance of enemy positions and strengths. We are also very adept at planning and executing any necessary stratagems. It will be child's play for me to plan the stratagem of discovering that I have an old acquaintance being nursed at the Institution.'

'You'll get me into trouble, you wicked man,' she scolded affectionately.

'Oh no.' He became very serious. 'That is the last thing that I would ever do, my dear. I would never risk harming a single hair on your head.'

He stepped close to her, so that their faces were only inches apart, and sincerity shone from his eyes. 'Don't be offended, my dear. But I have to tell you now that I've fallen in love with you, and I want you to be my wife.' He saw her eyes widen in shock. 'I know that I can't expect you to give me an answer at this moment, my dear. But please, please, please consider my proposal. I can't promise you wealth, or land, or any great value of possessions. But I can promise you my lifelong love and devotion, if you will honour me by agreeing to become my wife.'

Eugenia experienced a flurry of emotions: joy battling with doubt, disbelief struggling against the knowledge that she *had* heard him correctly. She felt herself blushing and lifted her hands to her glowing cheeks.

'Look at me,' she muttered. 'I'm behaving like a silly schoolgirl, aren't I?'

'You can behave in any way you wish, my

dear.' He smiled fondly. 'It won't, make a tuppence of difference to the way I feel about you.'

She drew several long, deep breaths to calm her racing thoughts and slow her pounding heartbeat. Then told him, very honestly, 'Of course I'd like to marry you, Louis. But I think it best if you take more time to consider. We've only known each other for such a very brief time, a man like you can have his pick of young, pretty girls.'

'I've not the slightest interest in young, pretty girls, my dear,' he asserted with an equal firmness. 'It's you I want.'

'I'm a spinster, well past the bloom of youth. I have no home, and my only income is a small annuity. You have everything to lose and nothing to gain by tying yourself down with me,' she argued doggedly, even though in her heart she was torturing herself by doing so.

He cupped his hands gently over hers. 'If you do not agree to marry me, then I shall have nothing but sadness and loneliness to look forward to. We can wait for as long as you wish before we wed. I can be the most patient man in the world, if only I know that someday you will become my wife. I beg you to tell me now that you will marry me.'

Eugenia was weakening fast and, sensing this, Louis Nolan pressed harder. 'Say that you'll become my wife. Say it now. Say it, I beg you, say it!'

'Yes, I'll marry you. But be warned, all that

I can promise to bring to you is my lifelong love and devotion.'

His eyes danced with delight and he kissed her full on the lips. Eugenia revelled in that kiss until the mocking applause of the crowd made her realize how raffishly unladylike she was being.

Laughing uproariously, Louis Nolan bowed to the onlookers, then, linking her arm, he proudly led her through the crowd.

Rosie's bruised head was aching as she loaded the empty beer kegs back on to the carts.

Henry Peebles came walking up to her. 'I'm sorry for getting you into trouble with your man, Rosie. That wasn't my intention.' His florid features were sympathetic.

Looking levelly at the man she said without resentment, 'You and I both know what your intention was, Henry Peebles. It was to try and get in between my legs to pleasure yourself.'

'That's true enough, girl,' he admitted with a rueful grin. 'And I can't be blamed for wanting to have you. There aren't a man in the regiment who wouldn't jump at the chance of having you.'

'Well, neither them, nor you, will ever get that chance. I believe in being faithful to my husband,' she stated firmly.

'That's to your credit, and I don't doubt you. But I'll tell you this. That man of yours don't deserve you. I didn't like him from the first moment I clapped eyes on him, nearly four years past, and I ain't changed my mind. He's a pig! And if I come to hear that he's knocking you about too much, then I'll make it my business to make him pay a price for it. Remember one thing, and I'm speaking the God's honest truth now. If you ever needs me as a friend, then I'm here for you.'

Before she could make any reply, he turned about and walked away.

Thirty

Cavalry Barracks, Hounslow,
April 9th, 1854

'It's come, Bronton! It's come!' Cornet Peter Barryton's boyish face was flushed with excitement as he burst into Charles' room. 'I've just seen Fothergill. We are all ordered to assemble immediately in the common room.' The diminutive slender youth was almost dancing with joy. 'We're going to war! We're going to fight the Russians. Isn't it wonderful news!' He rushed out of the room shouting, 'We're going to war, you fellows. We are to assemble immediately in the common room. We're going to war!'

Charles sat staring at the open book on his lap, thrilled that the long wished for moment had finally arrived. He drew a deep breath to steady the thudding of his heart and made his way downstairs to the assembly.

In the crowded room it appeared that practically every officer in the regiment was present. The hubbub of their excited voices was deafening, and their smiling faces and outbursts of laughter made the gathering a festive occasion. The noise quieted a little when the colonel entered, but it took the harsh shout of Philip Fothergill to create silence enough for the old man's tremulous voice to be heard clearly.

His parchment-hued features contained a rare ruddiness of colour, and his enthusiasm was patent.

'As you all know, gentlemen, Her Majesty's government, in conjunction with the French, declared war ten days ago on the Russian Empire. Within the last hour, the despatch that we have all been eagerly hoping for has been delivered into my hands.' He waved a sheet of notepaper above his snow-white head. 'The Twentieth are ordered to reinforce the Expeditionary Force in the East. We are to furnish two service squadrons. In total, three hundred and twenty officers and men, and two hundred and eighty horses.'

A cheer erupted, forcing the old man to stop speaking. He waited, smiling, until the noise subsided. 'We are to take transport from Portsmouth in two weeks' time. Our eventual destination is the port of Varna in Bulgaria. There we shall join up with the rest of our army, the French and the Turks, the objective being to halt the Russian advance across the lower Danube.'

Another cheer silenced him once more. When he was able to, he continued with a sly quip. 'I must confess, gentlemen, that the presence of so many of you here in the barracks today is most gratifying to me. It proves my theory that nothing serves better to bring officers prematurely back from leave than to offer them the opportunity to teach Johnny Foreigner some manners.'

This was met with full-throated laughter and, pleased by the reception of his joke, the old man chuckled. 'I suggest that you use the rest of the day to celebrate these happy tidings. It will be time enough tomorrow to begin the preparations for departure. I bid you good day, gentlemen.'

He left to yet another cheer, and then the gathering began their celebration, mingling together in happy laughing groups while perspiring orderlies rushed to serve the champagne that was being called for on all sides. For the remainder of that afternoon and evening the hierarchical structure of the mess was disregarded and superiors and inferiors became a brotherhood of comrades. Captains laughed and joked with cornets; majors toasted lieutenants.

The paymaster, the quartermaster, the riding master and all commissioned ex-rankers of lowly origins were treated as social equals by titled aristocrats, their anecdotes listened to and applauded. For Charles Bronton these were the happiest hours he had known in the mess since joining the regiment, and for the first time he experienced a sensation of comradeship with his fellow officers.

The other ranks also cheered when they were paraded to be told that the regiment was going to war. It was a welcome release from the harsh, monotonous grind of barrack life. They cheered even more loudly when, on the orders of Colonel Forrester, they were issued with an advance of pay so that they also could enjoy a night of celebration.

The pubs and drinking dens of the small town made ready to profit from this unexpected good fortune. Within hours, the mean streets and alleys were thronged with reeling, singing, drunken soldiers. Savage brawls continually erupted, glasses and windows shattered, men fought like wild beasts with fists, boots, teeth and belts, and the provost sergeant and his regimental police savagely clubbed down the offenders and dragged them bleeding and senseless back to the already packed cells of the guardroom.

In the fetid barrack rooms the women and children clustered around the wavering light of tallow candles, fearful about their now uncertain future.

'How many of us will be let to go, Dorcas?' Rosie asked.

The older woman had been a soldier's wife

since her twelfth birthday, and Murphy was her fourth husband. All her previous husbands had been drafted overseas and all had died there.

'That's hard to say.' She shrugged. 'We has to draw lots for it. I've drawn lots three times, but I was in the infantry then. They used to let six women to a company go. But trust my luck, I was left behind twice to be chucked on the parish. We nearly starved to death, me and my kids did.'

'But we'em not Foot, we'em Horse,' Nell Harrison objected, her baby sucking hungrily at her flaccid breast. 'There's a hundred men to a company of Foot, aren't there, and only sixty-odd to a troop of Horse. What if they says that only three or four from each troop can go? There's well above a hundred women in this barracks, and only four troops to be sent.'

Dorcas Murphy sniffed loudly and wiped her broken nose on her sleeve. 'Then you'll just have to hope that you're one of the two, won't you, Nell?'

'Me and my kids are going to die if Augustus leaves us behind.' The other woman in the group, Annie Bartleet, sounded near to tears.

Dorcas Murphy regarded her with good-natured contempt. 'Well, Annie, the amount of time that you and Augustus spends on your knees praying to God, I should think you'd not have a care if your man leaves you behind. God's sure to look after you, aren't he? You keeps on telling us that you're one of His chosen lambs.'

Annie began to sob and Dorcas scolded her sharply. 'There aren't no use you piping your eyes, girl. You're just going to have to do what the rest of us has got to do, and that's hope to Christ you gets lucky in the draw. Because if you don't, then it's out on the streets you go.'

Rosie was very thoughtful. She had missed her last period, and was certain that she was again pregnant. 'But why can't the ones who aren't drawn to go just stay on here in barracks until the regiment comes back?'

'Because a woman and her kids am only allowed to stay if her man's still with her. Them whose men stay here at the depot can stay on. But them whose men has gone has to leave the barracks, because some pious idiots in the government reckons if us women stays here by ourselves we'll all be flogging our mutton and causing all sorts of other trouble.'

Rosie frowned in disgust. 'How do they do the draw?'

'Well, the ones that I was in, they just writ the names down on bits of paper, screwed them up and chucked them into a shako. Then the names was pulled out one at a time.' Dorcas grinned at the memory. 'It aren't half a game, I can tell you, when the last name's been drawn. Those who aren't drawn don't half kick up. There's bloody hell to pay.'

'Who does the drawing?'

'Well, the company sarn't-major did ours,

232

so I expect it'll be the troop sarn't-major who'll do it for us. That'll be Henry Peebles, won't it?'

'It's not fair. They ought to take us all,' Nell Harrison whined. 'I don't know what I'll do if I'm not drawn to go. What'll happen to me and me kids?'

'You can go back to your family,' Dorcas suggested, and the other woman shook her head.

'No I can't. They disowned me for marrying a soldier. I tried to talk to them after I wed, but they wouldn't even look at me. They said I was nothing but a redcoat's whore and they never wanted to see me again. They're very religious, you see.'

Dorcas cackled with laughter. 'Well then, take Annie back with you to talk to them. She's been washed in the blood of the lamb like they has, so she'll soften their hearts towards you.'

'It's nothing to joke about,' Nell retorted angrily. 'What am I going to do with three little ones to feed?'

The fat woman's frizzed mass of greasy hair moved slowly from side to side. 'You'll have to throw yourself on the parish. I don't know what else you'll be able to do, my wench.' Dorcas sounded resigned. 'I'm bloody glad that all my kids am grown-up and making their own ways in the world, so if I don't get drawn to go I've only got meself to worry about.'

Rosie was as worried as her companions,

but accepted that, for the time being at least, there was nothing that could be done to alter the situation. She reached for her shawl and said, 'I'm going to treat us to a drop of gin, girls. I don't see why we shouldn't try and enjoy ourselves like the blokes are doing.'

She hurried through the barrack lines towards the block that housed the senior NCOs. From the lighted windows there came the sounds of singing and drunken voices, and the high-pitched screeching of a woman berating her husband. Rosie could not help but smile wryly. It was Peter Moston's wife, Hetty, a foul-mouthed harridan who ruled her husband with a rod of iron.

She went to the rear door of the men's wet canteen and bought two bottles of cheap rotgut gin from the civilian sutler who ran the place. She could hear the uproar within the canteen and knew that the guard would have to come and clear the place when it came to closing time. She also knew that anyone in the barrack rooms unfortunate enough to be sober would get little or no sleep that night.

Every pay night was the same. When the drunken men came back to their quarters, riot would ensue. Old and new scores would be settled in violent clashes, the stinking urine tubs that were placed for use at night in the rooms would inevitably be tipped over, and the floor would be awash with urine, faeces and vomit. The noise and uproar and fighting would continue until the last drunken man fell into sodden sleep.

She hugged the bottles of gin to her breasts. They were the women's escape route from the violence and uproar of the coming night. The raw spirit would make them so drunk that they would lie in a comatose stupor, oblivious to the hell that raged around them.

She looked across the parade ground to the serried lights of the huge officers' block. 'I'll bet none of your women will have to go through what we have to. They'll not be drawing lots, will they? I wish I'd been born lucky and was living in the lap of luxury, like you lot. I'll bet it's not rotgut that you're swilling down your gullets tonight, neither,' she thought enviously.

Meanwhile, in his small room on the top floor of the officers' block, Charles Bronton was lying on his bed, snoring loudly, with an empty champagne bottle clutched in his hand. He was dreaming, vivid, colourful, exciting dreams of battles and glory. A smile touched his lips. Glory! Battles and glory!

In her bedroom at the Institute for Sick Gentlewomen on Harley Street, London, Eugenia Pacemore knelt on her knees in the darkness, her hands tight clasped before her.

Earlier that evening a cavalryman from Hounslow Barracks had brought her a letter from her cousin, Charles, telling her that he was being sent to war. Louis Nolan was already in Turkey, having been ordered there to buy replacement horses for the coming campaign.

'Dear God, please keep Louis and Charlie safe through this war. Please God, keep them safe. Bring them back to me, I beg you, bring them back.'

Thirty-One

Hounslow Barracks, April 17th, 1854

Rosie bent over the great iron cooking pot hanging from its chain above the fire. She stirred the greasy mass of meat and potatoes bubbling in the pot and, satisfied that the food was cooked, called to the other women.

'Alright, girls, let's dish it out. The men will be back in a minute.'

The women brought the tin basins to her and she ladled carefully measured portions into each, trying as best she could to ensure that each basin contained the same proportions of meat, potatoes and broth.

The men returned, dusty and sweaty from hard riding, just as the last basin was ranked with its fellows upon the tables. The room was a hubbub of noisy talk and laughter, and the clattering of accoutrements being discarded. The men were in uniformly high spirits. They, in sharp contrast to the women, were not dreading the day of departure to the

East. For them the war meant travel, adventure, accelerated promotions, a chance to gain glory, and above all else, the prospect of loot.

'Do you think we'll get rich?' a younger soldier asked eagerly.

'You'll get my boot up your backsides if you don't all shut up and let me get this grub dished out,' Jack Collier interrupted. 'And since you've got so much to say, Conky, then you can do the calling.'

'Why me again?' the old veteran complained.

'Because you aren't got eyes on the back of your head.' Jack Collier grinned. 'Now get against that bloody wall and get on with it, will you. We're bloody starving.'

To a chorus of jeers and catcalls, Conky White went to the end of the room and stood with his face to the wall so that he could not see what was happening behind him.

Jack Collier pointed at random to one of the basins, and asked, 'Who shall have this?'

'Cooper,' White replied instantly, and the named man took the basin.

Collier pointed at another basin. 'Who shall have this?'

'McKinley.'

The named sandy-haired Scotsman poked at the grey-looking portion of meat in the basin, and swore. 'Sod this for a game o' sodgers! This is all bone!'

'Then break it open and suck the marrow out of it,' Collier told him.

The routine of question and name continued until every basin had been distributed, and although some men cursed and grumbled at what they received, no one questioned this method of distribution. It was mere chance that dictated at any meal which men received the worst or best pieces of meat, and over a period of time the good and bad luck evened out among them.

The women waited patiently for the men to finish eating, as only then would they divide what was left in the cooking pot between themselves and the children.

The door opened and Corporal Smailes peered into the room.

'What's you come pestering us for, you tosser?' was the roar that greeted him.

He grinned and saluted. 'Thank you for that courteous welcome, my lords, ladies and gentlemen. His honour, Troop Sergeant-Major Peebles, has just confided in me that the orders for the route have come. We're marching to Portsmouth tomorrow.'

The men cheered.

The women exchanged troubled glances.

'How many of us are to go?' Dorcas asked.

'Only two to a troop.' Smailes grimaced sympathetically. 'Major Fothergill's set the number. The draw's to take place tomorrow morning straight after Stables. Each troop is to do its own drawing. So Peebles will be doing yours.'

He withdrew, leaving a tense silence behind him that was broken by Dorcas Murphy hissing angrily. 'That bastard, Fothergill! There's fifteen wives in this troop, and thirteen of us 'ull be kicked out on the street by this time tomorrow. Homeless!'

Homeless! That final word struck deep into Rosie, forcing her to face the harsh reality that over the last four years this troop, this regiment, had become both home and family to her. Her life in barracks had been hard, squalid and rough, but she had also found warm comradeship and a sense of security. She had known that if she were taken ill then the other women in her troop would care for her. If she had a child, and she were to die, those same women would care for her baby, and raise it with their own. As for her marriage, Rosie was able to philosophically accept that that relationship could be much worse than it was. As a husband, Jack Collier was bearable enough.

Now, however, she faced a fearful prospect. If she was not drawn to go with the men, then she, and the child growing in her womb, would be left friendless, shelterless, and virtually penniless. She might find work of some sort, but as her pregnancy advanced, she foresaw her only options being prostitution or the workhouse, and both of those options would inevitably doom her unborn child to a life of grim hopelessness.

Rosie put both hands protectively over her womb, vowing silently, 'We'll go with the regiment, baby. I'll find a way to make sure of that.'

Thirty-Two

It was nine o'clock, the smaller children were in bed asleep, and the women were sitting around the table in a pool of light shed by the single oil lamp. The men were either on guard duty or in the wet canteen, from which they would return at ten o'clock for the final roll call of the day.

Normally the women would be talking as they darned and sewed, but tonight they were silent, each trapped in their dread of what might happen early the next morning.

Rosie had been racking her brains for hours, examining and rejecting ideas of how to ensure that she would accompany the regiment to the East. There was one idea, however, which persisted in her mind.

The faint chimes of the great clock upon the turret of the guard room penetrated the room, and Rosie counted their number. The hour was getting late, and she knew that if she was to have any chance of influencing the draw she must act now. She finished sewing on a shirt button and bit through the thread with her sharp white teeth. Folding the shirt, she put it on top of the pile of clothing and got to her feet.

'I'll take this lot across to the sergeants' mess.'

'I wouldn't bother.' Dorcas scowled malevolently. 'Let the bastards wait till tomorrow.'

Rosie stretched and yawned. 'No, I'll go now and get the money off them, because if I get chucked out of here tomorrow there's some of the buggers who'll weasel out of paying me. You know what they're like.'

'Don't I just!' Dorcas gusted irritably.

Moonlight silvered the roofs of the barrack blocks and Rosie deliberately kept in the shadows as she walked quickly towards the sergeants' mess. She had no wish to meet and be forced to talk to anyone, she wanted only to concentrate on what she intended to do.

Dim lights glowed from the windows of the tall block and the noise of laughter and singing sounded from the ground floor where the bar was situated.

'I hope he's not drunk,' Rosie thought, then smiled mirthlessly. 'But perhaps it'll be better if he is. Drunk and randy.'

Standing just inside the main entrance, she waited until one of the mess servants appeared. 'Will you tell Sergeant-Major Peebles that I need to speak with him urgently. I want paying for this lot.' She indicated the bundle of clothing beneath her arm.

The man nodded and disappeared down a passageway, from which Henry Peebles emerged a few minutes later, in shirt-sleeves, his breath smelling of rum, his eyes glistening from the effects of the alcohol.

He frowned at her. 'What do you want with me, Rosie Collier? It had better be something important, because I don't like being disturbed in my off-duty time.'

For a brief instant Rosie's determination wavered, and she felt like running away. But the knowledge of the child in her womb forced her on. 'I want to ask you a favour, Sergeant-Major.'

'And what might that be?'

She looked about her and, lowering her voice, said, 'It's a very private matter. Is there somewhere we can talk without being seen?'

He pointed to the next building, which was a stables and hayloft. 'We can go in there.'

Inside the stables was a shadowed gloom filled with the warm sounds and smells of the horses in their stalls.

Rosie wasted no time. 'I want you to fix the draw tomorrow so that I can go with the regiment.'

'And how can I do that, with everybody in the troop watching me like bloody hawks?' His tone was jeeringly dismissive.

'You're the flyest bloke in the regiment, Henry Peebles,' she told him bluntly. 'I know that if you want to, you can make sure that I get drawn to go.'

He shrugged his thick, muscular shoulders. 'That's as maybe. But why should I do any favours for you?'

'Because you told me once that if I ever needed a friend, I could come to you.'

'But you haven't been acting very friendly

to me lately, have you?'

Rosie drew a deep breath, and for the sake of her unborn child, smiled invitingly at him. 'I can be very friendly to you. You'd still love to get between my legs, wouldn't you?'

'Of course I would,' he admitted readily. 'You're the best-looking woman in the regiment.'

'Well then, if you agree to get me drawn to go, you can have me,' she said plainly. 'And I'll make sure that you enjoy it. But only for the one time.'

He made no reply, only stared at her questioningly. After a while she felt driven to demand, 'Well? Do we have a bargain?'

He grinned. 'We might have, Rosie. But we'll need to get the terms straight between us first. I might get the taste for you so bad that one time won't be sufficient for me. I might want you on a regular basis.'

She shook her head. 'No, that's not on. Not while I'm still wed to Jack. He's not always good to me, but I won't pay him back in that way. So it's one time only. You can take it or leave it.'

He chuckled. 'Fair enough, Rosie. I'll take it.'

He moved to her and fondled her breasts. 'Come on, we'll go up to the hay store. We shan't be disturbed there.'

She moved away slightly. 'How do I know that you can be trusted to keep your side of the bargain?'

'You don't.' He grinned. 'You'll just have to

take that chance, won't you?'

She stared hard into his face, and her instinct, honed and sharpened by harsh experience, told her that she could trust him.

In the hayloft she let him strip the clothes from her body, and his breathing quickened as he felt the firm, tender flesh beneath his hands. He took his own clothes off and drew her down on to the sweet-smelling hay.

To Rosie's surprise, he proved a gentle lover, and despite her conscious effort to remain physically and emotionally detached, she gradually found her body responding to his loving, and her own passion mounting as he thrust ever deeper and faster into her, and before he was done she had cried out in climax and clutched his body close.

They dressed in silence, Rosie uneasy at her passionate reponse to his love-making. Never before when she had been forced to prostitute herself had she responded so. She felt guilt, not because she had allowed the man to use her body, but because she had taken pleasure from it.

'I'll go first,' Peebles told her. 'Wait a few minutes before following, and make sure that no one sees you.' He moved to the ladder that led down to the ground and turned back as he reached it. 'Don't worry, Rosie. I'll make sure that you get drawn to go.'

On sudden impulse she asked, 'How about my room mates, can you do anything for them?'

'Jesus Christ!' he exclaimed. 'That wasn't

part of our bargain.'

'Please,' she cajoled.

He gave a sigh of exasperation. 'I can't promise anything ... But I'll see what's to be done. I'll do me best for you, Rosie.'

She suddenly remembered the bundle of clothing. 'Can you take these to the mess for me?'

'God's truth!' he cried, but took the bundle and disappeared from her view.

She smiled, feeling for the first time the warmth of liking for the man.

After waiting a few minutes, she cautiously climbed down the ladder, and peeped out of the stable doors. She jumped with shock as a loud clatter sounded behind her. She swung about and cried out in fright as a solid black shadow loomed up before her.

'Don't be alarmed, Rosie. It's only me. The horse butted me over.'

She recognized the voice. It was Arthur Sinclair, the recruit she had given a bed to long months before.

'I wasn't spying on you and Peebles, Rosie. I couldn't help hearing you. I was in here when you both came in. I brought some sugar lumps for the bay mare. She's not been well lately, and I was worried about her. Only I had to sneak in because I'm on guard duty, and if I'm caught in here I'm in trouble. I was going to go when you went up to the hay loft, but two of the sergeants and their wives were talking outside the mess, and I'd have been seen.'

She swallowed hard, afraid of what this discovery might bring upon her head. 'What are you going to do?' she asked nervously.

'Do?' He sounded puzzled. 'I don't understand, Rosie.'

'What are you going to do about me and Peebles?' she repeated.

She felt his hand upon her shoulder. 'Whatever you and Peebles were doing is your own business, Rosie. I'll not breathe a word.'

'Really?'

'Really. You were kind to me when I first came here, Rosie. And I never forget a kindness. So put your mind at ease. No one will ever hear a word from me.'

'Oh, thank you.' She felt weak with relief.

'I've got to go,' he said, and after checking that all was clear outside, he crept away.

Rosie drew several long, deep breaths, willing her jangled nerves to be calm, and then slipped out and hurried back to her barrack block.

'Stand by your beds!' the duty NCO, Sergeant Peter Preston, shouted as he came stamping into the room with a jingle of spurs. 'Get that bugger on his feet!'

The drunkenly snoring man was dragged off his bed and propped upright at its end.

'Listen for your names!' The sergeant began to read from the list he was carrying. 'Ainsworth?'

'Present, Sarn't.'

'Calderhead?'

'Present, Sarn't'

'Cullen?'

'Present, Sarn't.'

When the roll call was complete the sergeant grinned sardonically. 'Make the most of your comfy beds tonight, my lads. It'll be a long time before you sleeps in such luxury again. And you married men had better make sure that you empty your bollocks, because there's little chance of you having your women to shag tomorrow night. They'll more than likely be in some other bloke's bed by then.'

'Well there's no danger of your missus being in some other bloke's bed, is there, Sergeant? She's too ugly for anyone to want her.' The room erupted with jeering laughter.

The sergeant continued to grin sardonically. 'That's the good thing about having an ugly missus, my lads. They never gives you cause to be worrying about them opening their legs for other men. Not like some women I could mention. Aren't that right, Corporal Collier?'

Lying in bed behind the curtain, Rosie could hear everything that was being said, and she caught her breath, her heart thumping in trepidation. Had Henry Peebles been bragging about having had her? Had Arthur Sinclair told other men about what he had seen and heard? If either of them had been talking, and Jack Collier came to hear of it, then she dreaded what he might do to her, especially if he was in one of his drink-fuelled moods.

She strained to hear her husband's reaction to Preston's baiting.

'That's very true, Sergeant Preston, very true indeed. It's a great worry being married to a good-looking woman.' Jack Collier's tone was respectfully subservient. 'So you take good heed of Sergeant Preston's advice, lads. If there's a choice between marrying a good-looker or an ugly pig, then do what he did, and marry the pig.'

His gibe ignited a howling storm of applause and laughter, and he shouted above the noise, 'Are we dismissed from roll call now, Sergeant?' But Preston had already accepted defeat and left.

Rosie sighed with relief, and her tense body relaxed. The blanket curtain was pushed aside and Jack Collier, still chuckling with satisfaction, lurched to the narrow bed. He leered lustfully down at her. 'If you're wearing anything, my sweetheart, then get it off.'

She obeyed without demur, sitting up in bed and pulling her gown and undershift over her head, then lying back to wait while he undressed.

Their conjugal relationship was, and had always been, very straightforward. She lay beneath him, he entered her after little or no foreplay, and as soon as he had satisfied himself, he rolled off her and went to sleep. Although she could have wished for a more tender, less selfish lover, she was grateful that Jack Collier never forced himself upon her, or made any perverse or sadistic demands upon her. Brothel-hardened as she was, the inescapable fact that his grunts and gasps and the creaking of the bed could be clearly heard throughout the long narrow room didn't bother her. It was an unavoidable concomitant of barrack life.

Tonight, however, Jack Collier did not roll over and fall asleep as soon as he had spent himself inside her. Tonight he cuddled her close, and whispered, 'I'm dreading tomorrow. I can't a-bear to think of having to part from you. I know that there's lots o' times it might not seem so, sweetheart, but I do love you, you know. I don't know what I'll do if I have to leave you behind tomorrow.'

His unguarded confession deeply touched Rosie, causing her to feel a pang of guilt that she should have taken pleasure from another man's loving such a short time before. For a fleeting instant she felt the urge to reassure him, to tell him that Henry Peebles had promised that she would go with the regiment, but she bit back the words, scolding herself fiercely.

Long after Jack was snoring in his sleep, Rosie lay racked with worry about what the morning might bring to her and the child within her womb.

Thirty-Three

The two service squadrons marched out of Hounslow Barracks at eight o'clock in the morning en route for Portsmouth. At the same hour the women and children were ordered to muster in front of the sergeants' mess to take part in the drawing of lots.

'Why do they send the men on ahead, Dorcas?' Rosie was curious.

'Because there's some blokes who'll desert if they knows their wives and kids are going to be left behind. So the officers likes to get them all safe on board transports, before they comes to know if their wives are going with them or not.'

'But they could still jump overboard and desert,' Rosie pointed out.

'Maybe. But it's a bloody sight harder deserting off a ship than it is on land.'

The crowd of women were silent for the most part, faces pale with tension, many carrying babies in their arms and with small children hanging on to their skirts. The children, conscious of their mothers' strained nerves, were also infected with the prevailing sombre mood, some whimpering, others nervously sucking their thumbs, all of them preternaturally subdued.

Rosie was afflicted with an uneasy sense of guilt as she looked at Annie Bartleet's wan features and cluster of timid children.

'I've done wrong to try and cheat her of a fair chance to go,' she thought.

She looked beyond Annie Bartleet to where the foul-mouthed, evil-tempered, childless Hetty Moston was standing with a group of clone-like cronies, and felt her guilt lessening.

At the main barracks gates, Charles Bronton watched the rear of the column of squadrons disappear from view, then turned his horse and trotted towards the sergeants' mess.

It was not really necessary for him to be present at the women's drawing of lots, which he found an unpalatable procedure, but he felt it necessary to satisfy himself that the draw was made fairly. Unlike some of his fellow officers, Charles did not dislike or despise the soldiers' women, for all that they were largely drawn from the lowest levels of society. But he paid them little or no attention as individuals. They were merely part of the backdrop of regimental life.

When he reached the mess he found that a table had been set up behind which a seated clerk was writing the women's names on scraps of paper, then screwing them up tightly and placing them in an upturned shako.

Henry Peebles, acting as scrutineer, stood looking over the clerk's shoulder, in company with Regimental Sergeant-Major Shrive, an ageing, bow-legged veteran.

The two NCOs saluted as Charles came up.

'If you please, Mr Shrive, I want to address the women,' Charles called.

'Very good, sir!' Shrive scowled at the crowd. 'Be silent for the officer!'

Charles reined in and looked over the expectant mass of faces before him. 'Listen carefully, all of you. It has been decided that because there are large discrepancies in the numbers of women in each troop...' He paused, realizing from the blankness of some of the women's expressions that they had no understanding of what the word discrepancies meant. He began again. 'It has been decided that the fairest way of making this draw is not by individual troops, but instead by drawing from the total of the two squadrons.' A wry smile touched his lips. 'Those of you who are not clear as to my meaning may ask the women around you.'

There was an immediate clamour of questions and answers, which persisted until Shrive bellowed angrily. 'Be silent! Be silent for the officer, damn you!'

'With respect, sir.' It was Hetty Moston who shouted. 'What's to be done for them who ain't drawn to go?'

'They'll be left to starve, like always,' another woman shouted, and this provoked a loud outburst of angry agreement from the women.

'Shut your mouths! Show respect!' Shrive

grew purple with fury. 'Show respect for the officer!'

'It's alright, Mr Shrive.' Charles waited patiently for the outburst to quieten. Then he explained, 'Those who are not drawn to go will be issued with official claim warrants to be presented at their home parishes where they have the right of settlement and relief. They will also be issued warrants entitling them to claim casual relief from those parishes they must travel through en route to their home parishes...'

'Begging your pardon, your honour, but what about those of us who're Irish?' Dorcas Murphy asked. 'How do we get back to our parishes across the water?'

'Well, you can either swim or fly, Paddy. Take your pick.' Hetty Moston and her cronies cackled with laughter, and were instantly showered with epithets by the Irish-women in the crowd.

'Be silent, all of you! The next woman who opens her mouth gets her name chucked out of the draw and gets no warrants at all! I mean what I say. Make no mistake about it,' Shrive threatened.

A sullen silence descended, broken only by the shrill wailing of a baby and the snuffling whimpers of some of the children.

Charles Bronton could not help but feel pity for the plight of the Irishwomen, and was relieved that he could offer them some help.

'We officers have subscribed to a hardship fund, which will be administered by our regimental agents in London. Those of you who need to take passage on board ship may apply to their office for assistance.'

He signalled to Henry Peebles. 'Commence the draw, Sarn't-Major.'

'Very good, sir.' Peebles grinned at the women. 'There are twelve names to be drawn, ladies. If any woman's name is called and she don't make answer, then another name will be drawn in her place.'

Peebles lifted the upturned shako and shook the contents, then took out one of the pellets of screwed-up paper and opened it, shouting the name written there.

'Martha Sykes?'

'I'm here! I'm here!' the woman shrieked in delight, uncaring of the envious scowls and barbed comments from her immediate neighbours.

Three more names were called, and with each successive disappointment the mood of the crowd became uglier. Tension gripped Rosie, tightening her throat, constricting her breathing.

'Dorcas Murphy?'

'I'm here, glory be!' the big Irishwoman bellowed with pleasure. 'That husband o' mine 'ull not be getting shot of me this time, will he?'

Another five names were called, and Rosie's fears that Peebles had cheated her hardened to angry conviction.

'Annie Bartleet?'

'I'm here! Oh thanks be to the Lord God!

I'm here, Sergeant-Major! I'm here! Thanks be to the lamb of God!'

Peebles chuckled grimly. 'I do believe that you are here, Annie Bartleet! And the next and last name is...' He took the final pellet of paper and opened it, then paused before shouting, 'Rosie Collier?'

'I'm here!' Relief flooded through Rosie, a relief so intense that it made her feel momentarily faint and light-headed.

'No! No!' Nell Harrison howled like a wounded animal. 'We should all go with the regiment! It aren't right to leave us behind! It aren't fair!'

'When does we ever get treated fair?' another woman shrieked.

There came screams and shouts of protest from the crowd, some of the women tearing at their hair and clothes, wailing in frantic despair. The babies and children, frightened and bemused, added their squalling cries to the tumult.

'Let's you and me get out o' this.' Dorcas Murphy took Rosie's arm and pushed through the heaving pandemonium.

As they broke clear they almost collided with Henry Peebles, who winked at Rosie but passed on without speaking. Dorcas saw the wink and she stared questioningly at Rosie, but waited until they were out of anybody's earshot before demanding, 'Did you have anything to do with fixing the draw, Rosie?'

'How could I?' Rosie asked hotly. 'I was standing next to you, wasn't I? How could I have had anything to do with fixing the draw?'

'Well, it's awful rare aren't it? There's more than a hundred names in the hat, and there's three names from our room drawn out of it. You and your best mate in the regiment, which is me. And Annie Bartleet, who you've always had the soft pity for. It's awful rare, so it is.'

Elation suddenly swept over Rosie, and she laughingly agreed. 'So it is, Dorcas. It's awful rare!'

Thirty-Four

The Port of Varna, Bulgaria,
early July, 1854

Varna's narrow streets were choked with waggons and animals and people, and the humid smoky air was rancid with a miasma of foul stenches. Sewage festered in open channels. Savage dogs fought to tear at dead animals rotting in the gutters, their snarls mingling with the babel of a score of tongues.

Turks, French, Bulgars, British, Greeks, Egyptians, Maltese, Jews, Tartars, black faces, white faces, brown faces, multi-hued uniforms and clothing merged to create a shifting, swirling kaleidoscope, and as Charles Bronton guided his horse through the maelstrom he was assailed on all sides by strident street vendors and whining beggars.

At the house used for Lord Lucan, the British Cavalry Commander's headquarters, he was received by an elegant, pink-cheeked, drawling young captain wearing the scarlet tunic of the Dragoon Guards, who then left him to wait for nearly two hours in a small bare ante-room.

Eventually he was summoned into Lord Lucan's presence. Lucan was tall with long black side-whiskers, sweeping mustachios and balding head. His manner was irascible and his voice hectoring. He made Charles repeat his report on the sudden death of Colonel Forrester from fever, and while he listened he constantly muttered angrily to himself and ejaculated expletives. When he had heard enough, he barked at Charles. 'You are dismissed.'

Outside once more, the elegant Dragoon Guardsman smiled patronizingly at Charles. 'His Lordship has taken an uncommon shine to you, Bronton. I've rarely seen him act so condescending toward a fella.'

Charles replied with deliberate irony, 'Yes, I thought he condescended to me extremely condescendingly.'

The pink features stared doubtfully after him as he left. Outside in the street he heard his name called.

'Bronton? Charles Bronton?'

He reined in and looked around at the jostling noisy crowd.

A tall, heavily bearded Bashi-Bazouk was standing at his side, smiling up at him. The man wore a short embroidered jacket, baggy trousers and a huge turban. Around his waist was a broad sash with pistols, knives and a yataghan stuck in it, and bandoliers of cartridges criss-crossed his chest. In his hand he carried a Minie rifle. At the man's back was a murderous-looking pack of Bashi-Bazouks, equally colourfully dressed and heavily armed.

Charles stared hard, and then grinned in recognition. 'Major Beaston! How are you, sir? And how is Captain Nolan?'

'It's Colonel Beaston now, Bronton, and Nolan is very well. He's been appointed to the staff, and at present he's in Turkey buying remounts for the cavalry. Come, let's go somewhere we can sit and talk and have a drink.'

Charles happily agreed, and within minutes the two men were seated in a mosaic-walled café sharing a bottle of raki and smoking cheroots.

William Beaston listened in silence while Charles explained his errand to Varna, and then scowled savagely. 'Our commanders claim that lack of transport prevented them moving to reinforce the Turks at Silistria. It would be comic if it weren't so tragic. Nolan is having the devil of a job to find remounts, but there are plenty of packhorses to be had, yet Nolan cannot obtain the necessary authorization to buy any pack animals. What prize buffoons our leaders are!'

'Well, the war seems to be virtually over anyway, now that the Turks have given the Russians a beating,' Charles said. 'And I've seen nothing of the action.'

Beaston shook his head in emphatic contradiction. 'This war is only just beginning, my friend. We are going to invade Russia. Even as I speak there are ships reconnoitring the coast of the Crimean peninsula seeking a suitable landing point for the army. It is pretty well decided that we are to attack the Russian naval base at Sebastopol.' He paused. 'But you are to say nothing of this to anyone until the official announcement is made,' he warned.

'But when is it to be?' Charles asked excitedly.

His companion shrugged. 'Hard to say. Later rather than sooner, I would guess.' Seeing Charles's disappointment he smiled in sympathy. 'But I have hopes of seeing some action before then. The French are going to strike against the Russians on the line of the Danube. Marshal St Arnaud is impatient to win some glory, and he's preparing to send infantry divisions across the Dobrudja province. The Bashi-Bazouks are to provide the advance cavalry screen, and I am to command a regiment of them.'

'How I wish I were in your place!' Charles exclaimed. 'I would give ten years of my life to see some action. Eighty miles north of here the Turks were fighting and we did nothing, and if I have to sit on my arse doing nothing for any longer I think that I'll go stark raving mad!'

One of Beaston's men, a huge, coal-black Sudanese, came to tell him something in guttural Arabic. Beaston dismissed the man with a wave of his hand, then grinned at Charles. 'I have to leave you now, my friend.'

They shook hands and parted. Charles finished his drink and went outside to his tethered horse. He was just about to mount when there came a sudden loud commotion further down the street, and he heard a woman's voice shrieking furiously.

'You dirty, thievin' little haythen! I'll tear your balls off for ye!'

Curious to see who this English speaker was, he pushed through the quickly gathering swarm of eager onlookers.

'I'll teach you, you thievin' haythen!' Dorcas Murphy's left hand was gripping the small Turkish soldier's throat, choking off his guttural cries. Her right hand was between his legs, savagely twisting his genitals.

Rosie Collier was belabouring the soldier's shaven head with a thick stick, and Annie Bartleet, a baby in her arms, was weeping and wailing in concert with the children gathered around her skirts.

The encircling crowd were laughing and clapping, cheering on the female combatants.

'What's brought this about?' Charles asked

a red-coated British soldier who was standing laughing with two comrades in the forefront of the circle.

'Johnny Turk tried to snatch a bundle from one of 'um, sir. But the fat 'un and the little 'un was at him as quick as ratting terriers. He'll know better in future, won't he, sir. Our army women ain't soft targets. They knows how to fight.'

Charles could not help but smile wryly to himself. As he looked more closely at the women, recognition came in a flash. 'They're from the regiment. I've seen them at Hounslow, haven't I? But what the hell are they doing here in Varna?' He stepped out 'That's enough! Let that man go!'

He was forced to shout several more times before the two women realized who he was and ceased their attack, allowing the Turk to scurry away, groaning and nursing his bleeding pate and sore genitals.

Rosie was flushed with exertion and excitement, her long auburn hair flying loose about her shoulders, and Charles Bronton thought how surprisingly fresh and attractive she was for a common soldier's woman.

'What are your names?' he demanded. 'And what are you doing here in Varna? Why aren't you with the regiment at Devnya?'

Rosie told him their names, and who their husbands were, and then explained that they had been forced to sail from Portsmouth on a separate transport, which had deposited them at Gallipoli. From there they had eventually

261

managed to get a passage to Scutari transit camp in Turkey, and then finally on another vessel to Varna.

'We only left the ship this morning, sir. We were trying to get to the regiment. That Turk said he'd guide us, but then he tried to make off with our things.' She indicated the blanket-wrapped bundles of possessions and pleaded, 'Can you help us to get to the regiment, sir? We're not safe travelling by ourselves, are we? Three unprotected women.'

Charles thought of the battered Turkish soldier, and smiled ironically. 'Unprotected? I believe that if you two were issued with muskets and bayonets you'd be capable of taking on the entire Turkish Army.'

Rosie giggled and, seeing her white, even teeth, Charles was again struck by how very desirable she was, and found himself thinking that she was wasted on a coarse common soldier such as Jack Collier. She'd be much better off as the mistress of someone like himself who could truly appreciate her sensuality.

He guiltily quelled that thought as unfitting for an officer and a gentleman, and that same guilt impelled him to say, 'Very well. I will arrange transport and escort you to the regiment myself.'

Rosie beamed her gratitude, and once again he found himself regretting that both the Queen's regulations and his own personal honour as a gentleman prohibited any sort of carnal relationship between them.

Thirty-Five

The British cavalry encampments around the town of Devnya were little more than twenty miles from the coast. Charles Bronton hired an ox-cart to carry the women and children, and the long wooden-wheeled vehicle drawn by eight oxen took three days to make the journey.

Rosie was not irked by the tortuous progress, however. She drank in the beauty of the countryside they passed through. It was hilly and green, with lakes and streams and blue mountains on the distant horizons. There was an abundance of bird life. Storks flew in long lines, eagles soared and buzzards, vultures and kites scoured the wide plains. The trees and bushes were alive with green and yellow orioles. Jays, woodpeckers, grosbeaks and warblers sang and chattered through the days, and doves and partridges provided good eating for hunters.

She hadn't yet discovered that with all this beauty there came also torments and menaces. The military camps were swarming with huge voracious ants and were plagued by fleas, slugs, snakes and leeches. Clouds of biting flies continually attacked men and horses, driving both humans and animals half mad. The water supplies had been contaminated by the armies. Malarial fevers were laying men low, amoebic dysentery and cholera were on a rapid increase, and deaths were mounting. The horses were also fast declining, and on the voyage out from England so many horses had died or been injured that none of the cavalry regiments were able to keep all their men mounted, even though those regiments had left England woefully understrength as it was. They numbered little more than two full squadrons, comprising two troops each, instead of the recommended war establishment of four squadrons.

The small cavacade reached the camp of the 20th Light Dragoons late in the afternoon of their third day of travel. Of the three women, only Annie Bartleet voiced her joy at being so close to reunion with her husband.

Dorcas Murphy rolled her eyes in sarcastic reaction to Annie Bartleet's tearful protestations of thanks.

'Jaysus Christ! She loves the bones of him, don't she! Speaking for meself, I'd be as happy sharing me bed with the Devil, as sharing it with that rotten drunken bastard of mine. What say you, Rosie?'

Rosie smiled thoughtfully. She had never been in love with her husband, but she felt that she owed him her loyalty and support. 'Jack's alright,' she answered. 'I could have had a lot worse than him.'

The Irishwoman leered salaciously. 'And at least he gives you plenty of the needful, don't he? I can't remember the last time that my man give me a good shagging.'

A hundred yards from the rigidly aligned rows of bell tents that comprised the 20th Light Dragoons' encampment, Charles Bronton spurred ahead. As he reined in at the guard tent, Cornet Peter Barryton came hurrying to speak to him.

The youth was resplendently uniformed and accoutred, the only concession made to active service being the removal of the flowing white plume from his shako.

'Hello, Peter, you're duty officer?' Charles asked.

The youth shook his head. 'No, there's been a punishment parade called. Fothergill has just ordered summary punishment for three of B Troop. Corporal Collier and Privates Murphy and Rawlings.'

'Corporal Collier?' Charles was shocked. 'But he's a steady man. What happened?'

'The usual thing. The three of them were in the village this morning, drunk on raki and knocking the locals about. Sergeant-Major Peebles saw them and ordered them back to camp. They abused him, and Collier offered to fight him. So, naturally, he had them arrested. Fothergill has awarded them fifty each. And you'll be needing another corporal for B Troop, because Collier's lost his stripes of course.'

'Dammed fool. He would almost certainly

have made sergeant within the next few weeks, we're losing men so fast.' Charles shrugged. 'Ah well, they've got off lightly. Fothergill could have ordered a court martial, and then it would have been two hundred and fifty lashes. I'll ask Fothergill to give Finch a chance as corporal, and Bartleet can take the trumpet in Rawlings' place.' He took off his shako and mopped the sweat from his forehead with a piece of towelling.

'Oh, by the way, your servant's gone down with the fever. You'll need to replace him also.' Barryton chuckled. 'It's not one of your better days, is it?'

Charles cursed irritably, and swiped without effect at the cloud of flies buzzing around his head. 'No, it isn't. I can't even kill a damn fly.'

Peter Barryton's expression became tense and nervous. 'I hate seeing the men flogged, Charles, it turns my stomach.'

'It doesn't do much for my appetite either.' Charles sighed regretfully. 'But you know what many of the men are like, Peter. They live for the drink, and once they've had a skinful they become wild beasts, and wild beasts are only kept under control by fear of their masters' whips.'

He stared sombrely at the youth. 'But it is our system that keeps them behaving like wild beasts, Peter. I met the author Captain Nolan once. It is his belief that only when we begin to treat the soldier and his family with kindness and respect will we have an army that will not need to be flogged. Its soldiers will be self-disciplined and efficient, because they will have a proper respect for themselves.'

A trumpet shrilled the assembly call, and Charles grimaced ruefully. 'However, until that happy day dawns, we shall just have to continue flogging the poor devils.'

The loud creakings of the lumbering ox-cart sounded behind him, and he frowned with concern. During the journey from Varna he had come to like Rosie Collier for herself, appreciating her lively mind, good humour and the unfailing kindliness she showed towards the other women and children.

'This is a sad reunion for her,' he murmured, and signalled the cart to halt. 'Collier, Murphy, I've unfortunate news for you both. Your husbands are to be punished for serious misconduct. The parade is forming now, so I would suggest that you keep the children out of sight and earshot to avoid unnecessarily distressing them.'

'What's Jack done?' Rosie's heart sank.

Bronton related what he had been told.

'Oh my God!' Rosie shook her head in dismay. 'He's a good man, until he gets the drink inside him. It'll be his ruin.'

Dorcas Murphy only shrugged. 'That bastard Murphy is more trouble than he's worth. It's me that has to look after the bugger after he's took a flogging.'

The parade was formed in a hollow, three-sided square, and on the open side three sets

267

of tent poles had been roped together to form triangles. A small procession came marching from the guard tent.

The provost sergeant led, followed in single file by the three prisoners, hands bound behind their backs, bodies stripped to the waist. The prisoners were flanked by an escort with carbines at the high port, and bringing up the rear were the farrier sergeant and farriers.

All eyes rested on the three short-stocked whips in the farrier sergeant's hand, each whip with its nine long thongs, each thong knotted nine times along its length.

Major Philip Fothergill stood in company with the officers some yards from the triangles. Closer to the triangles, Charles Bronton and the surgeon waited.

The procession halted and the escorts spreadeagled the prisoners on the triangles, securing ankles and wrists with pieces of rope. Michael Rawlings was white-faced with fear and visibly trembling. Colum Murphy was grinning defiantly. Jack Collier was sullenly scowling.

Whispers hissed along the ranks and the NCOs bellowed for silence.

Charles Bronton's gaze wandered, and he frowned with pity as he saw over the rows of tall shakoes the small group of women and children clustered on top of an empty transport waggon, some weeping, others staring with wide eyes and pale, worried faces. His attention focussed on Rosie Collier's strained features, her hands clutched tightly together between her breasts.

The provost sergeant approached the group of officers and saluted. 'Prisoners made ready for punishment, sir. Shall it be one at a time, or simultaneous, sir?'

'Simultaneously,' Fothergill snapped. 'But hold fast a moment, Sergeant Jenkins.' He stepped out from the group of officers and turned to face the ranks. 'Parade! Attenshun!'

Spurred heels jingled in impact, bodies stiffened into rigid statues.

'Take heed of what I say.' Fothergill's acidic voice carried clearly through the humid air. 'You have grown slack in turn-out and discipline. But I will tighten you up, if I have to flog every man here to do so.'

At that moment a man in the far rank, tormented beyond endurance by a stinging fly, slapped at his cheek.

'Sergeant-Major!' Fothergill barked.

'Sir?' Henry Peebles stamped forward and his arm flashed up in quivering salute.

'Place that man under close arrest. Bring him before me tomorrow morning for sentence.'

'Very good, sir!' Peebles flashed another quivering salute, and bellowed, 'You two men there, escort the prisoner to the guard tent. At the double, damn you! At the double!'

The unfortunate man was hurried away at a run, and the ranks stood wondering on whom the axe would next fall.

Fothergill nodded to the farrier sergeant.

'Carry on.'

The grizzled-haired old veteran took wads of leather and pushed them between the teeth of the prisoners. 'Bite hard on it, lads,' he told them gruffly. 'It'll help you bear the pain.'

Colum Murphy spat the wad out. 'I don't need to bite on nothing,' he jeered. 'The cat's not been fashioned that can draw a whimper from me.'

The NCO glanced at the mass of scar tissue on the man's back, and said with genuine admiration, 'No, I don't reckon it has, Murphy. You're a hard one, and no mistake.'

To the pallid-faced, trembling Michael Rawlings, he said, 'Don't try counting the strokes, lad. Just stick it out. It'll be over sooner than you thinks.'

He took station some yards distant and ordered the farriers, 'Do your duty.'

The thongs whirled high in hissing unison and slashed down with savage force. A low-pitched growl rose from the ranks.

'One! Two! Three! Four! Five!' The farrier sergeant, hardened by the countless floggings he had administered during his long service, stood impassively counting in measured cadence.

By the twelfth stroke the prisoners' backs were a criss-crossing mass of plum-coloured weals, the bites of the knotted thongs bringing oozing blood, and every stroke that followed cutting deeper into flesh. Blood spattered upon the farriers' arms, faces and shirts, and ran down to soak the prisoners'

270

overalls.

Michael Rawlings was writhing and shrieking in agony. He lost bladder control, and urine pooled around his feet, snaking in thin winding rivulets across the dusty ground.

Cornet Peter Barryton gagged and heaved and hurried from the ground to hide his vomiting. A young soldier in the ranks toppled over in a faint. Some men looked away from the bloody backs. Others growled with hatred for those who had inflicted the punishment. Some stared with stolid indifference, and a few men's eyes glistened with obscene excitement.

Rosie was silently weeping for her husband's agony and humiliation, tears running down her cheeks, but she could not turn away. Charles Bronton saw her suffering, and hated what he was witnessing, but steeled himself to show no emotion.

Colum Murphy lifted his sweat-soaked face to the skies, and bared his teeth in snarling defiance. Grunting as the thongs bit into his torn flesh, he gasped out, 'That's it! Lay it on! Lay it on, you bastard.'

Jack Collier stood in silence, his head bowed, eyes tight closed, face contorted, his body shuddering at each slice of the whip, his teeth grinding into the thick leather wad until it was a shredded soggy pulp.

'Forty-nine ... Fifty!'

'Punishment completed, sir.'

'Thank you, Sergeant Jenkins.' Fothergill had watched calmly, secure in the conviction that he had acted in the best interests of regimental discipline and order.

Buckets of salted water were brought and thrown on to the bloodied backs, then the prisoners were untied and taken away. Michael Rawlings had to be supported by his escorts, but Jack Collier and Colum Murphy struck the proffered helping arms away and walked with heads held high, glorying in the muted covert plaudits of their comrades.

'Sergeant-Major, give the men an hour of the rapid drill,' Fothergill instructed, and then he and his officers strolled from the ground while behind them Henry Peebles' bawled commands sent sweating, panting men in motion like frenzied marionettes.

'Come on, Rosie, dry your eyes,' Dorcas Murphy admonished sternly. 'You've seen a flogging before. Why do you let this one upset you so?'

'Because it's the first time I've seen my own husband flogged, that's why!' Rosie sparked defiantly.

'Well, get used to it.' The Irishwoman showed no sympathy. 'Because if your man don't watch it, he'll be getting plenty more where that came from. I've seen it all before, girl. Once a good steady soldier gets the lash, it seems to do something to his head, and before you know it he turns into a "Queen's Hard Bargain". So you'd better try and talk some sense into Jack's head before he drags you both down.' The Irishwoman took hold of Rosie's arm and pulled her along. 'We'll get across to the hospital. That's where they'll be took.'

'What about Annie's kids? She might be needing help with them,' Rosie said.

Dorcas chuckled grimly. 'There's no need to worry about the kids, my jewel. They're safe and well, because by now Annie 'ull have washed 'um all in the blood of the lamb, and saved their souls for 'um.'

The regimental hospital consisted of four bell tents placed in isolation from the encampment. They were crammed full of men suffering from fevers, dysentery and the Bloody Flux. A little distance apart lay two blanket-wrapped corpses awaiting burial. The stench of excreta and rotting bodies polluted the area and clouds of voracious flies hummed and buzzed and continually tormented the sick and the few who attended them.

Outside one tent the youthful assistant surgeon was smearing ointment across Jack Collier's ravaged back when Rosie and Dorcas arrived.

'Oh Jack, why do you have to drink so much? You know how it changes you.' Rosie was torn between worried concern for him and angry resentment that he should have behaved so stupidly.

His sweaty face was pale and drawn with pain, but he tried to force a smile. 'Now don't have a go at me, Rosie. I'm real glad you've come at last. I been worrying about where you might be and if you was alright or no.'

'Are you their women?' the surgeon asked, and when they nodded he handed Rosie the small wooden box of ointment. 'Then you can look after them. I've other men to attend to who are here through no fault of their own.'

Dorcas snarled aggressively at Colum Murphy. 'What did I ever do to deserve a rotten husband like you?'

He returned her aggressive snarl. 'You kept on living, instead o' jumping into your grave like a Christian, you bloody cow.'

Jack Collier winked at Rosie. 'There now, ain't they a happy, loving couple. They're a shining example to us all.'

His brave attempt at humour dissolved Rosie's anger and resentment, and she softened towards him. 'I'll finish spreading this, and then I'll get some cloth to cover your back,' she said as, gently and carefully, she began to dress his wounds.

Thirty-Six

British Cavalry Camp, Devnya,
August, 1854

'For as much as it hath pleased Almighty God of his great mercy to take unto himself the soul of our dear brother here departed, we therefore commit his body to the ground...'

Charles Bronton recited the prayer from memory. 'Earth to earth, ashes to ashes, dust to dust; in sure and certain hope of the resurrection to eternal life through our Lord Jesus Christ.' He closed his eyes in thought. 'I should have been a damned parson.'

He continued to the end of the burial prayer and nodded to the corporal lined up with the firing party to one side of the open grave. The man saluted.

'Prime and load ... Ready ... Present ... Fire!'

The ragged volley of shots echoed across the green hills and the breeze skittered on the surface of the lake, and that same breeze caught up and wafted away the small grey-black clouds of smoke discharged by the exploding cartridges.

'Prime and load ... Ready ... Present ... Fire!'

Twice more the volley echoed, and then the firing party shouldered their carbines and were marched away by the corporal. Charles followed them.

'Get it filled in! Move yourselves, you idle bastards!' Henry Peebles bellowed. Jack Collier and Colum Murphy stamped the blades of their long-handled shovels into the heap of loose earth and began to throw the spoil down upon the blanket-wrapped corpse of ex-Regimental Sergeant-Major Shrive.

'Why are you rushing so to cover poor old Shrive up, Henry?' Trumpet-Major Joseph Blackstone chuckled. 'He's not about to jump out of there, is he?' He tapped the three stripes surmounted by a crown on Peebles' arm. 'Are you scared he might rise from the dead and stop you adding the fourth stripe? The poor old sod wasn't even cold when you stripped his chevrons off his tunic, was he?'

Peebles' strong yellowing teeth bared in a savage grin. 'I've been waiting a long time to get to be regimental sergeant-major, Joe. Can you blame me for being a bit impatient to get them off the useless old bugger and put them where they rightly belongs?'

'Well don't jump the gun, Henry,' his friend cautioned. 'You haven't got the RSM's place yet. There's a couple of others in the running for it.'

The fitful breeze died away and the intense heat again exerted its untempered, stifling grip. Sweat rolled down the labouring privates' faces, dripping from their chins, running into their eyes to fiercely sting and smart.

'Jaysus, it's hotter than hell,' Colum Murphy complained. 'I could almost feel jealous of old Shrivey. He's a bloody sight cooler down there than we are up here.'

Jack Collier smiled sardonically and, pausing from work, stared at the two NCOs. 'Will you be saying a private prayer over the grave when we've finished here, Sergeant-Major? A prayer of thanksgiving perhaps?' he asked with exaggerated respect.

Peebles appeared puzzled by the question. 'Why should I be doing that, Collier?'

'Well, Sergeant-Major, if God hadn't taken Mr Shrive so quick, you might well have taken a fever and died yourself before having a chance of gaining the fourth stripe. The notion come to me that you might want to give thanks to God for his goodness. He must know how much you deserves to take Mr Shrive's rank. Seeing as how much service you've had with them toy soldiers in the yeomanry.'

'Jaysus!' Colum Murphy exclaimed in shock at his comrade's foolhardy audacity.

Joseph Blackstone erupted with raucous laughter.

Peebles' expression displayed no reaction and when he spoke his tone was equally expressionless. 'As soon as you've made up Mr Shrive's grave and mounded it all tidy,

277

you can dig another one next to it, Private Collier. And you can help him, Private Murphy.'

'Oh Jaysus, Sarn't-Major, me back's broke already from digging this 'un,' the Irishman complained plaintively. 'It'll take hours. The ground's awful hard. It's like iron, so it is. And me hands are blistered raw to the bone.'

'It had better not take hours, Private Murphy.' Peebles smiled almost pleasantly. 'Because I'm marking the pair of you down for guard duty tonight, and your turn-out had better be up to scratch, or you'll be in real trouble.'

'But we was both on outlying picket last night, Sarn't-Major,' Murphy protested. 'And we was on the night guard on Tuesday as well.'

'Well, I'm very relieved to hear that, Private Murphy.' Peebles was smiling broadly now. 'It's took a weight off my mind that has, knowing that you've had the practice before, so you'll be able to carry out the duty to my satisfaction.'

The smile abruptly vanished, and he barked, 'I'll be coming back up here to measure the grave, so you'd best make a proper job of it if you know what's good for you.'

The two NCOs turned and marched from the row of fresh raw graves. Once they were out of earshot, Murphy hurled his shovel to the ground and furiously cursed his friend.

'Bloody hell, Jack, why couldn't you keep that tongue of yours still? If you wants to keep on fighting a war with that bastard, then fight it by yourself and don't drag me into it with you.'

Jack Collier only grinned savagely. 'If ever we gets into a battle, then I'll put a ball into the back of his head.'

After a moment or two, Colum Murphy laughed. 'Well, you'll have to be quick about it, Jack. Because I'm intending to do the very same thing meself.'

'Then maybe I'd best do it without waiting for a battle.' Jack Collier's eyes were murderous. 'Because I want that bastard's blood, more than I've ever wanted anything else in my whole life.'

'In the meantime, I've got some pressing business to attend to.' Murphy suddenly began to dig out the earth covering one end of Shrive's corpse.

'What the hell are you doing?' Jack exclaimed in amazement.

The Irishman kept on shovelling the earth out until he had uncovered the blanket, then ripped through the thin fabric and extracted two bottles. Grinning broadly, he handed one bottle to Jack.

'I put these in here when I sewed the old bugger in it. I reckoned that we'd need a wee drink or two, because funerals always gives me a powerful thirst. And I had the notion that Peebles 'ud keep us up here sweating.'

'Good on you! You're a true Christian, Paddy.' Jack Collier pulled the cork from the bottle with his teeth and took an eager gulp of its contents.

Thirty-Seven

'Trumpet-Major? Trumpet-Major?' Rosie came out of the tent when she saw Joseph Blackstone passing. 'Have you come from the graveyard? Is my husband still up there?'

'He is that. And he's likely to be up there for a couple of hours yet, my wench.' Blackstone appreciated a pretty face, and had a soft spot for this young woman. 'You might make a start on cleaning his kit, because he's down for the night guard. And your man is as well, Dorcas.'

Dorcas had come to the tent flap, and when she heard this information she cackled with raucous laughter. 'I bet that pleased the bastard, didn't it. I don't think! And he can clean his own bloody kit. I'm not his servant.'

'Suit yourself,' Blackstone retorted as he walked on. 'But Peebles is going to be inspecting them, and if your man isn't up to scratch then he'll most likely be getting his hide scratched by the Drummer's Daughter again.'

'Good!'

'Now you don't mean that,' Rosie remonstrated.

'Maybe I don't, and maybe I do.' The Irishwoman's fat face creased with laughter. 'But seeing as it's pay day tomorrow, and I'll be wanting the price of a drink, I'd best keep the bastard sweet, hadn't I?'

The two women spent the next few hours burnishing, polishing, washing and brushing their husbands' elaborate uniforms, accoutrements and saddlery equipment. The shadows of afternoon were lengthening by the time they had finished.

'They should have been back long before now.' Rosie peered out of the tent flap towards the high ground where the graveyard was situated. 'They must be starving hungry.'

'So am I.' Dorcas rubbed her huge belly. 'I hope Annie's got the grub ready. I could eat a scabby babby. Let's get to the cookhouse and make sure that the greedy buggers don't eat our rations as well as their own.'

Suspicion as to the reason for her husband's non-appearance was beginning to plague Rosie. 'You go on ahead and save my share. I'm going up to the graveyard and see what's keeping them.'

'Ahh, that's the right stuff, that is. The right stuff!'

The cords stood out in Colum Murphy's thick throat as he swigged from the bottle of raki.

'Leave some for the rest of us, you paddy

pig!' Jack Collier snarled and snatched at the bottle, but he was so drunk that he missed his aim and toppled forwards to sprawl face downwards on the ground. The circle of crouching men roared with laughter, and Murphy blinked owlishly at the fallen man.

'What's you doing down there, Jack? It's not like you to go to kip with drink still left in the bottle.'

The group were in a shallow dip in the ground just beyond the horse lines where the beasts, covered in blankets and rags in a vain attempt to keep off the swarming flies, stamped and squealed in distress under the onslaught of their biting tormentors.

Rosie had to pass the horse lines en route to the graveyard, and heard the laughter as she approached. Her face twisted in both anger and dismay. By the time she reached the dip, her husband was on his feet again, sucking greedily at the bottle of raki.

'Jack!' she shouted angrily and ran down the slope to grab the bottle from him.

He stood swaying, staring at her in fuddled shock.

'Look at you!' she stormed at him. 'You're down for night guard and you're as drunk as a bob 'owler. Do you want to go on the triangle again?'

His bloodshot eyes blinked slowly, then narrowed threateningly. 'Give me that bottle.'

'No!' She shook her head, her long hair shining in the sunlight as it tossed from side to side.

'You're showing me up,' he said. 'Now, I won't tell you again. Give me that bottle back.'

A hush had fallen on the rowdy circle and the men watched intently. In their rough world the man was expected to be the master of his woman, and any man who failed to demonstrate that mastery became an object of scorn and ridicule to his fellows.

Jack Collier stepped close to his wife and glared into her tense face. Again she stubbornly shook her head. 'No, you shan't have it.' She upended the bottle and a concerted bellow of outrage erupted from the watchers as the liquid splashed on to the ground.

Collier's eyes blazed and he punched her with all his force, catapulting her slender body back and over. As she lay, half-stunned and helpless, his boot thudded into her body again and again until the other men rose and pulled him back.

Winded and wracked with pain she lay gasping for breath, drawn up into a foetal position, her arms wrapped instinctively in a protective shield around the child in her womb.

Another bottle of raki had been produced and she remained ignored as the men passed it from hand to hand and their raucous jests and laughter sounded once more. As soon as she was able, she crawled on hands and knees up the slope, then got to her feet to stagger back towards the tents.

A hand stopped her, fingers cupped and

lifted her chin, and Henry Peebles scowled down at her. 'Who done this to you, Rosie? Was it your man?'

'It's none of your business,' she spat.

His fingers gently touched the painfully swelling flesh around her left eye. 'You'll be needing a leech on this,' he told her. 'You'd better come with me to the surgeon.'

'No. I don't need any surgeon. Just leave me be, will you?'

'Why did he hit you? Is he drunk again?'

His tone was sympathetic, and Rosie was weakened by that sympathy. A sob tore from her throat, and she blurted out, 'It's the flogging that did it. He isn't the same as he was before. It's like the Devil's got into him. He doesn't seem to care about anything other than swilling drink down his throat.'

'I've seen it happen a lot of times, Rosie,' Peebles told her solemnly. 'A man can be a good soldier and conduct himself well, and then he gets a taste of the cat, and it changes him for the worst.'

'But it was you who got him flogged,' she accused.

'Oh no!' He shook his head emphatically. 'Oh no! He got himself flogged, Rosie. I gave the three of them the chance to go back to their tents, and it was your man who got saucy. I'd no choice but to report him.'

Rosie reluctantly accepted this truth, but still challenged him. 'But why do they need to flog men like they do?'

He shrugged. 'What else can we do with the

bad 'uns?'

'But Jack's not a bad 'un!' she protested loyally. 'That was the first time he'd ever done anything wrong. Why couldn't they just take his stripes away? Why did they have to flog him like he was an animal? He's not like Colum Murphy and that crowd. He's not a bad 'un like them. And the bloody officers get drunk all the time, don't they? Why aren't they flogged for it like the men are?'

Peebles' manner hardened abruptly. 'That's enough of that sort of talk, girl. Officers are officers, and the men are the men. It's not your place to question how things are done.'

She rounded on him, spitting like a savage alley cat. 'You bloody officers are all the same, aren't you? Only looking out for yourselves. You don't care what happens to anybody else, just so long as you get your promotions and keep the stripes on your arms.'

She turned as if to run from him, and he grabbed her arm to hold her back. Bending so that his face was only inches from hers, he growled fiercely. 'I didn't get my stripes and crown by arse-licking. I earned them by good soldiering, and I'll keep them by more of the same. My dad was a soldier, and his dad before him. I was born in the barracks. That was a hard school to be raised in, and I knew from when I was a babby that the Drummer's Daughter was the schoolmarm. Now, if your man was stupid enough to get a dose of the Drummer's Daughter, then that's his own fault, and nobody else's. So you take my advice, girl, and keep that lip of yours buttoned up, because if I hear you bad-mouthing the officers again, it'll be your back that'll be getting flayed.' He pushed her away from him, turned on his heel and left her.

Her roused gutter devil was not intimidated by his threat. 'I'll say whatever I want to say,' she shouted at his retreating back. 'I'm not afraid of you or the bloody officers!'

He gave no sign of having heard her, only continued steadily on his way. She hissed in frustration and for a moment was tempted to go back to Jack Collier and make another attempt to stop him drinking. But then the painful throbbing of her damaged flesh brought home the futility of that action. All she would gain would be another beating.

She started to walk towards the tent she shared with the other women and children, but then on impulse changed direction and went up the hillside towards the expanding burial-ground halfway to the summit. At the end of the row of raw grave mounds a solitary figure was sitting. As she approached him, Arthur Sinclair turned his head and smiled in welcome.

'And what brings you up to this hill of sorrows, Rosie?'

'I just fancied a bit of peace and quiet,' she told him, and seated herself beside him. 'It won't disturb you, me sitting here, will it, Arthur?'

'Of course not. I'm always happy to be in

your company.' He studied her swollen, discoloured eye and grimaced with concern. 'You and Jack been quarrelling, have you?'

She sighed and nodded. 'He's swilling the pongalo down again and he's marked for night guard. His back's still not healed, and he's heading for another flogging as sure as God made little apples.' She shook her head helplessly. 'I don't know what to do about him, Arthur. It's like the Devil's got into him, and he won't listen to anything I tell him any more. When I try to stop him getting himself into trouble, I get my eye blacked.'

She took a short clay pipe and a piece of plug tobacco from her skirt pocket. 'Let's have a smoke, shall we?'

Sinclair readily assented.

'Why couldn't I have wed a real gentleman like you, Arthur?' Rosie smiled wistfully. 'I'll bet you've never raised your hand against a woman in your life.'

'No, I haven't,' Sinclair confirmed, smiling, 'but I have to confess that there have been times when I've been sorely tempted to do so.'

Rosie finished filling the bowl of the pipe, then struck a lucifer match and held the flame against the tobacco, sucking hard until it was drawing well. She blew out a cloud of smoke and passed the pipe to Sinclair, and for some time they sat in silence, passing the pipe between them, exhaling clouds of blue smoke that wreathed above their heads in the still air.

Rosie's eyes had been regarding a tiny grave mound set apart from the rest, and she muttered sadly, 'Do you know something, Arthur, there are times when I have to wonder why God makes women suffer so. Poor Annie Bartleet's heart broke when her baby was laid to rest here, and now another of her children is dying.'

She turned and counted the row of graves. 'Eleven of the lads gone already, and half the troop down with sickness. The French are dropping like flies with the cholera, and they say that it's now striking our regiments as well. I think that we'll be lucky if any of us leave here alive, never mind healthy.'

'I don't think we'll remain here much longer, Rosie. From what I hear we shall soon be invading the Crimea.'

'Where exactly is the Crimea?' she asked.

'Over the sea to the east there.' Sinclair pointed.

'Why should we be going there?'

'Because it's part of Russia. We shall be taking the war into their homeland.'

'I wish I was educated like you,' she said wistfully. 'I've hardly any learning at all. I feel very stupid and dense.'

'Oh no, you're not. You're one of the cleverest people that I've ever known.'

'How can I be clever, when I'm not educated?' she disputed.

'Let me assure you, Rosie, that some of the most highly educated people are among the most stupid. In knowledge of life, you far excel them. And that gives you more good sense and wisdom than the vast majority of the scholars I met during my years at university.'

'Good sense and wisdom.' She echoed his words despondently. 'I don't think that I've got much of either. And if I have, it hasn't done me any good so far.'

He sat motionless, looking at her sad face. A poignant yearning filled his heart, and he murmured, 'I truly wish that I'd met you years ago, Rosie, before I ruined my life.'

'And what difference would our meeting then have made?' She smiled.

'I would have asked you to marry me, Rosie, and perhaps followed the path my parents wished for me to take.'

'What did they want you to do, Arthur?'

He grimaced ruefully. 'My family wanted me to enter the Church. I'm descended from a long line of clergy. My father is a bishop. Do you think that you would have enjoyed being a parson's wife?'

The sheer incongruity of the suggestion made Rosie giggle with ironic amusement. 'No, Arthur.' She shook her head. 'I don't think that I would ever have made a suitable wife for a parson.'

A trumpet call echoed from the encampment, bringing her back to reality. 'I'll have to get back to camp. I'm going to go and ask Peebles to take Jack off the night guard. Here, you finish this.' She handed him the clay pipe and, lifting her skirts, ran from the graveyard.

Arthur Sinclair watched her go, and silently cursed the fate that had made her another man's wife.

Henry Peebles was alone in his tent, sitting on his bedding roll, when Rosie thrust her head through the tent flap.

'Can I have a word with you?' she asked.

He nodded impassively.

'Look, I'm sorry about what I said to you before. It was wrong of me.'

'That's right, it was,' he agreed, and his eyes held a gleam of satisfaction. She was about to speak again, but he gestured her to be silent.

'If you've come to ask me to overlook your man being too drunk for guard duty, then save your breath. He's going to be meeting the Drummer's Daughter again. That's as sure as there's a sun in the sky.'

'But another flogging could finish him for good!' she protested desperately. 'Just let him off the guard duty this once, and I'll make sure that he behaves himself in the future.'

'And what's in it for me, Rosie?' A smile was hovering upon his full lips. 'What advantage do I get if I let the bugger off?'

Rose had already steeled herself to face the inevitable. To save her husband from the flogging that she truly believed would bring irreparable damage to his personal pride and morale, she was fully prepared to pay whatever he demanded of her. She knew that she had only one thing to barter with: her sexual desirability. She drew a sharp breath and stepped fully into the tent, letting the flap drop behind her.

'You can have me again,' she told him levelly. 'You can have me right now.'

He grinned wolfishly and came to his feet. 'Now, I've got to admit that that's a very tempting offer, Rosie.' He stepped close and his hands moved to cup and fondle her firm breasts. She remained submissively still. Then his hands dropped, and he shook his head. The wolfish grin still bared his teeth, but his voice was gentler now.

'I'm not going to take advantage of you, Rosie, much as I'd like to, because there ain't going to be any guard mounted on this camp tonight.'

'No guard mounted?' Rosie was a little bewildered by this abrupt change.

'The regiment's just received orders to march back to Varna. I've already sent men to round up your bloke and his mates. So you'd best get off, and just make sure the bugger is able to stay on his horse for the march.'

Rosie experienced a confusion of emotions. Relief that Jack was not going to be punished was uppermost. Relief also that she was not going to have to act the whore again. But also there was a growing realization that she had misjudged Henry Peebles' character.

Sensing her confusion, Peebles chuckled. 'There now, Rosie, I'm not such a wicked, conniving bastard as you thought, am I? It might even be possible that I've got a bit of decency hidden deep inside me, mightn't it?'

'Yes, it might,' she admitted.

'But that's a fact that's got to stay a secret between you and me, Rosie. Because if it ever becomes common knowledge, then I'll lose my reputation as a hard, cruel bastard, and I can't afford for that to happen.'

He pushed her gently from the tent. 'Now, get your bloke ready for the march, because if he ain't, I'll have to have him.'

Thirty-Eight

Scorched by the brazen glare of the sun, enveloped in clouds of choking dust, seventy thousand men and seven thousand horses marched towards the port of Varna. Funnelling along the rutted roads from the north, the south and the west, the sweating, cursing soldiers of Great Britain, France and Turkey trudged for hour after hour, leaving in their wake a trail of human debris, men too weakened by fever to march on, or dead or dying from the cholera.

Some miles to the rear of their regiment, and on foot, Rosie, Dorcas and Annie Bartleet, each carrying a child in their arms and laden with their bundled possessions, were making slow and weary progress through the rolling countryside in company with the other regimental women.

A battalion of French infantry had traversed that way earlier, and some blue-tunicked, red-trousered soldiers struck down by the cholera were lying in their own excreta and vomit at the sides of the road. The dead were shrivelled and dark-faced from loss of bodily fluids.

Rosie wanted to help those men who were still alive, but the surgeons had warned that the cholera was highly infectious, and so she dared not risk going to their aid and endangering the health of the children. A sense of guilt assailed her as men gestured or croaked pleas for water, and she tried not to look at them as she passed by.

'That's one of our lads ahead there.' Dorcas pointed to a prostrate man in the dark-blue uniform of a Light Dragoon, who was lying face downwards some yards from the roadway. The women exclaimed in consternation and came to a halt, all eyes scrutinizing the man.

'Who is it?'

'Does anybody know him?'

'Oh God! I pray it's not my Augustus!' Annie Bartleet wailed hysterically. 'Dear God, don't let it be my Augustus! Don't let it be my Augustus.'

'Shut your bloody rattle, will you!' Dorcas reproved irritably. 'It's a pity he couldn't have laid face upwards, then we'd have been able to see who it is.'

'Somebody ought to go and have a look,' one woman said, and others agreed with her.

'Yeah. Somebody should go and look closer at him.'

'It could be one of our husbands.'

But, restrained by fear, no one ventured to move nearer. Then the man's hand moved and they cried out in shock.

Rosie had found it very difficult to refuse help to the Frenchmen, and she knew that if she passed this man from her own regiment without trying to help him, the guilt would haunt her for the rest for her life. Fighting to control her fear, she passed the small child she was carrying to another woman, and went towards the man.

'What the bloody hell are you doing?' Dorcas demanded incredulously. 'D'you want to catch the cholera?'

'Of course I don't,' Rosie answered over her shoulder. 'But he's one of our own. I can't just leave him here without trying to help him.'

She came to a standstill a couple of steps away from the man, and noted that around him there were no traces of the opaque, dirty-white fluid that cholera victims vomited in copious amounts.

Keeping her distance, she circled him so that she might see his features, and gasped in dismay when she saw it was Arthur Sinclair.

'Who is it?' a woman asked.

'It's Arthur Sinclair, from our troop.'

There were exclamations of relief, and Annie Bartleet cried out, 'Thank You, dear Lord. Thank You for saving my husband.

Thank You, dear Lord!'

'If I was you, Annie, I shouldn't spend too much breath thanking the bugger!' Dorcas frowned grimly. 'If the cholera's got among our troop, we could be finding your man laying in the dirt afore we gets much further along this bloody road.'

Rosie had been closely studying Arthur Sinclair's features, noting that his red-flushed face was not the dusky hue of cholera victims.

She went to him and knelt down to place her hand on his forehead. His skin was dry and burning-hot to her touch. Some twenty yards away from her was a clump of tall bushes, and she called to the other women.

'Will you come and give me a hand to shift him into the shade of those bushes?'

'Bugger that for a game of soldiers!' Megan Morgan, a buxom Welshwoman, answered. 'I'm not chancing getting cholera.' The other women loudly voiced their agreement with her.

'I don't think it is cholera. I reckon it might only be a fever that's taken him,' Rosie told them.

'And pigs might fly, girl. But I've never seen them doing so.' The Welshwoman shook her head. 'I don't care what you thinks he might have took. I'm not risking my neck.' She walked on along the road, and was immediately followed by all the others except for Dorcas and Annie Bartleet.

Dorcas gently put down the child she carried, and bawled after the retreating women.

'Wait for Annie, she needs a hand with her kids.'

Megan Morgan came back to lift the child and carry it on. Annie Bartleet was reluctant to leave her friends, but Dorcas pushed her. 'Don't you moither your head about me and Rosie. You've got your kids to think of. Get on your way now.'

The frail-bodied young woman was near to tears as she obeyed. The big Irishwoman came to Rosie and pushed her aside. She stood briefly staring at the comatose man, and then nodded.

'I reckon you're right, Rosie, it don't look like the cholera. But I don't reckon it's fever, neither. It looks more like the sunstroke.'

Stooping, she lifted Arthur Sinclair in her arms as if he were only a small child, and carried him into the shade of the tall bushes. Rosie could only shake her head in wry admiration of her friend's physical power. Dorcas began to strip the tight-fitting uniform from Sinclair, grumbling as she did so.

'It's madness expecting the lads to march and fight in this bloody heat wearing thick clothes like this.'

Stripped naked, Sinclair's body was lithe and muscular, startlingly white in contrast to his suntanned head and forearms, and Dorcas grinned in relief.

'Well he aren't shit himself, has he? So it aren't the cholera. He's got a sweet body. I wouldn't mind having a roll in the hay with him meself.'

She took her water canteen and, pulling his mouth open, dribbled water between his dry, cracked lips, then emptied the rest over his head and face.

'Give me your canteen, Rosie, and then look to see if there's any pool or stream around here. If it is the sunstroke that's took him, we needs to cool him down real quick, afore it kills him.'

She poured the water from Rosie's canteen down the length of Sinclair's torso and vigorously fanned air across his wet skin with her shawl.

'Where did you learn how to treat the sunstroke?' Rosie asked curiously.

'In Jamaica when I was with me second husband. He took the sunstroke one day. But it wasn't the sunstroke that killed him. It was the rum. Now go and find some water.'

Rosie stared across the rolling landscape and saw in the distance a huddle of buildings, their outlines shimmering in the hot air. Reasoning that where there were buildings there must be a water supply, she headed towards them, hurrying as fast as she could, the exertion bringing sweat pouring down her face and body.

As she got nearer to the buildings she saw that they appeared to be deserted and derelict, the tiled roofs collapsed, the mud and timber walls tumbledown. But still she pressed on, although her hope of finding water there was fast diminishing.

From hidden vantage points among the

ruined walls, keen eyes watched her approach, and when she got close enough, bodies began to snake sinuously outwards from those vantage points, utilizing the plentiful concealment of the uneven ground, tall grasses and thick shrubs to encircle her.

Rosie was breathing hard when she slowed to a halt a few yards from the nearest ruined building, and used her shawl to wipe the sweat from her face and throat while she peered about her. Although the area appeared to be deserted, a sense of uneasy foreboding suddenly afflicted her. It was unnaturally quiet, unnaturally still. There were no birds fluttering overhead, no rustlings of small creatures in the undergrowth, only a faint humming noise emanating from the innumerable hovering flies.

She wanted to turn away and leave this place, but the thought of Arthur Sinclair's desperate plight kept her here. For his sake she must find water. Urging herself onwards, she moved hesitantly towards the wall, then shrieked in fright as turbaned heads suddenly appeared over the battered, ochre-coloured bricks, and grinning bearded faces confronted her.

She turned to flee, only to meet a ring of men closing fast around her, blocking any chance of escape. For a fleeting instant terror threatened to engulf her senses, but she fought to keep her wits about her. Realizing that her only hope of escaping unscathed from this situation lay in trying to outwit them, she stood motionless, struggling to hide her fear.

The men closed the imprisoning circle and also came to a standstill. Wearing Turkish-style clothing, festooned with weapons, and uniform only in their filthy, stinking hairiness, she guessed that they must be Bashi-Bazouks, the Turkish irregular cavalry, notorious for their pillaging and raping.

Her heart was pounding rapidly and fear shuddered through her, but she forced herself to smile. 'I'm English. I'm a friend. I need to find water.' She pointed towards the distant roadway. 'There are many English soldiers over there, waiting for me to return.'

There was a rapid exchange of guttural talk and laughter, and then they jostled to crowd tightly around her. The foul stench of their bodies filled her nostrils. A greasy hand reached for her face. She struck it aside and shouted, 'I'm English. I want to speak to your officer!'

The huge, swarthy man roared with laughter, spraying spittle through jagged teeth black with decay.

An arm clamped across her throat from behind, choking off her cry of protest. Her legs were kicked from beneath her and brutal hands pinned her to the ground. With the expertise of practised rapists they spread-eagled her, holding her arms and legs wide apart, clamping her head so that she could not bite, using a knife to rip her clothing apart.

The sight of her shapely breasts and smooth belly and thighs provoked exclamations of lustful admiration. The huge, swarthy man stripped himself of his weaponry, untied his waist sash and unbuckled his belt to allow his voluminous pantaloons to fall down his thighs.

Rosie closed her eyes, praying fervently in her mind. 'Please God, don't let my child be harmed. Please don't let this harm my baby!'

Her childhood years of bitter experience came to Rosie's aid, and saved her sanity. She knew that she could survive rape, that this abuse of her body would not destroy her mentally or physically. For the sake of her unborn child she would come through this. She deliberately relaxed her muscles and, as she had done so many many times before, divorced her mind from her body, escaping from the present evil reality.

The huge man drew a deep, slobbering breath, lowered himself between her legs and readied himself to enter her, taking time to savour what was to come.

Just then a big, shaven-headed negro burst through the staring crowd, grabbed the huge man's head and jerked it backwards. A steel blade flashed in the bright sunlight and blood spurted through the huge man's long beard. Howls of fright and shock erupted and the men holding Rosie abruptly released their grips.

She opened her eyes in bewilderment to see the huge man still kneeling between her legs, both hands clutching his throat, blood spurting through his fingers, his eyes bulging, while all around the crowd scattered.

Rosie scrambled backwards and got to her feet, crouching low, trying to make sense of what was happening. She saw men fleeing from the knife-flailing onslaught of the big negro who wore the blue frock coat of a Turkish officer, and other men cowering on their knees as he passed, their hands clasped high before them as though begging for his mercy.

Seizing her chance, she ran, arms and legs pumping, her ripped dress and petticoat flying out behind her like fluttering wings, terrified that at any moment she would hear the thudding of pursuing hoofbeats.

Gasping for breath, her muscles rapidly tiring, she ran up a long slope and at its summit saw the winding roadway in the distance, and clouds of dust rising from it marking the progress of marching men. She glanced quickly behind. There was no sign of anyone coming after her, and she marvelled at how far away the huddle of ruins appeared. Terror had remarkably fuelled her speed. Unable to distinguish the clump of bushes where she had left her friends, she ran towards the roadway, changing direction so that she could intercept the head of the dust-shrouded column, driving her aching body as fast as she was able.

She was within a hundred yards, and could see that the men on the road were cavalry, when a small detachment broke away from the column and came trotting towards her. She felt like sobbing with relief when she recognized the busbies and dolmans of British hussars.

Slowing to a walk, clutching the torn edges of her clothing together, she called out, 'Can you help me? Please can you help me?'

The youthful corporal leading the detachment reined in. 'Who are you? What's happened to you?'

Rosie told him about her near rape and pleaded for help in finding her friends. Her story brought growls of anger from her listeners, and the corporal said, 'Don't you fret, my duck. You're safe now.'

He issued orders and the men spread out and began to search the terrain parallel to the roadway, shouting for Dorcas by name.

'I've got to report to my officer.' The corporal galloped back towards the halted column, and Rosie wearily followed, parched with thirst, her skin thick with sweat-caked dust.

When she reached the leading section, Rosie was greeted by wolf whistles and lewd invitations as the men caught glimpses of her bare legs and body through the gaps in her torn clothes.

The young, dashingly mustachioed captain frowned doubtfully as he listened to Rosie. 'And you claim that a negro intervened to save you? Why did he do so?'

She could only shrug. 'I don't know, sir.'

'Frankly, I find it hard to believe what you've told me.' The captain sniffed superciliously.

Rosie's anger flared. 'I'm not lying! Look at my clothes! Are you stupid enough to think that I've torn them myself? I'm telling you the truth!'

The man's bulbous blue eyes hardened, but before he could answer her, one of the hussars who had been searching for Dorcas and Arthur Sinclair rode up to report that they had been found further along the roadway.

'Well, at least that part of your story has been verified,' the captain acknowledged grudgingly.

She flung out her arm and pointed to the ridge she had crossed. 'If you cross that high ground over there, you'll see the ruins where those men are. If you catch them you'll find that I'm telling the truth.'

'My orders are to get to Varna as quickly as possible, and I'm not prepared to waste valuable time seeking the fellows that you claim to have attacked you. I'm sure that it's not the first time you have quarrelled with men. Women of your class constantly brawl with your menfolk, don't you?' The captain turned away from her, shouted an order to resume the march, and trotted on.

Rosie was momentarily stunned with disbelief at such cavalier treatment. Then a white-hot fury burgeoned in her, and she shouted after him. 'You rotten bastard! You wouldn't treat one of your own class of women so, would you?'

The men trotting past her laughed and jeered, and she felt like hurling herself at them. The youthful corporal kneed his horse to shield her from the column and, bending low from the saddle, hissed urgently, 'Hold your tongue, my duck. He's a vicious bad bastard and he'd have you flogged as soon as look at you.'

Rosie was trembling, her self-control strained to near breaking-point.

'Listen to me, my duck, I'm on your side.' The corporal radiated sympathy. 'My mate is with the escort to the waggons, they're about a mile behind us. His name is Michael Riley. You stop him when he comes along, and tell him that Tommy Cunningham says that you and your mates are to ride on the waggons as far as Varna. Have you got that? Tell Michael Riley that Tommy Cunningham says you and your mates are to ride on the waggons as far as Varna.'

Gratitude for his kindness overtook her fury, and she nodded and thanked him.

'I've got to get going, my duck. Good luck to you.' With a parting smile he left her and she moved back from the roadway and turned her back to the curious stares and comments until the column had passed. Only then did she walk along the road to meet up with Dorcas.

Thirty-Nine

Varna, August, 1854

The embarkation of the army was progressing with a painful slowness, the long lines of men, horses and guns having to be transhipped by lighters from the wooden jetties out to the steamers and sailing ships that were at anchor in Varna Bay.

Cholera had ravaged the sixty thousand British, French and Turkish troops camped in and around Varna. To make matters worse, a great fire had recently destroyed much of the timber-built township, and looters had sacked what remained, so now no shops or stores remained open and trade had come to a standstill, leaving the soldiers no opportunity to buy any food to supplement their rations. What was still plentifully available, however, was strong liquor.

Charles Bronton stood outside his tent in the cold darkness listening to the songs and laughter of the men around the campfires, and could only marvel at their cheerfulness. Every day they were burying comrades who had been struck down by the cholera. The camp hospital tents were crammed with the sick and dying, yet the men remained in good spirits. He smiled wryly. It was good spirits engendered by strong spirits. He didn't care to think about how low their morale would become should the supplies of raki dry up.

Rosie came from the darkness and sat beside her husband by the fire.

'Where've you been?' Jack Collier demanded.

'At the hospital to see Arthur Sinclair.' She filled a clay pipe with tobacco and, lighting it with a burning brand from the fire, took several puffs before handing it on to her husband.

'How's he doing?' Dorcas asked.

'He's still very weak, but he says he's feeling a lot better.' Rosie was pensive. 'I saw Conky White on my way back. He says that the lads buried this morning have already been dug up and the blankets pinched.'

Her words provoked a round of curses.

'It'll be them Bashi-Bazouks again.' Jack Collier glowered. 'Instead of just disbanding 'em, they should have shot each and every one of the bastards. They're only good for dog meat.'

'Well I'll tell you now, if I catch any of them dirty thievin' Turkey bastards sneaking around here, I'll put a ball in their heads for them, no danger,' Colum Murphy vowed. 'I'd sooner we were fighting on the Russkies' side against the haythen Turkey bastards.'

There was a chorus of agreement. The

majority of the British and French soldiers felt a contemptuous dislike for their Turkish allies.

'Mind you, when it comes to giving the lads a Christian burial, the bloody frogs aren't much better,' another man stated. 'The bloody harbour's full of them, all bobbing about like corks.'

The cholera had been taken on board the transports, and the men dying on the ships were being buried at sea, sewn up with a weight in a blanket and tipped overboard. The French were not swaddling and weighting their dead sufficiently, and many of the French corpses had slipped from their shrouds and risen to the surface, where they floated, gruesomely rotting.

'By Jaysus! I shouldn't like to end up floating around in the water like that, with all the fishes chewing on me arse,' Colum Murphy said.

'You got no cause to worry. You're so full o' wind that you'll just float up into the clouds,' Dorcas gibed.

There was an outburst of laughter, and the general mood lightened again.

Outside his tent, Charles Bronton had been joined by Philip Fothergill, whose promotion to lieutenant-colonel of the regiment had recently been confirmed.

'Good evening, sir.' Charles stiffened to attention.

'I've just returned from headquarters, Bronton. We are to embark on the *Simla* the day after tomorrow. The army is to land on the Crimea peninsula and take Sebastopol.' As always with Charles, Fothergill's manner was stiffly formal.

'That's good news, Sir.' Charles was both pleased and relieved. 'Every day we remain here weakens our strength.'

Fothergill continued without acknowledging Charles's remark. 'Because of restrictions on space, we are to leave our heavy baggage and spare mounts, to be shipped separately. Lord Raglan has also instructed that no sick men and no women or children are to accompany the regiment.'

'What about our hospital cases, sir? Does his Lordship intend that they are to be shipped on to Scutari?'

The other man frowned irritably. 'Whether they are or no will be for the commander of the Varna garrison to decide, Mr Bronton. My orders are to embark only our fit men on the *Simla*. I suggest you begin to make all arrangements as quickly as possible. Goodnight to you.'

He stalked off, leaving Charles greatly troubled by the implications of these new orders.

'This is a bad thing. We shouldn't be leaving the women to shift for themselves in this God-forsaken hole!'

Forty

Port of Varna

'Not taking us?' Dorcas Murphy exclaimed incredulously. 'Not any of us?'

'That's what I said, didn't I?' A haggard-faced woman disgustedly hawked and spat into the dust. 'They ain't taking us. They say there's no room on the transports.'

'That can't be right,' Megan Morgan protested.

'Oh, can't it now, Taffy?' the haggard woman challenged aggressively. 'Then why else are all of us stuck here like mawkins?'

Rosie stared around her at the large crowd of dirty, travel-worn women and children who were gathered on an open stretch of land some distance from the landing stages where the troops were embarking.

'Our regiment went on board ship yesterday,' the speaker continued angrily. 'But there's some of these wenches has been here for days. And none of the bastard officers has done anything to help us. We've had no ration issue nor nothing.'

'That's as maybe, but they can't separate us

from our men for good,' Megan Morgan argued.

The haggard woman grimaced sourly. 'They already has done, Taffy. There's your blokes over there.' She pointed towards the lines of men and horses converging on the landing stages. 'And you're here, and that lot are there to keep you apart.' This time she pointed to the motionless line of red-coated infantrymen forming a human barrier between the women and the landing stages. 'And don't you go thinking that they'll let you pass through them. One poor wench got her jaw broke yesterday when she tried to get to her bloke.'

'Oh, dear God! What's to become of us!' Annie Bartleet wailed in despair. 'We'll all die here! We'll all die! God save us! God save us!'

Her outburst set her children off into fits of crying, and Dorcas scolded her. 'Shut your bloody skrawking, Annie Bartleet! You ought to know by now that it's no use you asking that useless old bugger up in the sky for help.'

Rosie gathered the distressed children to her and tried to comfort them. 'It will be alright, sweethearts. There's no need to be upset. Everything will be alright. Don't cry now. Don't cry.' But even as she uttered the soothing words, she feared the worst.

On the nearest landing stage, Charles Bronton was overlooking the sling-loading of horses when he was approached by Henry Peebles.

310

'With all respect, sir, the married men have asked me to speak with you about their wives and children. They're very worried about leaving them here. They were wondering if you might intercede with the colonel on their behalf and get permission for the families to come on board with us.'

Charles grimaced uneasily. He was unhappy about leaving the women and children in such a plight, believing that they should at least be transported back to the British base in Constantinople. But as an officer he could not be seen to be questioning the orders of the army's high command. He chose his words carefully. 'The order has come from Lord Raglan's headquarters, Sergeant-Major. I'm afraid that Colonel Fothergill cannot countermand it.'

'With all respect, sir, supposing Colonel Fothergill was to approach Lord Raglan in company with the other regimental COs. Might not that have some influence on his Lordship?'

Charles had in fact already suggested this mode of action to Philip Fothergill and had been sarcastically rebuffed. Fothergill had witheringly pointed out that unquestioning obedience to orders could not be demanded from the common soldiers if their officers were seen to be questioning those same orders, and that Charles should have known better than to make such a stupid suggestion.

'Well sir?' Peebles pressed, and Charles, feeling trapped by the rigid code of discipline,

311

reacted with angry resentment.

'Just obey your orders, Sergeant-Major.'

'Yes, sir!' Peebles saluted smartly and marched away.

Charles turned his attention to the loading of the horses and tried without success to dismiss his feelings of guilt.

As he left the landing stage, Henry Peebles was accosted by Augustus Bartleet.

'Any joy, Sarn't-Major?'

Peebles shook his head, and the other man's face creased with anxiety.

'Is there nothing at all to be done, Sarn't-Major?'

'Not unless they promotes me to command the army, Bartleet.' Peebles grinned mirthlessly. 'And I haven't heard that they intends to do that.' He walked on, leaving the disconsolate man miserably staring across at the distant crowd of women and children.

Henry Peebles had his own reasons for wanting the women to accompany the regiment. He wanted Rosie Collier for his own woman. When the regiment went to war there would be opportunities to dispose of Jack Collier, and Henry Peebles was grimly determined that if the Russians or disease did not kill Collier, then he would himself. He was confident that once widowed, Rosie would readily agree to his proposal of marriage.

He came to a standstill, thinking hard, rapidly formulating and rejecting schemes to keep Rosie with the regiment. He saw a small

312

cavalcade of horsemen approaching the landing stages, and smiled as a fresh idea flowered. 'That might just do it.'

He headed purposefully towards the crowd of women and children, his eyes searching for Rosie Collier.

It was Dorcas Murphy who noticed his approach, and went to meet him. 'Are you bringing good news, Sarn't-Major?'

He came to a halt and waited for the Irishwoman to reach him, then spent some time whispering in her ear.

When he went back towards the landing stages, she hurried to tell Rosie and the other women.

'They're going to leave us here, girls. The bastards are meaning to abandon us. There's been no orders to give us shelter, or rations even. We'll all bloody well starve to death!'

There was an eruption of shrieks and cries of outrage and despair.

'Listen to me! Listen to me!' Dorcas bawled as she raised both arms and pointed them towards the cavalcade of horsemen approaching the landing stages. 'D'you see them bowsies? That's the bloody general and his bloody staff. Let's go and tell him what we thinks of what he's doing to us.'

A unified roar of assent came from the group and, led by Dorcas, hundreds of women coalesced into a human battering-ram, charging the line of sentries, knocking men down, trampling over them, running to surround Lord Raglan and his staff, shrieking

313

and screaming, pleading to be taken aboard the transports.

For long minutes the staff officers were trapped in a seething, deafening pandemonium, until organized squads of soldiers came to their rescue, brutally forcing a passage of escape.

A satisfied smile hovered around Henry Peebles' lips. Dorcas Murphy had followed his instructions to the letter. When the general and his staff came past him, galloping back towards the town, Peebles could clearly see the shock on many of their faces, and was hopeful that Lord Raglan, having experienced at first-hand the distressing effects of his order, might now feel obligated to countermand it and allow the women and children to accompany the army.

Within the hour fresh orders came from headquarters. As many as possible of the women and children were to be crammed into the remaining transports after the embarkation of the troops had been completed.

Henry Peebles decided to act immediately, however. He gathered his own regiment's women and children together and led them on to a landing stage.

The lighters were being rowed by seamen from the allied fleet. Peebles had a few quiet words with a mahogany-featured petty officer, money changed hands, and the party were taken on board a lighter and rowed out to a steamer. The petty officer escorted the women aboard and brusquely ordered them to go to the foredeck and stay there.

'If you don't stay quiet and still, you'll be put ashore again,' he warned.

A column of lighters filled with red-coated infantrymen came alongside the vessel.

'Are our men not sailing on this ship?' Megan Morgan asked.

'No. They're to be carried on the *Simla*. We got no space for horses.'

'Oh my God!' Annie Bartleet wailed tearfully. 'When will I see my Augustus again? Oh my God!' Her three children immediately burst into tears and, swearing angrily, the petty officer went away.

'Shut your bloody noise, Annie, or I'll bloody well clout you meself,' Dorcas threatened.

Rosie smiled and cuddled the crying children. 'We'll find your dad as soon as we land on the other side. Don't worry, we'll find him, certain sure,' she assured them.

The hours passed and ship after ship slipped anchor and sailed to join the great convoy rendezvous. It became obvious that despite the changed orders, there would still be many women left behind, unable to obtain passage. They milled around the landing stages, sobbing and screaming in anger and despair.

Rosie and Dorcas stood together at the taffrail of the steamer, staring at the unfortunate women left on the shore.

'God help the poor souls,' Rosie muttered.

'Well, let's hope he does, because there's

nothing we can do for 'um, my wench.'
Dorcas put her meaty arm around Rosie's
shoulders and hugged her. 'Let's just thank
our lucky stars that we're going wi' the
regiment, and not being left here like them
pitiful craturs.'

'Oh, believe me, I'm very thankful that
we're going with the regiment, Dorcas. But I
feel so sorry for those poor souls.'

Forty-One

Calamita Bay, Crimea
September 14th, 1854

The night was pitch-black, the wind howled
and torrential rain lashed down, saturating
the thousands of tentless, shelterless men and
animals spread across the beach and the
treeless hinterland.

'I never thought I'd ever say this, Rosie, but
I wish with all me heart I was back in Varna,'
Dorcas muttered through her clenched teeth.

Soaked to their skins, shivering with cold,
the two women sat huddled together in the
middle of the infantrymen they had sailed
with.

'Me too,' Rosie agreed. 'We should have
stayed on the transport with Annie Bartleet

and the kids. At least we'd be dry and warm.'

'Oh no, we shouldn't!' Dorcas said vehemently. 'If we hadn't got off it when we did, I'd have swung for the whining cow.' She mimicked Annie Bartleet's wailing voice. '"Oh Augustus! Augustus! When will we meet again, Augustus, my beloved?"'

Despite her physical misery, Rosie couldn't help but giggle. 'She was truly heartbroken at not being allowed to land, though.'

'I'll bet she's glad now that her kids aren't stuck out in this bloody storm,' Dorcas rejoined.

When the fleet had arrived at Calamita Bay that morning, orders had been issued that women with children were to remain on board the transports to be carried back to the British base at Scutari.

The soldier sitting next to Rosie suddenly lifted his saturated blanket from his head and threw it on the rain-puddled ground, grumbling loudly. 'This thing's no cover at all. Why the bleedin' hell didn't they land our tents? The bleedin' frogs and Turks landed their tents, and they're tucked up as snug as bugs in rugs, while we'em getting drownded out here. Why didn't they land our tents?' He went on to answer his own question. 'I'll tell you why, shall I? It's because the frogs and Turks are better organized than us. Our bleedin' officers couldn't organize a piss-up in a brewery.'

'Any more o' that sort o' talk, Private Conway, and I'll be organizing a flogging for you,' a sergeant shouted, and the soldier subsided into sullen silence.

Dorcas leaned forwards. 'Youse have to look on the bright side, my bucko. With all this rain around we can quench our thirsts, can't we? Them last couple o' days on board, when the water run short, I was parched dry wi' eating that salt pork.'

Rosie pressed her hands against her stomach, her fingers feeling for the rounded swelling that was her child. 'At least you're warm and snug in there, aren't you, my honey?'

She allowed her mind to drift into fanciful imaginings of what her child would look like. These day-dreams were a pleasure in which she frequently indulged. She was convinced that her child would be male, and that he would become a soldier. Rosie would not conceive of him following any other profession. In her mind's eye she created images of a tall, handsome, stalwart young man, dressed in the splendid full dress uniform of a Light Dragoon officer. She knew that it was very unlikely that he would ever become an officer, but in the privacy of her dreams she could create any scenario, and indulge her wildest hopes.

She became so immersed in her dream-world that the rains and winds ceased to trouble her.

'What bedtime stories I'll have to tell him. Of the wonderful sights I've seen, and the foreign countries I've travelled to, and all the different races and peoples I've met with. I'm glad that I'm married to a soldier. Just think how dull life would be if I was married to a factory hand, or a clerk, or a servant. I'm glad that I'm an army woman,' she thought.

'I wonder if our regiment will be landed tomorrow, Rosie?' Dorcas intruded upon her day-dreams, bringing her back to the reality of the foul night.

'I wonder if they had any cholera on board the *Simla*,' Rosie murmured with concern.

The vessel they had travelled on had been struck by cholera. Several men had died and been buried at sea and since landing, many other men had fallen sick but the surgeons could not treat them because the medical stores had not been landed yet.

'It's true what this fella here said,' Dorcas whispered hoarsely. 'Our officers are useless at organizing anything. We ought to have had a few tents landed at least.'

Rosie could only nod her head in rueful agreement, and silently pray that dawn would come soon, bringing with it sunlight and warmth.

Forty-Two

The sun was high and hot and the allied army was on the march. Huge phalanxes of men, horses and guns advanced, sunlight glittering upon steel bayonets, flags flying, bands playing, drums beating.

The Light Cavalry Brigade covered the flanks of the army and Rosie and her friends were trudging behind the infantry alongside a few horse-drawn baggage carts that had been commandeered from the local Tartar population. The carts were already fully loaded with cholera victims who were dropping all along the line of march. The women were doing what little they could to relieve and aid the sufferers.

Although she pitied the sick and dying men, Rosie could not help but be thrilled at the magnificent spectacle of the long ranks of scarlet and blue and green traversing the rolling ridges as far ahead as she could see.

'Look there!' Dorcas pointed eastwards. 'It's them Cossacks again. The cheek of them! Staring at us like we was a bloody circus!'

Rosie peered at the rising slopes of the low hills, shielding her eyes with her hands, focussing her gaze on the distant group of

320

horsemen who were sitting motionless on their small shaggy ponies.

'Why don't our lads go and kill the buggers?' Megan Morgan demanded indignantly. 'It's not right letting them cock a snook at us like this.'

'Don't talk so stupid!' Dorcas scoffed. 'Youse have seen the state of our horses. It's all the pitiful craturs can do to carry the lads, let alone raise a gallop. Are all the bloody Taffys as stupid as you?'

'Don't you call me stupid again, you Bog Irish cow, or I'll knock your block off for you.' The Welshwoman brandished her clenched fist.

'It's me that'll be knocking your block off, you Welsh mare!' Dorcas retorted.

Rosie interposed herself between them. 'Give over, both of you! We're here to fight the Russians, not each other.'

'Yeah, and it's us Paddies that'll be doing most of the fighting, like we always does.' Dorcas glared.

'Oh no!' Megan Morgan shook her head in emphatic contradiction. 'You Paddies 'ull be hiding behind us Taffys, like you always do when there's a bit o' fighting to be done.'

'You women there! Keep moving, damn you!' The shout came from a mounted commissariat officer who was following the carts.

The women simultaneously united against him.

'Don't youse be becalling us, you bloody bean-counter!' Dorcas roared.

321

'No! Not unless you fancies your chances at fighting us, you counter-jumper!' Megan Morgan shook her fist at him.

'Good on you, Megan. We'll teach him some manners.' Dorcas grinned savagely.

'That's right, Dorcas. We'll make him wish he'd stayed at home. Come on, you bloody nancy boy!'

'Yeah, come on and let's be having youse!'

Shoulder to shoulder they boldly faced their new-found common foe. Scowling, he circled his mount around them at a safe distance and cantered towards the leading cart.

Elated by their victory, Dorcas and Megan linked arms and marched on in triumph, their quarrel forgotten.

As the march continued, columns of smoke began to rise in front and to the eastern flank of the army where the Russians were burning villages and farms to deny the allies their use.

The carts trundled over the ridge of a hill and Rosie saw before her a wide treeless plain traversed by the narrow stream of the Bulganek. There was a single bridge with a white-walled, apparently untouched building beside it. The banks of the stream were covered with a seething mass of red-coated soldiers desperate to quench their raging thirsts. Away to Rosie's left, a large village was in flames and on the slopes of the undulating hills beyond the plain were several dark masses of horsemen.

The young officer commanding the carts' escort of infantry peered through his field-glasses, and exclaimed excitedly, 'They're Russians, by God! Russian cavalry! We'll see some fun now!'

Rosie's heart pounded with excitement as she saw several squadrons of the Light Brigade push forward towards the enemy.

'Is it our lads going forwards?' she wondered aloud.

The young officer smiled kindly at her. 'What's your regiment?'

'The Twentieth Light Dragoons, sir.'

'Here, take a look for yourself.' He handed her his field-glasses.

She focussed on the distant figures, and recognized the blue tunics and tall shakoes of Light Dragoons. 'I can see them. Our regiment.'

Dorcas crossed herself. 'Holy Mary, mother of God, please watch over the lads, and keep them safe.'

The officer took back his field-glasses and resumed his own scrutiny of the action. During the next half-hour he gave a running commentary to the eager listeners clustered around him.

'It looks like there is firing from our men ... It looks like the Russians are bringing up infantry. Thousands of them ... Our cavalry are retiring ... The Russians have unmasked a battery of artillery ... The guns are firing at our cavalry ... Our cavalry are in very good order ... A few of our horses and men hit by the look of it ... No panic there, though. The men are as steady as rocks ... Some of our infantry and guns are moving up in support ... Our horse artillery have gone into action ... The Russians are retreating ... We've won! We've won!'

His listeners cheered vociferously, but Rosie did not join in the cheering. She was trying to come to terms with the jarring realization that, although her husband had faced possible death or mutilation – indeed might even now be dead or wounded – no thought of him had crossed her mind. Not even when the officer had said that there were casualties. Guilt struck her. 'I never gave a thought to Jack, did I? I was only worried for the regiment. What sort of hard-hearted bitch have I become, not to be worried for my own husband?' She sighed despondently. 'I've got to try and be a good wife to him, even if I don't love him. I owe him that much.'

The army remained in position, ready for battle, until the last Russians had disappeared across the hills, then orders were given to make camp for the night.

Rosie and the women found their regiment's bivouac and helped the men to gather small shrubs, nettles and grasses to fuel the cooking fires. The rations of salt pork, biscuit and rum were issued, and the staves of the casks and boxes were broken up and added to the poor flames, which gave out barely enough heat to warm the meat.

Many of the men were disgruntled because they had not been allowed to charge the Russians, and the general atmosphere was sullen.

'They should have let us have a go at the Russkies,' Augustus Bartleet complained. 'We was just sitting there like Aunt Sallies!'

'The foot-sloggers are becalling us for useless peacock bastards.'

'Never mind, boys,' Colum Murphy consoled. 'There's always tomorrow. They might have run away today, but we'll catch up with them again tomorrow, and Lucan will have to let us loose on the bastards then, won't he?'

Jack Collier had only passed the briefest of greetings with Rosie and was sitting some distance away from her, but when darkness fell he came to touch her shoulder, and when she looked up he jerked his head in signal for her to follow, and led her away from the bivouac.

They passed close to the campfire where Henry Peebles was sitting with some other senior NCOs, one of whom muttered enviously, 'Look at that lucky bastard, Collier, taking his missus off for a shag. I wish I had a juicy little piece like that.'

'I don't know why she stays with the miserable drunken sod.' Sergeant Peter Moston glumly shook his head. 'There ain't no justice in this world, boys, when Jack Collier has got a sweet piece like that for a wife, and I got that vile cow that I'm wed to.'

'Well in your case, you being such an ugly bugger, it had to be any port in a storm, didn't it, matey?' another jeered, and there was an outburst of raucous laughter.

Some distance from the outermost

campfire, Jack Collier halted and brusquely told Rosie, 'This'll do. Lie down.'

A sense of sadness swept over her. 'Can't you even kiss me, Jack? Can't you even tell me that you care for me?'

He frowned in puzzlement. 'What's brought this on?'

She sighed, and shook her head. 'You just use me, Jack. You make me feel as if I'm nothing more than a piece of meat. And what about our baby? I'm getting near to my time.'

His frown of puzzlement became one of anger, and he snapped, 'I can't be doing with this rubbishy talk, Rosie. Now lie down and lift your skirts.'

In resignation, she obeyed, and lay passively while he roughly satisfied himself upon her body. When he had climaxed and withdrawn, he got to his feet and buttoned up his trousers.

She lay motionless, making no attempt to draw her skirt down to cover her naked belly and thighs.

'Cover yourself up, will you.' he growled impatiently. 'Don't lie there like a bloody whore. It aren't decent.'

In silence she stood up, rearranged her skirts, and followed him back to the bivouac. 'You made your bed, girl. Now you must lie on it,' she accepted stoically.

When Rosie seated herself by the side of Dorcas at the campfire the Irishwoman nudged her and whispered enviously.

'You don't know how lucky you are, girl,

having a man who still wants to give you some loving.'

The irony of the situation brought a mirthless smile to Rosie's lips. 'Oh, but I do, Dorcas. Believe me, I do.'

A spattering of raindrops fell and Dorcas grumbled. 'Looks like another damp night for us, girl. No wonder me bones is aching.'

Tentless and shelterless, the men and women wrapped themselves in blankets and great coats and settled themselves on the bare ground to try and snatch a few hours' sleep. But even in these brief hours of uneasy respite, the cholera and fevers still gathered their harvests, and many who lay down to sleep would wake no more.

Charles Bronton came to find Henry Peebles. 'The men are to be roused three hours after midnight, Sergeant-Major, without drum or bugle calls. It appears that the Russians have amassed upon the heights beyond the Alma River. We shall have a battle tomorrow without doubt.'

Peebles stared across the dark landscape to where, some six miles distant, myriad Russian campfires twinkled upon the high plateau to the south.

'Let's hope his Lordship makes proper use of us then, sir. It isn't good for our morale to hold us back and let the foot-sloggers do all the fighting.'

Charles frowned and warned curtly, 'Do not let me hear you comment again on the use that his Lordship makes of the cavalry, Sergeant-Major. Your only duty is to obey your orders without question.'

Peebles stiffened and saluted smartly. 'Yes, sir.'

As Bronton walked away, Henry Peebles scowled sourly after him, muttering beneath his breath, 'Oh, I'll obey my orders alright. Even though they're issued by a pack of brainless idiots, who don't know their arses from their elbows.' Then his thoughts turned to the prospects of battle, and he grinned savagely. 'With any luck it'll be Jack Collier's last day on this earth.'

Forty-Three

The army had risen long before dawn, and then had waited. And waited. And waited.

At ten that morning the order had come to advance, and the troops had marched for-wards to attack the Russians at the Alma River, leaving the women behind with the baggage carts on the camping ground. They had also left a trail of fallen men, stricken with the cholera.

The army's women had gone to the aid of the sick and dying men, taking them water, fashioning litters from shawls and sticks and carrying the men to the shore from where the boats could carry them to the hospital transports in the bay.

It was nearly five o'clock in the afternoon when the rumbling echoes of distant gunfire finally died away.

Rosie, Dorcas, Megan Morgan and three women from A Troop were returning from the shore, exchanging anxious glances.

'I hope it's all over,' Dorcas declared, and the other women shared in that fervent hope.

The heat of the sun and the gruelling toil of carrying the heavy makeshift litters for mile upon mile had taken toll on Rosie, and she felt near to exhaustion. 'Whether it's over or not, I've got to sit down for a bit,' she sighed wearily.

'Wait till we gets to our carts, Rosie. They're only the other side of that little ridge,' Dorcas urged. 'We can get something to eat and drink then.'

'Yeah, come on, Rosie. We're nearly there,' Megan Morgan encouraged. 'Here! Grab hold o' me arm. I'll pull you along.'

Rosie was in awe at the women's physical strength and seemingly inexhaustible stamina. But her pride prevented her from accepting Megan Morgan's offer.

'I'll be alright, Meg. It was only a passing weakness. I'm alright now.' She forced her aching body onwards.

Over an hour later, as they topped the ridge, they heard cheering and saw knots of gesticulating men clustering around mounted lancers among the lines of carts.

Rosie's eagerness to know what had happened momentarily overcame her weariness and, tapping her last dregs of strength, she hurried down the long slope to be enveloped in an excited tumult of shouts.

'We've won!'

'The Russkies are in retreat!'

'There's been thousands of the buggers killed!'

Dorcas pushed her way through the crowd surrounding the nearest lancer and grabbed the man's knee. 'What about the Light Brigade? How did we get on? Have we lost many?'

The man bared his teeth in angry disgust. 'We aren't lost any. The foot-sloggers have took a lot o' casualties, but we only watched! The whole of the Russki army was running away, and we weren't let off the leash to finish them off! We're the laughing stock of the army, so we are. We just sat and watched while the foot-sloggers did all the fighting for us!'

When Rosie heard his words her tense body sagged in thankful relief that the regiment had come through unscathed. But Dorcas shared the lancer's rancour, and came back to her friends, fuming angrily. 'What's the matter wi' our generals? They're old women, so they are! A pack of old women!'

'But aren't you glad that the lads are all safe?' Rosie challenged.

'O' course I'm glad, but that's not the bloody point, is it!' Dorcas scowled indignantly. 'It just aren't right for the foot-sloggers to get all the glory, and we gets none! How can we hold our heads up among the army now?'

'You're right, Dorcas! It's a bloody disgrace, so it is!' Megan Morgan was equally furious. 'I wish now that I'd married that guardsman who wanted me, instead of bloody Dewi Morgan.'

A mounted staff officer came galloping towards the carts, shouting for them to advance to the Alma. He reined in beside the women. 'You'd best come as well. There are many wounded to be attended to.'

'How far is it to the field, sir?' Megan Morgan asked.

'About six miles,' he informed them and rode away.

'Come on, girls, let's get going. We can be there long before the carts,' Dorcas urged. 'With any luck we might find something worth having on them dead Russians.'

Rosie reluctantly shook her head. 'I'm going to have to get a ride on the carts, Dorcas. I'm nearly done in.'

Several of the other women also refused to move until they had rested. Dorcas grimaced with contempt for their weakness. 'Suit yourselves, but there'll be nothing left worth having by the time you gets there. Them thieving frogs will have taken it all. Come on, Megan. Me and you'ull go and get rich by ourselves.' The pair hurried southwards.

It took nearly three hours for the convoy of

carts to make their tortuous progress to the Alma, and Rosie would never forget the scene of human carnage and destruction that met her eyes.

Two villages were in flames on the near side of the steep-banked shallow river, palls of black smoke rising high into the azure sky. On the hillsides beyond the river, and in the vineyards on each side, lay thousands of dead, dying and wounded British and grey-coated Russians, the scarlet coats of the British reminding Rosie of the fields of red poppies through which she had wandered as a child. Further to the east she could also see the blue coats of the fallen French.

The regimental bandsmen were already collecting the wounded and bringing them on stretchers to the hastily erected hospital tents, where the surgeons practised their brutal art, cutting through mangled flesh, sawing through shattered bones, tossing the amputated legs and arms on to ever growing heaps. The carts were immediately pressed into service to carry the treated wounded to the shore three miles away to be picked up by the boats.

A sweating, harassed surgeon, his arms red to the elbows with blood, asked Rosie and her companions, 'Will you take water to the men lying upon the field? That is the greatest kindness you can do for them at present.'

The women hastened across the wooden bridge and began their task. From all sides came groans and cries of terrible suffering and the occasional scream. When she reached the first clusters of fallen men, Rosie came to an abrupt standstill, horror-stricken by the hideous sight. Bloodily shattered faces, contorted limbs, mouths gaping in soundless cries of agony, dismembered bodies everywhere.

'Come on, Rosie. Anybody 'ud think that you'd never seen a dead man before. These poor buggers can't harm you. They're only hunks of meat in a butcher's field now. So get on and help the poor buggers who're still living, instead o' just standing there,' Dorcas admonished sharply.

The remonstrance steadied Rosie's jangling nerves and she began her task of mercy, searching out the living from the dead. Soon she found she no longer looked at the mangled corpses as objects of fearful horror, but instead as merely lifeless men.

The bulk of the army had advanced to take station on the highest plateau, but there were many officers and soldiers who also remained to bring water to the wounded. A corporal wearing the dark green uniform of a rifleman pointed higher up at the hillsides where swathes of Russians lay.

'Give them Russkies a wide berth, sweetheart. Some of the wicked bastards have shot our lads in the back after they've been given water,' he warned Rosie.

From further up the hillside came the sharp report of a rifle shot, and the corporal peered in its direction, exclaiming angrily, 'That could be another one. I hope it's one of our lads that's fired, and not a Russki.'

To Rosie's side a young soldier croaked for water, and she knelt in the pool of blood that had oozed from the torn wound in his side. She gently lifted his head and held her canteen to his dry, cracked lips. He took one single mouthful of water, choked and coughed and, as the liquid bubbled from his mouth and ran down his chin, he died.

'Oh no!' she exclaimed in distress. 'He's died still thirsty. The poor lad.'

'Well there's plenty more who are thirsty,' the corporal told her gruffly. 'So go and see to them, and save your tears for later.'

Rosie did not resent the man's harsh tone. She knew that he was right. This was not the time for tears. Tears were of no use to suffering men. She rose to her feet and moved to the next wounded man.

She lost all count of hours, all count of the number of hurried journeys she made down to the river and back up the hillside, all count of the men she tended to. Night came and still devoted teams of helpers moved across the battlefield, carrying the wounded on stretchers to the hospital tents where the exhausted surgeons toiled by candle and lantern-light. Rosie met Dorcas Murphy and Megan Morgan who were acting as stretcher-bearers.

'Did you get rich?' she could not help but ask.

'Did we bollocks!' Dorcas scowled indignantly. 'The bloody Jocks and Guards and them Zouaves had got the best pickings! We'll see you later, my duck, we got to get this poor soul down to the surgeons.' The women disappeared into the darkness with their comatose load.

Rosie continued searching out the wounded from among the dead until utter exhaustion forced her to stop. Then, wrapping herself in a great coat taken from a dead man, she lay down by the side of a small drummer boy who in the delirium of dying was calling for his mother. Rosie cradled him in her arms, soothing him until he lost consciousness and then fell into uneasy sleep herself.

She awoke in the cold grey of approaching dawn, and saw that the boy had died. She gently closed his staring eyes and straightened his limbs, then covered him with the great coat and went down to the river to refill her canteens with water. It would take all day, the coming night and another day before her work was done, the dead mass-buried in large pits, the wounded shipped out. Only then would Rosie and her friends go back to the regimental lines to rejoin their husbands.

Forty-Four

The Institution for the Care of Sick
Gentlewomen, London, Mid-October, 1854

When she had finished work for the day,
Eugenia Pacemore went to her room and sat
reading and rereading the two letters she had
received that morning. One letter was from
Louis Nolan, the other from Charles Bronton. The main content of both letters was
angry diatribes against the senior commanders of the army in the Crimea. Both men
complained bitterly that the British army was
being decimated by the lack of sufficient
medical care for the sick and wounded.

Eugenia's smooth brow creased with anxious concern. During the past week, the
London Times newspaper had published
despatches from its war correspondent,
William Howard Russell, furiously castigat-
ing the abysmal lack of provision for the
treatment of the British casualties from the
battle of the Alma. His reports had created a
furious uproar throughout the country. These
letters from her loved ones were confirmation
that Russell had not exaggerated his accounts

of the terrible sufferings of the British sick and wounded, in sharp contrast to the French casualties, who were provided for by an efficient ambulance and medical service.

There was a knock on the door, and Eugenia opened it to face the tall, slight, grey-eyed superintendent of the Institution.

'I hope I'm not disturbing you, Miss Pacemore.'

'Not at all, ma'am. Do come in, please.'

Florence Nightingale entered and seated herself on the edge of the bed, gesturing for Eugenia to take the solitary chair. She smiled with satisfaction, disclosing perfect white teeth.

'I've just returned from meeting with Mr Herbert. Everything is finally arranged for our journey to Turkey, Miss Pacemore.'

Sidney Herbert, the Secretary at War, was a personal friend of Florence Nightingale. He was being held responsible for the plight of the British wounded, and it was he who had persuaded the government to finance her going out to Turkey to help in the hospital at Scutari.

'We leave for France tomorrow morning, travelling via Boulogne to Paris, where we shall spend the night. Then on to Marseille the following day. We shall stay there for four nights and then sail aboard the *Vectis* mail boat to Constantinople.' She paused and looked intently at Eugenia. 'Have you any doubts about coming with me?'

'None whatsoever,' Eugenia assured her.

'It's my dearest wish to go with you.'

'Good! And in return may I say that I am well content to have you included in our party.' She frowned. 'I thought that when our committee advertised for nurses we would have no difficulty in recruiting the numbers we wanted, but sadly that wasn't the case. Most of those who applied were totally unsuitable.'

'How many of us are there?' Eugenia asked.

'Including myself and my old housekeeper, Mrs Clark, we shall number forty. There are ten Catholic nuns, eight Sellonite sisters, who've had experience in nursing cholera victims, six Anglican sisters from St John's House, and fourteen professional nurses. The Protestant Institution flatly refused to place their nurses under my absolute control, so of course I refused even to consider allowing any of them to join our party.' She rose to her feet. 'Until tomorrow morning then, Miss Pacemore. I suggest that you go early to bed, because we shall be leaving at an early hour.'

'I will, ma'am. Goodnight to you.'

Eugenia moved to the window and looked out on to the rain-wet street, excitement coursing through her. 'What an adventure this is going to be. Surely there will be opportunity to meet with Louis and Charles. Perhaps they can get leave to come to Constantinople. Or perhaps I might be able to go to the Crimea to visit them.'

Her thoughts turned to Florence Nightingale. They were approximately the same age, both gently born, both trained in nursing at the Kaiserswerth Institute. Yet although Eugenia had tremendous respect and admiration for the other woman, she knew that they could never become close friends. She was always aware that behind Florence Nightingale's frail and gentle exterior, there was a hard core of self-centred, steely determination. Although invariably polite and gently spoken to her staff, she brooked no familiarity from her underlings or social inferiors, and was a strict disciplinarian.

Eugenia smiled wryly and, going to the small bedside table, picked up and scanned the detailed contract that all of the party had been made to sign.

Nurses must be of good character and mature years. They will receive 12 to 14 shillings a week, with bed and board. This sum will be increased to 16 to 18 shillings after three months' good conduct, and further increased to 20 to 22 shillings after a year's good conduct.

The nurses must submit absolutely to Miss Nightingale's orders. Any misconduct may be punished with instant dismissal, and the dismissed woman will have to travel back to England as a third-class passenger on salt-meat rations. If a nurse is invalided home, however, she will have her expenses paid for first-class passage.

Nurses are allowed a moderate ration of strong drink. One pint of ale or porter with dinner. Half a pint of either brew at supper, or one glass of Marsala wine, or a single ounce of brandy.

No nurse, under any circumstances, may leave the hospital alone. She must either be in the company of the matron, Mrs Clark, or at least three other nurses.

A uniform will be issued, but the nurse must provide her own underclothing, four cotton nightcaps, a carpet bag and an umbrella. No coloured ribbons are allowed to be worn. The nuns and sisters will wear the habits of their various religious orders.

Eugenia unenthusiastically regarded her newly issued uniform, which was hanging from the door hook. She thought it very plain and ugly. It consisted of a shapeless grey tweed dress, a grey worsted jacket, short woollen cloak and a plain white cap. There was also a holland scarf to be worn over the shoulders with the words SCUTARI HOSPITAL embroidered upon it.

She busied herself in making final preparations for the journey and then went to bed. But she could not sleep, her mind too full of excited speculations about what she might find facing her in far-off Turkey. The prospect of meeting with Louis Nolan and her beloved cousin, Charles, filled her with joy.

'Maybe Louis and I will get married in Constantinople. Wouldn't that be so romantic!'

She accepted with equanimity the unromantic reality that she would be helping to nurse sick and wounded men, witnessing horrific sights, surrounded by indescribable suffering, and almost suffocating in the dreadful stenches of death and decay. Only scant months before, she had volunteered to work side by side with Florence Nightingale in the vilest slums of London, where there had been an outbreak of cholera. She had helped to care for the human dregs of the slums – men, women and children considered by respectable elements of society to be lower than brute beasts.

It was during that period that a mutual respect between herself and Florence Nightingale had been forged and tempered as if in a furnace. Eugenia knew with utter certainty that they would both be able to endure whatever ordeals might lay ahead.

During the long, sleepless hours of that night, Eugenia thought about the fellow members of the party. She had already met most of them, and now with sardonic amusement she anticipated what a shock some of these women would receive when they discovered just how their conception of nursing differed from Florence Nightingale's. She was still smiling in mischievous anticipation when sleep finally took her.

★ ★ ★

The first clash of temperaments occurred early the following morning when the party assembled at London Bridge station to take the train to Dover.

The Anglican and Sellonite sisters protested indignantly that they were high-born ladies, and as such could not be expected to sit in the same carriages as low-born professional nurses. Their spokeswoman haughtily declared that when ladies associated with hired nurses, the distinctions and privileges of social class must be maintained. The ladies should not be expected to do menial work. They should have the best quarters and food, and all their washing, mending and cleaning should be done for them by the hired nurses.

The hired nurses – poor and humble women from the lower classes, conditioned from birth to accept the contemptuous strictures of their social superiors – made no protest. They were only too conscious of the low regard in which society held them.

Inwardly seething with anger, Eugenia had witnessed the ladies' arrogant behaviour; and when the 'ladies' spokeswoman graciously invited her to share their carriage, she refused frostily. 'No thank you. I fear that the air in your carriage will be too preciously rarefied for my comfort. I prefer to sit with the hired nurses. I am, after all, receiving wages for this work.'

She took her seat among the nurses, who were pleasant enough in their manner towards her, but still there was an uneasy

342

atmosphere in the carriage, conversational exchanges stilted and cautious. Eugenia regretfully realized this was created by her presence. These women would never be able to accept her as one of their own and be completely at ease in her company. The gulf in birth and breeding between her and them was too deep and too wide to ever be successfully bridged.

The reception that greeted the Nightingale party when they reached Boulogne lifted Eugenia's spirits. They were given a hero's welcome, and men and women alike struggled to carry their baggage. The hotel owner refused to accept payment for their meal, and placed his establishment at their complete disposal.

The ladies snobbishly refused to sit at dinner with the hired nurses, but to Eugenia's immense satisfaction, Florence Nightingale displayed her moral stature by waiting in person on the hired nurses, and taking her own meal with them, much to the discomfiture of the ladies.

At Paris and Marseille the party was met with more popular acclamation, and Eugenia found herself enjoying it tremendously. Capping that enjoyment was the knowledge that every hour brought her closer to reunion with the two people whom she loved above all else: Louis Nolan and Charles Bronton.

Forty-Five

Light Brigade Camp, Kadakoi, Crimea
October 25th, 1854

In mid-October the prevailing winds had shifted to sweep down from the north, and although the days were still tempered by sunlight, the nights had become bitterly cold.

Before dawn, in the tent which she shared with her husband and six other men, Rosie sat alone mending a torn shirt by the light of a solitary candle. The icy wind buffeted the canvas walls and draughts shivered the candle flame. Rosie completed her task and bit through the thread, then laid aside the shirt and blew on her cupped hands, rubbing them together to warm her chilled fingers.

The tent flap was pushed aside and the blanket-wrapped bulk of Dorcas Murphy appeared.

'Jaysus! It's bloody freezing out there!'

'It's not much warmer in here.' Rosie smiled ruefully.

'Ah well, the sun 'ull be up soon.' The Irish-woman sat down on the ground facing Rosie and held her hands over the candle flame.

344

'Then we'll go down to the harbour and see what we can find. I want to be well away before Murphy comes back, because if I see his ugly face again this morning I'll put me fist into it. He was like a bear with a sore head when he got up so he was. The miserable bastard! The way he goes on at me, you'd think it was my fault that we're stuck starving wi' the cold and hunger in this God-awful country. I told him to blame bloody Raglan and Lucan and Cardigan for the state we're in, not me ... I reckon we'll all be dead soon, the way things are going.'

Rosie sat listening to her friend's familiar litany without comment. Colum Murphy's discontent was shared by virtually the entire army. After the victorious battle at Alma River, the allies had advanced on Sebastopol, but had not assaulted the city. Instead they had taken position to the south of Sebastopol and captured the small port of Balaclava to use as the supply base for the British and Turks, while the French had established their base further to the west at Kamiesch Bay.

Heavy guns had been laboriously transported over the tortuous single track from Balaclava harbour up to the high plateau overlooking the city's fortifications, and everyone was confident that after a bombardment the city would fall. But after weeks of bombardment nothing had been achieved. The high morale following the victory at the Alma had been eroded by the ever-worsening cold and hardships, and sickness had again begun to decimate the regiments. To make matters worse, there were reports that a large, fresh Russian army was gathering a few miles to the east of the British base. This forced the Light Brigade to move out long before dawn every morning and picket a ridge of high ground a mile to the east of the Kadokoi camp, a miserable, teeth-chattering duty that their commander, Lord Cardigan, did not share, since he remained ensconced in luxurious comfort on his private yacht in Balaclava harbour, and never ventured out before sunrise and a hearty breakfast.

The tent flap opened again and Megan Morgan, wrapped in blankets, came in. 'We've lost another from the troop. Gussie Bartleet. The cholera took him last night. Still, it did me a bit o' good. I got his baccy, and three new clay pipes as well.'

'Oh my God!' Rosie exclaimed in concern. 'What will poor Annie and her kids do now?'

The Welshwoman shrugged. 'They'll be alright. From what I hear, the girls at Scutari are having a good time of it. Living like toffs, so they are, wi' the pongalo coming out of their ears, having any man they fancy. I wish I was there meself.'

'And me as well, girl,' Dorcas muttered in heartfelt agreement.

Dawn came and the wind dropped. From the siege lines to the north came the reverberating echoes of cannon fire. But this didn't perturb Rosie or her friends; the sound of cannon fire was the familiar accompaniment to their lives here.

The three women left the camp and made their way along the muddy track that led to Balaclava three miles distant across the undulating plain. The narrow way was thronged with lurching ox waggons and horse-drawn carts. There were numerous squads of soldiers, their once-fine uniforms now threadbare and discoloured, and the inevitable strings of sick and wounded men, some litter-borne, others limping and crawling, and yet more crammed into carts.

At one point Rosie and her friends encountered a group of soldiers' women at the side of the track, clustered and crouched around a young girl lying upon the muddy ground, her eyes screwed shut, her thin face a pallid grey hue.

'What's the matter? Has she got the cholera?' Dorcas asked.

As she voiced the question the girl writhed and screamed in agony.

'No. She's having a babby.' The woman shook her matted mop of hair and frowned. 'It's breeched and already dead, I reckon, and there's nothing more we can do to help her. She'll not be long in this life; she's lost too much blood.'

As the three friends moved on, Rosie carried the picture of the young girl's grey features vividly in her mind, and fear flooded through her.

'What about my own baby? Will it be born in the mud like that poor girl's? Will it live?'

she wondered to herself.

They climbed up a hill and saw beneath them the village and harbour of Balaclava. The once-pleasant small town had been ransacked, the doors, windows, rafters of the houses taken for firewood, its population of immigrant Greeks expelled. Many of the ruined houses were now packed with fever-stricken Turkish soldiers, and the narrow streets and alleys had become running sewers. The narrow land-locked harbour was crammed with shipping, its waters a sink of stinking filth, dead animals and rotting offal. There was noise, bustle and vitality on all sides. Supplies were being landed and taken by fatigue parties out to the rows of commissariat store tents. Drafts of fresh troops were disembarking, pristine in scarlet tunics and white pipeclayed accoutrements. Harassed commissariat conductors were checking supply lists and hurling abuse at their fur-capped Tartar labourers.

As Rosie and her friends made their way through the streets, they were continually invited to buy foodstuffs, sweetmeats, liquor, tobacco and dozens of other items from the Levantine traders who had flocked into the town to replace the original inhabitants. But the three women had come to buy a particular commodity, opium, and the trader they sought was a Turkish woman known as Madam Turgut.

They skirted the landing quays and went along a winding alley to enter a small tumbledown, derelict church topped by a half-shattered onion dome.

'Hello, English ladies. You come to see Madam Turgut again. That's good. That's good.' A small, rotund, black-eyed woman came smiling from the gloomy shadows to greet them, her teeth shining white in her swarthy face.

The air was thick with the acrid scent of opium smoke and the haunch of goat flesh roasting over the fire at the far end of the long room, its juices falling to hiss and crackle in the flames.

There were several blue-uniformed Turkish soldiers reclining against one of the side walls, some sitting puffing on hookah water-pipes, others lying comatose in glazed-eyed, drugged stupefaction.

The opposite wall had a curtained lean-to erected against its entire length, divided into separate cubicles, and from behind the thick curtains came grunts and hoarsely gasped cries.

Madam Turgut giggled and made lewd gestures with her hands. 'Soldier men like to jig-a-jig. My girls earn much money.' She winked at Rosie. 'I tell you, lady, you are very pretty. You could earn much money from jig-a-jig if you come here and work for me. You are so pretty and young that you need jig-a-jig with officers only. Not with soldier men.'

The woman was giggling like a mischievous gamine, and her good humour was so infectious that Rosie couldn't help but be amused at her manner. 'I'm a respectable married woman. I only do jig-a-jig with my husband.'

The three of them sat down on the floor around a hookah and took turns drawing the water-cooled smoke deep into their lungs. As the drug took effect, a feeling of contented lassitude crept over Rosie.

They shared a second pipe and Rosie lay back in somnolent torpor, all the trials and tribulations of her life slipping away. She felt happily at peace and lost all sense of time, drifting between sleep and wakefulness for hours.

It was dusk when her dreamy somnolence was disrupted by the entrance of a man wearing the blue frock coat and red fez of a Turkish officer. He strode past the women and began to shout at the soldiers, kicking them to their feet.

The soldiers came stumbling past Rosie, heading for the door. The officer crossed the room and began to tear aside the shielding curtains of the cubicles, shouting furiously all the while. Women shrieked and naked men hurriedly left, carrying their clothes, some trying to drag on trousers and tunics.

'What's happening? Why's he doing this?' Megan Morgan demanded of Madam Turgut.

The small woman confronted the officer and there was a rapid exchange of questions and answers. Then he brushed past her and disappeared outside.

'What did he say?' Rosie asked.

'He say there has been a big fight by the Fedoukine Hills and many Russians and Turks and English horse soldiers have been killed.'

Megan Morgan was grim-faced. 'Horse soldiers! That could be our lads. Come on, girls, we'd best get back to camp straight away.'

Darkness had fallen when the three women reached the sloping road from Balaclava and climbed to the high plateau of the plain. They passed close to an entrenched battery of Royal Marine artillery and Dorcas shouted to the gunners.

'What's been happening?'

'The Russians come across the Causeway Heights, and the bloody Turks ran away from the redoubts there. But the Jocks stopped the Russian cavalry over the far side of Kadakoi camp, and then below the Fedoukine Heights our cavalry pushed the rest of the Russians back.'

'How about our cavalry, did we lose many?' Rosie called.

'We've heard that the Heavies didn't lose many, but the Light Brigade have took a right hammering.'

Rosie's heart thudded with apprehension and she hurried on.

When they came in sight of Kadakoi camp, Rosie's dread increased. There were no camp fires burning, despite the bitter cold of the night.

'Jaysus! Is there nobody there? Have they all

351

been killed?' Dorcas exclaimed.

'For Christ's sake, don't say that, it could make it come true,' Megan Morgan reproved sharply.

But when they got closer, Rosie could make out dim figures moving and cried out in relief. 'Look there, I can see some of them.'

They reached their own troop's tent line to find a group of men talking in low voices. Rosie could hear a woman sobbing inside one of the tents.

Colum Murphy detached himself from the group of men and came to meet his wife. 'Where the hell have you been?'

'That's none of your business,' she retorted fiercely.

'Where's the rest of the boys?' Megan Morgan questioned. 'Where's my Dewi?'

Murphy's voice softened. 'He's dead, Meggy. There's only us few here still standing from our troop. The rest are dead or wounded, except for one or two that might be took prisoner. We got slaughtered.' He smiled grimly. 'But we did our duty, and so did your Dewi. You can be proud of him.'

'Are you certain sure my Dewi is dead? Couldn't he just be wounded?' Megan Morgan quavered.

Colum Murphy put his hand against his chest, which was heavily caked with dried blood. 'I'm certain sure that he's dead, Meggy. He was my front man and a cannonball hit him. This is his blood.'

Megan Morgan's features crumpled in grief

and harsh sobs tore from her throat.

'What about my husband?' Rosie asked.

'I don't know. He was still alive when we reached the Russian guns, but then I lost sight of him.'

Rosie found herself guiltily wishing that she could feel grief or worry. Instead she felt only the regret that if Jack Collier were indeed dead, then her baby would never know its father.

'What happened to the brigade then? How did we come to lose so many?' Dorcas asked. The men took turns to describe what they had experienced, and the story gradually took shape.

The Light Brigade had been ordered to charge against Russian guns at the far end of a long, shallow valley. To reach these particular guns they were forced to run a gauntlet of devastating fire from more Russian guns and rifle pits on both sides of the valley. After taking their objective they were counter-attacked by overwhelming numbers of Russian lancers and the survivors had had to cut their way through these fresh assailants to make their escape. 673 men had charged down that valley. Only 195 had returned and many of these were wounded. More than 500 horses were destroyed.

Rosie listened with ever-increasing distress. Many of the lost men had been her friends who, tough and brutish though some of them might be, had always treated her with kindness. Yet even now, she still felt no grief for her husband, and her guilt for this fact was troubling her.

'I'll get a fire going and cook some grub for us all,' Dorcas said.

'No you won't.' Henry Peebles spoke from the entrance of the nearest tent. 'It's been ordered that no fires are to be lit, and we've got to keep the noise down and be ready to stand to.'

'Why?' Dorcas challenged.

'Because the staff are expecting another attack.'

'But the lads need to have something hot to eat,' Dorcas argued.

'So do I, but orders are orders,' he snapped. 'So why don't you go and make yourself useful to the surgeons, because you're not needed here.'

Rosie had led Megan Morgan into a tent out of the biting wind, and she heard Henry Peebles' words. She felt that she must do something to atone for her lack of emotion over her husband's situation.

'I'm going to help with the wounded, Megan,' she said and returned outside.

Henry Peebles came up to her, staring intently into her eyes, and said in a low voice so that no one else could hear him, 'If Jack Collier has been killed you'll be needing another husband to take care of you, Rosie. I'll wed you as quick as I can, and you can share my bed in the meantime. I know you're carrying Collier's babby, and I don't mind raising it.'

Although Rosie was not prepared to play the hypocrite by pretending to love for Jack Collier, she still resented Peebles' assumption that she was eager to jump into his bed.

'If Jack is dead then I'm well able to take care of myself,' she answered coolly. 'And I will choose my own husband if I decide I want to marry again.'

He smiled bleakly. 'I just want you to know that I'm here if you want me.' He paused as if waiting for her reply, and when she stayed silent, went on, 'Listen, they're trying to arrange a truce so that we can collect our dead. I'll go and look for him for you.'

'There's no need for you to do that,' she snapped curtly. 'I'm well able to do it myself.'

'But there'll be some terrible sights in that valley, Rosie. Cannonballs smash men up. You don't want to see such things.'

'You're forgetting that I was at the Alma, Sarn't-Major. I've already seen what cannonballs can do to men's bodies.'

He shrugged his broad shoulders and accepted defeat. 'I was only trying to make things easier for you, Rosie, because I truly do care for you.'

Suddenly Rosie felt that she was being unduly churlish towards him. He was, after all, only following time-hallowed army custom. The vast majority of serving soldiers' widows remarried almost immediately within the regiment if they could find a man prepared to take them. Even those who had been in love with their deceased husbands

355

usually accepted that harsh necessity compelled them to take another husband as quickly as possible to ensure the security of food and shelter for themselves and their children.

'Look, I am grateful for your offer, Sarn't-Major, but it's not yet known whether Jack is alive or dead. In either case, he's still my husband, and it's my duty to try and find him, and if he's living, then I must try to help him. If he's dead, then I must at least wash his body and prepare him for his grave. If I don't do that, then I can't have respect for myself, or expect anyone else to respect me ... Now I'm going to go with Dorcas to see if we can help with the wounded.'

She walked away with the Irishwoman and left Henry Peebles staring pensively after her.

The Light Brigade regimental hospitals were a row of bell tents set up in the central square of the ruined village of Kadakoi.

Most of the wounded that had been brought here had already been treated and were lying outside the tents waiting to be transported onwards to Balaclava. Rosie and Dorcas went among them, searching for Jack Collier and other members of their regiment. Hardened though she was to blood and death, Rosie could not help but be shaken by some of the terrible head wounds that had been inflicted by Russian sabres and lances.

She found Conky White lying on his front. 'Do you know what's happened to Jack?' she asked, and he shook his head.

'Me and him were coming back from the battery when the Russki lancers came at us. His horse went down and I was too busy fighting for me life to see what happened to him after that. Sorry, my duck.'

In a lamplit tent, Assistant-Surgeon Alfred Bayliss of the 20th Light Dragoons was sitting on an upturned cask by the side of the improvised operating table: a wooden door. His hands, bare forearms and apron were caked with blood. He had a long, thin cheroot between his lips which he was smoking with much enjoyment. A middle-aged man with an eye for pretty women, he immediately recognized Rosie as she pushed her head through the entrance flap.

'Looking for your husband are you, Rosie Collier?'

'Yes, sir.' Her eyes fixed on the man who lay motionless on the improvised table, his head completely swathed in bandages with only a small hole left over his mouth for breathing.

'Well this isn't he.' Bayliss grimaced ruefully. 'This is Lieutenant Bronton.'

'The transports are here,' a voice shouted outside, and Bayliss rose to his feet.

'The sooner we get the poor fellows down to Balaclava harbour, the better for them.'

'Can I help, sir?' Rosie asked.

'Of course.' His face suddenly appeared drawn and aged with sorrow. 'Those that are dying can stay here, and be spared the further agony of being jolted about on a damned ox

357

cart. At times like this I wish that those arm-chair warriors who shout so loudly about the glory of war could be here to witness the price that has to be paid for that glory.'

'Will Mr Bronton live?' she whispered as they went outside.

'I'm confident that he will, but his features are most dreadfully mutilated. One eye is gone completely, and I fear for the condition of his remaining one. He might well be blinded.'

'That will be very hard for him. He was such a handsome man.'

Rosie was genuinely sorry for Charles Bronton, despite the social gulf between them. In her mind she questioned herself guiltily. 'Why is it that I can feel pity for an officer, and yet not care very greatly about my own husband?'

Driven by that guilt, as soon as the convoy of carts and mule-litters had been despatched, she borrowed a lantern and spare candles and trudged through the bitter winds of night until she reached the valley where the Light Brigade had been destroyed. There she searched among dead men and dead horses for long hours until the grey light of dawn, but nowhere could she find her husband.

Forty-Six

Malta, October 30th, 1854

Eugenia stood on the forward deck of the *Vectis*, gazing with delight at the honey-coloured palaces, churches, the great limestone forts and towering ramparts that surrounded the sun-sparkled waters of the grand harbour of Valletta. The harbour itself was a scene of bustling movement, with small, brightly painted row-boats swarming to and from shore to anchored warships. Steamships were heading to the open seas, smoke gushing from their tall funnels, naval cutters and gigs slicing through the gentle swell, their oars throwing up cascading showers of diamond-bright water drops.

Clustered around Eugenia, the three distinct groupings of black-habited Anglican sisters, white-habited Roman Catholic nuns and grey-uniformed hired nurses were awaiting the arrival of the boats which were to ferry them ashore for a sightseeing trip.

The storm-tossed voyage from Marseille had done nothing to thaw the snobbishly frosty relationship between the Anglican sisters and the hired nurses, who had slept and taken their meals in separate cabins. The Catholic nuns were somewhat friendlier, but their piety and the strict supervision enforced by their mother superior prohibited any general conviviality.

Eugenia had remained with the hired nurses, and the time spent in such close shipboard proximity had eased the initial resentment they had felt towards her, and had loosened the fetters of social convention. Now she was included in their general chatter, and sometimes coarse anecdotes. For her part, she was happy in their friendly companionship.

Her closest new friend was Mrs Jane Gibson, who had been a surgical nurse in several London hospitals. Jane Gibson was a plump, pretty, twinkly eyed woman in her mid-thirties, with a mischievous sense of humour, who candidly stated that after burying three husbands she was on the lookout for a fourth.

'But I'll not be marrying some young penniless buck for lust of his good looks and fine body this time, my dear,' she told Eugenia. 'I'm looking for an old, creaky-bodied bridegroom with plenty o' money and property to leave me. I want to be a widow of comfortable means this time, so that I can enjoy my freedom.'

'But he might live for many years,' Eugenia pointed out.

Jane Gibson winked roguishly, and ran her

hands down over her prominent breasts. 'If the first sight of these all bare in the candle-light don't give the old bugger a fatal heart attack, then I'll smother him with them.'

Eugenia laughed with her.

Florence Nightingale had been confined to her cabin with sea-sickness and the super-vision of the party had devolved upon her friend and aide, Mrs Bracebridge, whose attitude towards the hired nurses mirrored that of the Anglican sisters.

There was a stirring among the waiting women as Mrs Bracebridge bustled self-importantly on to the deck and, coming to stand in front of the hired nurses, directed them sternly.

'On shore, you women will be met by Major Varley of the militia, the gentleman who has very kindly agreed to conduct your tour of Valletta. I must impress upon you that Miss Nightingale expects the very highest stand-ards of behaviour and comportment during the tour. All Major Varley's instructions must be obeyed without question. Any conver-sation between yourselves must be quiet and seemly. No liquor of any type is to be imbibed or purchased. No tobacco or snuff is to be used or purchased. No foodstuffs are to be eaten or purchased. No greetings or remarks are to be exchanged with any common people, soldiers or sailors. You may, however, acknowledge respectfully any words that are addressed towards you by a lady or gentle-man of quality. Now, have you all fully understood these instructions?'

'Please, ma'am,' Jane Gibson enquired. 'Can I ask you something?'

'Well, Gibson? What is it?' Mrs Bracebridge glared impatiently.

Jane Gibson's tone and expression was one of humble anxiety, but her eyes twinkled mischievously.

'Please, ma'am, I'm worried that if a gentleman dressed like a gentleman of quality addresses himself to me, how am I to know whether or not he is a real gentleman? He might be an imposter, mightn't he, ma'am? I'm a very humble woman, ma'am, and I've no acquaintance with gentlemen of quality, ma'am. I don't think that I...'

'For heaven's sake, be quiet, Gibson!' Mrs Bracebridge flushed with temper as she heard the sly chuckles sounding from among the group of nurses. 'I do not believe that you will be addressed by any gentleman of quality, Gibson, so the situation will not arise.'

'Boats are coming, ladies,' a sailor shouted from mid-deck, and any further exchange between the women was cut short.

'Good morning, ladies. My name is Varley, Major Varley.' Face as scarlet as his coat, irascibly mannered, sweating profusely, the short, fat man introduced himself to his charges on the landing quay at the foot of the long, broad flight of steep, stone steps that led up to the streets and alleys of the city.

'You will do me the courtesy, ladies, of

keeping formation and maintaining discipline during this tour. Without formation and discipline it will become chaos. Now, follow me.'

He led the party up the steps to an open square and there marshalled them into the desired columnar formation. Anglican sisters in front, Catholic sisters at the rear, the hired nurses in the centre where they would have no opportunity for unobserved bad behaviour.

'Very well, ladies. Remember now, the maintenance of discipline and formation are paramount.' Taking station at the head of the column, he bawled, 'Black sisters! Forward march!'

The solemn Anglicans dutifully obeyed, and the grinning nurses followed, but the nuns seemed confused, some straggling after the column, others going back down the steps, and still others milling anxiously around their mother superior, waiting for her orders.

By now a crowd of soldiers, sailors, civilians and urchins had gathered to gaze at this strange spectacle.

'Look out, sir! You've lost half of your regiment!' a soldier shouted to the major, and the crowd began to laugh and jeer.

Major Varley's scarlet face darkened to purple and he bellowed, 'Halt! Halt, I say! Where are those damned white sisters? Where are they?' He scurried back, bawling at the top of his voice. 'Will you get into formation, white sisters! Join the column! Join the column! Stop this straggling! We must have discipline and formation! All will be chaos, else!'

'Join the column! Join the column! We must have discipline and formation!' Jane Gibson mimicked Varley's voice and, unable to control herself, Eugenia dissolved into helpless laughter.

It would be the last time for many months that she would experience such joyful amusement.

Forty-Seven

Constantinople, November 4th, 1854

Just after dawn, in blustering winds and teeming rain, the *Vectis* wallowed through choppy, white-capped seas to drop anchor off Seraglio Point. Despite the atrocious weather, the women rushed up on deck to gaze at the domes and minarets of the fabled city, and across the narrow Bosphorus Strait at the huge quadrangle of the Barrack Hospital with its four corner turrets that topped the high skyline on the opposite shore.

Over a late breakfast in the nurses' cabin, the talk was of how splendid the Barrack

Hospital appeared.

'It must be the biggest hospital in the world.'

'There must be room for thousands of beds.'

'The poor fellows will be pleased to see us, I'll bet.'

'If we're let to nurse them,' Emma Fowler, a tall, raw-boned woman, her face and hands roughened by years of hard toil, said doubtfully.

'And why should we not be let to nurse them?' another woman demanded.

'You heard what Miss Nightingale said up on deck, didn't you? She said that the strongest of us will be wanted at the washtub. Well, that'll be us hired hands, won't it? I can't see them la-di-dah bitches doing any laundering. They'll all be too busy mincing around reading their bibles and saying their prayers, while us lot does all the scrubbing and fetching and carrying.'

Her words brought resentful mutterings of agreement, and then Mrs Bracebridge came in. 'Get your belongings together. We are to move directly across to the hospital. There has been a battle in the Crimea and the wounded are expected to begin arriving here shortly.'

The news provoked excitement and bustle, but Eugenia experienced a shiver of premonitory anxiety, and followed Mrs Bracebridge out of the cabin.

'Do you have more details about the battle,

ma'am? Were our cavalry engaged?'

The other woman hissed impatiently. 'I've far too much to do to waste time in idle gossip about battles, Pacemore.'

Eugenia's fiery spirit rose at the woman's tone and she snapped curtly, 'I don't ask for the sake of gossip, Mrs Bracebridge. My cousin and another close friend of mine are cavalry officers serving with the army in the Crimea. Naturally I'm greatly concerned for them both.'

Mrs Bracebridge looked shocked. 'Officers, you say?'

'Yes, I do say.' Eugenia's premonition was now disturbing her greatly, and she was unable to dismiss it as mere fancy. 'So, can you please tell me anything further about the battle?'

The other woman shrugged. 'I only know what Lord Napier told Miss Nightingale when he came out to the ship this morning. Apparently the Russians tried to attack the harbour at Balaclava and were driven off. The Light Brigade of our cavalry were almost completely destroyed in a charge against the Russian guns. There is some talk of a dispute among our generals as to where the fault lies.'

'Oh my God!' Eugenia battled to keep her composure. 'My cousin is the adjutant of the Twentieth Light Dragoons. They're part of the Light Brigade.'

Mrs Bracebridge's manner suddenly altered, and she laid her hand sympathetically on Eugenia's shoulder. 'Now, try not to worry,

366

my dear. Your cousin may be perfectly safe and well. I don't doubt that when we arrive at the hospital we shall be able to find out very quickly who has been wounded or killed. Now I really must get on. There is so much to be done. Try not to worry.' With a final pat of sympathy she bustled away.

Eugenia knew that it was pointless to be fearful about her cousin, yet she couldn't shake off her premonitory dread. She was able to draw some comfort from the fact that Louis Nolan had told her in his last letter that he was employed on the staff of Lord Raglan.

'At least Louis would not have charged with the brigade. So he must be safe and well. Oh God, let them both be safe and well. Please God, let it be so.'

The rain had ceased and the gleams of sunlight momentarily lancing through the clouds did nothing to temper the cold wind. The procession of brightly painted caiques, small gondola-like boats, approached the wooden landing stage on the Asiatic shore of the Bosphorus. Oar blades struck against the floating bloated carcasses of dead animals, whose rotting flesh gave off a nauseating stench, while along the shoreline, packs of starving, mangy dogs fought over the carrion carried in by the waves.

As the shore came nearer, the women were able to see clearly the steep, rubbish-strewn muddy slopes that led up to the Barrack Hospital. A few groups of British soldiers stood on the slopes watching the boats coming in. Others were limping upwards towards the massive building, some being helped by comrades.

'I don't think I like the look of this, Genia.' Jane Gibson grimaced unhappily.

Eugenia made no answer. All her thoughts were on her cousin and Louis Nolan.

One by one the boats discharged their passengers and the women formed their separate groupings, each one carrying her carpet bag and umbrella.

'Look at that lot.' Jane Gibson pointed upwards to where a trio of haggard-looking European women dressed in tawdry finery were in heated dispute with a couple of soldiers.

'Prostitutes!' Emma Fowler ejaculated angrily. 'That's bloody shameful, that is! They'll be spreading the clap all through the army, so they will. As though we won't have enough work as it is.'

'Oh, come on now, Emma.' Jane Gibson giggled. 'You wouldn't begrudge these poor soldier boys a little bit of pleasure, would you?'

Florence Nightingale landed in company with Mrs Bracebridge and her husband. They led the straggle of women up the rutted track and through the mighty gateway of the Barrack Hospital, to be received with stiff formality by the bewhiskered, frock-coated Staff Surgeon Menzies and the military commandant, Major Sillery.

After the briefest of introductions, Florence Nightingale and the Bracebridges went off with the two men, leaving the rest of the party to be guided to their quarters by a blue-tunicked, elderly sergeant.

'I'm Sergeant William Thomas, late of the Twenty-ninth Foot, ladies, now in the Ambulance Corps, for me sins. I served twenty-five years in the old regiment, went to pension, and got brought back again. Her Majesty decided that to earn me pension I'd got to come out to this God-forsaken hole and do a bit more service. More than a hundred of us pensioners come out, and now we're nearly all dead – through overdoing the drink, mostly. But it saves Her Majesty the expense of our pensions, don't it? So it's brought some good to her, I suppose.' He paused, and his warm, gap-toothed grin embraced them all.

'I'll tell you something though, ladies. Despite what the medical gentlemen and our officers might be thinking, I for one am real pleased to see you lot. You're sorely needed. We're knee-deep in shit and blood here, and we need all the help we can get.'

Eugenia was touched by this first token of welcome they had received, and many of the women shared her sentiment. But some of the Anglican sisters displayed their displeasure at being spoken to in this manner by a social inferior.

'Will you now guide us to our quarters, my good man.' Sister Grace Pringle scowled.

'And spare us any more of your inane recital.'

His bleary eyes were amused as he looked at her horse-like face for long moments before replying pleasantly, 'I'm only a poor, ignorant old soldier, missy. So I don't know what inane means. But seeing as you're such a fine lady, I'll take it as a compliment, shall I?'

He turned to speak to the whole party. 'I'll give you a bit of a walk round, so you can learn the lie of the land and save yourselves getting lost when you're on your own. So come on with me, if you please.'

For Eugenia, the guided tour in Malta had been the source of unalloyed pleasure, with its beautiful buildings, laughing children and handsome people. This present tour, however, almost instantly became a cause for horrified shock and burgeoning anger. The sights, stenches and sounds she met with temporarily obliterated her anxieties concerning her cousin and her fiancé.

The building was situated in a quadrangle around a great central square, which was a sea of mud and stinking refuse. One entire side of the building was a fire-gutted ruin. There were more than two miles of vast, empty corridors, damp streaming down the walls, the tiled floors broken and misshapen. One wing of the building comprised a depot for troops in transit, another section was a cavalry-horse stables. Adjoining the depot was a canteen where rotgut spirits were sold. Beneath the building were huge, rancid cesspits that poisoned the air and a maze of noisome dark cellars where hundreds of army wives who had been forcibly separated from their husbands led a savagely harsh existence, many of them prostituting themselves to buy the drink and opiates they craved, leaving their neglected children to the mercies of others.

The cacophonous hospital wards were crammed with sick and wounded men being tended by untrained male orderlies, who were mainly drawn from the convalescents waiting to return to their regiments in the Crimea. Beds, bedding and clothing were in such short supply that hundreds of the patients lay on straw palliasses on the bare floors with only a great coat or blanket to cover them, still clad in the ragged, filthy uniforms they had arrived in. Filth, bad and insufficient food, swarming vermin, overcrowding and callous neglect brought death to thousands who, with proper care, would surely have lived.

The doctors and surgeons, plagued by shortages of medical supplies, battled manfully to save the sick and wounded, but the inadequacies of the organizational and commissariat systems ensured that their battles ended all too frequently in defeat.

When the party of nurses and sisters finally arrived at the great corner turret which was to be their quarters, each of them was silent and subdued, their spirits at a low ebb.

Their allotted five small rooms and kitchen did nothing to raise their low spirits. They were foul-smelling, dank and dirty, with no furniture except for a couple of broken beds and a few wooden chairs. Turkish style divans ran around the walls, and there was one small room set aside as a kitchen, but there were no cooking implements or pots. Before they had completed their inspection of the quarters, the women also became unhappily aware of the swarming bugs and fleas, and the scurrying of rats' feet in the black-shadowed spaces under the divan.

'These rooms are a disgrace! How dare you expect ladies to live in such a slum?' Sister Pringle angrily upbraided their guide.

'It's not me that expects you to live here, missy,' Sergeant Thomas said quietly. 'It's the commandant that's give you these quarters, not me.'

'Why haven't you had these room cleansed and furnished as befitting for ladies of consequence? I shall have you punished for neglecting your duty, my man. I have friends with influence.'

'It was no part o' my duty to have these rooms seen to,' the old man protested. 'So it's no use you threatening me, missy.'

'Missy? Missy? Whom exactly do you think you are talking to?' Sister Pringle's horsey face was livid with rage. 'How dare you address me with such insolent rudeness? I'm going to report you, and demand that you be punished for your insolence towards your betters.'

Eugenia had been distressed by what she

had found during the tour around the building, but now her anger found new focus. This elderly man had been the sole friendly face and voice that they had so far met, and she sprang to his defence. 'You're being unjust, Sister Pringle. How can you possibly blame the sergeant for the condition of these quarters?'

The woman stared at Eugenia in disbelief, and stuttered in fury, 'B–blame? B–blame? I shall blame whomsoever I choose to blame. So mind your own business, and remember your place, woman. Remember that you work for wages.'

'Remember my place?' Eugenia's temper flared white-hot and she stepped forwards to come face to face with Sister Pringle. 'My place, Sister Pringle, is the equal of your own as regards birth and breeding. But I am ashamed to acknowledge that I am of the same social rank as such a stupid, arrogant, useless creation as yourself. I've listened to your gibes and sneers directed against we hired nurses and kept my peace. But I tell you now that if I hear one more sneer or gibe issue from your lips, I shall give you the slap that you so richly deserve.'

Sister Pringle's eyes blinked in fear and she backed away.

'Kindly control yourself, Miss Pacemore.' The soft, low voice carried itself clearly to all ears.

'Miss Nightingale, I thank our dear Lord that you're here!' Sister Pringle exclaimed in

373

breathy relief. 'This woman was about to physically assault me! I do believe that she's gone mad!'

'Your beliefs as to Nurse Pacemore's mental condition are of no interest to me, Sister Pringle. But I will not tolerate discord and dispute among my staff. So both of you take heed of that. Now, listen to me carefully, all of you. Our arrival has not been welcomed by the gentlemen who command here. The work we are to do is still under discussion. So for a few days we must stay secluded in these quarters. Our food will be issued from the hospital kitchens and brought to us by the orderlies.' She glanced about her with obvious distaste. 'There are no furnishings or bedding available for us. In fact, there's very little of anything in this hospital. Even the water is rationed. We are to be allowed one pint each daily, and that must suffice for washing and drinking. There are no spare lamps or candles, so tonight we shall go to bed in darkness. There are no brooms, buckets or mops for our use, so you must cleanse these quarters as best you can with whatever old rags we can procure. Everyone is to share in the task of cleansing our quarters, no matter how exalted they may consider their station in life to be.'

She looked challengingly at Sister Pringle and her fellow Anglicans. 'Is that understood, Sisters?'

They made grudging murmurs of assent.

Florence Nightingale turned to Eugenia. 'I

wish to speak with you privately, Nurse Pacemore. Will you please come with me?' She led Eugenia upstairs to an empty room. 'The casualty list from the Balaclava battle was brought here last night on the fast steam packet. I've had the opportunity of scanning it, and I'm sorry to have to tell you that your cousin, Lieutenant Charles Bronton, has been severely wounded. He should be arriving here later this week.'

The news struck Eugenia like a physical blow, and her face drained of all colour. Florence Nightingale gave her a few moments to recover from the shock.

'If your cousin is sent back to England, would you wish to accompany him? If so, I am prepared to release you from your contract.'

Eugenia pondered this briefly. 'I'm very grateful for your kind offer, ma'am, but my cousin has always put his duty before any personal desires. He would be most displeased if I were not to stay here and do my own duty. I do not want to be released.'

'Good! Because I do not wish to lose your services.' The other woman smiled approvingly and dismissed her. 'You may go and help with the cleansing of the quarters, Nurse Pacemore.'

'May I request something else, ma'am? Do you know of an officer named Captain Louis Nolan? He is Captain Nolan, the author.'

'Indeed I do. I met him personally on a couple of occasions. Sadly, he was killed in the charge of the Light Brigade.'

'Killed!' The word reverberated like a deafening drumbeat in Eugenia's brain, shattering her control. A wave of giddy, sickening blackness engulfed her, and she crumpled senseless to the floor.

Forty-Eight

Kadakoi Camp, Crimea
November 5th, 1854

Long before dawn, Rosie awoke, chilled and shivering, her bladder uncomfortably full. She unwrapped the soiled, threadbare blankets from her body, clambered stiffly to her feet and, stepping carefully over her snoring companions, went out of the bell tent. Thick fog enveloped her and the air was icy-cold and damp, the darkness almost impenetrable to her sight. She cautiously made her way some distance from the tents before pulling up her skirts and squatting down to urinate.

As she made her way back, she passed Henry Peebles' tent and saw the luminous glow of a lantern and a shadow moving across its canvas wall. She halted and called softly, 'It's Rosie Collier, Sarn't-Major. Can I speak with you?'

'Come on in, Rosie.'

She entered and found him sitting bare to the waist on a wooden box, carefully passing a candle flame along the seams of a shirt to destroy the lice and their eggs.

'I'll tell you something, Rosie, this is one war that can't be won while we're here. For every louse I burn to death, another hundred enlist and come to plague me.'

'To plague all of us, Sarn't-Major,' Rosie responded ruefully. 'I'd give anything to be able to have a bath. I'm beginning to stink like a badger.'

He grinned and winked. 'Don't you worry, Rosie. You'll always smell as sweet as a flower to me. Now, have you come to tell me that you'll be my woman?'

'No, I haven't. I've come to ask you to let me borrow a horse for a few hours.'

'What d'you want a horse for?'

'To carry firewood. We've not a stick left to cook with, and the nearest brushwood is up in the hills east of the Second Division's camp. If me and the girls can have a horse, we can fetch a big load back.'

He looked at the visible swelling of her pregnancy. 'Are you able to do the work, Rosie? You're getting a bit heavy in the stomach, aren't you?'

She smiled and rested her hands on her stomach. 'He's carrying light and easy. Half the time I don't even know he's there.'

Peebles considered for a few further

seconds, then nodded. 'Alright, if you're sure. You can take Fothergill's. It's a bit lame but it can still walk.'

'But what'll he say if he finds out I've taken his horse?'

'He won't know. He went down to Balaclava last night and he's sailing for Turkey today to meet his missus in Constantinople. It wouldn't surprise me if he never came back. There's quite a few officers who've buggered off back to England for good.'

'Alright. Thanks.' She turned to leave, but he gestured her to stay.

'Hold on a minute, Rosie. You know that now your man's disappeared it's against the regulations for you to stay on here with the regiment. By rights you should be put off the strength. So why don't you agree to be my woman? I'd be able to fix it for you to stay on then.'

She shook her head impatiently. 'How can I be your woman when I'm still married to Jack Collier? You're talking silly!'

It was his turn to shake his head impatiently. 'No, I'm not, girl! Jack Collier isn't on the list of prisoners taken by the Russkies, and he's not among the wounded. So he's either dead, or he's deserted. If he's a deserter and we ever catch him then he'll be hung or shot, so he's as good as dead. Either way, it means that you haven't got a husband, and that babby you're carrying won't have a father. What sort of a life will the poor little soul have if it hasn't got a dad? And what sort

378

of a life will you have if you're chucked out of the regiment?'

These were questions that Rosie had been asking herself with increasing frequency during these last days. Questions which afflicted her with anxious forebodings. She hesitated uncertainly, and without conscious volition her fingers touched the brass button nestling on its ribbon between her breasts. Over the years she had come to superstitiously believe it to be her personal talisman, and to trust in its power to protect her.

Henry Peebles' eyes studied her intently as he tried to judge what effect his words were having. Then, goaded by his need to know, he asked, 'Well, Rosie? What do you say? Will you be my woman?'

She drew a long, deep breath, and shook her head. 'I can't. I can't be any other man's woman while I don't know what's happened to Jack. I'm his lawful wife, and I owe him my loyalty.'

'Jesus Christ!' he exclaimed irritably. 'You don't owe him anything! He served you like you was a dog. Beating you black and blue. Drinking all his money away. How can you feel any loyalty toward the bad bastard?'

She stared at him with wide, troubled eyes, and stammered, 'You don't understand!'

For a brief instant she was sorely tempted to tell him why she felt under such intense pressure to be loyal to Jack Collier. To tell him about her past. To tell him that Jack Collier had married her knowing what she had been.

That he had restored her self-respect by marrying her, had enabled her to hold her head high once more as a respectable woman, and above all else, shortly to be a mother whose child would never need to be ashamed of her.

'Then explain it to me, so I can understand,' he pressed.

She opened her mouth to speak, then clamped it firmly shut and ran from the tent.

Henry Peebles cursed sibilantly. Jack Collier's disappearance was an aggravating mystery to him. He had glimpsed the man for the last time when they were attacking the Russian gunners in the battery, but since then his fate had become a mystery.

'You bastard, Collier,' Henry Peebles hissed. 'You've become the torment of my bloody life.'

'How much further have we got to go?' Dorcas Murphy demanded. 'Are you sure you aren't gone and got us lost? I can't hardly see me own feet through this muck.'

Day had dawned but the clouds overhead and the fog blanketing the land combined to create a murky darkness, limiting visibility to scant yards.

'Yeah, does you really know where you're taking us to, Rosie? We'se been walkin' for miles up and down these hills and I'm near knackered,' Megan Morgan complained.

Leading the horse, Rosie snapped back at them impatiently, 'I've told you already where

380

we are. Up beyond the Second Division's camp on the Inkerman Heights. There's lots of brushwood in the gullies up here.'

'Oh yeah, and there's millions o' Russians on the other side of the Inkerman gorges, aren't there? You'll get us all killed, so you will,' Dorcas grumbled.

'Don't talk silly. There's no way the Russians can come across to this side,' Rosie said confidently. 'All the lads say that they can't.'

They breasted a rise and a breeze blew, thinning the fog and increasing their range of visibility. Rosie sighed with relief as she sighted a straggle of small scrubby oaks and brushwood some thirty yards down the sloping hillside in a broad gully.

'Look!' She pointed. 'There's our firewood, girls.'

'Let's get to it then,' Dorcas urged. 'Because I don't care what all the lads say, I still reckon we're too close to the bloody Russkies for my liking.'

Using the small axe and the two billhooks they had brought with them, the women chopped feverishly at the branches. Time passed and the heap of branches grew slowly larger.

'Jaysus! This is hard graft, right enough.' Dorcas wiped the back of her hand across her sweating forehead. 'I swear these branches are made of iron.'

As she spoke there sounded in the distance the thumping echoes of cannon shots.

They all stopped work to stand and listen

intently. More cannon shots sounded and then, much nearer, there was a rattling of musketry, but because of the hilly, gullied terrain and the veiling mist, they could not pinpoint which direction the sounds were coming from.

More muskets rattled, and were answered by the sharper cracking of Minie rifles. This time the sound seemed to come from the direction of their own journey.

'Jaysus! That sounds like it's between us and the camp,' Dorcas exclaimed. 'The Russkies must have come across the gorges.'

The two older women instinctively turned to Rosie for leadership.

'What shall we do?'

'Which way shall we go?'

Rosie saw the apprehension in their eyes and struggled to control her own rising fears. She forced herself to answer calmly. 'We've got nothing to worry about. We're well sheltered in this gully. So we'll load our firewood on the horse and just wait for things to quieten down. I'm not going to leave a single branch here after all the sweating we've done to cut the stuff.'

Her show of calm steadied her companions, and Dorcas grinned admiringly. 'Fair play to you, Rosie. You've a good head on your shoulders. You always know what to do.'

They used the ropes they had brought to tie the branches into bundles, and the bundles on to the horse's back. Then they sat down and smoked their clay pipes.

By now the distant cannon shots had become a constant thumping and the musketry and Minie rifle fire was a continuous rattling from seemingly every direction.

'Jaysus! There's an awful big battle going on. I wonder if our regiment is in it.' Dorcas frowned with concern.

'I shouldn't think so.' Megan Morgan shook her head. 'There's not enough of our lads left to mount a charge, is there?'

Shouts and the sharp cracking of Minie rifles sounded from nearby, and the next instant several men in the dark-green uniforms of British riflemen appeared on the skyline at the top of the slope. Muskets volleyed and two of the riflemen fell, one jerking spasmodically and shrieking at the top of his voice.

Rosie and her friends jumped up in shocked fear.

The riflemen ran down towards the gully as the grey great coats and flat, black-glazed hats of Russian soldiers suddenly appeared on the skyline.

Muskets blazed and a rifleman staggered, then pitched forwards on to his face at Rosie's feet, blood and brains leaking from his shattered skull. The horse screamed and reared as musket balls punctured its flank, then bolted into the brushwood and was trapped, thrashing frantically about in futile efforts to free itself, its high-pitched screams overlaying the hoarse shouts of the men.

The remaining six riflemen formed a line,

their bayoneted weapons menacing the mass of oncoming Russians who were hesitantly advancing down the slope.

'Why don't you shoot?' Rosie shouted desperately, and one man grunted.

'We got no ammo left. You'd best run for it.'

Rosie turned to her friends and with a shock of dismay saw Megan Morgan slumped on her knees, hands clutching her chest, blood spurting out between her fingers.

'Come on, lads!' the same rifleman shouted, and ran at the Russians. Howling savagely, his comrades followed.

A score of muskets exploded, smashing the charging riflemen to the ground, and Rosie felt a hammer-blow on her shoulder that spun her round and sent her crashing on top of Megan Morgan.

'Youse bastards! I'll show yez, youse fuckin' bastards!' Dorcas bawled in fury and, snatching up a fallen rifle, stepped forward to shield her friends. Half a dozen Russians rushed to attack her, and she managed to plunge the bayonet into one of them before their bayonets rammed into her body and she went down. Rosie had painfully levered herself upright, but a musket butt smashed into her stomach, leaving her doubled up in agony, unable to drag breath into her lungs. Another glancing blow struck her forehead, tearing skin and flesh, bringing blood spurting, and she reeled sideways and fell on to her back.

Her attacker stepped forwards and drew back his weapon to give the final death blow, then suddenly checked the plunge of his bayonet and stepped back a pace.

'What's up?' his companions shouted at him. 'Why haven't you finished her off?'

He crossed himself and muttered a brief prayer.

'She's got a baby inside her, and I don't murder babies in their mothers' wombs.'

Forty-Nine

The Battlefield of Inkerman
November 6th, 1854

The battle of Inkerman had been desperately close-fought. Outnumbered four to one, the British, later joined by the French, had taken heavy casualties, but the Russians had suffered three times as many, and all across the terrain, thousands of men lay in their own blood.

There were over 2,000 British wounded, and the medical services were overwhelmed. The surgeons, their assistants and the stretcher-bearers toiled until sheer exhaustion forced them to take a brief respite before beginning their work of mercy all over again.

Other troops dug great pits in which the naked dead were laid in close-packed rows and the cold, muddy earth spaded in to cover them.

Drawn by the prospects of loot, the human vultures who infested Balaclava came to join the camp, and sailors from the harboured ships swarmed across the litter of human wreckage, stripping the dead and dying men of everything they had, even their blood-stained clothing.

Isolated shots rang out as here and there the enraged fighting soldiers inflicted their own brand of sanguine punishment on the looters.

The four stretcher-bearing bandsmen shuffled wearily over the ridge and down the slope towards the gully, cursing angrily as they saw the shattered skulls of the dead riflemen.

'Some of these lads must have only been wounded. The bastard Russkies have crushed they heads in for badness.'

'Look! Down in the gully there!' one of them shouted. 'There's women there.'

They hurried into the gully, their rage becoming even more heated as they neared the women's bloodied bodies.

'The evil bastards, killing women like this. They'm worse than any wild beasts, they am!'

'Well, God help any Russki that I comes across this day, hale or wounded.'

Rosie was lying on her back by the rocky side of the gully, and one of the men went to look more closely at her blood-caked head.

'Bloody hell!' He expelled a noisy gust of breath. 'This 'un's still breathing.' The next instant he shouted in shock, 'She's moving as well! There's summat happening to her!'

The other men came pounding across to him. Their commander was a farmer's son, widely experienced in birthing animals, and within scant moments he recognized the import of Rosie's swollen stomach, writhing body and gasping moans.

'Her's whelping! Come out o' the way, you lot, and let the dog see the rabbit.' He took his bayonet and cut her skirt, parting it up to her navel. He saw the red-tinged watery discharge seeping down her inner thighs, and nodded with satisfaction at this proof of his accurate diagnosis. 'There now, what did I tell you? Her's whelping.'

'What shall we do, Bill?' the youngest of them quavered nervously.

'What shall we do, Bill?' Corporal Wilkinson mimicked jeeringly, his broad, red features grinning confidently. 'I'll tell you what I'll do, Bandsman Samuelson, you useless young fart, you. I'll bring this whelp out alive and kicking. I'se helped to birth more lambs and calves and piglets and colts than I'se had hot dinners. This 'un 'ull be a piece o' cake for me, because it'll only have two legs and two arms, and that's a sight easier than pulling out eight of the same.'

'I can't see her living through this,' another of the men said doubtfully. 'She's took a ball in the shoulder by the looks of it, and a crack on the head. Look how it's split open.'

'That's all the more reason for me to save

her babby, aren't it?' Bill Wilkinson answered sombrely. 'At least then her won't have carried it for nothing all these months, will her? And while I'm busy, you lot find out if these dead 'uns have got any valuables stowed away. Let's try and show a bit of profit for this day's work, shall we?'

For long long hours Rosie had lain, slipping in and out of consciousness, her mind peopled with surreal, constantly changing images over which she had no control – faces, scenes, the echoes of voices. At times she experienced faint glimmerings of lucidity, fleeting moments when she thought, 'I'm dying, aren't I ... This is death reaching for me.'

Yet during these brief moments she felt no fear, but only a calm sense of acceptance and relief that her unborn baby would be with her wheresoever she was bound.

She was aware of the labour pains periodically wracking her flesh, flooding and ebbing like tidal waves, but still they did not force consciousness upon her. Her mind remained in the grip of that surreal unreality over which she had no control.

The squalling cries emitted from the tiny wet scrap of humanity brought roars of delighted laughter from the men clustered around it.

'It's a boy. And a tough little bugger to have come through what he has. I was beginning to think I'd never get him out.' Bill Wilkinson beamed with satisfaction.

Using strips of rag, he tied the umbilical cord and separated it with his bayonet. Wrapping the squalling baby in a blood-stained shirt stripped from one of the dead riflemen, he gave him to another man to hold, then turned his attention to Rosie.

Crouching beside her, he expertly removed the placenta and staunched any further loss of blood. Lifting his canteen, he dribbled some water on to her face, using a piece of rag to gently wipe the blood and dirt away from her cheeks and closed eyelids to disclose the deathly grey hue of her complexion. He shook his head regretfully.

'Her looks to have lost too much blood, lads. I think her's nearly gone.'

'Her's done for, alright,' another agreed. 'Shame really, her looks to be a pretty woman.'

'What shall we do, Bill? It seems a bit cruel to jog her around. Might it be kinder to leave her here to die in peace?'

The corporal squatted back on his haunches, mulling over what to do with her, then he hawked and spat on to the ground. 'We'll take her, because I'm not leaving the poor little wench here for the carrion crows to rip her eyes out while she still might have a breath in her body.'

'But she'll be dead by the time we get her back to camp,' one man objected. 'So we'll be breaking our backs for nothing.'

The corporal rounded on him in a spurt of

anger. 'I don't give a toss about your back! If her dies, then her dies. At least we can make sure to get her buried like a Christian.'

'Alright, Bill, alright.' The man held up his hands to ward off the corporal's anger. 'Whatever you say, Bill.'

Corporal Bill Wilkinson stared sourly at the masses of wounded men lying around the 2nd Division's hospital tents waiting their turn for treatment.

'Put her down,' he ordered.

A youthful assistant-surgeon was moving among the casualties, briefly checking their wounds, deciding which ones might have a chance of living after surgical operation, and which cases appeared hopeless.

The corporal shouted to him. 'Mr Farquar, I've got a young woman here. Found her up on the heights. Do you think you could come and look at her? Her's just give birth to this babby.' He lifted the child for the surgeon to see.

The surgeon was intrigued. 'A woman given birth, you say? What the devil was she doing getting mixed up in the battle?'

His smooth, beardless features made him look like a young boy, but when he came to Rosie, he examined her with the confidence of a veteran doctor. Using a lancet to cut away her blood-saturated clothing, so that she was almost naked, he felt carefully with his fingers for broken bones, taking her pulse, pressing his ear against her breast to listen to her heartbeat, opening her closed lids to study her pupils.

'Will she live?' Corporal Wilkinson asked.

Farquar shrugged casually. 'That's in God's hands, Corporal. There are no broken bones as far as I can ascertain, and I don't think her skull is fractured. It appears that she's got a shot-wound in her shoulder. The ball will have to be extracted or the wound will turn gangrenous. But obviously she's lost a great deal of blood, which may have weakened her too much for her to survive the operation.'

'But you will try and do something for her, won't you, Mr Farquar,' Wilkinson urged.

The young man stared reflectively at Rosie's pallid, dirty, bloodstained face. 'She's a pretty little woman, even in the mess she's in now.' Then he nodded. 'Take her inside, Corporal, and I'll do what I can for her.'

In the tent, Rosie was placed on the planks of the makeshift operating table. Bill Wilkinson stroked Rosie's cold cheek.

'I don't suppose you can hear me, sweetheart, but I'm real sorry that I've got to leave you now. I only wish there was more I could do for you, but there ain't.'

Drifting in a dark void, Rosie could hear faint, muffled snatches of his words. She tried to answer, to call out, but her body refused to obey her mental impulse, and then all was dark and silent once more.

'What will you do with the child, Corporal?' George Farquar asked. 'Because in all truth I don't believe that this woman will survive a deal longer, do what I may to prolong her life.'

'Give him here to me.' Bill Wilkinson took the baby into his arms and cradled it close, grinning down at the tiny screwed-up features. 'I'll take him back to my missus, sir. Me and her 'ull care for him, and if his mam dies then we'll bring him up as our own, and when he's old enough he can 'list as drummer-boy in our regiment.'

'You're a good Christian man, Corporal,' Farquar said sincerely. 'But he needs a name, does he not?'

'Indeed he does, sir.' Bill Wilkinson chuckled. 'And seeing as this is where he was born, I shall name him Inkerman Battle ... Inkerman Battle-Wilkinson! Aren't that a fine name to have, sir.'

George Farquar roared with laughter, pulled out a golden sovereign from his pocket and handed it to the other man. 'It's the very finest of names, Corporal. And I beg you to take this and, when the boy is old enough to understand, give it to him, and tell him it is George Farquar's christening gift to Inkerman Battle-Wilkinson.'

Fifty

While the infantry and artillery battle was raging, the remnants of the Light Brigade had been posted on the flank of the fighting, and had had to endure being shelled and losing more men and horses from their pitifully scant numbers. They bivouacked in their position overnight and returned to their tents in the morning.

Henry Peebles immediately went to look for Rosie, but initially was not unduly concerned when neither she nor Fothergill's horse were anywhere to be found. He assumed that she must have gone down to Balaclava and taken the horse with her. But as the hours passed and morning became afternoon, he began to worry and went to talk to Colum Murphy.

'Where's your missus at?'

The Irishman scowled morosely. 'I've not seen hide nor hair of the cow since before dawn yesterday. Knowing her, she'll be on the piss down in Balaclava, and when I catch a hold of her she'll be feeling the weight of me fist.'

'Have you seen Megan Morgan?' Peebles asked.

'No. But she'll be with my missus and Rosie

Collier. They're as thick as thieves, them three.'

'I don't think that they're down in Balaclava.' Henry Peebles frowned, worried. 'Rosie Collier came to ask me for the loan of a horse, and I said she could have Fothergill's. Her and the others were going to collect brushwood. They'll have gone over to the heights for that. I reckon they got caught up in the fighting. Round up the lads and get saddled. I'll be back shortly.'

Peebles went to Lt. the Hon. Rufus Tytherleigh Bart, who was now commanding what was left of the 20th Light Dragoons, to report that three of the regiment's women were missing, and requested that he be allowed to go in search of them.

Rufus Tytherleigh bore little resemblance to the glittering dandy who had left England only months previously. His once-gorgeous tunic was now tarnished and torn, his trousers were civilian checks, his boots a labourer's hobnails. His dashing whiskers had become a straggly beard, his coiffed locks a greasy, matted tangle.

The young nobleman's outlook on life was as altered as his outward appearance. The sharing of hardships, of slaughter, of the moments of terror and wild exultation, had kindled in him a strong feeling of respect and admiration for the courage and endurance of the rough, uneducated, foul-mouthed men under his command.

The former Rufus Tytherleigh, who had

394

looked upon army women as worthless drabs and virtual prostitutes, would have refused permission for this search. The present Rufus Tytherleigh instantly gave permission, and took charge of the search himself.

'We'll divide the men between us, Sarn't-Major. My party will cover the area east of the Second Division. Your party will enquire of the burial parties and stretcher-bearers if they've come across the women.'

Within minutes the two parties of searchers had left the tent lines to go in their opposite directions.

The night was well advanced when Henry Peebles at last found the burial party that had laid two women in one of the mass graves.

'They was with some of the Rifles. Some stretcher-bearers told us where to find 'um.' The sergeant pointed across the moonlit rolling land. 'The grave's over there. About two hundred yards. Just keep in a straight line and you can't miss it. But you'll need to take shovels if you want to look at 'um, because my blokes covered it in. They'll be easy enough to find though, because we put 'um right at this near end of the top layer, and wrapped 'um in blankets.' He smiled mirthlessly. 'It 'uddn't be right to lay women down among a load o' naked men and not wrap 'um up decent, 'ud it? What 'ud all them bloody Bible punchers back at home say if we didn't bury our women wrapped-up decent?'

'Two women, you say?' Peebles asked

anxiously.

'Two women,' the sergeant confirmed.

'Did you see a horse anywhere near to them?'

'Yes, a dead 'un. It had cavalry trappings. But the bloody Russkies had cut all the best pieces of meat from it. Bad luck to the bastards! I'm become partial to a bit of fresh horse steak meself. Better than that bloody salt muck we gets issued with.'

Henry Peebles' heart sank. It seemed a certainty that the two dead women were those he was looking for, but where was the third?

'Could there have been another woman anywhere near? Perhaps she was still living and they took her to the surgeons.'

'Well, you'd have to ask them about that.' The sergeant pointed his hand and suggested, 'If I recollect rightly they was from the Second Div. You could ask at their hospital lines ... Anyway, in the meantime, you can use these shovels to dig up the ones we buried.'

The grim task of exhumation took little time. The layer of earth covering the grave was only inches deep.

Henry Peebles' heart was thudding with fearful dread as he watched the blankets being unwrapped, and he gusted an exclamation of relief when the moonlight silvered the distorted features of Dorcas Murphy and Megan Morgan.

Colum Murphy's brutal face betrayed no emotion, and he uttered no sound as he stared down at his wife.

Henry Peebles' anxieties for Rosie made him impatient to leave the grave and rush down to the hospital tents of the 2nd Division.

'You can cover them up again, lads, then go back to camp.'

One of the men started to rewrap the blankets around Dorcas, and Colum Murphy growled savagely, 'Take your hands off her. It's for me to do that.' He went down on his knees and tenderly cradled her face in his huge hands, muttering brokenly, 'I never told you before, Dorcas, but I love you well, and I'm sorry for all the badness I showed you. I'm truly sorry ... I swear it! Truly sorry, I am...'

Henry Peebles silently signalled to the rest of the men and led them away, leaving Colum Murphy to mourn his dead.

'Yes, Sergeant-Major, I did operate on a young woman earlier today. But I don't know her name, or which regiment she belonged to.' As he spoke, George Farquar, face drawn and white with weariness, was intently putting stitches through the bleeding stump of a chloroformed man's arm. 'She was a pretty creature though.'

'And how badly had she been wounded, sir?' Henry Peebles asked eagerly, sure now that the young woman must have been Rosie.

'I extracted a ball from her shoulder. Unfortunately the bone was badly broken. She was in a poor way, I'm afraid. Had a nasty contusion on her head, and had lost a deal of blood, and to make matters worse she had recently given birth as well. She was completely comatose, I didn't need to use the chloroform.'

Henry Peebles was momentarily thunder-struck by the news of the birth.

Farquar completed his task and instructed his assistant, 'Put a dressing on this, Mitchell.' Then he bawled loudly, 'You men outside there, I'm ready for the next.'

The grey-faced amputee was carried from the tent, and another shuddering, panting, half-dead man took his place on the blood-soaked planking of the table beneath the weakly wavering beam of the hanging lantern.

'Where is she now, sir? Does she still live? Is the baby alive?' Peebles hardly dared ask for fear of what he might be told.

Farquar stretched his arms wide and groaned. 'Dear God, I'm as stiff as a corpse!' Then he answered casually, 'The baby was taken by one of the stretcher-bearers, who seems to be a very kindly man. I wrote a note explaining what had happened to the child and slipped it into the woman's bodice, though I'm very doubtful that she lived to read it. As I've said, she was very low. How-ever, I had her forwarded on to the harbour. We're sending all the wounded that we can to Scutari, because we haven't got the facilities to care for them here in the Crimea.' He saw the raw anxiety in Peebles' expression, and went on almost apologetically, 'I did all that I could for her. Whether she lives or dies is in God's hands now. You will have to enquire down at Balaclava. I can't tell you more.'

'Yes, sir.' Peebles saluted. 'Thank you very much for your help, sir.'

All through that night and the following day, Henry Peebles scoured the fetid, shambolic environs of Balaclava and its harbour for sight or news of Rosie, questioning and badgering men already harassed beyond endurance by the enormities of the task they faced in finding space on the ships to load the thousands of the wounded and transport them to Scutari. There was no order or method in the embarkation of the casualties. There were no registrations of names, regiments, or even gender. There was only confusion and chaos.

Peebles searched through the casualty collection areas, pulling aside the coverings of the dead and living alike to stare into face after face after face. He bribed boatmen to row him out to the vessels lying at anchor, and at times his heart leapt for joy when he saw a woman's figure among the sick and wounded and thought that he might have found Rosie, only to meet with crushing disappointment as he looked into the eyes of a stranger.

His senses reeling from lack of sleep, his body almost totally exhausted, he was finally forced into the bitter acceptance that he would not find her. The only bleak hope left to him was the possibility that she had been put on to a ship that had sailed for Scutari before he had arrived in Balaclava. He could only cling desperately to this hope, and for the first time since he had been a child, pray to God, and beg Him that this might be so, that Rosie might be safely en route to Turkey.

It was with a heavy heart that he reluctantly journeyed back towards Kadakoi Camp.

Fifty-One

Barrack Hospital, Scutari
Monday, November 7th, 1854

Eugenia Pacemore stood in the ranks of nurses mechanically reciting the Lord's Prayer, but in her innermost thoughts she was desperately voicing a different prayer, over and over again.

'Please God, let Charles be still alive. Please God, let him come here alive.'

The ships bringing the wounded from the Battle of Balaclava had started arriving the day before, and the offloading of the men was in full swing. Still torn with her grief over Louis Nolan's death, Eugenia did not think that she would be able to bear the loss of her cousin as well.

Florence Nightingale remained motionless with her head bowed, eyes closed, hands clasped before her breast, and the nurses exchanged wry grimaces. These compulsory daily prayer meetings were irksome to the vast majority of them.

'We come here to look after the sick and wounded, not to bloody waste our time praying. Leave the praying to them Black Crows and them White Romans,' Emma Fowler whispered.

Florence Nightingale's eyes opened and fixed sternly upon Emma Fowler's face. 'Time spent in prayer is never wasted, Nurse Fowler.'

The tall, raw-boned woman was not abashed by this reprimand, however. 'If you please, ma'am, there's hundreds of poor men suffering and dying for want o' proper care in this hospital, and them from the Balaclava battle started arriving yesterday, and there's more coming in today...'

'Do you think that Miss Nightingale is not very well aware of that fact, Nurse Fowler?' Mrs Bracebridge interrupted angrily.

Emma Fowler defiantly turned on her interrupter. 'O' course I knows that she knows! And she knows as well that all we've done since we come here is to count and sort and mend old linen, and count and sort and count again the packets o' provisions. And while we're doing that, there are men dying for want o' proper nursing. So I want to know why we aren't been put to the work that we come here to do?'

The other two boldest spirits among the nurses, Eugenia and Jane Gibson, voiced their support.

'Yes, put us to our proper work, ma'am. We were forced to spend hours yesterday in church listening to the chaplain's sermon when we could have been helping with the men from the Balaclava fight.'

'Let us get to nursing the poor lads.'

'Be silent!' Mrs Bracebridge shouted furiously. 'How dare you behave in such a manner?'

'Wait, Mrs Bracebridge.' Florence Nightingale gestured the woman to be quiet. Then she addressed the room at large, her low, calm tones carrying clearly to all ears. 'I shall tell you why you are not being put to do the task you came here for. The medical gentlemen have refused to accept you on to their wards. They have also refused to make use of the comforts and stores that I purchased in Marseille. They say they cannot see that any advantage can be gained by utilizing our services. That they have no confidence in our abilities. That we are weak women, who lack the necessary strengths of character and physical endurance needed to face the horrors of war.'

A grim smile fleeted across her expressive features. 'There are moments when I confess that I feel that I am at war myself with these medical gentlemen. However, I do not intend to surrender to their prejudice against us. I intend that we shall remain secluded here in our rooms until such time as they realize their own folly and are forced to then invite us to work with them.'

Her penetrating gaze moved over them, appearing to momentarily centre on each individual, and with confidence ringing in her voice, declared, 'And that invitation will not be long in coming, ladies, I do assure you. So I would ask you to keep your patience, and to put your trust in me.'

At first there was no visible reaction, then first one, then another, then another indicated acquiescence.

'Thank you, ladies.' Florence Nightingale bowed her head in acknowledgement. 'Now you may get on with your various tasks.' She left the room.

Mrs Bracebridge glared at the three women who had spoken out. 'If any of you three dares to behave with such insolence again, I shall make an example of you, and you will pay a hard price, I promise you.'

Eugenia stepped forward. 'We intended no insolence, Mrs Bracebridge, I assure you.'

The woman's thin lips curled scornfully. 'So you say, Pacemore, so you say.'

'I do say, and truly mean it, Mrs Bracebridge,' Eugenia insisted quietly.

The woman turned to leave. 'May I have permission to go down to the landing stage, Mrs Bracebridge?' Eugenia asked.

'Certainly not!' the woman snapped curtly. 'You have just this minute heard Miss

Nightingale's order that you are to remain in these quarters in strict seclusion. Now get on with your work, all of you.'

Before Eugenia could speak again, Mrs Bracebridge swept imperiously from the room. The group of nurses dispersed, and only Eugenia, Emma Fowler and Jane Gibson remained in the small room, the heap of old linen awaiting sorting and mending. But instead of joining her friends in their work, Eugenia put on her cap and coat and draped the holland scarf around her shoulders.

'What are you doing, Genia?' Jane Gibson asked.

'I'm going down to the landing stage. Sergeant Thomas told me that my cousin wasn't landed yesterday. Perhaps he will arrive today, or at least I can find someone who knows of his whereabouts.'

'What if Bracebridge sees you going down there?' Emma Fowler said. 'The nasty bitch 'ull jump at the chance of getting you into trouble with the Nightingale. She'd like nothing better than to have you sacked for disobeying her.'

The warning caused Eugenia only a fleeting moment of hesitation. Tormented by over-whelming concern for her cousin, she was grimly determined to see him no matter what trouble she might get into. 'I'll just have to risk that.'

'Wait a minute, Genia.' Jane Gibson's eyes sparkled mischievously. 'You can't go out wearing our uniform. It'll make you too conspicuous. I've got a nice coloured shawl hid in my bag that you can use, and we can sew a piece of this linen over your skirt to hide it. And you must leave your cap off, and let your hair hang loose. From a distance you'll look near enough like one of the barrack women, so you won't attract any attention.'

Within brief minutes Eugenia's appearance was transformed, and with a giggle Jane Gibson produced a pair of long, dangling, shiny earrings.

'Here, put these on. They'll add the finishing touch.'

Eugenia could not help but smile wryly as she clipped the jewels on to her small earlobes. 'I've never in my life worn anything like these.'

'They was a betrothal present from my second husband. The only present the mean bugger ever give me.' Jane Gibson laughed. 'And he'd have took them back and sold them for drink if I hadn't kept them well hid.'

Emma Fowler came back from checking that the corridor and stairways were clear.

'You'd best hurry, Genia. Don't leave by the main doors. Sneak out through the ruined part. Make your way around through the shanty town, then cut across the burial grounds, and down to the landing stage. Keep off the main trackway and come back here the same way.'

Feeling like a naughty schoolgirl playing truant, Eugenia ran quickly down the staircase and along the maze of corridors that led to the burned-out section of the vast building.

Prior to the arrival of the British Army, the settlement of Scutari had consisted of the barracks and a few neighbouring dwelling places with no shops or markets, but its environs were the main burial areas for Constantinople. Vast cemeteries stretched southwards from the barracks in a macabre panorama of thousands of tombs and weeping willow trees, a virtual city of the dead.

Now, however, the establishment of the British Depot at Scutari had attracted hordes of the living, and around the barracks a large shanty town of sheds and tents, booths and stalls had sprung up, peopled by Turks, Jews, Greeks, Levantines, Armenians all eager to batten on the troops. Drink shops, dancing booths and brothels abounded and thrived, un-checked, un-regulated, un-policed.

Discipline was lax in Scutari, the majority of the regimental officers preferring to spend their time in the fleshpots of Constantinople across the Bosphorus Strait. With their officers mostly absent, many NCOs also took advantage of the opportunity to neglect their duties and enjoy themselves, turning a blind eye to the troops' misdemeanours. At any given time there could be three or four thousand soldiers in the Barrack Depot and Hospital, and at any given time hundreds of those soldiers could be found riotously drinking, fornicating and brawling in the rancid dens of the shanty town.

Eugenia pulled the shawl close around her head and shoulders as she picked her way through the mud-thick, filthy alleys.

A redcoat came reeling out from one of the drinking sheds as she passed and collided with her, sending her stumbling sideways, forcing her to throw her arms wide in an effort to retrieve her balance. The shawl slipped down from her head, and the redcoat squinted drunkenly at her.

'Well now, ain't you the sweet piece o' meat. Come here.' He grabbed her arm and jerked her to him. 'Come and have a drink wi' me, sweetie.'

'Let me go!'

She tried to tug free, but he was a big, powerful man and his other arm encircled her, his hand grabbing her buttocks, crushing her against his body.

'Come on inside and let's have a bit,' he grunted hoarsely, his foul breath gusting against her face. 'I'll pay you your price, don't fret.'

His slack, wet mouth clamped on her lips and she could taste the rotgut liquor he had drunk. She wrenched her head back and screamed in horror.

'Help me! Somebody help me! Please help me!'

'Don't play hard to get wi' me, you whore,' he snarled.

Some men and women stopped to watch,

but no one bothered to intervene. He lifted her off her feet and started to move towards the door of the shed. She struggled frantically, kicking and screaming at the top of her lungs.

'Help me! Please help me! Help me, somebody!'

Her shawl fell to the ground, disclosing her grey coat, and some of the threads tacking the piece of linen over her skirt broke and the linen peeled partially away.

A tall, fair-haired man in a long sheepskin coat suddenly blocked the redcoat's passage.

'Put her down, Mogsy!'

'What?' The redcoat blinked in surprise.

'I said put her down,' the fair-haired man repeated. 'She's not a whore, you drunken fool. Now put her down!' He reached out and dragged the redcoat's arms away to release Eugenia.

'What are you doing, Artie?' the redcoat demanded, more puzzled than angry. 'If you weren't me mate, I'd lay you out.'

White-faced, trembling uncontrollably, Eugenia's urge was to flee, yet some unaccountable force held her there, powerless to move.

The fair-haired man spoke gently to her. 'There's no reason for you to be afraid, miss. No harm will come to you.'

Against all reason, she found herself trusting him.

'What's going on here?' the redcoat, still

half-stupefied with alcohol, demanded plaintively.

'I've already told you, Mogsy. She's not a whore.' The fair-haired man's tone was controlled and patient, as though speaking to a child. He smiled at Eugenia. 'If I'm not mistaken, miss, you're one of the newly arrived Nightingale nurses, are you not?'

Beginning to recover from her terror, and somewhat calmer now, Eugenia realized that the man's diction was that of an educated gentleman, and answered him as such.

'Yes, I am one of Miss Nightingale's party, sir. I'm truly grateful to you for coming to my aid.'

Arthur Sinclair recognized that she was from the upper social classes, and bowed in courteous acknowledgement. 'I'm very happy to have been of some service to you, ma'am.'

'Artie? What's going on?' The big redcoat's drink-flushed features resembled a bewildered child's.

'Go on back to the hospital, Mogsy.' Arthur Sinclair patted the man's broad shoulder. 'I'll follow you there.'

'Alright, Artie. I'll go. But you won't be long, will you?'

'No, I won't. I promise. Go on now, there's a good fellow.' Sinclair gently pushed him, and the big man went shambling away along the alley.

'I can only tell you how sincerely sorry I am that this has happened, ma'am. But I beg you not to condemn Mogsy too harshly. The poor fellow took a ball in the head at the Alma, and sadly it's addled his wits. When he's in drink, he really is not responsible for his actions. Will you permit me to escort you out of here, ma'am? This place is really not safe for a lady to pass through unescorted.'

'That is very kind of you, sir. I would greatly appreciate your doing so. I'm on my way to the landing stage to meet the Balaclava wounded.' And so together they traversed the labyrinth of alleys without further incident.

When they reached the top of the steep decline leading down to the shore, Arthur Sinclair stopped and bowed. 'You will be safe now, ma'am. So I'll bid you good day.'

'Good day, sir, and thank you for your kindness.'

They parted and only then did Eugenia suddenly realize. 'How rude of me! I didn't even ask his name!'

She halted and turned to call after him. 'I am Miss Eugenia Pacemore, sir. May I ask your name?'

'Arthur Sinclair, ma'am,' he shouted with a final wave of his arm.

Hearing the shouting and bustle below, Eugenia's desperate hunger to see her cousin overcame her and she hurried on down the steep slope.

Turkish caiques were ferrying the wounded and sick troops from the ships to the shore. Turkish labourers then stretchered the new arrivals up the single rough trackway to the Barrack Hospital.

The landing stage was a maelstrom of noise and crowded confusion. Wounded men were screaming their agony like stricken animals as they were pulled from the boats and dumped on to stretchers.

There were several British redcoats and blue-tunicked men of the commissariat on the landing stage, but they were paying no attention to what was happening. They stood talking and laughing together, smoking their pipes and swigging from bottles of spirits.

As Eugenia came near enough to see what was happening, horrified disgust and anger filled her, and she marched up to the group to confront them.

'Why are you allowing our men to be treated so roughly by these Turks?'

Faces turned and curious eyes scrutinized her. Then one man grinned.

'Well the Turks ain't treating them half so rough as the Russkies did, so I reckon they'll do well enough.'

There was an outburst of raucous laughter from his companions.

'What are you doing down here anyway?' another man asked her, and leered suggestively. 'Is business slack up in shanty town? Are you come here to find customers?'

This brought more laughter, and a string of lewd comments. Realizing her own impotence, she could only glare at them and turn away.

She moved further along the landing stage to where the Turks were crowded together

411

waiting for the caiques to bring in more of the wounded and sick. She was surrounded by swarthy, whiskered faces, and guttural voices loud in her ears. She heard an English voice bawling furiously.

'Take your hands off me, you bastards, or I'll swing for you!'

She pushed through the crowd towards the voice and found herself face to face with a dark-complexioned man leaning on a wooden staff. She recognized his tattered, filthy, blood-caked blue uniform, with its distinctive silver braiding, and the silver-banded forage cap perched on top of his long, narrow head.

'You're in the Twentieth Light Dragoons, are you not?'

'Ahr, missy, I am.'

'Can you please help me?'

'Help you?' Conky White exclaimed irately. 'Help *you*? Can't you see this bloody stick I got, missy? It's me that needs help to get up that bloody hill there. If these bastards puts me on a bloody stretcher, they'll jog me to death, and me arse is killing me as it is, it's that bloody sore. A ride on a bloody stretcher 'ull be the death o' me.'

'I only want to ask if you know anything of my cousin,' she explained quickly. 'He's Lieutenant Bronton, and he's the adjutant of your regiment.'

Conky White reacted with surprise. 'Your cousin? Mr Bronton is your cousin?' His bloodshot eyes doubtfully regarded her clothing. 'Our adjutant is your cousin? But

412

you don't have the look of a gentry woman.'
'Take no heed to my appearance,' she snapped impatiently. 'I'm one of Miss Nightingale's nurses, and we don't wear the clothing of gentlewomen. Now, please, can you tell me anything about my cousin, Lieutenant Bronton?'

'Miss Nightingale's nurses?' he mused aloud. 'That aren't a regiment that I'se ever heard tell on.'

She had to struggle to stop herself shouting at him, and drew several deep long breaths before saying quietly, 'We're not a regiment. We're civilians who've come here to help nurse the sick and wounded soldiers. Please, I beg you, can you tell me anything about my cousin? I know that he was wounded at Balacava, and I've been told that he is to come here to Scutari.'

Conky White shook his head. 'He aren't coming here, missy. Him and some of the other officers who bin hurt has been took on to Malta, on board some toff's private yacht. The lucky sods. Living in the lap o' luxury, I don't doubt. The bloody ship that brought me here was a hellhole. Hardly any water or food, and what bit we got was stinking and rotten. And there was nobody to see to us. There was poor bloody soldiers dying every day and being chucked over the side like pieces o' dead meat.' He saw the distress on her face and his manner softened.

'You got no cause to fret about your cousin, missy. He got cut bad around his head, and

413

he lost an eye, so I was told. But apart from that, he warn't too bad. He'll be as right as ninepence in a few weeks, you'll see.'

'Malta? You're sure he's gone on to Malta?'

'I'm as sure he's gone on to Malta as I'm sure me name is Conky White, missy,' he stated positively.

She sighed in disappointment, but drew relief from what she had been told. 'Thank you very much for your help, Mr White. And now it's my turn to help you.'

She moved to stand alongside him, and drew his arm across her shoulder. 'Lean your weight on me, Mr White. Don't worry that I'll find you too heavy. I'm much stronger than I look.'

While Eugenia and Conky White were making their slow, painful progress up the track, Arthur Sinclair was standing at the main entrance of the Barrack Hospital watching the newly arrived casualties being stretchered past. Sinclair recognized one pallid-faced casualty and ordered the bearers to stop.

They obeyed, and carelessly dumped the stretcher on to the ground, causing the casualty to groan in pain.

'Hello, Tommy, you've lost your leg, I see.' Sinclair lifted the blanket and peered at the bloodied bandaged stump. 'How are you feeling?'

'Bloody rotten!' Tom Malkin croaked weakly. 'What be you a-doing here, Artie? I thought you was dead.'

'Well, it was touch and go for a while. I'm still marked down as convalescent, unfit for active service, so they've made me a hospital orderly. I'll get you put in my ward. I can make sure that you don't get cheated out of your rations then.'

He beckoned the bearers to come with him, and walked beside the stretcher down the long, broad corridors, listening to Tom Malkin's account of the destruction of the Light Brigade in the charge at Balaclava.

'It were bloody murder, Artie. We never stood a chance. That useless old bugger, Raglan, should be strung up by his balls for sending us into that valley – him and the rest of the bloody toffs on his staff. They're all useless, all of them!'

A sardonic smile touched Sinclair's lips. 'I quite agree, Tommy. Yet there are some who are saying that the charge was a glorious feat of arms.'

'Glorious?' Malkin's features twisted in a bitter grimace. 'I'll have to tell meself that when I'm trying to hop around on one leg, won't I? Trying to live on fourpence-a-day pension. Because I won't be able to find work, will I? No boss 'ull pay wages to a cripple. All I'll be able to do is to beg on the streets or go into the workhouse.'

Sinclair patted the other man's shoulder in sympathy, but could find no words of encouragement or comfort. He had seen too many crippled old soldiers begging in the streets.

'What's it like in here, Artie?' Malkin asked.

'It's a disgrace, Tommy.' Sinclair's features now twisted in a bitter grimace. 'A bloody disgrace.'

Fifty-Two

Scutari, November 20th, 1854

At midday, the small, weather-battered sailing ship transporting Rosie and other wounded from the Inkerman dropped anchor in the Bosphorus. A bad storm and continuously adverse winds had tripled the normal sailing time for the voyage.

Lying in the hanging cot in the cramped, dark cabin, Rosie was woken by the loud metallic rattling of the anchor chain, and she realized that the remorseless pitching and rolling of the ship's slow passage across the Black Sea had ceased.

As always on waking, her thoughts immediately turned to her baby, and she prayed fervently to God to protect him and his new guardian, Corporal Wilkinson. She also prayed for the surgeon, George Farquar, who had slipped a letter of explanation into her bodice before having her taken to the Balaclava harbour.

Rosie had been fortunate. The ship's captain had noticed her, a solitary woman among hundreds of wounded men, and had ordered that she be placed in a cabin, and that his own steward must care for her. For the first few hours of the voyage Rosie had remained semi-comatose, then gradually she had regained her full senses, along with the terrible worry and grief of being parted from her baby. Physically, she was in a parlous condition, feverish and drained of all strength, her wounded shoulder a constant, throbbing torment.

Two hours passed and then the cabin door opened and the steward came in. Sean Quinn was a runty, middle-aged, rat-featured product of the Liverpool slums, who had cared for Rosie as tenderly and devotedly as if she were his own daughter, ignoring all the proprieties of polite society by helping her to use the chamberpot, bathing her verminous naked flesh, and dressing her in his own long flannel drawers and vest. Carefully washing and brushing her tangle-matted hair until it shone, he spoon-fed her with whatever rough delicacies the ship's galley could produce. He sat with her whenever he could, and constantly tried to soothe her worries about her baby.

His discoloured snaggled teeth bared in a smile when he saw that she was awake. 'We'se got here at last, Rosie. I bet you'll be real glad to get off this rotten old tub, won't you? She rolls worse than a drunken Jack on the

Ratcliffe Highway.'

'I'll be glad to be on land again, Sean, but not to leave you,' she told him sincerely. 'I only wish that you were coming with me.'

'And so does I, Rosie. But it can't be so. As soon as we get everybody off, we're heading back to Balaclava. But see what I've brung you to go ashore in. Cut and sewed it meself.' He held up a roughly tailored dress fashioned from linen sheeting, and laughed ruefully. 'It ain't what the fancy Judies are wearing back home, but it'll cover your drawers and vest up well enough.'

This further token of his kindliness brought a lump to Rosie's throat and tears from her eyes. 'Thank you, Sean. It's lovely.'

His own eyes became watery and he swallowed hard, then scolded her with mock severity. 'Don't you go piping your eyes, girl. I don't want tear-stains all over me, I'm damp enough already. Now let's get you dressed and up on deck. The unloading's started. I'll wrap a couple o' blankets round you to keep the chill off.'

Wiry and tough though he was, the effort of carrying Rosie piggyback up the ladders to the deck sorely taxed Sean Quinn's strength, and he was panting heavily as he let her down.

There was a cold breeze blowing, but it was not its sharp-edged bite that sent a shiver through Rosie. It was the sight of the deck packed with a mass of filthy, verminous, suffering men, some crying out in delirium, others moaning in agony, others ominously silent and still.

Sean Quinn saw her dismayed expression. 'We're short-crewed, Rosie, and had to work the ship as best we could. There was nobody to spare to do much for these poor buggers, what with the storm and that. So there's been a lot of dying on this trip.'

Those men unable to scramble down into the tossing, pitching caiques were lowered by ropes, and Rosie could only marvel at the gritty stoicism they displayed as their helpless bodies were battered and banged against the ship's sides. She was more fortunate when it came to her turn. Sean Quinn made his shipmates lower him with her, and he used his body to cushion her against any impact. Then he forced the Turkish boatmen to make room for him to sit and cradle her in his arms during the passage to the shore.

At the landing stage, he commandeered a stretcher and settled her as comfortably as he was able. Taking her hands, he said sadly, 'I got to get straight back aboard, Rosie. Or the captain 'ull have my guts for garters. Good luck to you, my honey, and I hope with all me heart that we'll meet again some day.'

'I do hope so, Sean. I'll never forget how good you've been to me.' Rosie could not hold back her tears, and her last sight of his face was a blurred, distorted image.

Then he was gone and, feeling helplessly bereft and alone, she struggled desperately to stem her tears and face her uncertain future with courage. She lifted her gaze to the great turreted mass of the Barracks Hospital on the skyline, and wondered what might await her there.

Fifty-Three

The vile stench of the Barrack Hospital emanated like a putrid miasma beyond its high walls, and if the ships transporting the wounded and sick to Scutari could be likened to to the antechambers of hell, then within these high walls was hell itself.

The sudden influx of casualties from the Battle of Inkerman had completely overwhelmed the human and material resources of the hospital. The administrative system had virtually collapsed as one after the other the departments rapidly lost grip of the situation. The hospital had become a scene of chaos. The wards were crammed full, and hundreds of men were laid in rows along the corridors without pillows or blankets, their heads on their boots, their sole coverings the tattered, filthy, great coats or blankets they had been wrapped in since the battle. Dysentery raged and there were no chamberpots for the helpless, bedridden men, so they lay in their own foul body-wastes. The water pipes that flushed the privies in the turrets no longer worked, and the privies themselves had become stinking heaps of human excreta. The huge wooden tubs brought into the wards and corridors to serve as urinals were frequently left un-emptied for days on end, the acrid contents overflowing and pooling across the floors.

There were no rooms set aside for surgical operations, nor any operating tables. Amputations were performed in the wards and corridors on makeshift boards and trestles without even screens to shield them from sight, and the tubs of severed flesh and bone remained in situ until they too overflowed.

The hospital orderlies were detailed from men who were convalescing, or new recruits awaiting passage onward to their regiments in the Crimea, none of whom had received any training in caring for the sick and wounded. There were malcontents and malingerers among them who were prepared to rob their helpless comrades of any valuables and cheat them out of their rations.

Army regulations detailed the three types of diet a man was meant to receive in hospital: his normal rations, cooked by the hospital, half his normal rations, or a diet of liquid food. The surgeon could also prescribe extras for an individual man, such as arrowroot, milk puddings, port wine or brandy, milk, eggs, chicken, that could be obtained on production of a requisition chit.

Here in Scutari, these regulations were almost totally ignored. One sole kitchen catered for the entire hospital. There were no saucepans or kettles. The only cooking equipment consisted of thirteen coppers each holding little more than 220 litres, and fired by green wood. Once each day the ward orderlies would queue, sometimes for hours, at the purveyor's stores to draw the raw or salt-meat ration for their individual wards. The orderlies would take the meat to the kitchen, tie a scrap of rag, or other identification token, and chuck it in a copper. When the untrained cooks considered it cooked, the meat would be reclaimed by the orderlies and the water it had been boiled in was fed to the men on the liquid diet. Tea or coffee was then brewed in those same, unwashed, grease-caked coppers, and so rendered virtually undrinkable.

Each orderly took the food back to his ward and divided it among the men who, due to the lack of knives, forks or spoons, were forced to eat it using their fingers. Those who were asleep sometimes got nothing. Some orderlies would eat the sleeping man's ration themselves, or barter it for drink and tobacco. Any extras that the purveyor's stores managed to issue had to be cooked over stick fires in the wards themselves or out in the courtyard. Invariably, if port wine or brandy had been prescribed, the orderlies would drink it themselves.

The administration of medicines and the application of poultices, plasters, salves and ointments were also left to the orderlies, who, in their careless ignorance, would often make the patient take all the separate doses in one single draught.

Confronted with the dire, ever-worsening state of affairs in the Barrack Hospital, the medical director had given a grudging permission for the Nightingale nurses to help care for the sick and wounded, but with the proviso that they could only enter into a ward if the individual doctor in charge agreed to accept them.

In the small improvised kitchen in the nurses' quarters, Florence Nightingale had already directed that special diets should be cooked using the stores she had brought with her from Marseille. Buckets of hot arrowroot and sago laced with port wine were prepared daily, but then Florence Nightingale stubbornly followed her own private agenda, refusing to let her nurses feed the patients with this special diet unless an individual doctor issued a specific requisition for a specific patient. She was determined to force the medical staff to come to her for help, and it inevitably developed into a battle of wills.

On the dirty tiled floor of a crowded ward, Eugenia Pacemore and Emma Fowler were attending to one of the newly arrived Inkerman casualties.

'You'd best not come near me, miss. I'm swarming,' the young soldier lying on the tiled floor warned Eugenia, his face crimson with embarrassment. 'And I've messed meself a lot of times as well.'

She smiled reassuringly. 'Don't you fret about that. We've tackled lice and mess before, haven't we, Emma?'

'I'll say we have. Lice as big as mice, we've tackled, and mountains of mess. Now, let's get these rags off you, and then we'll give you a nice wash.'

'It ain't proper for you to be seeing my privates,' he protested weakly as she began to cut his filthy, tattered uniform from his body, but could offer no more than verbal objections because both his arms were bloody-bandaged stumps.

'Proper don't come into it, lovey,' Emma Fowler chuckled. 'I've seen more men's privates than you've ate hot dinners, I shouldn't wonder.'

With Emma Fowler's help, Eugenia was able to lift and manoeuvre him so that she could cleanse every inch of his skin.

'Please don't be embarrassed,' Eugenia told him gently as she sponged his genitals.

'What do you think you're doing, Pacemore, behaving with such shameless indecency?' a voice demanded shrilly.

Eugenia looked up into the scowling face of Mrs Bracebridge who was standing in the doorway with Sister Pringle.

'I'm bathing this poor lad, Mrs Bracebridge, as you can clearly see. He's only just come off the ship, and he's verminous. Doctor Grey has given us permission to do this.'

'You were fondling him intimately, Pacemore. I saw you doing so with my own eyes,' Bracebridge accused.

'It's not the young man's fault, Mrs Bracebridge. I heard him begging them not to strip his clothing off. That was why I ran to fetch you,' Sister Pringle interjected, her thin lips curled in spiteful satisfaction.

'And I am grateful to you for doing so, Sister Pringle. Very grateful indeed.' Mrs Bracebridge's head was wobbling from side to side, her face red with outrage. 'What have you to say for yourself, Pacemore?'

Eugenia's fiery temper sparked, but she kept her control. 'This young man is verminous, and he has lain in his own body wastes since the battle. I would be failing in my duty as a nurse if I were to leave him in such an unhappy condition.'

Mrs Bracebridge's head wobbled more violently. 'Duty? Your duty is to conform to the rules and regulations laid down by your superiors.'

'There is nothing in the rules or the regulations which forbids me to wash a patient who is unable to wash himself,' Eugenia argued.

'Our rules clearly state that a nurse must not do other than bathe the men's heads and hands. All other physical contact is strictly forbidden, except for spoon-feeding those men unable to feed themselves.'

'And reading them suitable passages from the Bible or some other spiritually uplifting work, Mrs Bracebridge,' Sister Pringle added.

'And that's all you're good for doing, aren't it, you useless crow!' Emma Fowler spat out contemptuously. 'Sitting on your lazy arse, reading a load o' tripe to some poor mother's son who needs proper care, and not the holy rubbish you spends all your time spouting out.'

'Hey, I'm all wet and freezing cold,' the young soldier reminded them plaintively.

Mrs Bracebridge did not deign to look at him. Instead she glared down the long ward to where an orderly was lying on his corner cot, smoking a pipe.

'You there! Orderly! Come here!'

The man levered himself upright. 'Are you talking to me, missus?'

'Come here this instant!' she shrilled. 'I have work for you to do.'

'I aren't got time for any bloody work.' The orderly clambered reluctantly off his bed and stood scratching himself. 'I've got to go and fetch the rations.'

'Do you dare to disobey me?' Mrs Bracebridge challenged indignantly.

The orderly grinned contemptuously. 'You can't order me about, you mouthy cow. You aren't got power to do that. So just piss off.' He bent and took a wooden bucket from under his bed, and sauntered away through the far door.

Mrs Bracebridge glared at the grinning faces staring at her from the crowded cots.

'Come on, Emma, let's get this poor lad dried and put a clean shirt on him.' Eugenia started to gently rub his goosefleshed skin with a strip of rough towelling.

'How dare you disobey me, Pacemore? I've ordered you to stop fondling that man,' Mrs Bracebridge shrieked, her mottled features twitching with fury.

Eugenia's initial anger had metamorphosed into a feeling of weary disgust with this woman, and she replied quietly, 'Mrs Bracebridge, if you can't be useful here, then just go away and let us who want to help do so without further hindrance.'

Mrs Bracebridge erupted into a furious tirade, but Eugenia deliberately ignored her and went on towelling the young soldier's naked white body. With mischievous pleasure, she took ostentatious care to thoroughly pat dry his genitals.

'Miss Nightingale shall hear of this, Pacemore. You are my witness to this woman's wicked defiance, Sister Pringle. Miss Nightingale shall hear of this directly. I'll have you discharged, Pacemore! I'll have you expelled from this hospital!'

Mrs Bracebridge stormed away with Sister Pringle at her heels in eagerly servile attendance.

'Do you reckon the Nightingale will order us home, Genia?' Emma Fowler wondered. 'She sent Nellie Jenks home for quarrelling with Bracebridge, didn't she?'

Eugenia sighed and shook her head. 'I don't know what she may do. To be truthful, I'm beginning to wonder what point is there in any of us staying here, if we're not permitted to practise our skills. You and I are experienced nurses, Emma. We can set fractures and dress wounds as skilfully as any of the dressers and assistant-surgeons I've met in this hospital. Yet we're not allowed to do so.' Her voice rose in angry protest. 'We're not even allowed to bathe the men properly. We can't even clean the floors! And all the time men are dying in here by the hundreds. Men who could have been saved and made well again...' Her voice trailed away as a sense of despair overlaid her anger, and she felt near to tears.

'There now, don't take it to heart so. It'll be all the same a hundred years from now, and there's nothing you or me can do about it,' Emma Fowler said philosophically. 'And at least we managed to wash this 'un, and get a clean shirt for him to put on. That's something to the good, aren't it?'

Eugenia snatched at this straw of comfort. 'So it is, Emma. So it is.'

After a fruitless search for a cot, they were forced to lay the young soldier on to a straw-filled palliasse in the corridor. They were making him as comfortable as possible when Mrs Bracebridge and Sister Pringle came hurrying up to them.

'Miss Nightingale says that you are both to return to your quarters this instant.' Mrs Bracebridge radiated a malicious pleasure. 'You're both to be sent back to England for your insolence towards me, and your flagrant disobedience of our rules. And I for one am very happy that you're going. You're not fit to do the Lord's work in this hospital. And let me make it very clear to you both that nothing you can do or say will save you this time. You are being sent back to England!'

Fifty-Four

The Turkish bearers carelessly dumped Rosie's stretcher down at the end of the line of newly arrived casualties outside the main entrance of the barracks. The hard impact jarred her wounds, causing her to cry out in pain.

It was several hours before a bulbous-eyed sergeant came out from the entrance and moved along the line of new arrivals, shaking his head and grumbling self-pityingly.

'I don't know why it's always me that has to sort it out. It ain't fair. It's always me that has the bother of sorting you lot out. I don't know where I'm going to put you all, and that's a fact.'

When he saw Rosie he halted abruptly, his eyes bulging even more prominently. He lifted his forage cap and scratched his bald head. 'And whose bright idea was it to send you to me? This is a bloody hospital for soldiers. And soldiers are men, ain't they?

429

And you're a woman, ain't you? What am I going to do with you? Where am I going to put you? You can't go into the wards with the men, can you? It wouldn't be right and proper.'

Feverishly weak and in terrible pain as she was, Rosie's self-control momentarily weakened and her eyes brimmed with tears. The sergeant saw her distress and became shamefaced.

'Now don't take on so, young woman. I don't mean to upset you.' He called over to the orderlies who were bringing out the corpses. 'Take this 'un down to the cellars. See if you can find somebody to see to her needs.'

'They can't see to their own needs. She shouldn't be sent down there,' one orderly grunted sourly, but he helped to carry the stretcher through the corridors and down flights of stone steps into the fetid gloom of the cramped chambers where hundreds of soldiers' wives and widows and their young children lived.

Rosie's ears were assailed by the noise of children wailing, women shrieking, raucous talk and singing and laughter. She saw women lying in drunken stupor and others in rags nursing squalling babies at their breasts. Several women accosted the orderlies, begging for money, liquor, opium, tobacco or food.

'What regiment are you?' one of her bearers asked Rosie, and when she told him, he bellowed loudly, 'Is there anybody from the Twentieth Light Dragoons here?'

They progressed from one chamber to another, and the orderly kept on bellowing the question until finally one haggard-faced woman sitting on the floor with her back to the wall, answered.

'I'm from the Twentieth.'

'Well this 'un is one of yours.' The orderly seemed relieved. 'Put her down, boys, and let's get out of here.'

As the men walked away, the haggard woman scrambled to her feet and came to peer curiously into Rosie's face.

'It's you, Rosie!'

Rosie nodded. 'It is, Annie.'

Annie Bartleet's features were pallid and dirty, her hair hanging in lank, greasy strands, her body emaciated and foul-smelling. Her eyes held a strange wild gleam.

'Are you alright, Annie? Are you poorly?' Rosie was concerned at the visible physical deterioration of the woman.

'Has my Augustus come with you?' Annie Bartleet asked anxiously. 'He said he was coming back to me today.'

Knowing that Augustus Bartleet had been killed in the charge at Balaclava, a tremor of unease passed through Rosie. She glanced about her at the huddles of women and children. 'Where are your kids, Annie?'

'Augustus is looking after them. He said he was bringing them back to me today. Is he with you, Rosie? Have you seen him

431

anywhere? He's got to be somewhere near, Rosie. He promised he'd come back to me today. He promised he'd bring my kids back to me.' With each sentence Annie Bartleet was becoming more agitated, gabbling her words, spittle spraying from her lips.

Rosie realized with dismay that Annie Bartleet's mind was unhinged. She sought desperately for words to soothe and quieten her, but could find none.

'I'm going to look for him. I'm going to look for my Augustus.' Annie Bartleet suddenly turned and scurried off, merging her frantic shouts with the general pandemonium. 'Augustus? Where are you? Where are the kids?'

Another woman came to stand over Rosie. 'What happened to you then, Rosie Collier?'

It was Hetty Moston, the foul-mouthed harridan widow of Sergeant Peter Moston. Although she had never liked this woman, Rosie was relieved to find another familiar face.

'I got shot at the Inkerman. Dorcas Murphy and Megan Morgan were killed. And then I had my baby. But he's back there being looked after by a man from the Forty-first.'

Hetty Moston saw Rosie's desperate anguish, and a hint of compassion entered her harsh voice. 'I'm sure your babby is better off where he is, than being here. Annie Bartleet's kids have all died from the cholera. It took the poor little buggers in a single day, so it did. That's what started to send the poor cow round the twist. And when the news come about her man being killed, that finished the job, and sent her right off her head. O' course, Annie ought never to have followed the drum, you know. Her's always been too soft and weak for army life...'

Hetty Moston's large, tobacco-stained teeth bared in a grim smile of approbation. 'But you're a tough nut, Rosie. You might look all small and soft and pretty, but underneath you're as hard as nails. You're the same as me. We was born to follow the drum, me and you. Born for it!'

Rosie's fingers sought the small round brass button nestling between her breasts. Tormented by mental and physical pain, weak and feverish, still Hetty Moston's words struck a chord within her.

'I do believe I was,' she muttered. 'Born to follow the drum.'

'Have you got any money on you?' Hetty Moston asked. 'Or anything that might be sold?'

'No. And I'm not hiding anything, so there's no use you searching me.'

The other woman shook her head and chuckled grimly. 'Don't worry, I wasn't intending to rob you. You and me has never been friends, Rosie Collier, but I don't rob from me own regiment. But if you has got anything valuable then you'd best shove it up your arse for safe keeping. Some of the bitches in here are bad enough to rob their mother's deathbeds.'

433

'I've got nothing, so you can leave me in peace,' Rosie reiterated. Faintness swept over her, causing her eyes to close and her body to sag.

Hetty Moston's drink-ravaged face scowled, and she swore a string of foul oaths. She turned on her heels and walked away, but then turned again and came back. She bent and dragged Rosie's stretcher against the wall. Startled by the jerking movements, Rosie opened her eyes.

'What are you doing?' she asked.

'I must need me head examined,' Hetty Moston snarled savagely. 'I'se got more than enough troubles looking after bloody Annie Bartleet, without having to look after you as well. I must be mental! You stay quiet now.'

Rosie's eyes closed once more, and her features took on a greyish hue. Hetty Moston's face was near to Rosie's wounded shoulder, and she sniffed suspiciously. Her fingers touched Rosie's forehead, and she muttered, 'You're burning up, girl.'

She carefully lifted the blankets and the white-sheet dress away from Rosie's shoulder and, with her nose almost touching the bloodstained bandages, sniffed several times. She straightened and shouted threateningly at the other women and children in the chamber.

'This young wench here is one o' my regiment. You all saw what happened to the last stupid bitch who made me angry. So don't none o' you try gettin' up to your thieving tricks with this wench. Just leave her laying peaceful.' Hetty Moston's glowering features gave emphasis to her threat, and there were quickly given assurances. She growled, then spoke to Rosie, who gave no sign of hearing. 'You'll be safe, Rosie Collier. Nobody 'ull dare interfere wi' you now you're under my protection. So you rest now, and I'll be back presently.'

Rosie had heard the words, but they held no relevance for her. She was floating through a velvety darkness towards a distant pinprick of white light, which slowly enlarged as she travelled nearer to it. She felt no fear, for somehow she knew that when she reached that light, when it engulfed her, then all her pain and anguish would be at an end. That within that light she would someday, somehow be reunited with her baby.

Arthur Sinclair was off duty and half-drunk in the depot canteen when Hetty Moston came in search of him. She pushed through the uproarious crowd of roistering soldiers and women and roughly grabbed his arm, causing him to spill the rotgut spirits from his mug.

'Damn and blast you, Hetty!' he upbraided her angrily. 'This drink cost me my last penny.'

'Shurrup and listen,' she snarled fiercely. 'I've got Rosie Collier down in the cellars.'

'Rosie? Rosie Collier?' He blinked in shock. 'What's she doing here?'

'She's dying, if I'm any judge,' Hetty Moston stated flatly. 'I can smell the gangrene on her. And if you wants to see her alive, you'd best come now.'

'Oh my God!' The words penetrated his drunken haze, sobering his reeling senses. 'Oh my God!'

Together they hurried down into the dark, damp gloom of the cellars.

Rosie was lying motionless. Hetty Moston snatched a stub of lighted candle and held its wavering flame close to Rosie's nostrils and her slightly open mouth.

'We're too late, her's gone,' Hetty Moston said quietly, and patted the man's shoulder. 'I know you thought a lot of her, Artie. Try and take comfort that she died nice and easy.'

He slumped on to his knees and kissed Rosie's cheeks, his tears dropping on to her still, peaceful face.

Fifty-Five

Early in the cold morning, the day after their confrontation with Mrs Bracebridge, Eugenia Pacemore and Emma Fowler left the Barrack Hospital, dismissed from their service with the Nightingale nurses. As they emerged, carpet bags in hand, from beneath the great archway, Emma Fowler spat out viciously.

'Well it's good riddance to that cow Brace-bridge and that Black Crow Pringle – and the bloody Nightingale as well. I'm glad to be leaving this hellhole.'

Eugenia's emotions were mixed. She was angrily resentful at being summarily dismissed, but at the same time was greatly looking forward to being with her cousin once more. With careful management, the income from her annuity and Peter's army pay would support them both until he was recovered from his wounds. Then she thought she would seek another nursing appointment.

Although it was barely dawn, a procession of stretcher-borne sick and wounded came winding up the trackway from the landing stage, and the loaded handcarts of the dead were being trundled to the vast cemeteries.

On impulse Eugenia said, 'I'm going to the cemetery, Emma, to say a last prayer over the poor fellows. Do you want to come with me?'

'I'm not a praying sort of woman, Genia, as you well know. But you go, and I'll pop into shanty town and buy a few bottles for the journey. I'll meet you down at the landing stage.'

It was a long walk through the acres of ancient and modern Muslim gravestones and tombs to reach the new British cemetery. Eugenia was following some yards behind a handcart of blanketed corpses that was being pushed and pulled over the rutted, muddy trackway by three sweating orderlies.

When she finally reached a recently opened

mass grave she waited until the orderlies had added their load of corpses to it and left. Then she moved to stand at the side of the raw pit and offer up a prayer for the souls of those who lay here. She felt sadness for the waste of so many lives and pity for the loved ones who were left to mourn.

Her prayer finished, she turned to retrace her steps, and saw some distance away a tall, fair-haired young man in a long sheepskin coat. He was standing in the section of the cemetery reserved for the individual graves of the officers.

She recognized him as Arthur Sinclair, and on impulse went towards him.

'Mr Sinclair? Mr Sinclair?'

When she reached him she noted that he was holding a small wooden cross and standing beside a freshly mounded grave.

They greeted each other cordially and, indicating her carpet bag, he asked, 'Are you leaving Scutari, Miss Pacemore?'

'Yes, I'm returning to England. I sail today. But I'm hoping to join up with my cousin in Malta en route. I came here to pray for these poor fellows who'll never see home again.'

'I'm under orders to leave also,' Arthur Sinclair told her. 'I'm sufficiently recovered to rejoin my regiment. I'm here on much the same errand as yourself.' He lifted the wooden cross to show her, and tears shone in his eyes. 'I'm going to put this on my dear friend's grave here. She saved my life.'

'She?' Eugenia asked.

'She was the wife of a comrade. I buried her here myself yesterday. I couldn't bear the thought of her being put into a mass grave. She deserves better than that...' Acidity crept into his voice. 'I hope that these officers and gentlemen will not object to a private soldier's wife sharing their last resting place, even if when alive they would not have deigned to share any sort of lodgings with the poor girl.'

'I'm sure they won't object, Mr Sinclair,' Eugenia said warmly. 'And I must now say goodbye to you, with all my best wishes for the future.'

They shook hands, and he bowed. 'Goodbye, Miss Pacemore.'

Suddenly curious, she asked, 'Your friend – what was her name?'

'Rosie. Rosie Collier.'

Poignant memories flooded into Eugenia's mind. Memories of the small, sweet-faced girl she had wanted so desperately to help.

'Rosie,' she murmured sadly. 'I knew a Rosie once. She was a small child then, and she'll be a grown woman now. Hardly a day passes when I don't pause for a moment and wonder what has become of her.'

'She'll be a happily married woman, with a house full of children of her own.' Arthur Sinclair smiled.

'I do hope so,' Eugenia said wistfully. 'Goodbye, Mr Sinclair.'

'Goodbye, Miss Pacemore.'

Eugenia walked, smiling, through the

thousands of tombs and gravestones, all depression lifted from her, driven out by the image of Rosie, happily smiling, with her small, sweet-faced children clinging to her skirts.

440